A Time to Be Born

★ NUMBER ONE IN THE AMERICAN ODYSSEY SERIES ★

A Time to Be Born

GILBERT MORRIS

Fleming H. Revell
A Division of Baker Book House Co
Grand Rapids, Michigan 49516

©1994 by Gilbert Morris

Published by Fleming H. Revell
a division of Baker Book House Company
P.O. Box 6287, Grand Rapids, MI 49516-6287

Second printing, July 1994

Printed in the United States of America

Library of Congress Cataloging-in-Publication Data

Morris, Gilbert.
    A time to be born/Gilbert Morris.
      p. cm. — (The American odyssey series)
    ISBN 0-8007-5497-2
    1. Stuart family—Fiction. 2. Family—United States—Fiction.
    I. Title. II. Series.
PS3563.08742T56 1994
813'.54—dc20   93-26089

To my wife, Johnnie
Forty-three years together–
and I've enjoyed every second of it!

CONTENTS

THE STUART FAMILY

William Stuart, 1852– , m. 1878, remarried 1905
    Marian Edwards, 1860–1905   Agnes Barr, 1875–

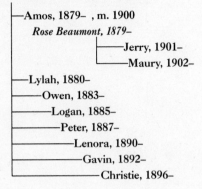

        —Amos, 1879– , m. 1900
        Rose Beaumont, 1879–
                    —Jerry, 1901–
                    —Maury, 1902–
        —Lylah, 1880–
        —Owen, 1883–
        —Logan, 1885–
        —Peter, 1887–
        —Lenora, 1890–
        —Gavin, 1892–
        —Christie, 1896–

A Time to Be Born

1900	1910	1920	1930	1940
Spanish-American War	Woodrow Wilson elected president	Lindbergh makes solo flight across Atlantic	The Great Depression	Polio epidemic ravages country
Boxer Rebellion in China	World War I	Stock Market crash	Franklin Roosevelt elected president	Japanese attack Pearl Harbor

Part 1
1897–1898

1960	1970	1980	1990	2000

Billy Graham launches major campaigns

racial segregation schools declared unconstitutional

Vietnam War

Martin Luther King Jr. assassinated

Jesus People revival among youth

Watergate scandal causes Nixon's downfall

Ronald Reagan elected president

Scandals involving TV evangelists

Bill Clinton elected president

AIDS crisis worsens

1

ESCAPE FROM THE MOUNTAINS

Owen Stuart never forgot the day his sister Lylah left the farm to go to Bible school in Fort Smith. The date—September 4, 1897—stuck like a burr in his mind, and he often wondered why he could remember that date, but could never remember the dates of wars or treaties or when famous people were born. Dimly he understood that Lylah's departure was a landmark occasion in the Stuart family history, for she was the first of the young ones to leave the remote recesses of the Ozarks for the world outside.

But though he always remembered the brilliance of the fall afternoon and the flaming colors of the hills that surrounded their farm that year, it was the memory of how he had found his sister—her bags packed to go to Bible school, out behind the barn smoking a cigarette—that had stayed with him.

Owen had gotten up early, unable to sleep, and had crept out of the loft where he slept with his four brothers—Amos, Logan, Pete, and Gavin. The rustle of his corn shucks mattress seemed deafening in the stillness, but he made his way to the door and crawled down the ladder into the main room, then left the house.

He loved the early cobwebby hours of the morning and was always the first to rise. A sharp pinching cold lay over the valley, the foretaste of winter, but he loved the air, thin and raw and bracing, containing the rich rank odors of the earth and the forest. For an hour he walked the trails that led away from the house, looking up from time to time to the thin glitter of the stars. The earth, still and motionless, seemed to be a dead ball rolling through dead space, but Owen was acutely aware of the movements around him—the patter of tiny feet, the rustle of brush as large animals passed through, the flutter of wings.

Finally at four, a first skim-milk color diluted the coffee-black shadows, and he made his way back to the farm. And it was then, as he left the trees that banked the log cabin in the rear, that he caught the smell of smoke.

At once he stopped, alert and careful as any animal, before he moved, catlike, to the barn. It was only a small affair, poorly built of rough-hewn pine beams and sheathed with slabs picked up from the mill. Even as Owen circled it, he noted that it was listing more than ever against the five thick saplings he had placed against the north side to brace it up. Without realizing it, he was stirred with a faint sense of dissatisfaction. *Looks like we could have a barn that could stand up by itself.* A vague thought of his father came to him, and he shrugged slightly, thinking, *I guess as long as Pa can find a party to fiddle at, this ol' barn's gonna have to take care of itself.*

The acrid odor of smoke led him to the rear of the structure, and as soon as he turned the corner, he saw the indistinct outline of a figure, low to the ground, and then: "Hello, Owen . . . come and have a draw."

A smile tugged at his lips, and he moved forward until he could make out the features of his older sister. She was hunkered down on her heels, back braced against the wall, and he chose that same position before answering.

"Guess you're up early to do your prayin' before you leave for Bible school."

Lylah Stuart was closer to this brother than to anyone else in the family. She grinned, recognizing the gentle jibe in his statement, then handed him the cigarette. "Sure. Have a draw, Owen."

Owen took the cigarette, studied it for a moment, then

took a long pull on it before handing it back. "Better than rabbit tobacco . . . or dried corn silk," he remarked. "Where'd you get a real cigarette, Lylah?"

"From Bob Briley . . . at the dance last week."

"Bob never gives anything away," Owen said, his voice clear in the cold air. "I can guess what he wanted in return."

A glint of humor lit Lylah's eyes and her lips turned up in a smile. "That's right. You know Bob pretty well."

She drew on the cigarette again, and as she expelled the smoke, Owen studied her. She was the handsomest member of the family, one of those truly beautiful girls who spring up among the hill people of Arkansas from time to time, almost as noticeable as an albino deer. Lylah had a wealth of auburn hair, a short English nose (as did all the Stuarts), full lips, a rich complexion, and a pair of violet eyes—deep, wide-set, and striking. She had come to womanhood early, and even the coarse homemade brown dress could not disguise the full roundness of her figure.

"Well, do you think Bob got what he wanted?"

Accustomed as he was to his sister's directness, Owen felt uncomfortable with the question. Although he was only fourteen, he had been aware for a long time that his sister drew men as nectar draws bees. But he refused to show his embarrassment. "Naw, I reckon not, Sis."

Lylah reached over and ruffled the boy's thatch of chestnut hair. "Glad you still have some confidence in your rowdy sister."

They sat there, comfortable with the silence that lay between them. As the sky grew brighter, they smoked and watched the world come to light. Finally a door slammed, and Owen rose to his feet in a single smooth motion. He had passed from babyhood, suffering little of the awkward stage that most boys struggle through—one day a baby, Lylah thought as she watched him, and the next a lath-shaped young man who was one of the most physical people she'd ever seen.

"Who is it?" she whispered, preparing to crush out the cigarette.

"Amos."

Lylah relaxed and, leaning back against the wall, waited as Owen hailed softly, "Hey . . . Amos, over here."

Amos Stuart, the oldest of the children at eighteen, looked up, saw Owen, and came at once to his brother's side. "Come on," Owen said, a grin on his lips. "Sister's holding services."

"I'll bet she is," Amos remarked, and followed Owen to where Lylah sat. "If Ma catches you smoking," he said, settling down against the rough siding of the barn, "she'll burn your backside."

"She won't catch me." Lylah offered the cigarette, adding, "This is the last time I'll ever hide behind the barn to smoke."

Amos drew the smoke into his lungs, handed the cigarette back, then remarked, "You'll have to hide someplace. I don't reckon they allow smoking at Bible school."

"That's their problem." Lylah shrugged.

"You'll get sent home," Amos argued. He was the logical member of the three, thinking things out carefully, whereas Owen and Lylah both leapt and then thought. He was no more than five ten and weighed less than 135 pounds. Lean as a hound, pared down by hard work, he was stronger than he looked. He had the same oval face, blond hair, and dark blue eyes of his mother.

"I'm never coming back here," Lylah announced flatly. "Except for a visit." She reached over and grabbed her brothers' hair, pulling them close in a gesture of affection. "I'm going to miss you two," she said, and despite the roughness of her caress, both Owen and Amos sensed a faint thread of apprehension in her voice.

They were very close, these three—closer to each other than they were to anyone else in their small world. Amos was close to his mother, but not in the same way that he was tied to these two who sat beside him in the growing light of dawn. Being more introspective than either of the others, he had thought much of what it meant—Lylah's departure. Moved by the plaintive note in her voice, he asked, "Lylah, why are you doing it—going away to Bible school? You don't have any more religion than a coonhound."

Amos's comment caused a quick flare-up of the temper that lay near the surface. "I guess I've got as much religion as you have, Amos Stuart!" she snapped.

"Well, that's nothing to brag about." Amos shrugged. "I never put up my sign for a preacher, and that's about all they put out at Bethany Bible Institute."

Owen shook his head, for he had been dreading Lylah's departure since hearing of it. "You'll go crazy, sister," he urged. "I know Ma gets on your nerves, all the time making us go to church . . . but you know what Don Satterfield says about that school." He pulled his lips together in what he considered a good imitation of the young man, his voice high-pitched with a twang: "Why, we get up and pray before dawn *every day* . . . and sometimes we pray *all night!* And there ain't no worldly stuff allowed . . . like smokin' and drinkin' and play-actin'."

Both Amos and Lylah giggled over the rendition. Satter-field, a lanky young man who had grown up in their valley, had fallen hopelessly in love with Lylah in the first grade, and she had used him shamelessly ever since. He had been at Bethany Institute for a year, studying for the ministry, and it had been at his fervent urging that Marian Stuart had per-suaded her husband to send Lylah away to the school.

But though Lylah laughed at Owen's mild mockery of Sat-terfield, she grew serious. Grinding the cigarette into the dirt with her heel, she rose and looked around at the farm. Both boys got up, watching as she let her eyes rest on the hills that stretched to the north and on the cotton fields with their skeleton-stalks, lifting grotesque arms as if in prayer to some dark god. Finally, walking slowly to the edge of the rickety barn, she stared at the house.

It wasn't much—just a dog-trot log cabin, with two big

rooms separated by a passageway. The roof was steep enough for a large sleeping loft, and at the back, William Stuart had added a room with a shed roof. There was no grace about the place, nothing to please the eye. Life in the mountains was too hard for refinements. Staying alive was a struggle, leaving no strength for the little touches that lay in Lylah Stuart.

She noted the few feeble pansies, purple and white and maroon, that remained of the small bed her mother had planted. Somehow that seemed to disturb her. She turned to Owen and Amos. "Be sure you dig Ma some flower beds next spring."

"Sure, Lylah," Amos said gently. Then he asked again, "Why do you have to go?"

Lylah looked around once more at the shabby outbuildings, at the razorback pig rooting into the earth, and said abruptly, "I'll never slop a hog again . . . or pick cotton or kill one of those skinny chickens!"

She broke off, but her brothers knew that the vow had risen from deep within, for she loathed farm life with all her soul. She hated the grinding work, the poverty, the lack of any color in the bleakness of their existence. Staring down at her hands, she touched the callouses made by ax and hoe.

Suddenly she looked up, and her voice was strange—strong as iron, yet somehow wistful and unsure. "I'd go *anywhere* to get away from here!"

At that moment, a door slammed, and the three started. Lylah took a deep breath, then said, "Come on. Let's go eat breakfast."

Amos and Owen followed her as she walked back to the house. She went inside, and Amos stopped at the woodpile. "Guess we better split some of this wood, Owen." The two of them picked up axes, and with practiced ease began splitting the wood. Good blocks of beech it was, and soon wedge-shaped lengths of the fragrant wood, splinterless as a cloven rock, fell away as they worked.

"I wish she wasn't going, Amos."

Amos stared at his younger brother, compassion in his dark

blue eyes. "Well, she is, and that's the end of it," he said heavily. "Now . . . this ought to be enough."

The two loaded their arms with wood and entered the large room which served for all the social activities of the family. As Amos dropped the firewood into the box by the stove with a loud rattle, his mother said, "Thank you, boys. Now, go wash up. Breakfast is about done."

Marian Stuart had been an Edwards before she married— a cousin of the famous preacher Jonathan Edwards. Though she herself never mentioned her famous relative, this perhaps accounted for her single-minded devotion to God. Her simple act of thanking Owen and Amos was typical of the touch of grace and gentility that rested in her, setting her off from most women of the mountains. It was more than kindness . . . though that was in it, as well. She was, Amos had often thought, in some ways like the rich ladies who had ruled the big plantations before the Civil War. Despite the poverty and hard work that had worn her down—that and steady childbearing—Marian Edwards Stuart possessed some fragile attribute that all real ladies have. Quality, some have called it, and though it is a rare enough and vague term, everyone who knew Marian Stuart realized that she could have fitted into a much higher sphere of life than the one she had occupied for most of her thirty-seven years.

She moved about the room, from the stove to the table, a tall woman with heavy ash-blond hair tied up in a bun. She had very dark blue eyes set in an oval face, with lines beginning to mark the smoothness of her skin. She was not thought of as a beautiful woman; rather, her features gave the impression of strength, having little of what was commonly called "prettiness."

"You sit down, Lylah. I guess we can wait on you your last morning at home." Marian smiled at her eldest daughter, coming over to brush a rebellious curl into place.

"Oh, Ma, I can't eat anything!"

Marian smiled, but ignoring the protest, called out, "Will!

Come and eat!" She looked around as her husband came into
the room. "We've got some of that sausage you and Lylah like
so much."

William Stuart, a handsome man of forty-five, was one inch
over six feet, lean and muscular. His reddish chestnut hair
had a slight curl, and it lay neatly on his well-shaped head. It
was marked by a white streak running from front to back on
the left side—a memento of the Battle of Five Forks, the last
battle of the Civil War. He had been only twelve, but had
joined up as a drummer boy when his father had been killed
at the Battle of Nashville. He had a short English nose, startling light blue eyes, a mobile mouth, and a rather prominent
chin with a deep cleft. This last trait he had passed along to
all of his children except Amos.

"Well, now," he said with a grin, "I guess we got to send
somebody off to school to get a first-rate breakfast around
here." He moved over and put his arm around Marian, who
flushed slightly and moved away. Quickly he sat down and
set his gaze on Lylah. "Well, daughter, last chance to change
your mind."

"Don't start on her, Will," Marian said quickly. She sat down
at the foot of the table and bowed her head. The rest followed
her example, and she prayed, "Oh, God, we thank thee for
this food and for every blessing. And this morning, we ask that
thou wouldst give traveling mercies to the children . . . and set
thine angels to watch over Lylah as she leaves us. Keep her
safe from all harm, for we ask it in the name of Jesus."

As soon as the prayer was over, Owen looked around the
table. "I'll be danged, Ma, if you ain't outdid yourself this time!"

Marian smiled, and as the family tore into eggs, sausage,
grits, biscuits, and pancakes with blackstrap syrup—she
picked at her own food. She let her eyes roam around the
table, studying each face:

*Will Stuart—as restless and unstable as the wind—he can play
any instrument, but he can't control himself.* Marian concentrated
on her husband's handsome features, thinking of how he

could be so charming, but with so little resistance to temptation. He was welcome at all the musicals and play parties and dances, she knew, for he was a fine musician and had a splendid tenor voice. *If he worked as hard as he played, he'd be a fine man,* Marian thought. He was sweet and thoughtful at times and worked for weeks without a break. But then, in one form or another, the weakness of his flesh would draw him down. Marian Stuart knew well the pitying looks she got from her friends . . . knew then that Will had been drunk or with another woman.

Marian shifted her gaze to her three oldest children. Amos, who was most like her, loved books the way a starving man loves food. But he loved his family more . . . enough to give up his chance at school to make a living out of the rocky soil that composed their hill farm. Marian felt his longings, this oldest son of hers. *He's got to have his chance . . . somehow he's got to have a chance!*

And Owen—not a thinker like Amos, though bright enough—he was the hunter, the fisherman, the one who won all the races and wrestling matches among his boyhood crew. He was, Marian thought, a great deal like his father, but she thanked God that the boy had received Will Stuart's better characteristics. Marian noted the firm line of the boy's jaw, took in the steady eyes, and thought with relief, *He'll be all right. He's not like Will . . . at least, not yet.*

There was Lylah, whose beauty frightened Marian, for she knew that beauty was a quality as dangerous as gunpowder to some women, and those who learned to use it could destroy a man as quickly as with a loaded pistol. *I wish she weren't so pretty,* Marian thought with pain. *She's going out into the world without God, and every man she sees will try to corrupt her.*

Her gaze fell on the others, the young ones:

Logan, twelve years old, resembled his father, but there was a calm steadiness in him that was lacking in the other boys. He was the mechanical one—the fixer and the inventor. Marian's eyes ran over the serious face, then moved to

Pete, aged ten. *Peter looks so much like my cousin, Jonathan*, Marian thought, *so tall but with the Stuart features*.

And Lenora, only seven, already showed signs of looking like her mother—same ash-blond hair, but with hazel eyes. Tall for her age, the child already possessed a strong maternal instinct.

Gavin, the only one in the family with dark hair and almost black eyes, sat next to Lenora. He was five years old and a throwback to Will Stuart's grandmother. "The black Stuart," he had been called, though he had the sunniest temperament of all the children.

Marian rose and went to pick up Christie, thirteen months. As she nursed her youngest, Marian admired the fine blond hair and the cornflower blue eyes regarding her solemnly.

Finally the meal was over, and Amos said, "I'll get the team hitched, Lylah. We've got a long trip, so get your stuff together."

Will leaned back in his chair, protesting, "If she's got to go, I should be the one to take her."

At once Marian said, "That fence on the north forty has got to be repaired, Will. We're going to lose stock if it isn't."

"Well, let Amos do it."

"No. Amos hasn't been to town for two years. He's worked hard, and he needs a little time off."

The older children recognized that this meant: *You can't be trusted to go to Fort Smith alone, Will.* And Stuart got to his feet and stalked out of the room.

"You want me to stay, Ma?" Amos asked.

"No, son, you go with Lylah. You two have a good time."

"Ma, let me go with them, please!" Owen begged.

Marian shook her head, but when she saw the sorrow on Owen's face, she changed her mind. "Well, I guess it won't hurt. You'll have to wear your best clothes, though, so go get ready."

At once Logan and the other children let out a whoop of protest, but they understood shortly that it was in vain. Marian shooed them out from underfoot, and managed to have one moment with Lylah. She helped the girl put her scanty wardrobe into a suitcase borrowed for the occasion, and said wistfully, "I wish you had some nice things, Lylah."

Lylah turned and hugged her mother. "Oh, Ma, it's all right!"

The two women held on to each other, for somehow both understood that this was a good-bye that covered more than a trip to Fort Smith.

The older woman voiced it. "You've not been happy here, Lylah. But I'm worried about you. The things you want so badly . . . they'll not make you happy, either."

Lylah braced herself for another sermon, her lips thinning, but her mother only said, "I'll pray for you . . . every day, daughter."

Lylah recognized her mother's inherent goodness, and a chill came over her as she thought of leaving the safety of this place. "Oh, Ma—I've got to go—I've *got* to!"

Marian held the girl close, smoothing her hair as she had not done for years. They stood there, and Lylah never forgot that moment. She little knew at that instant how many times she would go back and relive this scene, often with tears.

"I know you have to go," Marian said and forced a smile onto her lips. "And we both know you don't know God. Maybe you'll meet him at the school. But I know you'll find God, because he's given me a promise. He gave it to me the morning you were born, Lylah. I was holding you for the first time, and the Lord dropped a word into my heart. He said, 'This child will not have an easy way. She will wander far from me and from you. But I will bring her back. You will see her one day, a handmaiden of the Lord and a mother in Israel.'"

The words frightened Lylah. She'd never heard this before. But somehow it cheered her, too. "Try not to worry too much, Ma," she begged. She wiped the tears from her eyes, and soon the two women moved out of the house, where Amos was just driving the team up to the front of the house.

Will Stuart came back from the barn, and in one of his swift mood changes, smiled at Lylah. He hugged her, reached into his pocket and brought out something which he put into her hand. "Buy yourself something pretty," he whispered, and lifted her clear off the ground, her arms locked around his neck. "Don't forget the old man!"

Ten minutes later the wagon headed down the winding dirt road. Lylah looked back toward the house. All of them were waving, and she waved back, but then the timber closed in and she couldn't see them anymore. She sighed and settled into her seat between Owen and Amos.

"You sorry to be leaving?" Owen asked.

"Yes . . . but I've got to do it."

Amos stared out over the heads of the mules, his eyes thoughtful. "Sure," he said. "I know how it is, Sis."

Lylah felt a stab of sorrow for this lean brother of hers. For years she had known that Amos longed to leave the farm, to find his place in the world. But he had chosen to stay, sacrificing himself for her and the family.

Gently she put her hand on his arm, then whispered, "You'll get away someday, Amos."

He didn't answer, and the three of them rode down the rutted road, the harness jingling musically and the warm sun washing over them. Lylah was aware that there would never be a moment like this again—just the three of them. She wished that the journey would last forever, that she and Amos and Owen could be together always. But she knew that this was impossible, and she had to fight against a dark and foreboding fear that rose in her breast.

"Come on, now," Amos said, noting Lylah's sadness. "You've got plenty of time to be sober with those Baptists. But first we're going to have a rip-roaring time in Fort Smith, right?"

"Right!" Lylah agreed, and put an arm around each of her strong brothers. "One rip-roaring time for the Stuarts!"

2

A Christmas Time

Donald Satterfield was worried. He had been proud when the president of Bethany Institute had put him in charge of the group of students taking the trip to Little Rock for the annual meeting of the Arkansas Baptist State Convention in early December. He had glowed in the praise of Dr. Harry Barton: "Donald, you're the most reliable student at the institute. I know I can trust you to shepherd our young people well."

Satterfield, a serious young man, took his task as a sacred trust, and the fifteen students in the group had not only attended the sessions where rousing sermons were preached, but those less-than-exciting meetings where business took place.

That the group had done so was a tribute to the popularity of the young evangelist. Most of them had emerged from the hills, as had Satterfield himself, and had never seen a city the size of Little Rock. They had been awed by Fort Smith, where the most dynamic sight was the gallows where Judge Isaac Parker had stretched the necks of almost a hundred desperados harvested from Indian Territory. But Little Rock boasted such marvels as electric streetcars and a building six stories high.

"That building will fall," declared a bull-shouldered freshman ministerial student named Harold Pink. Pink was the one of whom the head of the Bible department had said, "Harold thinks the world's on fire, and he's the only one with

a bucket of water!" Now, staring up at the red brick building
that dominated Main Street, Pink added to his prophecy: "If
God had intended for man to live in tall buildings, he'd never
have put a stop to the Tower of Babel!"

But Don Satterfield had a far more serious problem than the
shaky theology of a rather thick-headed freshman.

One of his sheep—the only female of the flock—was missing.

"Has anyone seen Lylah?" Satterfield rushed into the lobby
of the First Baptist Church, his hair rumpled and his eyes
filled with anguish. It was the last night of the convention,
and when he had gone to the home of the family who had
kept Lylah during the visit, he was told that she had left early.
But the young minister had not found her at the church, and
he yanked at his hair nervously, saying to the others, "She left
the Whites' house in plenty of time to get here."

"I told you how it would be, Brother Satterfield," Pink said
ponderously. "As the Scriptures say, 'A wise man will attain
unto counsel, but stripes are for the back of a fool.'" Having
called his leader a fool in an acceptable manner, the burly
youth nodded, seeming to take pleasure in being the har-
binger of evil tidings. "She's probably wallowing in the flesh-
pots of this modern-day Sodom!"

"Oh, shut up, Harold!" Satterfield would not have spoken
so roughly if he had not been so worried. He scanned the
lobby frantically but saw nothing of Lylah. "You all go on in,"
he said. "I'm going to wait out here until she comes."

Henry Townes, Satterfield's second-in-command, was
more reassuring. "Oh, she's just late, Don. You know how
women are. You don't have to worry."

But Townes was right on only one count; he missed two
out of three. Lylah was certainly late, but Satterfield *didn't*
know how women were. And if he had known where she had
been all afternoon, he would have torn out his hair from worry!

With the possible exception of the state capitol, the
Lafayette Opera House on Capitol Avenue was the most or-

nate building in Little Rock. A large imposing structure in the Victorian style, it had succeeded in luring to the city the better road companies that were criss-crossing the nation at the turn of the century. In earlier days, it had hosted such giants as Sarah Bernhardt, Lillian Russell, and even an aging Edwin Booth.

Many thousands had passed by the opera house since it rose to dominate the wide street that led to the capitol, but not one of them had been so strongly affected by it as had Lylah Stuart.

She had been bored with the convention, as she had known she would be, and it was to escape boredom that she had pestered Don Satterfield to include her in the group. He had thought it was his own idea, of course. "The experience will do her good" he had told the president, not realizing that Lylah herself, using her feminine wiles, had planted that idea in his mind.

Satterfield, who had been hopelessly in love with Lylah for years, was sincere enough. He had been disappointed that Lylah had taken so little interest in spiritual things at the Institute. Oh, she had done well enough academically, for she had a keen mind. She had even memorized the kings of Judah and Israel with the dates of their reigns, rattling them off carelessly when called on. But she had attended only those services required by the code of the school. Satterfield had never once succeeded in getting her to attend any of the all-night prayer meetings, nor even one of his own meetings in the smaller churches of the area.

Nor had he any idea of the crashing boredom Lylah Stuart was enduring! But Lylah was too smart to behave in a manner that would send her back home to slop razorback hogs. She was a clever girl and played the role of "student at Bible school" as she had played other roles. Her boast to Amos and Owen that she would set the institute on its ear by doing what she pleased was not the way, and she knew it.

But the empty years loomed before her, as they do for men

and women in prison cells, and when the chance came to go to Little Rock she grabbed it. It took only a few soft words, a little pressure as she leaned against Don Satterfield, to get her way.

Her first train ride was thrilling. Snow began to fall as the train chugged toward Little Rock, and it was exciting to watch the dead-looking hills being transformed into smooth mounds of glittering white. The excitement of the train ride palled into nothingness, however, when Lylah passed by the opera house and saw the pictures plastered across the front of the building. She glanced up at the huge sign that read:

ONE ENGAGEMENT ONLY!
ROMEO AND JULIET
STARRING MAUDE ADAMS

Turning her avid attention to the playbill, Lylah studied the picture of the star. "Why, she's no older than I am!" she whispered aloud.

"And not nearly as pretty!"

Startled, Lylah turned to find herself facing a tall young man dressed in a thick fur coat. He was handsome, with chiseled features. When he took off his black bowler hat, he revealed a mass of black hair piled high in front in a pompadour. A pair of bold black eyes dominated his face, and when he smiled, Lylah knew she'd never seen such a perfect set of teeth!

"Miss Adams *is*, in fact, older than you are," the man smiled, and then his eyes took on even more of a sparkle as he added, "but she certainly is not as attractive!"

Accustomed as she was to subduing the young men who fluttered around her, Lylah was suddenly a little breathless, for this man was no callow student! He was very tall, and the diamond he was wearing on his right hand flashed as he gestured. Assurance flowed out of him, and the young woman knew that this man was more dangerous than any she'd ever met. *He knows how to handle women the same as I know how to handle men,* Lylah thought.

But there was enough audacity in her to cause her to hold up her head and smile—she knew what *this* did to men!—and she murmured, "My mother taught me not to talk to strangers—especially to those who tell lies."

The man threw back his head and laughed, delighted with her answer. "Your mother gives good advice," he said, "but I haven't lied to you."

"Yes, you have," Lylah said quickly, motioning toward the picture on the wall. "I'm not as beautiful as that lady."

"Have you ever seen her in person?"

"Well, no—"

"Well, *I* see her every day . . . and I swear on my grand-father's . . . nose," he substituted quickly, "that Miss Adams would give a year's earnings to have your coloring and those eyes!"

Lylah stared at him, ignoring the compliment, and breathed, "You *see* Maude Adams every day? Are you . . . an *actor?*"

Again he laughed, then reached out and turned her around. "My feelings are hurt!" he said, and pointed to a picture just to the left of the star's.

Lylah read the name aloud: "James K. Hackett—" then examined the picture. "It's you!" she cried, and turned to face the actor.

"In person!" He bowed gracefully, then asked, "And you are—"

"My name is Lylah Stuart."

"Well, Miss Stuart, I take it you haven't seen the play?"

"No, I haven't. Are you Romeo?"

"Well, no—" A frown creased his smooth forehead, and he bit his lips. "If justice were done, I *would* be in that role." Then he flashed those white teeth. "But many critics say that the part of Mercutio is far better than that of Romeo. Do you agree?"

"Oh, I've never seen *any* play, Mr. Hackett!" Lylah protested.

His heavy black eyebrows shot up. "Never seen a play?" he said in astonishment. "I can't believe it! What have you been doing all your life?"

An impulse prompted Lylah to invent a story about being the daughter of a wealthy man who didn't like plays, but she was too smart and too honest for that.

"I've been feeding pigs," she said with a sudden impish grin.

Her smile, Hackett found, was infectious. And she was a peach. He suddenly liked the girl's forthrightness. He shook his head. "My, that won't do! You'll have to come to the performance."

"Oh, I can't afford it," Lylah said at once.

"As my guest, of course." Hackett smiled. He reached into his pocket and came out with one of the complimentary tickets the actors all received. "Front row center." Seeing her reluctance, he added quickly. "After the performance I'd like to take you backstage to meet Miss Adams."

A verse of Scripture flashed into Lylah's mind: *There hath no temptation taken you but such as is common to man: but God is faithful, who will not suffer you to be tempted above that ye are able; but will with the temptation also make a way to escape that ye may be able to bear it.*

Lylah struggled, knowing that entering a theater was against all the laws of God she'd been taught. She was due at the church, and Don would be worried sick about her. Her mother would be grieved. No doubt there would be language that would offend the ears of a young lady. And certainly no green young girl should even *think* of putting herself under the power of a creature as attractive as James K. Hackett!

"I'll be honored to be your guest, Mr. Hackett," Lylah agreed, after a spiritual struggle that lasted all of fifteen seconds.

"Fine! Now you just come along with me, and we'll have something to drink before I have to change—"

Quickly the minutes passed until the curtain went up. And from that instant, time ceased for Lylah Stuart.

For three hours the actors moved and spoke and fought and loved. Their strong voices flowed over the stage, the language of Shakespeare sometimes caressing Lylah's ears like sweet drops of rain on dry earth, other times falling like blows that crush and maim, as the Capulets and the Montagues raged at one another.

When Romeo got his first glimpse of Juliet, his words came to Lylah like magic:

> O, she doth teach the torches to burn bright!
> It seems she hangs upon the cheek of night
> Like a rich jewel in an Ethiop's ear—
> Beauty too rich for use, for earth too dear!

And when Juliet, in the balcony scene, mourned that the one she loves is the sworn enemy of her family, Lylah wanted to cry out—

> O, be some other name!
> What's in a name? That which we call a rose
> By any other name would smell as sweet.

But it was in the death scenes that Lylah felt most keenly the power of poetry and drama. She did not know the play and supposed that somehow Romeo and Juliet would overcome all their difficulties and live happily ever after. When Romeo came to the tomb and found Juliet apparently dead, Lylah delighted in the first of the scene, especially the speech that Romeo made:

> Eyes look your last!
> Arms, take your last embrace! And, lips, O you
> The doors of breath, seal with a righteous kiss
> A dateless bargain to engrossing death!

But when Romeo killed himself, Lylah was struck dumb, unable to speak, hardly able to think. To complete the tragedy, Juliet, finding the dead body of Romeo, stabbed herself with his dagger, crying out, "O happy dagger! This is thy sheath. There rust, and let me die."

Lylah began to weep, overcome by grief for the young lovers. And when Hackett found her, he was shocked to discover that the young woman had been so affected by the play.

"Why, Miss Stuart, what's this?" he whispered, taking both her hands. The tears were running down her cheeks, and the worldly actor thought he'd never seen anything more innocently beautiful in his life than the soft, damp eyes of Lylah Stuart!

"I can't . . . help it!" Lylah moaned.

"Well, now, you come and meet Miss Adams. She'll be flattered that her performance has been so effective."

And so she was. Maude Adams, though only thirty years old, had received applause from royalty and admiration from many, but she was genuinely touched when she saw the trembling lips of the beautiful young girl. Realizing that Lylah was beyond speech, she took her hand, then kissed her on the cheek. "It's good to see that what I do on the stage has some power to move young people."

"Oh, Miss Adams," Lylah whispered, "it's the grandest thing there is!"

Maude Adams stared at the young woman, then shifted her gaze to Hackett. "Well, she certainly has the beauty for the stage, hasn't she?"

Lylah had dreamed all her life of something like this! She lifted her glorious eyes to Maude Adams and said, "I want that more than anything!"

Hackett squinted as if in thought. "Why, certainly, Miss Stuart! And if you come to New York, Miss Adams and I will be glad to help you find your place in the theater!"

Maude Adams knew her man, however, and warned, "It takes more than good looks to become an actress, Miss Stuart." A peculiar light came to her eyes, and she added softly, "More hearts are broken by this profession than any I know of. Better for you simply to come and enjoy the plays, than to risk letting your dreams get broken."

After Hackett led her out of the dressing room, he said, "Let's have a bite to eat."

"All right." Lylah was like a woman in a trance. She lifted her face to Hackett. "Will you help me get on the stage if I come to New York with you?"

Hackett blinked. He was a womanizer, and this girl was a rare prize to add to his collection. But he was shrewd enough to know that while a one-night affair in a hick town was one thing, to take a young woman to New York was something entirely different.

"Well . . . your parents would have to—"

"I have no family," Lylah said. "I have nobody to care."

"Nobody at all? Well, come along then and we'll talk about it—"

"Donald Satterfield?"

Satterfield, his mouth drawn tight, leapt to open the door of his hotel room. The others had gone on the 8:00 A.M. train to Fort Smith, but he had stayed behind. All day long he had walked the streets of the city, finally returning to his hotel room in despair, not knowing what else to do.

Opening the door, he found a young man standing there holding an envelope. "You Don Satterfield?"

"Yes! Yes, I'm Satterfield."

"Fellow asked me to bring this to you."

Satterfield took the envelope and ripped it open, ignoring the messenger's outstretched palm. With disgust, the young man whirled and stalked away down the hall. The note was not long, and Satterfield's hands trembled as he read it.

Don, I'm leaving college and going East where I've been of-fered work. I've never fitted in at school, and have been unhappy there. Don't try to find me. I'll write when I get settled. Please go see my folks. Tell them I'll write soon. You've been so nice to me, Don. Thanks for everything.

Lylah

P.S. President Barton,—it wasn't Don's fault that I left. He did his best for me, so please don't blame him for this. It's my own decision.

Satterfield read the note twice before its meaning sank in. Then he looked up, and seeing the messenger was gone, tore down the steps and caught the young man as he was leaving the hotel.

"Who gave you this note?"

"Can't remember... but two bits might improve my memory." The messenger grinned, took the money Satterfield gave him, then shrugged. "I don't know his name, but he's one of them actor fellows playing at the opera house." He stared at Satterfield, who wheeled around and ran out into the cold air. "Hey!" he called out. "Ain't no use goin' down there! The whole crowd left last night on the train for the East!" Then he shrugged, snapped the money smartly, and went out whistling "Buffalo Gals."

It was Owen who first heard the voice calling. He got down from the chair where he was tying a rope of stringed popcorn on the top of the fir tree he had placed in the corner. The other children were milling around, helping him decorate the Christmas tree, and he had to shove his way through them to get to the door. "I'll bet that's Lylah coming!" he said, excitement in his voice.

The others crowded around him, but when Owen saw the horse and rider pounding over the hard-packed snow, he said, "It's not Lylah."

Amos came to stand beside him, followed by Will and Marian. "That's Don Satterfield," he said with disappointment.

"I hope Lylah didn't get sick and have to stay at school for Christmas holidays," Marian said.

Will Stuart shook his head. "Something's wrong . . . that's sure." He stepped forward to greet the visitor, calling out, "Get down, Don."

They all watched as the lanky young man dismounted awkwardly. His nose was red with the cold and his lips were blue. "Hello . . . " he said, and the very diffidence of his voice was as strong as an alarm bell to the adults.

"Where's Lylah, Don?" Marian demanded at once. "Is she sick?"

"No . . . well, I don't think so." Satterfield glanced at the children, and felt worse than he ever had in his life. "Can't you send the little ones in, Mr. Stuart?"

"You young 'uns go inside," Will ordered, and the severity of his tone was enough to send the smaller children inside. Owen stayed where he was, defying his father's stern gaze. Finally, when the door was shut, Stuart asked in a hard voice, "All right, Don. Let's have it."

All of them expected Satterfield to say that Lylah was dead. Such sudden deaths were not uncommon in their world. They all willed him to say something less tragic. So it was, that when Satterfield had finally stammered out his story, all of them felt a little weak.

"She's alive," Amos said, relieved. He stood there while Satterfield almost wept as he told how he'd tried to find Lylah. Amos watched the reaction of the others, but something was growing inside him—a vague notion at first, but a notion that had grown solid as granite by the time Satterfield turned to go. "Don, what's the names of those actors?"

"Well, the star was a woman named Maude Adams. But it was one of the men who sent the note. I asked around, but nobody knew them. Nobody noticed Lylah when they left to go to the train."

"You say they was all headed back to New York?"

Satterfield nodded. "I found out that much from the man

who manages the theater. He said Little Rock was the last stop for the play, and that they'd all be goin' back to New York." He waited for Amos to speak. When he did not, Satterfield rode away, anxious to leave the family.

Owen had been watching his brother's face. "You're going after her, ain't you, Amos?"

Amos nodded. "Yes, I am."

"Amos, you can't go!" Will Stuart spoke up.

"Work's all done, Pa. I'll be back for spring plowing."

"But you don't have the money to go to New York, son!" Marian said. "Besides, if you did get there, it's a mighty big place, and you don't know a soul. How would you ever find one girl in a place like that?"

Amos Stuart lifted his head and a bright purpose burned in his dark blue eyes. "I got enough for train fare saved back, for most of the way. I'll catch rides for the rest of it. And as for finding Lylah, why, you've always said nothing is too hard for God, ain't that right?"

"That's right, Amos!"

"Well, Ma, I'll do the looking . . . and you do the praying!"

3

A ROOM IN NEW YORK

When Amos Stuart stepped off the murky, smoke-blackened train in New York City and into the bright sunshine, he looked like a coal-heaver who had neglected to wash up after his day's work. His hands and face were streaked with smoke and dust, his white linen shirt was wrinkled and smutty, and his brown suit was disheveled.

Amos had been on the train for four days and nights but had not gone to bed at all, for he had no funds to use the sleeping car attached to the train. He *had* left home with a little more than he had expected, for his father had given him fifty dollars—a princely sum indeed for a poor hill farmer.

"I'd just waste it, Amos," his father had said, as he had thrust the small roll of bills into the boy's shirt pocket. "Find our girl, that's what's important."

In addition, Don Satterfield had pressed thirty dollars on him. Amos had tried to refuse, knowing that it was the young man's tuition money, but Satterfield had insisted. "I feel responsible, Amos. Just wish it was more . . . besides, God told me to give it to you."

The extra money had been enough to pay Amos's fare all the way to New York, but as he stepped off the train, he had only thirty-two dollars to his name—not nearly enough for his return fare. He kept the money concealed in a leather tobacco bag, suspended by a string around his neck. There had been no privacy in the day coach of course, and he wondered how many people had lost their watches and pocketbooks while traveling.

He kept a six-chambered revolver in his pocket, also a gift from his father, who had warned, "Them city folks are slick, Amos. They'll steal the gold out of your teeth!"

While Amos had no gold in his teeth, he had taken the revolver, for it could be sold for cash in the city. It wasn't uncommon for the people of the hills to carry firearms; there was no law against it, and as he stepped to the ground and found himself caught up in a milling crowd of people, the weight of the weapon gave him a little more confidence.

He reasoned that the passengers would be headed for town, so he allowed himself to be carried along with the stream. As he moved off the brick-paved surface, he listened to the fascinating sounds of voices. The people spoke much more rapidly here, he noticed, and there was a hard edge to their dialect that contrasted sharply with the soft drawls of his own people.

When he passed through the station—bigger than any building he'd ever even seen—and moved outside, a hack driver, an old man with an Irish brogue, spoke up. "Cab, sir? Take ye right uptown!"

Amos hesitated, then asked, "How much does it cost?"

"A dollar."

Amos thought of his dwindling supply of cash and shook his head. "I guess not."

The cabdriver took in the rumpled suit, the shabby carpet-bag, and grinned. "Come to get rich in the big city, have ye?"

Amos returned the smile. "No, I'm just looking for someone." He looked around with perplexity, then back to the cab driver. "Can you tell me where the opera house is?"

The cabbie's grin broadened. "*The* opera house, is it? Why, me boy, there's at least *twenty* of 'em . . . maybe more!"

"Oh." Amos was so weary from his journey that he could not think straight. "Well," he said slowly, "where's the biggest one?"

"Down on Broadway," the Irishman replied. He was a

shrewd-looking old man, but there was a kindly gleam in his sharp eyes. "Look, me boy, you'll walk your shoe leather off gettin' there. Get up on the seat of the cab. Any fare I pick up will have to go in that direction."

"I don't have the money."

"And did I ask ye for any?" the cabbie asked indignantly. "Me name is Mack Sullivan and I've got a couple of boys of me own, out in the world someplace. I'd like to think that if I give a young fellow a helping hand, why, the good Lord will cause somebody to do the same for them. Besides, I wudna do it if I hadna liked your face. Up with ye now," he ordered, seeing a couple heading his way.

As Amos listened to Sullivan chattering away on the trip downtown, he studied the outlying sections of New York and was disappointed. Some of the areas they passed through were no more than a hodgepodge of wooden and brick buildings, huddled together without harmony or design. Most of the wooden houses were unpainted, and they had the sodden appearance that comes from long exposure to the weather. Some of them leaned crazily to one side or hung over the street, looking as if a little push would knock them down.

As they rattled toward the heart of the city, however, the slums gave way to more attractive neighborhoods, most of the houses made of brownstone. Bells began to ring, and the cabbie nodded. "Time for church." He gestured toward a large, handsome building, built of wood and painted gray. Many people were making their way along the street on their way to the services. Nearly all the men wore tall silk hats and the long, double-breasted frock coats known as Prince Alberts. The ladies' skirts were so long they touched the ground, and some of the women themselves looked deformed.

"Why do those women have such big rear ends?" Amos inquired.

Mack Sullivan stared at him in amazement, then began to laugh. "Why, that's the style, me boy! Bustles, they call them things. Womenfolk don't wear such things where ye come from?"

"No. A woman would get laughed out of town if she put on a thing like that!" He stared at them, shaking his head in disbelief. Some of the bustles were so exaggerated they stuck out twelve, fifteen, or even twenty inches behind their wearers. "Why are they in such a hurry, all of them?"

"Hurry?" The Irishman looked at the crowds surging like a human tide down the street, then shrugged, "They ain't in no hurry, me boy. I guess folks just move faster in the city than they do on the farm." He stopped two blocks later, hopped out, and handed the lady down. Then, after taking his fare, he climbed back onto the seat. "Well, now, me guess is ye don't know a soul in this town."

"That's right."

"Not much money and no place to stay?" Without pausing for an answer, Sullivan went on, "Well, I think ye'll not be stayin' at the Ritz. Maybe ye'd like to find a cheap place?"

Amos quickly let it be known that this was his desire, and the old man drove along the streets, dropping comments rapidly, stopping at last on a street lined with rows of smoke-stained houses that almost rimmed the curb. With practically no yards to play in, the children were playing in the streets, in the dirty slush of snow that was banked up on the sidewalks.

"Italian people." Sullivan nodded. "Good folks, most of 'em, but a little too high-tempered. Most of 'em are poor, and sometimes they take in a boarder or two. Nothin' fancy, ye understand. Just a cot, maybe, and whatever they have to eat at their table."

"Do you know any of them, Mr. Sullivan?"

"Well, now, not to put too fine a point on it, me boy, I *do* have a slight acquaintance with one of 'em." He pointed with his buggy whip toward one of the narrow houses, the steps crowded with an assortment of youngsters. "Anna Castellano is her name. Her poor husband—bless his soul!—was took off by the grippe two years ago. The poor woman does the best she can, but it's a hard life fer a woman alone in the world." Sullivan shrugged his thin shoulders, adding, "It'll be about the cheapest thing ye can find, me boy."

"Just what I need," Amos said. He picked up his bag, got down, then reached up to shake hands with the Irishman. "I didn't think city people were so friendly, Mr. Sullivan," he said. "I'm beholden to you."

"Ah, now, there's them that'll take advantage, me boy," Sullivan warned. "Ye get your business done and skedaddle back to the farm! Now, be sure to tell Mrs. Castellano that Mack Sullivan sent ye."

"All right . . . and thanks." Sullivan whipped his horse up, and Amos moved to the stoop where half a dozen black-eyed children, all with ragged black hair, stood staring at him. "Your Ma at home?"

"Yeah, she's awashin' in the back yard," replied the largest of the children, a girl of about fifteen. "You hafta' come this a-way."

The houses were built without walk spaces, so Amos followed the girl through the house. The rest of the troop followed, speaking loudly, half in English and half in Italian.

When Amos stepped out the back door, he saw a heavyset woman wearing a black coat with a yellow scarf around her head, pummeling clothes in a black pot. The smoke from the fire under the pot curled around, and as she turned her face to avoid it, the sight of a strange man made her eyes grow narrow.

"Whatta you want?" she demanded in a throaty voice, thickened by an accent.

"I'm looking for a place to stay," Amos said quickly. "Mack Sullivan said you might have a room."

The suspicion disappeared from the woman's round face at once. "Mary Elizabeth, come watch-a the fire." As the largest girl separated herself from the others and went down the steps to take the stick, the woman met her at the foot of the stairs and climbed up, holding to the rail. "A room? No gotta room."

"Oh. Well, I guess—"

"No gotta room, just for *you* . . . but you can maybe sleep with-a Nick and Mario, my boys."

"Oh, that'll be all right, Mrs. Castellano," Amos said quickly.

"You pay one dollar every day . . . and you eat at our table." She was not a handsome woman, but there was a pleasant air about her. Her face was marked with care, but she had large attractive eyes, the darkest Amos had ever seen. "Come on, I show you the room."

Amos followed her up two flights on the narrow staircase, then onto a narrow, dark hall with two doors on each side. Opening one of the doors, she gestured. "You take-a that bed," she said. She studied his soot-stained clothing, and said abruptly, "Take off-a your clothes."

Amos froze, the blood rushing to his face. He had heard that there were bad women in the big city, but Anna Castellano had not seemed a likely version. He began to edge toward the door, and the woman, seeing the shocked look on his face, broke into a peal of rich laughter. Her large body quivered, and she finally wiped her eyes and gave Amos a merry look. "I'm-a glad to see you're a nice-a boy. But you're safe with Mama Anna. I just think you're pretty dirty. I wash-a your clothes, and *you* can wash on the back porch."

"Oh—" Amos felt like a fool and said so. "I'm sorry, Mrs. Castellano."

"Just call-a me Mama Anna." She smiled. "Take your clothes to Mary Elizabeth . . . then wash-a your face."

Mama Anna's brusque orders somehow relieved Amos. He grinned as he changed into his other clothes. *Always good for a fellow to have a ma around to look after him.*

He went downstairs and handed his clothes to the girl— all except his underwear, which he had decided to wash himself. He washed up in the kitchen, where the smell of fresh bread baking in the oven brought an ache to his throat, he was that hungry. Anna must have sensed this, for she set him down. "You no eat breakfast? I fix-a you something."

As Amos forced himself to slowly eat the bread and stew she put before him, he listened as the woman chattered. The children came and went, scurrying around so fast Amos couldn't get a head count. He finally figured out that there were five little ones, with two older children. When he finished his meal, the warmth of the kitchen and the fullness of his stomach, combined with his long journey, began to bring an overwhelming desire for sleep.

Mama Anna, seeing his eyelids droop, said, "Now, you go to bed."

Amos mumbled his thanks and stumbled up the stairs, so overcome with fatigue that he could barely remove his shoes. He rolled onto the cot, pulled a worn blanket up to his chin, and promptly lost consciousness, slipping away into a black hole that closed upon him instantly.

Well . . . I got here, Ma. Now get those prayers to going!

Amos was awakened by the sound of voices. At first he thought he was back in the loft with Owen and his other brothers. But as he slowly pulled himself back to consciousness, he became confused, for the voices were strange to him. He sat up, bolt upright, to find a young man about his own age sitting cross-legged on a cot across from his. On the third cot a boy with the same curly black hair and smooth olive features regarded him steadily.

"Hello." The older one nodded. "You finally wake up?"

Amos was exhausted and, when he looked out the window, he saw that it was still dark. He arched his back and felt for his money pouch. "I guess so. I was on the train for four days . . . didn't sleep much."

"Four days? Where'd you come from?"

"Arkansas."

"Yeah? That's way out in the sticks, ain't it?" The young man shrugged, adding, "My name's Nick."

"I'm Amos Stuart." Amos was hungry again, and the smell

of some rich food wafted into the room, increasing his hunger. "Is it time to eat?"

Nick laughed, exposing a perfect set of white teeth. "Sure. Come on and let's get started before it's all gobbled up."

He led the way down the stairs and into the largest room in the house. The dining room was dominated by a large rectangular table flanked by an assortment of chairs, all occupied by either resident Castellanos or boarders. This last group included Amos and two young women, who shared a room down the hall from him. They were both plain and poorly dressed, but each of them gave Amos a calculating look as they ate.

The meal was spaghetti, served in two large bowls, kept filled by Mama Anna or Mary Elizabeth. There was plenty of fresh bread with butter, and water to drink.

Nick watched with amusement in his dark eyes as Amos poked at his portion of spaghetti cautiously, not knowing how to handle it. "You never ate spaghetti before?"

"No, I never did."

"Here, wind it around your fork like this." Nick demonstrated his technique, and Amos awkwardly succeeded in transferring a sizable portion of the slippery tubes into his mouth. "You like?"

"It's real good."

"Glad you think so." Nick winked at the others. "You're gonna' see a lot of it around here."

After supper, Amos walked down to the grocery store with Nick. They were scarcely out of sight of the house when Nick stopped and turned to face Amos. The gaslights were on—a marvel to Amos—and the yellow glow seemed to give the face of young Castellano an oriental cast. He was smoking a cigarette, and he let it dangle from his lower lip as he spoke. "This ain't your home ground, Amos," Nick said in a tight voice. "So I'm gonna give you one little bit of advice."

Amos was taken aback by the young man's rather abrupt manner. "I'd appreciate it," he said carefully.

"Keep your hands off my sister."

For one moment Amos thought Nick was joking, but there was no humor in the lean face turned toward his. "Mary Elizabeth? Why, she's just a kid!" he protested.

Nick shook his head. "She's filling out, and I wanna be sure you know what's what." He took a long draw on the cigarette, tossed it onto the hard-packed ice, then stepped on it, grinding it beneath his foot. "Us Italians are kinda funny. We fight a lot with the Jews and the Irish . . . but that don't mean nothin' usually. But we believe in family, see? Anyone who hurts one member of the family . . . well, he's got the whole bunch of us to fight."

Amos thought of his own family. "Why, we're like that, too, Nick. Back home, I mean." He had thought to keep his reason for coming to the city a secret, but an impulse overtook him. "The reason I'm here, Nick . . . my sister Lylah ran off with some man. I'm here to get her and take her home. And if the guy objects, I'll make him wish he'd never been born!"

Nick was studying the newcomer's face carefully and seemed to be testing the quality of his words. Liking what he saw, he allowed a smile to tilt the corners of his lips. "That why you're packing a gun?" he asked quietly. Then catching Amos's expression of outrage, he explained, "Yeah, I know about it."

"You went through my bag?"

"Naw, I didn't. It was Mario, my kid brother. He's only six, and you know how kids are . . . always into everything. Hey, it's okay," he said quickly. "Another thing about us Italians, we don't squeal on our friends." He waited for a moment, then nodded. "You're okay, Amos. Any guy who sets out to get the rat who ruined his sister is okay in my book. Anything I can do, you let me know. I mean, like if you find the guy, and he's too tough, I got some friends who'll turn him wrong side out."

Amos felt a warm glow, for he knew that Nick was not the sort who made such offers casually. "I'll remember that, Nick.

And if anyone insults Mary Elizabeth, I'll hold him while you
cut his ears off!"

Nick laughed, delighted with the idea. "Ho, that's the way
I like to hear a guy talk!" Growing serious, he turned and
asked, "You got any idea about how to find your sister?"

"Not much . . . except the guy she ran off with is an actor
of some kind. And I know the name of the woman who was
the boss when they were in Little Rock."

"Shouldn't be too hard." Nick shrugged. "You find the
woman, she names the punk, and we go get him. It'll be
easy!"

But it was not easy, as Amos soon discovered.

On Monday morning he set out to find Maude Adams.
Following instructions from Nick, he made his way to the
section of New York where most of the city's theaters and
opera houses were located. Going into the first one he came
to, Amos found a fat man wearing a black derby and sitting
at a desk. "I'd like to see Miss Maude Adams."

The fat man took the cigar stub out of his mouth, studied
the ruby tip, then set his pale blue eyes on Amos. "So would
about a million other guys," he remarked, and replacing the
cigar, resumed reading his newspaper.

Amos's temper flared, and he leaned forward. As his coat
fell open, the fat man's gaze took in the revolver Amos had
stuck into his waistband. The man sat upright, eyes bugged
out. "Hey, I didn't mean nothing, mister!"

"Neither did I," Amos said, but there was something in his
eyes that frightened the man at the desk. "I only need to ask
her a simple question."

"Yeah . . . sure." The fat man nodded, speaking rapidly.
"What you need to do is go down to the Victoria Theater.
Miss Adams won't be there, but you talk to a man named Joe
Rossi. He's a close friend of hers and can put you in touch."

"Thanks." As Amos turned to leave, the fat man said, "I
wouldn't flourish that gun in front of Joe. He's a pretty tough

article." As soon as Amos left, the fat man scribbled something on a scrap of paper and called out, "Hey, Pierce, take this note over to Joe Rossi at the Vic, will you?"

A grizzled old man with a patch over his left eye shuffled in, a broom in his hands. He took the note, stuffed it into his shirt pocket and left, grumbling about the cold.

"I hope Joe shoots that kid." The fat man smiled wickedly, then returned to his paper.

"Look, kid, lemme put it to you like this . . . there ain't no way I'm gonna tell you where Miss Adams is."

Joe Rossi had stood up when Amos entered his office. He had the note from Ed Bains, warning him that a yokel with a gun was making noises. He left his own hand in his right pocket, clutching a derringer . . . just in case.

He was a tough man, and a careful one, having been many things in the past, and he knew men well. The young man who stood before him was clean-cut and seemed to be a good type, but Rossi could see the bulk of the revolver beneath the thin coat the boy wore.

Amos was aware of the man's hard eyes, and didn't know what he'd done to make him angry. "I just need to ask her one question," he said quietly.

"What question?"

"I–I can't ask anyone except her." Amos bit his lip. "I know she's a famous lady and probably all kinds of people pester her. But I've got a problem, and she's the only one who can help me."

Rossi decided the boy wasn't dangerous. Removing his hand from his pocket, he sat down and waved toward the chair. "Sit down, kid . . . and let's talk. What's your name?"

Amos gave his name and sat there, twisting his soft cap in his hands as Rossi questioned him and trying to think of another way to find Lylah. But it seemed almost impossible. Finally he got to his feet. "Sorry to have bothered you, Mr. Rossi."

Rossi let the young man get to the door, then made a decision. "Stuart . . . wait a minute!"

"Yes, sir?"

Rossi rose and motioned toward his desk. "Miss Adams is out of the country. But if you want to write her a letter, I'll see that she gets it."

Amos thought quickly, then nodded. "I'd appreciate that, Mr. Rossi." He sat down and wrote a few lines, folded the paper, and handed it to Rossi. The older man took it and held it in his hand. "Leave your name and address. I'll send for you if she answers this."

Amos jotted down the Castellanos' address, then looked up. "How long do you think she'll be gone?"

"Maybe a month, maybe two."

Rossi turned away in dismissal, and Amos left the office, feeling defeated. *I can't stay here two months! he thought. I'm broke!* But then he remembered Lylah's face, and his jaw hardened.

He walked back to the Castellanos' house and, when Nick came home, he told him what had happened. "I've got to stay here until I hear something. Do you know where I can get work?"

Nick nodded. "Sure, you can work in the bottle factory with me." He frowned and stared down at his hands. "But you won't like it, Amos."

"Can't be any worse than plowing new ground."

"You'll see!"

A NEW ARRIVAL

A voice was calling his name, but Amos clung stubbornly to sleep, fighting for oblivion as a dreamer fights for his dream. Hands pulled at him, and he made a few feeble spasmodic blows that accomplished nothing.

"Lemme sleep!" he mumbled, burrowing his face in the pillow, trying desperately to will away the voice and the hands.

But the hands persisted, grabbed his shoulders and pulled him upright, and Amos squinted, recognizing the features of Nick Castellano. "Come on, Amos, pile out of there!" Nick said, and when Amos tried to break away, Nick braced himself and gave a rough jerk, pulling Amos half out of bed. "Better hurry up, or they'll dock your pay!"

Amos groped around in the murky darkness, fingers stiff with cold as he fumbled for his clothes. They lay on the floor where he'd let them drop the night before, stiff and dirty and cold, so that he shivered as the cloth touched his bare skin. They smelled rank. *Got to wash my clothes after work*, he thought. *Can't live like a pig!* He had only two sets of working clothes, and his first two weeks on the job, he'd washed one set every day, but that had taken too much energy, until now he usually went dirty . . . except for those times Mama Anna or Mary Elizabeth took pity on him and threw his stiff pants and shirt into the family wash.

When he was dressed, he stumbled out of the small room, casting one envious glance at Mario's sleeping form. *I'd give anything to be able to stay in bed and sleep!* He went downstairs, stood beside Nick at the mirror over the washbasin, and the two of them shaved in cold water, the dull razor raking Amos's skin and making his eyes water. After he finished, he slumped at the table with Nick and gulped down the coffee Anna set out, then silently ate the hot mush and rolls that comprised their usual breakfast. It was the last hot food he would have for fourteen hours, so he chewed slowly, trying not to think of the long day stretching before him.

Swallowing their last bite, they got up and took the small paper sacks Anna gave them. She kissed Nick. "I'll see you after work, *bambino mio.*"

Nick was embarrassed as always by her caress. He pulled away, grunting, "Yeah . . . okay, Mama." Anna patted Amos on the shoulder and smiled. "I put half an apple in your lunch, Amos."

"Thanks, Mama Anna." Tired as he was, Amos came up with a faint smile for her, then turned and followed Nick out of the house.

It was bitter cold, had been since the new year of 1898 had descended on the city. A fresh snow had fallen, laying a glittering white icing over the old covering of dirty yellow. It had stopped snowing, but the wind cut through Amos's thin coat and rasped against his throat and lungs like a razor as he breathed. His rough shoes were so worn that, despite the pieces of leather he had inserted to cover the holes in the soles, he could feel the cold dampness seeping in. When he inadvertently stepped onto a sheet of ice that broke beneath his weight, he felt icy water fill his shoes and knew he was doomed to have aching cold feet all day.

The two young men trudged along the murky streets, past block after block of tenement houses, saying nothing at all to each other. They were part of a silent stream of laborers, clothed in black and muted by the cold and the dullness of fatigue, who moved like specters toward the big smoke-stained buildings that blotted out the darkness of the sky.

As they approached the building, Nick burst out in a spasm

of defiance, "I ain't gonna stand this no more, Amos. This is my last day at this dump!"

Amos turned to stare at him. "You're quittin'?"

Nick glared at the bulk of the dark, many-eyed building, whose opaque windows seemed to glare blindly back at him. He cursed roughly, then shook his head, and when Amos asked what he was going to do, replied sharply, "I'll get by . . . and I'll make more dough than I ever made before, too, see if I don't!"

Amos said nothing, but he had not been unaware of the strain between Nick and his mother. Their arguments had been loud and frequent—she, accusing him of running with a wild bunch and warning him that he'd get into trouble if he didn't watch out; Nick, shouting that he was old enough to choose his own friends.

Amos had gone with Nick a few times and had formed a low opinion of Nick's crowd. At least, they didn't appeal to *him*. None of them had jobs, yet they had good clothes and money for beer and dance hall girls. They were all Italian, of course, and Amos had felt out of place, preferring to stay home after the first two or three times. He knew they were hooked up with some sort of shadowy organization that had its roots in the old country, and Nick had warned him, "Don't get crossways with nobody in this crowd, Amos. They got connections."

Nick need not have worried, for Amos had neither time, money, nor inclination to join that crowd. He was an intuitive young man and understood that they were on the fringe of lawlessness. But the few times he'd tried to mention his uneasiness to Nick, the other boy had only laughed at him.

A shrill whistle split the air just as the two young men entered the building. They hurried across the massive room, lit only by a few gaslights along the wall. Getting a hard look and a curse from their foreman, they took their places.

The work was simple enough, for all Amos did all day long was to tie glass stoppers into small bottles. He carried a bundle of twine at his waist and held the bottles between his knees so that he could work with both hands. Sitting in this cramped position, his shoulders began to ache after only a few hours. And by glancing around at his fellow workers— some of whom had done nothing but this monotonous work for years—the fear took root that he would become like them, gnomes with rounded backs and blunt faces, devoid of all other interests in life.

Amos was strong, but not particularly dexterous. His father, with his nimble musician's fingers, could have tied twice as many bottles. Added to his native ineptness was the freezing cold in the unheated factory. Amos had tried hard at first, but his numb fingers just would not do the work quickly, though he stared at them and willed them to go faster. It grated on him that the young woman next to him could tie three hundred dozen bottles a day.

She was a frail thing, with a hollow cough and two red spots on her cheeks not made by cosmetics, but her fingers flew, the string and bottles seeming to unite magically, flowing from her hands in a steady stream. She had attained a machine-like perfection. All movements of her thin fingers were automatic, and her eyes were blank as she worked, so it seemed to Amos she was becoming a machine herself.

As for Amos, he worked under high tension and grew so nervous that his muscles twitched in his sleep, and even when he was not working, he could not relax. He longed for the farm, for the hardwork at home had been a pleasure. The sharp biting cold of the Ozarks had not been like this deadening cold inside the musty building: That air had been invigorating, while the damp cold of the factory seemed not only to numb his fingers but his brain as well.

All day he tied the little bottles, stopping only for thirty brief minutes at noon to eat the sandwich and the half an apple. He washed it down with bitter-tasting water from the water can, then went back to the second half of his ten-hour day.

By the end of his workday, Amos's senses were dulled, his

fingers stiff and sore, and he knew that he would go back to the house, eat, and go directly to bed. He tried to think of some way to do what he had planned—to spend part of his time searching for Lylah. That grand scheme had lasted only a few days, for he was so exhausted at night that he could not force himself to go out and look for her. The search was, in any case, fruitless, for the only clue he had to her whereabouts was the theater, and by the time he walked to Broadway, it would be too late to make any inquiries. As for days off, he was barely making enough now to pay his room and board and to put aside a small amount for emergencies.

While he was struggling with this problem, Amos became aware that something was happening just to his left.

The superintendent, accompanied by a burly man in a suit and tie, was standing beside a small boy named Fred. When someone whispered, *"That's the inspector!"* Amos stopped work and turned to watch the little group.

The inspector caught Fred by the arm, peered at him intently, then asked, "How old are you?"

"Fourteen!" the boy replied, and would have said more, but was cut off by a dry hacking cough.

"I know this boy," the inspector said sternly. "He's twelve years old. I've had him discharged from three factories this year." He turned to the superintendent. "You'll have to let him go."

"No, we ain't got enough to eat at home," Fred protested. "I got to work!"

The inspector eyed him critically. "Look at him! Got rickets . . . and probably consumption to boot."

"Please, mister!" the boy cried. "I got to work! Ain't nobody but me got work, and I got a sick ma and a baby sister."

"Get him out of here," snapped the burly man.

The Stuart breed had been subject to fiery fits of white-hot anger over injustices for longer than Amos knew. His forebears were Scotch Covenanters who had incarnadined the soil of their native land over such as this. And as the big man started to turn away, a red curtain seemed to fall over Amos Stuart's eyes. He dropped the bottles in his hands to the cement floor, ignored the tinkling sound as they shattered, and leapt to grasp the inspector's arm.

"Inspector of *what*?" Amos demanded. "If you're supposed to inspect this place to see that working conditions are decent . . . all you have to do is look around . . . if you're not blind, that is!"

Startled, the big man tried to pull his arm away but found it gripped by fingers of steel. He looked wildly at the superintendent who was just as stunned.

"Are you supposed to see if women and children, many of them sick, are being overworked?" Amos raged. "Well, look around you, Mr. Inspector!" Amos used his free hand to make a sweeping gesture.

Work had stopped now, and every eye was turned toward the scene.

"That's the stuff, kid!" Nick shouted. "Tell the dirty rotters how it is!"

The superintendent came to himself and reached out to grab Amos, but was struck with an iron forearm that knocked him on his rear. He let out a yelp of pain, and the muscular inspector chose that moment to hit Amos in the neck with his big fist. Amos was driven to his knees, and the big man drew back his foot to administer a kick. But at that moment Nick came up and caught him over the ear with the edge of the stool he'd been sitting on. The man went down like a felled ox, and Nick shouted something in Italian. Then he grabbed Amos, a wild grin on his face. "Come on! They'll call the cops now!"

Amos's head was still spinning, but Nick guided him through the factory to the outside. The sky was growing dark, and the cold bit at them, but Nick beat Amos on the back as they lurched along. "You got *machismo*, kid! Come on!"

When they were clear of the area, Amos asked, "Will they arrest us, Nick?"

"Naw. They might send some of the cops looking for us,

but I got some pull with the boys now. They'll slip him a few bucks and he'll report that he couldn't find a trace of us." Nick gave his friend a proud look. "That's the way it's going to be with me, Amos. You get on the inside . . . and nobody can touch you!"

"The inside of *what*?" Amos asked, puzzled.

At once Nick's lips grew tight, and he shook his head. "Don't worry about it, kid. I'll take care of you." He smiled then, adding, "You're a pretty quick guy, you know? Real speedy, the way you clipped that super! Guess I'll have to call you 'Speed' Stuart from now on."

By the time they got back to the house, the excitement of the adventure had worn off, and Amos was beginning to realize that he'd lost three days' pay because of his escapade. He ate supper, half-listening as Nick told the story of their great revolt and he noted that the two female boarders and Mary Elizabeth were watching him with new interest.

But after he went to bed, Amos lay awake worrying, long after Nick and Mario's breathing grew even and regular. *I'll have to go back home*, he concluded. But everything in him rebelled at the idea of giving up. Buried beneath Amos's easygoing manner was an iron-hard stubbornness that would not let him quit as long as he was able to function. He racked his brain, trying to think of a way to stay in the city. Finally, a strange thought came to him—such an unusual thought, for him, that he grinned at his own foolishness.

The thought, however, refused to go away, and he lay there quietly, pondering what he should do about it. He even thought about praying for help from God. He moved restlessly, but the idea seemed to bore into his mind, and he almost said aloud, *Pray to God for help? Why should he help me? All I've done is go through the motions . . . never had anything real . . . not like Ma's got.*

He drifted into a light sleep at last, only to awaken soon after with the same impulse nagging at him. Half in disgust at what he considered a weakness, he whispered, "Oh, all right, then—God, help me get a job!" Another thought came to him, and he added, "And I want a job that pays plenty . . . and one where I can do something I'm good at and like to do." He did smile then, and as sleep came rushing back, he whispered, "Now, then—let's see how you manage *that* little trick!"

Amos slept until nearly nine o'clock the next morning, but his first thought when he finally opened his eyes was: *I asked God to get me a job!*

He sat up abruptly, remembering his prayer, and for a time didn't move, thinking how ridiculous the whole thing was. But he didn't feel like laughing, and when he went downstairs and coaxed Mama Anna into fixing him a late breakfast, he had the courage to mention his idea to her.

She listened carefully, then nodded. "Yes . . . I pray for you, Amos. God . . . he's-a *bigga* God!"

Amos stared at her. "My ma always says so, Mama Anna."

An hour later he was walking the icy streets, ignoring the cold wind and trying to decide which way to go. He knew he could find work at the jute mill or one of the other factories, but they were as bad as the glass factory. His pace slowed, and he walked aimlessly for almost an hour.

As Amos walked, he studied his surroundings, thinking he might see something that would suggest a job. But nothing came. By noon, he was cold, hungry, and discouraged. *Guess it was just a fool idea after all—me praying,* he thought wearily. *Well, there's still the jute mill. It's either that or go home with my tail between my legs like a whipped hound.*

First, he decided to enjoy at least this one day of freedom and spent twenty cents at a small café for a big bowl of hot soup and all the homemade bread he could eat—plus two big mugs of steaming hot black coffee. He made the meal last as long as possible, then walked outside, pulling his coat around him. It had occurred to him while eating that he would go back and ask Mr. Rossi if he'd heard from Miss Adams, so he made his way toward the theater district.

Rossi, however, was not in, and Amos knew it was useless to

ask the man who told him so. He left the theater and walked
slowly down the street, his head down. He'd turned to walk
back toward the jute mill after all, when he heard someone call
his name. Looking up, he saw Mack Sullivan perched on the
seat of his cab, waving at him.

Amos crossed the street and climbed up at the Irishman's
invitation. "Been wanting to see you, Mack. Wanted to thank
you for steering me to Anna's house."

Sullivan's face was blue with cold . . . all except his nose,
which was bright red in the cold air. He grinned, pulled out
a bottle and offered it to Amos. "Sure, me boy, no trouble
a'tall. Have a drink. No? Then I'll be havin' two for meself."
He swallowed the whiskey, did a strange little contorted jig,
and made a grotesque face as the strong drink hit his stomach. "Begorra . . . that's horrible stuff!" he gasped.

"Why do you drink it if it's that bad?"

"I'm a weak man," Mack acknowledged solemnly. "Well,
now, Anna tells me you're a foine young man."

"I'm a fine young man without a job, Mack."

"Do ye tell me that?" Sullivan was so surprised he took
another swig of the potent liquor, and after performing his
anguished jig, said, "I thought ye was working at the glass
factory with Nick." He listened carefully as Amos explained—leaving out some of the details—how he and Nick
had parted company with their former employer.

The stubby Irishman studied the young man with his
bright blue eyes. "Now, wait—" he began, pulling his brows
together and beating his head with his fist. "Come out, devil
of a thought!" He pulled out the bottle, scowled at it ferociously, and after a gulp and a dance on the seat, cried out,
"I've got it!"

"Got what, Mack?" Amos asked, amused at the little man's
antics.

"Why, it's something I heard only yesterday . . . no, it was
two days ago! Never mind, when I heard it, I thought of ye."

He grinned at Amos. "Would ye be for knowin' anything about horses, me boy?"

"Why . . . that's the *one* thing I do know something about, Mack!"

"And is it that ye can ride the beasts?"

Amos smiled at Sullivan. "If it's got hair and four legs, I can ride it, Mack." It was not boastfully said, but it was true enough. Amos had never had a horse of his own, but they'd been a passion of his always. He'd learned to ride the neighbors' horses, and by the time he was fifteen, he was racing with grown men, making a little money on occasion. But mostly he rode for the joy of it.

"Well," said Sullivan, "Will Pegeen heard that the fellow who worked for the big stable out on the east side got his leg busted. Pegeen told me they was lookin' to hire a man to take care of the ridin' horses."

"Where is it, Mack?" Amos asked.

Sullivan, after taking a small libation to celebrate, lifted his whip. "Hang on, me boy . . . it's this Irishman who'll have ye there in no time a'tall."

"I canna hire you if you canna handle the animals, Stuart," Jamie McClendon said, the burr of the Scots thick on his tongue. He was a small, spare man with steady gray eyes and a firm jaw. "Some of me horses are high-spirited, ye see, and some are jumpers. Besides, I do some horse-breaking. That's how that fool Murphy got his leg broke. He couldna stay on a horse with spirit."

Amos had found the manager of Greenlee Stables saddling up a large roan stallion and had asked for work at once. "Give me a chance, Mr. McClendon." He saw the man framing a negative and spoke up before McClendon could turn him down. "Give me your worst horse. If I can't ride him, I'll be on my way."

The manager liked the idea. "Weel, now, I'll just see what kind of a rider ye are. "Simpson," he called out to one of the hands who was forking hay, "put a saddle on Prince." Then he turned back to Stuart with a warning. "This is no job for a lazy man. There's more to it than riding a horse, ye see."

Amos held out his hands, palms upward. "Anybody around here got hands any harder than these?" he demanded. "I didn't get these callouses at a play party, Mr. McClendon!"

The Scotsman peered at Amos's hands from beneath beetling eyebrows. "Gud enough. But first ye ride Prince."

"And I get the job if I stay on?"

"I'll recommend ye to the owner . . . which is all it'll take."

Amos nodded, answered a few questions about his past, and five minutes later the stable hand came around the corner, leading a big black gelding. Amos studied the horse, admiring the powerful hindquarters and the round barrel but didn't miss the wild-looking eyes and the roman nose.

He approached the horse quietly, gathered the reins, and mounted in one swift motion that brought a look of approval to McClendon's eyes. Then Amos spoke to the big horse, nudged him with his heels, and was not entirely unprepared when the animal lunged forward. Within five strides he was running full tilt around the track.

"Hey, Mr. McClendon," the stable hand said, "that fellow can get hurt!"

But McClendon saw that the rider was sticking like a burr on the back of the gelding, and he noted with approval that Stuart was moving his body with the horse, in perfect timing with the long strides. *Weel now . . . the lad has been on a horse before, it seems,* he thought. He studied the action of the horse, and when Prince came around in a thunder of his powerful hooves, the manager saw that Stuart was in perfect control. He had never allowed the horse to get the bit in his teeth— a favorite tactic of the gelding. And on the next circle of the track, McClendon saw what he'd been looking for—the trick Prince had used to eliminate Murphy. He came crashing toward the rail, intent on raking his rider off his back. But it didn't work with this man.

"Good lad!" McClendon whispered as Stuart yanked the horse's head around, forcing him away from the fence.

McClendon waved at Stuart, who brought the big horse to a halt ten feet away. Even then the black gelding tried to buck, but all he got for it was a hard yank on the reins that brought him to an abrupt halt. Amos slid to the ground, handed the reins to McClendon, and grinned. "You didn't mention he'd try to rake me off on the rail."

"No, I did not," the dour Scot snapped back. "I can't use a man who's not as smart as the horse under him." Then he unbent a bit, and a slight smile touched his thin lips. "But ye done well, Stuart. The job's yours if ye want it."

"I'll take it!"

McClendon shook his head. "With a name like Stuart, I thought ye'd be a Scot. But ye haven't even asked about the pay."

"Well, whatever it is, Mr. McClendon," Amos said, "it's more than I'm making now. And there's no job for me better than working with horses."

"Aye, that's true," McClendon nodded, pleased with the answer. "Weel, now, come tomorrow morning, and we'll put ye to work."

When Amos returned to where Mack Sullivan was waiting, he was hard put not to yell and do a dance himself. "I got the job, Mack!" he cried, and his eyes were filled with joy. "I got it . . . thanks to you!"

"Did ye now? Well, that's foine, me boy!"

They drove back toward town, and when Amos finally descended from his state of euphoria, he suddenly had a thought that brought a frown to his face. "Mack . . . do you believe in God?"

"Do ye take me for a fool? Of course I believe in God!"

"Well, he talked to me last night," Amos announced. He told of the incident, concluding thoughtfully, "It all seems like sort of an accident. I mean, I just happened to meet you, and you just happened to have heard of a job I'd be good at."

But Amos was very serious when he said, "I guess there's more to religion than I thought, Mack."

"I hope ye learned a lesson." Mack nodded, and added in a pontifical voice, "Go to church and never forget that the good Lord is up there, watchin' ye all the time." The saintly expression was replaced by a look of impish glee as he pulled out his bottle and asked hopefully, "Have a drink?"

Amos laughed and shook his head. He knew the whole thing would be explained away by many, but he could not forget how strange it was—that God would make him pray, and then give him the very thing he made Amos pray for!

I'll have to write Ma a letter, he thought happily. *She'll probably say, "Well, what's so wonderful about that? Isn't it what I've been telling you for years!*

Later, after celebrating with Anna and the family, Amos found paper and a pencil and wrote it all down in a letter to his mother. That night when he went to bed, he prayed awkwardly, "God, you know how dumb I am, but I'll never forget what you did for me today . . . never!"

5

ROSE

James McClendon, the dour little manager of Greenlee Stables, was a staunch Calvinist as were his forefathers. Thus it was that only two weeks after Amos Stuart came to work with his horses, he was heard to mutter under his breath: "It was all in God's will—that clumsy oaf Murphy breaking his leg—all so the bonnie lad could come and take proper care of the stock!"

Amos, if he had heard McClendon's reasoning, would have probably agreed. After the dull laboring in the glass factory, it was nothing less than joy for him to ride the spirited thoroughbreds each day. He soon proved he was not too good to muck out the stables, as well. Indeed, he was such a hard worker that he drew dark looks from the other hands. He stayed over often, sleeping in McClendon's office on a cot, and within three weeks it was to Stuart that his employer turned to find out whatever he wanted to know about the horses. Amos knew them all, and cared for them as if they were children.

One Friday he exercised Prince, unsaddled him, and gave him a good rubdown. Afterward, he went to the office and used some of the manager's paper to write a letter home.

Dear Ma and Pa and all,
    I wish I had news about Sister, but so far have not been able to learn anything. As I told you before, sooner or later Miss Adams will have to come back to New York. Mr. Rossi told

me her new play will be opening here in three weeks, but said she might come back earlier to practice. I guess you'll have to keep on praying, Ma, and I'll keep on looking.

I love it here at Greenlee. Imagine getting paid for riding fine horses! If Mr. McClendon knew how much I love it, he'd probably cut my wages. But he's already given me a raise (which the other men didn't like, I'm afraid), and I'm saving money for tickets home when I find Lylah.

I miss all of you and long to see you. This big city is something to see, but I miss the mountains. Well, I'll write as soon as I have found out something.

He signed the letter, "Your loving son, Amos," and sealed it. At that moment the manager came in. "Can you sell me a stamp?" Amos asked him.

McClendon opened the desk drawer, produced some loose stamps, and handed one to Amos. "I'll hold the cost out of your pay. Now, go home." The man hesitated, then a glint of humor flickered in his sharp eyes. "Never did I think I'd have to tell a hand to quit work, but I don't want ye to burn out."

Amos smiled. "No danger of that." He put on his coat and left the office, whistling as he went.

The sky was lowering, and before he got halfway home, a cold drizzle began to fall. Soon his clothes were soaked, and water dripped down his neck and through his cap.

He had reached Fifty-first Street when he saw a woman struggling along, headed in his direction. The rain was falling harder now, and her clothing was as bedraggled as his own. Coming up even with her, he saw that the weight of the suitcase she carried was pulling her to a starboard list.

He hesitated for one moment, then stepped up beside her. "That's a pretty heavy suitcase, ma'am. Can I help you with it, wherever you're going?"

The woman had not heard him approach and turned sharply to face him. She was, Amos saw, very young, and there was a hint of fear in her voice as she said quickly, "No! I–I can carry it."

"Well—" Amos shrugged and turned to leave.

He had only gone a few steps when she hailed him. "Please . . . can you tell me if there's a rooming house around here?"

"A rooming house?" Amos wheeled around and stepped back to the girl. "You're looking for a place to stay?"

The cold wind whistled around the corner, keening a thin, high note, and the young woman suddenly set her suitcase down and rubbed her aching arm. She wore a cloth coat, faded and shapeless with the weight of the water that had soaked it, and the cloth hat on her head had collapsed, making her look rather ridiculous. But there was nothing ridiculous about the expression on her face, for it was obvious to Amos that she was not only exhausted, but frightened as well. Strands of dark hair had escaped the pins that anchored them, and now fell limply around her oval face. Her eyes were very large and appeared, in the murky darkness, to be as black as a woman's eyes could be. But at the moment they were filled with apprehension. She had a wide mouth, and her full underlip was trembling so badly, either from fear or fatigue, that she suddenly bit it nervously.

Seeing her condition, Amos thought quickly, then came to a decision. "Look, you'd better come with me to my boarding house. I don't know if there's a room for you, but Mrs. Castellano knows the neighborhood. She can help you. Here . . . let me carry that. We've got to get out of this rain before both of us drown!"

It may have been the mention of another woman . . . or perhaps it was the firm way in which Amos snatched up her suitcase and took her arm . . . but the young woman responded faintly, and with a note of hope, "Thank you."

They were still three blocks away from the house, and the downpour grew steadily worse. So by the time Amos had escorted the girl up onto the stoop and was opening the door, they were as wet as if they'd been thrown into the river.

"I'm Amos Stuart. What's your name, miss?"

"Rose Beaumont."

The warmth from the house was a relief. As soon as they stepped inside and closed the door, Anna appeared from the direction of the kitchen. "Amos," she exclaimed, "you're wet to the skin!"

"Yeah, I am. Mama Anna, this is Miss Rose Beaumont. She needs a room."

Anna leveled one look at the girl's soggy form, and took charge, fussing over her. "Look at you!" she scolded. Taking Rose by the arm, she hauled her off toward her own bedroom, which was on the first floor. Over her shoulder she threw Amos a withering glance. "Well don't just stand-a there! Bring-a the poor girl's suitcase!"

He grinned and followed obediently, depositing the suitcase in Anna's bedroom.

The heavy woman snatched it from him, then shoved him toward the door. "Get yourself outta those wet clothes! You wanna get sick?"

Amos shrugged, calling back as Anna pushed him outside and slammed the door, "Nice to meet you, Miss Beaumont!"

Anna turned to the girl who was standing motionless in the center of the room. "You get-a yourself dried off and into something warm," she commanded brusquely, digging out a thick towel from the drawer of an ancient oak chest. "Dry your hair good, yes? I come back and get-a you when it's time-a to eat."

"I–I don't have much money—"

Anna gave an expressive shrug and said with disdain, "You gotta eat, no?"

As the door closed behind her, Rose Beaumont stared blankly at it, then without warning, her shoulders began to shake and her eyes burned with hot tears she could keep back no longer. Blindly she moved to the bed, slipped to the floor, and pressed her face against the coverlet, muffling the sounds of her weeping.

Taking a deep breath, Rose came to her feet and wiped her tears away with the towel Anna had left. Then she opened the sodden suitcase, took out dry clothes, and put them on the bed. After glancing toward the door, she stripped to the skin, dried quickly, and donned fresh underwear and a plain brown dress. She had not slept in two nights, and the warmth and comfort of dry clothes soon combined to produce a delicious drowsiness. But she shook off the temptation to sleep and began to dry her hair.

Standing in front of the mirror, she pulled out the pins, and her hair fell to her waist in thick waves, raven black. When it was as dry as she could get it, she got her comb and brush from her suitcase. As she brushed the long tresses, she tried desperately to think, but her mind seemed drugged, she was so tired.

Rose's arms grew weary, and as she coiled her hair into braids, then pinned it into a halo, she began hoping that the woman called Anna would have a place for her. She dreaded the thought of going out into the cold and wet again. But did she have enough money? The thought of the slender packet of bills—less than ten dollars—floated before her, and a choking fear rose in her throat.

Rose closed the suitcase and set it on the floor. It was in her mind to go outside and talk to Mrs. Castellano, but her legs were too weak to support her. *I'll sit down and think about what to say*, she decided. *Maybe I can help with the housework and cooking to pay for my room and board—*

Sinking down on the faded and rather lumpy upholstered chair by the window, she stared out at the rain, which fell in slanting lines. The darkness was complete now, and the yellow gaslight just outside was an orange globe of light, a luminous cloud. There was something hypnotic about the warmth of the room, and she closed her eyes, leaning back with her head against the chair. The rain made a silvery tattoo on the glass, like the brush of angel wings, she thought.

Without willing them, memories came trooping into her

mind, like specters. She thought of her home, the dingy little border town in Texas. It had been a prison to her since early childhood, and she had always disliked the sterile desert and the tawdry streets. But now there was a certain nostalgia in the memory. *At least I had a place there!*

There was no place for her in that town now. Her only tie had been her mother—and the thought of her mother brought a stab of grief, sharp and keen. Maria, half Spanish and half Irish, had not been a good woman. Rose had known that much for a long time. A hard drinker, she could not say no to men—a trait which had brought her many beatings from her husband Earl, a slab-sided, pale-eyed man with a cruel mouth.

The vision of her stepfather brought an involuntary shiver to the girl. He had been prevented from actually molesting her, Rose knew, only by her mother's dire threats. The very first time Maria caught Earl at it, she had waited until he was asleep and poured scalding water over his chest. He had been so badly burned that it had been two weeks before he recovered enough to take his revenge. Then he had grabbed Maria and hit her.

"Go ahead," she said, glaring up at him. "Beat me half to death. But sooner or later I'll get well and I'll catch you asleep, and then I'll pour the scalding water on your *face*!"

Earl had not beaten her, for he understood that his wife would do exactly as she promised. Maria had added, "Touch Rose one more time, and you'll have to feel your way around . . . because your eyes will be burned out!"

Rose thought of the years after that, when she had felt her stepfather's pale eyes following her. Mercifully, he had been restrained by his knowledge that Maria would scald him if he bothered her.

Just then a bolt of lightning split the sky, illuminating the room for an instant, then the thunder cracked, seeming to shake the very foundation of the house. Rose shrank back in the chair and remembered her mother's funeral, for two weeks ago, it had been interrupted by a thunderstorm just like this one. *Her funeral—only two weeks ago!*

Rose seemed to see her mother's fresh grave, turning slowly to mud as the rain-soaked men shoveled in the dirt. And at once her unwilling mind formed another image of the episode three days later, when her stepfather had come to her room late at night. She seemed to hear the sound of his footsteps again, to hear the door creaking open. And then his voice whispering to her before his groping hands had found her.

She had screamed and rolled out of the bed, then run wildly toward the door. He had been so drunk he had missed the grab he made at her. Then, when he tried to take the stairs two at a time in pursuit of the terrified girl, he had fallen headlong. Rose had seen him bang his head on the tread, then laboriously crawl to his feet. She could never forget how he had stared at her with his loose mouth and wild eyes. "Go on—run! But I'll get you! I'll get you—!"

He had lumbered off and fallen into a drunken coma, and Rose had crept back to her room, dressed, and packed a suitcase.

She had saved a little money, enough for a one-way fare to New York. It had been a desperate venture, for all she had was a name and an old letter from her mother's half-sister who lived in New York. Rose had never met the woman, but she was the only relative she could run to. So she had come to the city with a few dollars and a tattered envelope with her aunt's name and address.

Bitterness scored the girl's lips as she closed her eyes, for the thought of her "aunt" was still rank. She had found the woman, but it had been worse than Texas. Her mother's sister was living with a man, keeping him by her earnings from hustling drunks at a local saloon. After one look, Rose had turned and fled, not even telling the woman who she was.

She had stayed for one night in a cheap hotel, another in the train station. It had been dangerous, for men approached her constantly, forcing her to flee. A kindly policeman had an-

swered her inquiry for a section of the city where she might
find a cheap room, and it had taken all her strength to get as
far as she did before the rain caught her.

The rain pattered on, and she thought of the young man
who had come to her aid . . . what was his name? Amos something. She was surprised that she had trusted him. But he
hadn't been like the others . . . not like them at all—

She dropped off to sleep sitting bolt upright, but jerked
spasmodically when a hand touched her shoulder. "Well, now,
you fall asleep, eh?"

"Oh!" Rose leapt out of her chair, looked around wildly,
then smiled sheepishly. "I–I guess I did."

"You come-a with me." Anna led Rose out of the bedroom.
When they entered the dining room, Rose flushed as every
eye turned toward her. "This is Miss Rose," Anna announced.
"Don't be bothering her, you hear me? Let-a her eat!"

Rose was extremely grateful for Anna's warning, for she
had no desire to talk to anyone. Slipping into the chair between a boy of about six and another somewhat younger, she
kept her eyes down, looking up only when necessary. She
noted the good-looking young man sitting next to Amos and
the two young women who were devouring their food. She
herself ate the spaghetti, beets, and cabbage slowly not because she had no appetite, but because she didn't want to appear greedy.

The conversation flowed around her, and once she looked
up to find Amos watching her. "Better than getting soaked,
isn't it, Miss Rose?"

"Oh, yes!" she answered, and gave him a brief smile. "I
don't know what I would have done if you hadn't come along,
Mr. Stuart."

Nick, too, had been eyeing the girl openly, impressed by
her good looks. When Amos told him of the incident, he had
failed to mention her smooth olive skin, the fine sweep of her
cheeks, the black hair, and especially the lustrous black eyes,

which she kept downcast. *What a pippin!* Nick thought. *Wish I'd been the knight in armor to rescue this one!*

Aloud he asked, "You been in New York long, Miss Rose?" He ignored his mother's frown and when Rose replied that she'd only arrived a short time before, he nodded. "Well, you'll have to let me show you around. A pretty girl like you has no business walking around this burg alone."

Rose smiled briefly, but made no answer. To head off Nick's approach after the meal, she made a beeline for Anna. "Mrs. Castellano, could I talk with you for a minute . . . alone?"

"Yes. Nick, you help Mary Elizabeth with the dishes."

"Aw, Ma!"

"Come on, Nick." Amos grinned. "I'll help, too."

When Anna and Rose had achieved some privacy in the small parlor, the young woman faced the older one. "Mrs. Castellano, I don't have very much money and I don't know anyone in New York." Rose lifted her head, and a rosy blush colored her cheeks, for she was shamed at having to beg. "I–I'm strong and used to hard work. If you'd let me stay here until I find a job, I'll help you with the housework and the cooking."

Anna admired the young woman's spirit, but was troubled. "Rose, I no gotta place for you."

"Oh, please! Just a place on the floor in here! Don't make me go—"

Anna, with her tender heart, could not bear the sight of the girl's tears. "Now, wait," she said quickly. "I don't have-a no more rooms, but if you don't mind sharing an old woman's room—"

"Oh, no!" Rose made an impulsive move to hug Anna, and the woman melted.

"You gotta some trouble, Rose? You stay with us. The good Lord, he knows how to fix it!" She held the girl, made motherly noises as Rose clung to her. At last she gently moved away. "You go to bed now, child. Tomorrow we talk."

Rose nodded, grateful she didn't have to face the rest of the family or the boarders.

She went at once to the room, accompanied by Anna, who turned back the covers. "You gotta warm gown? No? You wear one of mine." She smiled to see the girl's slim form. "It'll be big enough for you, I think!"

Ten minutes later, Rose lay buried in the thick feather bed and felt her tense muscles beginning to relax. She tried to stay awake, but the rain, still falling, danced on the window, and the last thing she remembered was the round, kindly face of Anna Castellano.

6

ENCOUNTER AT THE WORLD THEATER

A mos, saddle Prince!" James McClendon said, excitement gleaming in his eyes. "The secretary of the Navy, Theodore Roosevelt, is coming with a party . . . we'll need to saddle every horse that can walk!"

Amos had never seen the little Scotsman so worked up, and he threw himself into the task. By the time the three big carriages drew up, he'd harried the other hands into action so that nearly every animal was saddled. He himself held Prince's reins, for the big gelding was subject to uncertain behavior.

The owner of the stable, Mr. Harold Greenlee, was an ardent student of politics and an equally enthusiastic supporter of Theodore Roosevelt. He walked with the secretary from the carriages to the yard, leading an entourage of a dozen or so.

Greenlee spoke to the manager at once. "Are the horses ready, James?"

"Aye, they are, sir."

"Greenlee, I want the liveliest mount in your stable!" The secretary of the Navy spoke in a rapid, rather high-pitched voice. He was, Amos noted, of no great height but gave the impression of tremendous strength. Amos had read of his passion for boxing and hunting and horses, and now as McClendon said, "Bring Prince up, Stuart," he stepped forward.

Roosevelt stared at the animal, then grinned. The secretary had big, square teeth, and his eyes gleamed behind his spectacles. "Fine-looking animal," he exclaimed, then took the reins from Amos. He swung into the saddle with practiced ease, and as Prince took a quick step to the side, Roosevelt pulled him up sharply. He winked at Amos. "A little of the Devil in this one, eh?"

Amos nodded. "Right, sir. Watch him . . . he'll try to rake you off on the fence."

"Will he? Bully! I like a horse with spirit." He nodded, adding, "Thanks for the tip, young man!" Then he kicked Prince with his heels and shot out of the yard at a hard run.

The rest of the party were still trying to mount up, and for a few minutes, Amos and McClendon were busy getting them all into the saddle.

One of the party, a woman, stood back, giving the mount Amos held for her a rather skeptical look. "I'm not a very good rider," she admitted. "Is this one gentle?"

Amos had been too busy to give the woman more than a passing glance. Now he did so. She was young, no more than twenty-one, and very attractive. Light brown hair, dark brown eyes, a trim figure. "Well, miss—" Amos hesitated. "Thunder's a good horse, but a bit of a handful at times."

"Oh, dear!"

Amos saw her distress and quickly attempted to put her at ease. "I could get you a gentle animal, miss."

"Would you?" The woman's relieved smile came at once. "I think that might be better." When Amos led Thunder toward the line of stables, she fell into step beside him. "I'm sorry to be so much trouble."

"No trouble, miss," Amos replied. "Won't take but a second, and Lady will give you no problem." He tied Thunder and led the small mare out of the stall.

As he put the saddle on, the young woman laughed shortly. "I'm not really a part of the secretary's party. I guess I'm a party-crasher." Seeing Amos's look of surprise, she smiled and introduced herself. "My name is Virginia Powers. I'm a reporter for the *Journal*."

Amos had cinched the saddle and was slipping the bridle on, but at her announcement, he stopped dead still and turned to stare at the young woman.

She laughed then, a delightful tinkling sound, and gave him a roguish look. "I know what you're thinking," she said. "She doesn't look like a reporter!"

Amos was forced to smile. He shrugged, continuing to fasten the bridle. "To be truthful, I didn't know there *were* any women reporters. But I guess that's about the best job in the whole world."

Struck by Amos's comment, Virginia Powers narrowed her gaze. "You think so? Are you interested in becoming a writer?"

Amos nodded but didn't elaborate, saying only, "Let me help you up, Miss Powers." He waited until she approached, and when she stood beside him, noticed that she was pale. A thought occurred to him. "Have you ever ridden a horse?"

"No . . . and I'm scared to death of that beast!"

Amos stared at her, then shook his head. "You don't *have* to ride, do you?"

"Yes!" An intense determination fueled Virginia Powers, one that did not hide her fear, however. She took a deep breath and then looked up at Amos. "I'm not actually a reporter . . . not yet anyway," she confessed. "William Randolph Hearst is my uncle. Do you know who he is?"

"Yes, Miss Powers," Amos answered. "I've read a lot about him."

Everybody in New York knew about the man who had dropped like a bombshell into the life of the city. Hearst had used his family fortune to buy the *New York Journal* and had started a crusade to make it the most successful newspaper in the country. These tactics included the use of enormous black headlines, colored paper, full-page editorials, illustrations, and colorful cartoons. The rivalry between Hearst and Joseph Pulitzer for supremacy in the newspaper world had become so heated that almost everyone in the state kept up with it.

Virginia shrugged her shoulders and her lips grew firm. "It's like you thought . . . there aren't any women reporters. But I kept after my uncle until last week he finally agreed to give me a chance." She eyed the mare with apprehension. "He said if I could get an interview with Mr. Roosevelt, he'd put me on the staff . . . so, you see, I've just *got* to get on that horse!"

"You can do it, Miss Powers," Amos said quickly. "Look, let me help you on, and I'll ride right beside you, all right?"

"Oh, would you?" Virginia's smile was brilliant. "What's your name?"

"Amos Stuart. Now, put your foot in my hand . . . that's it—" She was a small woman, and he lifted her slowly and carefully upward. "Just put your leg over the saddle. That's it. See how steady Lady is? Now take the reins and let me get mounted—" Amos quickly swung into his saddle and brought Thunder around beside the mare. "Just touch Lady with your heels, and she'll move along. But don't be afraid. She's too old and sedate to do anything so vulgar as running away."

Virginia sat in the saddle, spine rigid and face pale, expecting the worst. But before they had gone more than a dozen yards, she exclaimed, "Why, this is *easy*!"

Amos led the horses out of the yard, and soon they were trotting beneath the trees that overhung the bridle path. The young woman was so delighted with her progress that Amos was pleased.

As she relaxed, she began to talk about her plan to get the secretary off to one side for at least a few minutes. "Just that much would be enough for Uncle William."

Amos shook his head doubtfully. "I don't know, Miss Powers. The secretary rides like a cowboy—which they say he *is*. Be quite a trick to catch up with him on Lady."

But Amos had underestimated this headstrong female. Virginia Powers came from a wealthy family, where she had gotten her own way more often than not. She was, moreover, a very attractive young woman who had learned how to handle men. She turned to Amos, studying his lean form, and his rugged good looks. "Amos, if you'll help me corner Roosevelt . . . maybe I can get my uncle to give *you* a job on the *Journal*."

Amos looked dubious. "I don't have enough education for that, but I'll help *you* if I can." He smiled at her, unaware of how appealing he was, with his ash-blond hair falling over his forehead and his dark blue eyes shining. "Look, there's one stretch of the bridle path that's different. It's so overgrown that nobody can do more than walk his horse through. Let's go, and we'll waylay the secretary there."

Anticipation brought a glow to Virginia's face, and she agreed at once. "Oh, Amos . . . let's do it!"

He led her to the uncleared section. "We'll pull back into the trees," he explained. "I'll keep an eye out, and when Mr. Roosevelt comes along, we'll step in front of him. The path is too narrow for him to pass both of us . . . so you'll have a few minutes to talk to him."

As they waited, Virginia began to question Amos, and despite his reticence, she had soon pried his life story out of him.

He laughed. "You'll be a good reporter. I never told anyone so much about myself in my whole life!" Then he lifted his hand to signal silence and cocked his head toward the path on the left. "It's him!" he said, excitement in his voice. "And he's all alone! Come on!"

Amos brought both horses into the narrow path, just as Roosevelt's horse approached at a fast trot. "Hullo! Is it you, Miss Powers?" Roosevelt asked in a booming voice.

Virginia turned in the saddle and smiled sweetly. "Why, Mr. Roosevelt, it's you! I'm sorry, but I'm such a poor rider that I had to ask this young man to help me."

Roosevelt grinned at Amos. "You were *exactly* right about this horse, young man! He jolly well *did* try to rake me off!"

"You ought to be used to that, sir. What Prince did was

nothing compared to what some of the city bosses and congressmen have done to scrape you out of the way!"

His reply delighted Roosevelt. He threw his head back, and his hearty *"Haw! Haw!"* rocked the woods. "What's your name, young man?"

"Amos Stuart."

"Well, Amos, you're dead right! I've stirred up a hornet's nest . . . and plan to do worse!" Here the path widened slightly, and Roosevelt brought his horse up beside Amos's. His small eyes twinkled as he demanded, "And do you think I'll win an office in the next election?"

Amos had read much about Roosevelt and had a ready answer. "Well, I don't think you'll be secretary of the Navy for long—" Amos waited out the dark scowl that came to Roosevelt's fleshy lips, before adding, "I think the bosses will get you into the race for president of the United States . . . just to get rid of you around here."

Again, Roosevelt was delighted. He grinned ferociously at the pair. "I'd *like* that!"

"Maybe I can help, sir," Virginia ventured.

"Help me become president?"

"Yes, sir. I'm a reporter for the *Journal*."

Roosevelt frowned, distaste in his face. "Not a very dignified paper."

"No, but people read it," Virginia shot back. "And William Randolph Hearst is my uncle . . . and you'll have to admit that *he* could help you!"

Roosevelt studied the young woman with more care. He had ambition enough for ten Caesars. But unlike most politicians who bray that they are in politics only to *help* people, Roosevelt really *meant* it!

Born into a wealthy family, Roosevelt had been a sickly child. He had determined to become a hard, tough, healthy man, and had made himself so by vigorous exercise and discipline. More recently, he had brought that same fortitude into his political life, fighting his way through the crooked machinery of New York, shouldering his way into the office of New York City Police Commissioner. Success in this post had brought him to the attention of the new president, William McKinley, who had appointed him assistant secretary of the Navy. But everyone knew that this was not Roosevelt's goal, for he made no secret of the fact that he intended one day to occupy the highest office in the land.

And Roosevelt knew the power of the printed page. Publishers of popular newspapers such as Joseph Pulitzer's *World* and Hearst's *Journal* were enormously influential in politics.

"So . . . Hearst is your uncle?" Roosevelt asked. "Well, now, what does he think of my new programs?"

The three rode along, Roosevelt both listening and speaking with enthusiasm, and by the time they got back to the road that led to the stable, Virginia had her story. "You'll see your views in the *Journal* tomorrow, Mr. Secretary."

"Bully! Bully!" Roosevelt nodded, then cast an inquiring glance at Amos. "Now, Stuart, the truth! Did you show this young woman how to ambush me on the path?"

Amos nodded. "I'm afraid I did, sir."

"You rascal!" Roosevelt laughed. "I like to see a young man with initiative! But if I were you, I'd make Miss Powers buy me a steak for it!"

Roosevelt galloped off, and when he was gone, Virginia turned to Amos. "I'd like to, Amos," she said with a warm smile. "Buy you a steak I mean."

"Oh, you don't have to do that."

Virginia stared at him. She was puzzled by his manner, for she was accustomed to the brash assurance of the young men of her set. Stuart was not only attractive in appearance, but something about his modesty pleased her. When he helped her off the mare, she grasped his arm. "I've got to go write this interview . . . and I owe it all to you. Tonight I have to attend a play, so I can review it for the paper. I've got two tickets, and you're taking me."

Amos shrugged. "I don't have anything to wear."

Virginia liked him the better for admitting it. "Then *get* something," she insisted, and kept on, until Amos finally agreed to meet her at the theater.

"I guess you're used to having your own way," he said. "Well, I'm used to doing what I'm told, so I suppose it's all right. I'd really like to see a play. I've never seen one."

"Well, you won't see much of a play tonight," Virginia told him. "It's a real stinker, from what I hear. But we'll have fun, and afterwards we can get a sandwich or something. You can help me think up bad things to say about it in the review." She turned and put out her hand. "I'll see you tonight . . . and thanks a million, Amos!"

She left, and later when Amos was putting the horses into their stalls, McClendon stopped by. "Well, he's something, Secretary Roosevelt, isn't he?"

"Sure is," Amos agreed, but his thoughts were on the problem of what to wear when he met Virginia Powers at the World Theater.

Amos arrived at the theater at seven, an hour earlier than Virginia had mentioned. He had spent most of the afternoon buying a new suit and the shirt, tie, and shoes to go with it. He had also gotten his hair cut, and as he entered the lobby, was feeling a little disgusted with himself. *What a fool I am! Spending all my money on this outfit . . . when I'll never come to a fancy place like this again!*

He had convinced himself that Virginia Powers would not even show up. "Just putting me on," he muttered sourly. He stood with his back against the wall, watching the people stream into the theater. He was a little shocked at the dresses some of the women were wearing. Many of them were in the now-familiar bustles, the trains of their dresses dragging the floor. But others wore the new "sheath" gown, a simple tube made of fabric that reached from the hips to the shoetops. The garment had all the charming contour of a gun barrel, and was so tight that the wearer could not take a long step.

Still others wore a type of blouse with holes punched in the fabric. These were made of thin semi-transparent material, and were called "peek-a-boo" blouses, so Amos learned.

He stared at the hairstyles, not knowing that the one he disliked most was called a Psyche knot, created by folding back the woman's long hair upon itself and giving it various twists until it stood in a short club-like protuberance behind or above the head. Amos thought he'd never seen anything uglier, and hoped that none of his sisters ever appeared in public in such a getup.

By eight o'clock he was ready to leave, convinced he'd been tricked, but at that moment Virginia came through the door. She looked around the room, her eyes falling on him, but she showed no sign of recognition. *Doesn't even know me!* Amos thought bitterly. He moved toward her, and when he was five feet away, he saw her eyes open wide and her hand go to her breast in a gesture of shock.

"Why, Amos!" she whispered. "I didn't *know* you!" She looked at him, taking in the lean figure, enhanced by the trim gray wool suit, the shiny black shoes, the well-shaped cut of his hair. "Clothes *do* make the man!" she murmured, shaking her head. She had been prepared for a rather embarrassing time, expecting Stuart to come in a cheap suit, his hair ragged and unkempt.

Amos could see that she was pleasantly surprised. "You look very nice indeed."

"So do you, Miss Powers."

"Oh, you can't call me that!" she protested. "I'm Virginia." She took his arm. "I'm sorry to be late. But we're just in time for the play." At her nod, an usher stepped forward and led them down the aisle of the theater.

The World was neither the largest nor the finest of New York's many theaters. It had been once but was now surpassed by newer structures. But it was more than adequate, with its enormous crystal chandeliers, its padded seats, and rich-looking purple curtain. Amos sat down next to Virginia, staring at the crowd—then the curtain went up and the play started.

The play was "The Bride Elect," starring Christie Mac-Donald and Frank Pollack. It was a drama, set in Europe, and the colorful costumes dazzled Amos. Not only that, but it was a musical. This too was a source of amazement to him, for he had never heard an orchestra.

As the play unfolded, Amos found himself caught up in the action, unaware of Virginia's secret amusement. *He's so innocent*, the girl was thinking. *It might be fun to make something of him. He looks well enough and he seems bright.*

At the intermission, when they went outside, she smiled at his enthusiasm. "I'm glad you like it, Amos. When it's over, we can go out and write the review. You can say the good things, and I'll say the bad things."

But they never wrote that review, for the next act was barely underway when a troop of six young women in beautiful dresses came on and began to sing a number. At her side, Virginia felt Amos stiffen, and when she turned to look at him, she saw that he was not smiling. In fact, he looked ill.

"What is it, Amos?" she whispered urgently.

Amos tore his gaze from the stage. She could tell that he was in a state of shock. "That's—that's my sister up there!"

Virginia turned to stare at the stage. "Which one?"

"The one in the yellow dress."

Virginia examined the young woman carefully. "The one you came to New York to find?" she asked, remembering what he had told her earlier. "She's so beautiful!"

Amos had not told Virginia the whole story. He had simply said that his sister had run away from home, not mentioning the fact that she had left with a man. Now he said hoarsely, "I've got to talk to her!"

He actually rose, and Virginia was aware that he was going up on the stage! "Wait! You can't talk to her *now*! We'll go backstage after the play. I've got an appointment with Christie MacDonald."

The play moved along, but Amos heard nothing more. Lylah! He stared at her, unable to believe his eyes. She looked so–so different. Older, somehow, and more alive. He tried to think what he could say to her when they met, but his mind was still reeling. He was so confused that, when the curtain came down, and the actors took their bows, he was unprepared for Virginia's suggestion. "Come on, Amos. We'll go backstage."

Still in a daze, Amos let her pull him along and found himself at the side of the big stage, just behind the edge of the curtain. The houselights were up, and he looked down the row of actors and actresses who had gone out to span the stage, bowing at the applause.

Then the curtain came down, and he saw Lylah. She didn't notice him at first, since she was laughing and talking with a young woman as she left the stage. As she approached the place where Amos was standing, however, she lifted her eyes and saw him. She stopped dead still; the smile suddenly disappeared from her face, and her lower lip began to tremble.

The two stared at each other, cut off from the rest of the crowd as if they had been on the moon. Neither of them could speak, and Virginia watched, breathless, sensing the drama of the meeting. *They're very close*, she thought with great insight, *and she's hurt him terribly*.

Then Lylah squared her shoulders, held up her head, and came to stand before her brother. "Hello, Amos," she said quietly. She didn't reach out to him, and saw at once that he was incapable of action. "Wait for me. I'll change and we'll go talk."

She left, and Amos stood looking after her, his face strained and pale.

"Amos, I've got to go interview Miss MacDonald," Virginia began. "You'll want to visit with your sister alone, anyway—" She hesitated, then added, "I want to see you again. If I come to the stable tomorrow, can we talk?"

Amos blinked, wrenched his thoughts back to the young

woman at his side, and nodded slightly. "Of course—" He broke off, then passed his hand over his forehead. "I'm sorry to spoil your evening."

Virginia put her hand on his arm, feeling a sudden, unaccustomed rush of pity for him. "It'll be all right," she whispered. "Be gentle with her, Amos."

"Why, sure I will," he said, and then she was gone. He moved back, getting out of the way of the stage hands who were hauling on ropes and moving the scenery around. He was grateful that he had a few minutes to compose himself, for seeing Lylah had shocked him terribly.

He was over the worst of it when she came out, wearing a dark gray dress and a black coat. "Amos, there's a café down the street," she said. "We can talk there."

He walked out of the theater with her, not saying a word until they were outside. "I'm glad to see you, sister," he finally said, not looking at her.

"How did you know I was in the play?"

"Oh, I didn't. Just happened to come."

They spoke no more until they were seated at a table in the café. They ordered coffee and sandwiches, and when the waiter was gone, Lylah spoke. "How long have you been looking for me? I know that's why you're here in New York."

"I left home almost two months ago." Amos could not help himself, but leaned forward and put out his hand. She put her hand in his, and he groaned. "Oh, Lylah, why did you do it?"

Lylah held her brother's hand, her face ashen. She had been almost as shaken as Amos at the moment of their meeting. "I can't explain it. It–it was something I had to do." Then she whispered, "Do–do you hate me, Amos? Do you all hate me?"

"No! Never that, sister!"

Tears filled Lylah's eyes, and she let them overflow. "Never hate me, Amos. Love me . . . even if I can't be what you want me to be."

They sat there talking for a long time. The food came, but

they ignored it. They drank cup after cup of coffee, Lylah telling of her experience, her great adventure. As she spoke of life in the theater, her eyes glowed, and Amos knew she would never come home.

Then Lylah began to question Amos, and he spoke diffidently of what he had done since leaving home. She drew out of him more than he wanted her to know, more than he knew himself.

"Amos," she said with dawning conviction, "you'll never go back to the farm!" She saw his head snap up, saw the impact of her words in his widening gaze. "I know you, Amos. You've hated that farm . . . more than me, I think. And when you talk about writing, your whole soul spills over!"

"Why, Lylah," he said in a shocked tone, "I've *got* to go home. They can't make it without me."

"Yes, they can."

A sudden resolve formed in Lylah's mind. It was something she'd thought about for a long time. Now she was fully determined. "Owen can help more, Amos. You've got a good job . . . and that girl can help you get on at the paper. And I'll help, too. I'm not making much, but I can send a little, and Pa can hire a man if he has to."

Amos could not speak. He had put his dreams away years before. Buried them and kept them firmly in the grave. But now . . . he began to breathe a little harder, and he asked hoarsely, "Lylah—do you think it can happen?"

Lylah loved her brother deeply. It hurt her to see the longing on his face. A great joy swept over her as she thought, *I've hurt them all . . . but if I can help Amos, that will make up for some of it.*

She took his hand in both of hers, leaned forward, and whispered, "We're a pair of rebels, big brother. But we're going to make it, you and me!"

7

"REMEMBER THE *MAINE*!"

The feeble February sun was a pale and pallid disk that seemed to be made of ice rather than fire. It dropped behind the low-lying hills just as Owen emerged from the woods and crossed the yard. He tossed the sack of rabbits down on the table beside the house, then went to the front.

As soon as he opened the door, he was met by his mother who was smiling. "A letter came from Amos today. We were waiting for you to come home before we opened it."

"Let's read it now, Ma!" Logan yelped.

"No, let's eat first," Owen countered. "I need to thaw out and get something hot in my belly."

"It's all ready." Marian got them all seated, and they ate the venison steaks doused in white gravy. There were the usual loud arguments between the younger children, and Owen listened as his father told about a bear that he'd seen a mile away from the house.

When they finished, Marian sat down and opened the envelope. She took out the two sheets of paper and held them up so that the yellow light from the coal-oil lamp fell on the clear, firm writing. She began to read, slowly and carefully:

Dear Folks,

I hope you are all well and that the winter has not been too hard on you. I have been in good health, and though the weather is colder here, I do not mind it.

My new job is turning out fine. As I think I told you,

Virginia spoke to her uncle, Mr. Hearst, about me, and he was
so pleased about the way I helped her get the interview with
Mr. Roosevelt that he gave me a part-time job on his newspaper, the *New York Journal*. As I told you, it was mostly just
cleaning up down at the paper, but Virginia has helped me
with my writing, and now here's my big surprise: I wrote a
piece about the police chief . . . and Mr. Hearst liked it so
much he put me on full time!

It was hard for me to say good-bye to Jamie, he's been so
good to me. But he's happy for me. I'll write more later when
I get settled.

"I don't like the sound of that." Owen frowned. "It sounds
to me like he won't be coming home." He was slouched down
in his chair, his brow furrowed. Owen had missed Amos more
than any of them—except for Marian, of course. "He keeps
talking about that woman, Virginia Powers. I'll bet she's sweet
on him. Well, go on, Ma, let's hear the rest of it."

This means I won't be coming home as soon as I thought.

"See? What'd I tell you?" Owen interjected.

But the good news is that I'll be able to send more money
home. Maybe you can hire a man to help you with the spring
plowing. If I do well, Virginia says her uncle will give me a
raise, so I can help with the expenses there—maybe even
send Owen to college.

I was glad to get your letter, Ma, and especially glad to hear
that Lylah had written. She left New York last week, going
with a group of actors on a traveling road show. We've seen a
lot of each other since I ran across her in the theater. As I said
before, there's no hope that she'll come home—not now, anyway. She's not making much money, but she says the star of
the show likes her and has given her a small speaking part in
the play. I'll sure be glad to see it, but I worry about her, as you
all do.

That's about all, I guess, except to tell you about one of

the boarders here at Mama Anna's. She came here about two months ago, and we've gotten to be good friends. Her name is Rose Beaumont, and she is all alone in the city, having lost her parents recently. I had the chance to do her a favor, and she's been very grateful. Unfortunately, she had to go to work in that terrible bottle factory where I punched the manager. It's wearing her down, just like it did me. Nick and I take her out to eat sometimes, not together, of course. Anyway, I'm trying to find a better job for her. You might put her in your prayers, Ma. She could sure use it!

Well, good-bye for now. I enclose twenty dollars and will send more in two weeks. Owen, don't shoot all the deer in the county. Save a few for me!

Marian put the letter down on the table, and looked across at her husband. "Will, Amos won't be back for spring plowing. We'll use this money to hire a hand to help you."

Will Stuart nodded thoughtfully. "Guess you're right, Marian. He ain't thinking of this farm."

Pete Stuart had listened carefully to the letter. Now he spoke up. "It sounds like Amos has another girl, don't it?"

Marian studied the letter and replied slowly, "Amos always did have a soft heart. I reckon he's just trying to look out for this Rose girl."

Owen rose abruptly, and climbed the ladder into the sleeping loft. Seeing him go, Will was thoughtful. "Marian, it was worse than we knew—Lylah running off the way she did." It was bad enough for her to go, but now we've lost Amos for good." He motioned toward the loft. "Owen—he'll be the next to leave. We'll be lucky to keep him until he's eighteen."

"I know, Will." Marian looked out the window, and it seemed she was trying to see through the mountains that separated her from Amos and Lylah. She sighed heavily, then turned away, her face sad. "It's all in God's hands."

"Oh, Amos, I'm too tired to go out tonight!"

Rose had come home, exhaustion evident in every line of

her slender figure. She had just managed to wash up when Amos came to remind her that they were going out to eat and then to see a play.

Amos insisted. "I know you're tired, Rose, but you don't have to work tomorrow. And you need to have a little fun." He finally persuaded her, and knowing that she had no energy left for walking, Amos splurged recklessly on a cab.

He took her to an inexpensive café, where Rose brightened up, warmed by the good food and pleased by Amos's constant stream of talk—mostly about his job. As she sipped her tea, he told her with great animation of the Spanish crisis.

"You see, Rose, the Spaniards have been persecuting the Cuban people. They've sent a general named Weyler— 'Butcher Weyler' he's called—and he's slaughtered the poor Cubans by the thousands! Well, my boss, Mr. William Randolph Hearst, has stirred up the American people. He sent the best artist in America to sketch the horrible atrocities, so that Americans can see what's going on down there." He fumbled in his pocket, came out with a portion of a newspaper, and showed it to her. "Look at this!"

Rose stared at the picture of a beautiful, demure, young girl, standing naked and helpless as a rugged Spanish soldier pawed through her clothing. "Why . . . this is awful!" she cried.

"Terrible! And that's not the worst of it!" Amos's eyes glowed with righteous indignation as he recounted the murders of "Butcher Weyler." "Well . . . anyway," he said, "I'm hoping Mr. Hearst will send me to Cuba."

Rose was instantly alert. "I'd hate to see you go, Amos. I–I don't know what I would have done without you."

She looked so innocent and vulnerable sitting there that Amos reached over and took her hand. "Oh, Rose, it was nothing. What I really want to do is find you a better job." He studied her face, seeing her fatigue. "I know what that place is like. You've got to get out of there."

"It's hard." Rose sighed. "Much harder than any work I've

ever done. All I do is work all day, come home and fall asleep, then get up and start all over again."

"Well, I want you to forget that blasted factory for tonight." Amos got to his feet and pulled her up with him. "We're going to see a show and have a great time. Come on!"

They left the café and, thirty minutes later, were seated in the Stellar Theater, waiting for the curtain to go up. Rose, who had never seen a play, was as dazzled as Amos had been a few weeks earlier. The play, *The Devil's Disciple*, was by an Irishman named Shaw. It was a rousing comedy set in the days of the American Revolution and delighted both Amos and Rose.

After the play was over, they strolled out onto the street, reliving their favorite parts. It was late, but Amos wasn't ready for the evening to end. "Before we go home, let's go get something warm—some hot chocolate, maybe."

Rose protested, but Amos was still charged with excitement, and she gave in. They were walking along the street when a voice called out, "Hey! Amos!" They both looked up to see Nick crossing the street, dodging the buggies. He was wearing a sporty-looking suit, with a new derby cocked over his right eye. "Look at the two o'you." He laughed. "Out on the town!"

"Hello, Nick." Amos smiled back. "We've been to see a play."

"Yeah? Well, come on, let's get something to eat." He stationed himself on the other side of Rose. "How come you go out with this guy? Don't you know you can't trust a rebel? Now a nice hometown boy like me . . . you can put yourself in my hands and be sure nothing's gonna go wrong."

They smiled at his foolishness, and when he motioned toward a brilliantly lit establishment, Amos was uneasy. "That's a saloon, isn't it, Nick?"

Nick punched Amos's arm and grinned. "Saloon? Why, they serve the best steak in this old town in Charlie's Place! Come on inside and I'll prove it."

Amos glanced at Rose, who was waiting for him to decide.
"Well, we're not really hungry, but we'll go in for just a few
minutes." They followed Nick and were promptly escorted
to a good table. Nick seemed to know the manager, Charlie
O'Steen, and remarked, "He's a good egg, Charlie is . . . and
always has a good show."

Nick bullied them into ordering steaks with all the trim-
mings. But it was soon evident that Charlie's Place was more
than a restaurant. As they were waiting for their food, a sudden blast of music interrupted their conversation.

"Charlie's got a great idea here," Nick said. "Guy can eat,
have a drink, and see a swell show, all for one price." He
sipped at his drink, and nodded toward the stage, which took
up one end of the large room. "This is a great show . . . you're
gonna love it!"

Amos and Rose watched as the entertainers came on. It
was a revue, with singing, dancing, and several comedy
sketches. The star was a slender fellow by the name of Eddy
Sparks. Eddy had a fine voice, and his specialty was singing
love songs to an attractive young woman . . . or several of them.
In most of the numbers, the stage was filled with these girls,
either singing along with him, or cavorting about, kicking up
their heels.

After the show, which lasted forty-five minutes, Nick
winked at them and got to his feet. "Hey, Eddy!" he called
out. "Come over and meet some friends of mine."

To the surprise of both Amos and Rose, the entertainer
turned his head, and seeing Nick, smiled and walked over as
the rest of the troupe left the stage. "Hello, Nick."

"Great show! Just great, Eddy!" Nick beamed. "Want you
to meet some people. This guy you better watch out for—
Amos Stuart, a big-shot reporter on the *Journal*."

Sparks put out his hand, his mobile lips curving into a
smile. "I always treat the gentlemen of the press right. I get
better reviews that way."

"And this is Miss Rose Beaumont."

Sparks bowed, smiled again, and cocked his head to one side. "Did you enjoy the show, Miss Rose?"

"Oh, yes!" Rose had forgotten her fatigue, and the excitement of the evening had heightened her color, so that the glow in her cheeks set off her black hair and her unusual eyes. She smiled, revealing even white teeth. "You sing so well, Mr. Sparks."

"Put that in your review, Mr. Stuart," the actor said quickly. He was regarding Rose in a peculiar manner, and asked abruptly, "Are you in show business, Miss Rose?"

"Me! Oh, no!" Rose blushed slightly, which only increased her charm. "I only work in a factory."

Sparks made a show of indignation. "What? A factory? Why, that's a crime against nature!" He made a sweeping gesture toward the stage. "Not one of those girls is as attractive as you!"

"You offering her a job, Eddy?"

Sparks nodded instantly. "As a matter of fact, one of our young ladies is leaving the company. Would you be interested in a change of professions, Miss Rose?"

Rose gasped and shook her head almost violently. "Oh, I couldn't! I mean, I never learned how to sing or dance or anything like that!"

"Neither did most of the girls you saw tonight," Sparks said dryly. Then he brightened. "But the girl who's got to be replaced is more decorative than talented. She's the one I sang to." He frowned slightly. "You don't like garlic, do you?" Without waiting for a reply, he rushed on, "She does a simple little dance once in awhile, just with the other girls, nothing complicated."

"What's the pay?" Nick demanded.

"You her agent?" Sparks grinned. "Well, the job only pays twenty dollars a week." When he saw Rose's eyes grow wide and her mouth form a perfect O of surprise, he pressed his advantage. "Of course, the hours aren't long. From seven until eleven. We do the show twice each night. But you can sleep 'til noon if you want to."

Rose thought of her mornings, when simply getting out of bed and staggering down to the factory took all her strength. Sleep until noon! But she was too shy, and whispered, "Oh, I just couldn't do it."

Nick was right at her side, urging her. "Can't do it? *Sure* you can, Rosie! Why, I could do it myself . . . except I'm not as pretty as you—"

He laughed at his own joke and kept urging her, until finally Amos interrupted nervously. "Nick, don't say any more. Rose doesn't want to do it."

Nick stared at him, temper flaring in his dark eyes. "Oh? And she *does* want to work herself to death in that factory? Amos, stay out of this."

Sparks intervened. "Hey, don't get mad, okay?" He smiled at Rose. "Miss, if you want to try it, I'll give you a couple of days to think it over. I'd like to have you . . . but you might as well know that acting is a hard world. Lots of fellows will promise you you'll be a star, but you probably won't. Too much competition. This job here isn't like trouping all over the country, though. Home every night . . . and no funny business with my company," he added, looking meaningfully at Amos. "I'm a happily married man, and I don't allow my people to fool around." He bowed. "Good to meet you both. Come and see me if you change your mind."

After Sparks left them, Nick was apologetic. "Well, sorry I blew my top, Amos."

"It's okay, Nick. I—I can see what you mean. And the guy seems pretty regular to me."

"What he said about the girls, it's on the level." Nick nodded, then laughed. "I tried to buddy up to the little blond with the green dress, and it was no sale!"

Amos finally managed to pry Rose away from Nick, who said it was too early to go home. Finding a cab, they rode through the dark streets, saying little. When the cab stopped in front of the house, Amos jumped out and helped Rose down. She stood there as he paid the driver, then the two of them climbed the steps.

"I'm so tired," Rose murmured, "but it's been a wonderful evening, Amos." She turned to face him, and the silver of the moon was reflected in her eyes. "Everything seems so . . . strange."

Amos stood close enough to smell the fresh scent of her hair and to catch the glints of light in her green eyes. A silence lay over the street. Only the faint echoes of the horse's hooves floated on the night air. "You look very pretty tonight," he said softly.

Rose touched his cheek and smiled again without answer. And then Amos reached out with both hands and cupped her shoulders. Her eyes flew open, but before she could speak, he pulled her to him and kissed her.

Rose, taken totally off guard, did not resist. As his lips fell on hers and his arms tightened around her, she felt a sharp pang of fear. But her anxiety quickly fled in the gentleness of his embrace, and she sensed a strange security such as she had never known before. His lips were firm, and she found herself responding to his kiss. For a long moment they stood there, holding each other. Finally, one of them, and they never knew which one, broke away.

"Rose," Amos whispered huskily, "I never knew a girl could be so sweet."

Rose was glad the night was dark, so that Amos could not see her cheeks, for she felt them grow warm. "I–I must go in," she murmured, but before she stepped inside, she gave him a sweet smile. "Thank you for taking me out, Amos."

She moved quickly into the house, went at once to the room she shared with Anna, and tried to get undressed and into bed without waking the woman. When she lay down and pulled up the warm covers, Rose lay still for a brief time, thinking of the evening. But sleep came quickly, for she was exhausted, and her last impression before she drifted off was Amos Stuart's kiss.

✱   ✱   ✱

The next day was Sunday, and Rose was strangely quiet, having almost nothing to say to the children or to Anna. Anna, of course, noticed, quickly dismissing her silence as the result of too little sleep the night before.

But the next morning, when Anna came to awaken Rose, she was shocked when the girl sat straight up in bed, a determined expression on her face.

"Anna, I'm not going to work at the bottle factory!" When Anna stared at her, disbelieving, Rose tried to explain. "I can't stand it anymore!" She hesitated. "Maybe Nick told you about the job at the restaurant."

Anna shook her head firmly. "That's-a no good, Rose! No young girl can stay nice in a place like that!"

But Rose had made up her mind. She waited until noon, walked into town, and found Eddy Sparks rehearsing a song. "Why, it's you!" Getting up from the piano, he raised one eyebrow. "Changed your mind?"

"Y–yes, I have."

Sparks was a kindly man, and he knew the girl was nervous. "Well, sit down and we'll see what we can do."

An hour later Rose left Charlie's Place and went to the Castellano house. "Anna, I'm moving," she said. "This place is too far from the restaurant. Mr. Sparks fixed it so I could room with one of the other girls in the company."

Anna saw there was little she could do to persuade the girl differently. "I hope you come and see us often, Rose."

Rose gathered her few belongings, and when she left, gave Anna a tremendous hug, then fled from the house.

"I gotta pray for that girl," Anna vowed. "She's gonna need it, I think."

A clear starry night with a moon hanging overhead like an immense yellow globe—that was the setting in the harbor of Havana, Cuba, on Tuesday, February 15, 1898. The U.S.

battleship *Maine* hung motionless on her anchor, her great bulk shrouded in darkness. Officially she was on a "good-will" visit, but everyone knew she had been sent by Washington to show this country's readiness to protect American lives and property, by force, if necessary.

The crew was asleep, except for a few on watch. Captain Charles D. Sigsbee was at his desk, writing a letter to his wife. The Marine bugler began taps . . . and the captain paused to listen.

And then it happened.

A thundering explosion shook the *Maine* from bow to stern. Many smaller jolts followed as the ship's ammunition caught fire and exploded. The shells went off one after another, spraying red-hot splinters in every direction. Lights went out, and clouds of black, suffocating smoke filled the spaces below decks. The vessel listed to port and began to sink. Within seconds her dying noises were intermingled with the sounds of dying men. Captain Sigsbee groped his way through the blackness. Coming out on the main deck, he saw that nothing could be done to save the *Maine* and gave order to abandon ship.

Daylight revealed the destructive scene. The *Maine* had settled into the harbor's muddy bottom, leaving only a mast and part of her upper deck exposed. Smoke still curled from the wreckage, and there was a strange gurgling sound—air bubbles escaping from the flooded compartments. Of the 350 officers and men aboard, more than 260 were killed by the explosion or drowned in the aftermath.

America went mad with fury over the sinking of the *Maine*, encouraged in this fierce anger by the scorching stories reported in the *New York Journal*. William Randolph Hearst saw that his hour had come, and his flaming editorials created a spirit of aggression across the country.

On the night the *Maine* blew up, Amos was at Charlie's Place, watching Eddy Sparks's show. To be more specific, he was watching one member of the show. He came in most nights, and had for over a month, ever since Rose had joined Sparks's company.

On that night after the show, he took Rose out for a late supper, and when they had eaten, the two of them walked the streets. Finally they went back to Rose's hotel, and when they got to the entrance, Amos said with some agitation, "Rose, I've got to talk to you."

She hesitated, then relented. "There's a parlor on the second floor. Nobody is ever there this time of night." She led him up the stairs and as soon as they were in the parlor, Amos turned her around to face him. "Rose, I don't know but one way to say this." She had never seen him so flustered. Finally he blurted it out. "I want us to get married!"

Rose stood there in shock. His proposal had been totally unexpected, and she began to tremble. "But, Amos, we've known each other such a little while—"

"Does that matter?" Amos demanded. He grasped her arms, and pulled her close. "Ever since the first time I kissed you, I haven't been able to think of anything but you!"

Rose stood helplessly in his grip, her mind spinning. She liked him so much, and he had been so kind to her. They had seen each other four or five times a week since she had moved uptown, and yet, she could not give him an answer.

"Amos, I don't think we're ready for marriage . . . at least, *I'm* not." She spoke quickly, but when she was finished, she saw that he was not deterred.

"Think about it, Rose," Amos said. "I know it's sudden, and I know we'll have to wait a long time. But if I just knew you'd be mine someday I could do *anything!*"

He left then, and went home to bed, though neither of them slept much that night. They were so young, and neither of them had any real experience in love. Rose was very much afraid and she had no one to turn to, no one to advise her. Amos was afraid, also, but he was an intense young man, knowing only one method to get what he wanted—to strive for it with all his might.

Amos Stuart never knew what might have happened if the *Maine* had not been sunk. He often wondered about it in the years that followed. What he did know was that he was called into the office of William Randolph Hearst two days after the sinking of the *Maine* for an unexpected interview.

His heart began to beat like a drum when his editor gruffly said, "Come along, Stuart. Mr. Hearst wants to see you."

"I suppose you're wondering why I want to see you?" said Hearst, when Amos stood before the publisher.

"Well, sir, I can't think you'd go to all this trouble to fire me," Amos replied, licking his lips nervously. "So you must have an assignment for me."

Hearst was not a jovial man, but he allowed himself a slight smile. "Yes, I do. You understand there's going to be a war with Spain?"

"Yes, sir. No way to avoid it."

"All right, here's what I want," Hearst said crisply. "I want one of my reporters in the ranks. Not as a reporter . . as a soldier, telling what the war looks like to him."

"That's a great idea, Mr. Hearst . . . and I'll do it!"

Hearst was caught off guard by Stuart's swift acceptance. "Now, hold on. It's going to be a *real* war, Stuart. You could get killed."

"On the other hand, sir," Amos shot back, "if I don't get killed, I may get some great stories for the *Journal*."

The publisher and the editor exchanged brief nods. "All right, now here's what I want you to do. The secretary of the Navy, Theodore Roosevelt, is going to get into this thing. He wants to be president of the United States, and the best way to do that is to become a war hero. You join his outfit. It'll be in the thick of things."

"I know the secretary slightly, Mr. Hearst," Amos said, enjoying the surprise on the publisher's face. "You may have forgotten my part in Miss Powers' interview with Mr. Roosevelt."

"I *had* forgotten!" Hearst exclaimed. "Would he remember you?"

"Oh, yes." Amos nodded. "He came back to ride at Greenlee Stables a few times, and I always saddled up for him. He teased me a great deal about Miss Powers."

"Get into his outfit," Hearst said instantly. "I'd think he'd choose cavalry, fancies himself some kind of cowboy. He knows you're good with horses, so he might take you. That way, we could get the stuff straight from the top."

The three men planned their strategy for over an hour, and when Amos left, Hearst shook hands with him. "My niece thinks you're quite a fellow, Stuart," he said. His cold eyes fixed Amos firmly. "Do a good job on this one . . . and we'll see what we can do for you."

But Amos did not leave New York the next day. Nor the next week . . . nor even the next month. He waited until Theodore Roosevelt issued a call for his Rough Riders, and then sought an audience with the secretary. It was a short interview.

Amos offered his services, and Roosevelt, desperately in need of all the experienced help he could get, accepted him on the spot. "Capital!" he exclaimed. "I must have Prince, and you'll take care of the horses for all our officers. It'll be *Sergeant* Stuart now!"

Amos went at once to Hearst, who was delighted beyond bounds, then he sought out Rose.

"I'll be leaving soon, Rose, to go to the war," he said. "Won't you say you'll marry me when I come back?"

"Oh, Amos . . . I can't!"

Nevertheless, when Amos left New York on May 7, 1898, with the Rough Riders, Rose could not bear it. She clung to him, weeping, and promised, "I'll marry you when you come back, Amos . . . if you still want me to!"

And Amos Stuart rode off to war, with the memory of her kiss, and knew that he would not get killed, for he had too much to live for!

8

San Juan Hill

Never had so many hare-brained schemes for winning a war surfaced than after the sinking of the *Maine*! Buffalo Bill Cody, the old Indian fighter and showman, promised to kick the Spaniards out of Cuba with thirty thousand "Indian braves." Frank James, who'd ridden the outlaw trail with his brother Jesse, offered to lead a regiment of cowboys. The Sioux nation announced that they were ready to go on the warpath and take Spanish scalps. Mrs. Martha A. Shute of Denver, Colorado, wanted to form a troop of cavalry made up entirely of women. And William Hearst suggested a regiment of all-star athletes—prizefighters, wrestlers, baseball players, football players, rowers, runners, gymnasts. Our athletes, he boasted, were practically bullet-proof. They would "overawe any Spanish regiment by their mere appearance. They would scorn Mauser bullets!"

President McKinley ignored these goofy schemes, calling instead for 125,000 volunteers. He could have asked for a million, for at least that many flocked to the recruiting office. In one of his early stories, Amos explained why so many young men sought so desperately for a chance to die:

> Twenty-five years ago such a call would not have worked. At that time the Civil War had only been over for eight years. Memories of the struggle were still vivid, and only lunatics dreamed of repeating such an ordeal. But time has passed and the memories of the horrors of that war have faded. Veterans,

eager to recapture their youth, look back on it as an adventure filled with romance and glory. Our young men, raised on heroic war stories, long for adventures of their own, and so they flock into the recruiting stations, many of them trying *anything* to pass the physical. One man drank a gallon of water to meet the minimum weight requirement. Another, undersized by three-eighths of an inch, lay in his bed for three days in the hope of "lengthening" his body. It didn't help—and in years to come he may well be glad of it, for he may be living instead of a few dried bones covered by a blanket of sand in Cuba!

The last sentence was stricken by William Randolph Hearst, who did more than any other single man to bring on the war. When Frederick Remington had first been sent to draw scenes of the conflict, he'd found little to sketch and had wired back to Hearst, "There is no war!" Hearst had fired right back, "You furnish the pictures and I'll furnish the war!" Even after the sinking of the *Maine* could not be proven to be the act of an enemy, but an internal explosion, Hearst ignored that fact and continued to beat the drums for war.

Of the thousands of young men who volunteered, the luckiest were accepted into the First United States Volunteer Cavalry Regiment, more commonly called the Rough Riders. Theodore Roosevelt was invited to command, but he refused, claiming lack of military experience. Colonel Leonard Wood thus became the official commander of the Rough Riders, but everyone in the country knew that Roosevelt was its true leader.

Roosevelt had tremendous influence, of course, and within two weeks the regiments received the best of everything. Whole trainloads of supplies were rushed to its training camp in San Antonio, Texas. There were plenty of horses and the men were issued the Krag, the best rifle of the day.

Roosevelt wanted the regiment to represent the "best" elements in American life, which meant two types of people. The first he termed the "gilded gang"—men like himself, who were wealthy and educated, eager for a good fight in the service of their country. A list of their names read like the Social Register, many of them graduates of Harvard and other Ivy League schools. Some were bankers and stockbrokers and lawyers, and their number included a world-champion polo player and a national tennis champion.

The backbone of the regiment, however, was the kind of men Roosevelt had known during his ranching days—westerners, sons and grandsons of the pioneers. A colorful lot, they went by such names as "Cherokee Bill," "Happy Jack," "Dead Shot Jim," "Lariat Ned," "Rattlesnake Pete," "Weeping Dutchman," "Prayerful James," and "Rubber Shoe Andy."

They came from the Rockies and the Dakota Badlands, from Texas, New Mexico, and Colorado. The regiment boasted eight sheriffs, seven army deserters, and an unreported number of outlaws. Most of them were bowlegged and all were more comfortable on horseback than on foot.

A week after Roosevelt arrived in camp, he could call the name of every man in the regiment. He'd sit atop his favorite horse, Little Texas, his high-pitched voice rattling the horses and confusing their riders. But the men loved him! When he appeared, they didn't cheer or applaud. They blazed away with their six-shooters, causing a stampede.

By the end of May, Roosevelt had forged them into a real fighting force. And the troopers showed their affection for Roosevelt by calling themselves "Teddy's Terrors," "Teddy's Texas Tarantulas," "Teddy's Rustler Regiment," and "Roosevelt's Rough 'Uns" . . . but in the end, they were the Rough Riders.

When the regiment left for Tampa, Florida, on May 28, Amos, like all the rest of the men, was at a fever-pitch of excitement. They traveled south in seven flag-draped trains, and were greeted by large crowds all the way to Florida. At one of the stops, a young man named Faye O'Dell nudged Amos. "Come on, Amos, let's let them gals have their way. They wanna kiss some real heroes!"

Amos grinned, liking the young man very much. The two of them got off the train where townspeople were handing out watermelons and buckets of iced beer. The local drum-and-bugle corps made a racket loud enough to raise the dead, and as O'Dell had said, the pretty girls in their straw hats and bright gingham dresses were ready to greet the heroes. One of them, a very pretty redhead, threw herself into Amos's arms, kissed him firmly, then began to work her way through the crowd of yelling soldiers.

O'Dell, an undersized product of New York, grinned and winked at Amos. "Hey, this sure beats workin', don't it, Amos?" He snatched a chubby girl, kissed her noisily, then as the call from the sergeant came, reluctantly let her go. As the two of them climbed back onto the coach, he said regretfully, "Sure wisht this war had come along sooner, Amos. I been wastin' my life up till now!"

But O'Dell wasn't so exuberant after a few days in Tampa, a small, dusty, Gulf Coast town. As Amos wrote in a story:

> Life in camp is worse than any of the soldiers had imagined. Only one small railroad line leads to the camp, and the lack of water makes life miserable. Supplies clog up, and many go without food and equipment. With inadequate sanitary systems and the lack of clean water, dysentery and typhus are laying many low. Accommodations are so bad, many are sleeping on cement floors with newspapers for covering. The refuse from thousands of animals not only stinks to heaven, but pollutes the water supplies. To die for one's country in battle is one thing–but to die in squalor because of insufficient or corrupt leadership is tragedy!

As Amos half-expected, Hearst sent back a biting comment on his piece: "Stuart, either tell the story of this glorious war in a positive manner, or don't bother to send any more stories!"

Amos showed the wire to Colonel Roosevelt, who was always interested in the public relations of the war. "Hearst doesn't give a continental for this country!" Teddy snapped, his smallish eyes blazing with anger. "All he wants is to sell more newspapers." But then he grinned at Amos. "You write it as you see it, Sergeant! When we swing into action, you'll be the most famous correspondent in the country!"

But Amos knew he could not afford to write it as he saw it, not if he wanted to keep his job as a reporter for the *Journal*. Hearst was a tyrant, firing men for far less than that.

As the days rolled on, Amos grew glum, not only because of the tight-rope he was walking with his news stories, but because of the disturbing letters he was receiving from Rose ... or *not* receiving. At first she had written regularly, but after a letter in which she told him that Eddy Sparks had left Charlie's and she was out of a job, she wrote less often. Two weeks later, he heard from her again. "I've got a job with a stage company," she reported. "It means going on the road—like Lylah. The manager agreed to give me a trial, so I'll have to do good to stay with the company—" From that point on, her letters almost stopped.

He got only three more before leaving for Cuba—one from Detroit, one from Cleveland, and one from Atlanta. All were brief and factual, giving only the bare details of her travels and her work. In the last one Amos received, she wrote:

"Amos, I am not sure about our getting married. We haven't known each other very long, and we're both young. You may be gone a long time ... though I hope not. Let's think about it and when you get back, we'll see."

It was a blow to Amos, and Faye O'Dell took note. "What's wrong with you, Amos?" he asked a few days later. "You look like you lost your best friend."

"Oh, just worried about the war, I guess," Amos replied, not wanting to share his news with anyone.

"Well, looks like we'll see the elephant pretty soon," Faye said, his homely face aglow with excitement. "Everybody says we'll ship out this week."

The rumors, for once, were right. While inspecting the horses, Roosevelt told Amos personally, "Stuart, get the animals ready for a sea voyage." His big teeth gleamed as he grinned. "We'll ship out on Saturday—and about time, I say!"

Amos worked hard preparing the stock and seeing to the food and equipment necessary to care for so many animals. But on the day before they boarded ship and cleared the harbor, he got a letter from Nick which troubled him. Nick wrote in his atrocious hand:

Hey, Soldier Boy! I guess you'll be mowing those bean-eaters down pretty soon, so be sure and get one for me! Sometimes I wish I was there with you, but then I wake up and know it's not for me. We're all doing fine. Mama says to tell you she says fifty Hail Mary's for you every day, so you ought to be safe, right?

Haven't seen Rose since she left for her tour, but a guy came into the bar the other day—fellow I know named Danny Beers. He's an actor, and he's just left the bunch Rose is with. Said he couldn't stand the star—a guy named Hackett. Well, while we was talking, he mentioned Rose. Didn't know I even knew her, and I didn't let on. Didn't sound too good, Amos, to tell the truth. He said the manager of the troop she's with is pretty bad—likes to chase women. I asked him if Rose had fallen for him, and he said it looked like it. Way he put it was, "This guy Hackett don't keep his actresses around unless they come across. He said Rose was drinking some, too, which is a shocker, ain't it? Don't sound like our Rosie. But when a girl is all alone in the world, she's a pigeon for a good-looking guy.

I hate to tell you this, but you've got a right to know. I'll see if I can get in touch with Rose. Do what I can to wise her up. Take care of yourself. Don't get killed on me! Get that thing over and hurry back home.

Amos wrote at once to Rose, but he had no time to do more than scribble a few lines, for the army was on the move. Everything was confusion. The ships would hold only sixteen thousand of the twenty-seven thousand men, so entire regiments had to stay behind, and there was a scramble for places among those who did go.

The Rough Riders, not to be denied their chance at glory, simply hijacked a steam launch. Tired and hungry, to them the ship seemed like heaven. And when an officer from another regiment came along a few minutes later to claim it, Roosevelt flashed his best Toothadore smile. "Yours, you say? Do tell. Well, we seem to have it, don't we?"

On the evening of June 14, thirty-two transports blew their whistles, weighed anchor, and began to move. They carried the largest military force that had ever left American shores. Once clear of the harbor, they were joined by fourteen warships, where the flotilla formed three columns and steamed southward under a canopy of stars.

"I don't care if I get shot by a greaser," Faye O'Dell moaned. "That couldn't be no worse than this blasted boat!"

Amos was inclined to agree. The two of them had come topside to lean on the rail, sick of the stifling hold where they slept in bunks three levels high. Most of the men had been sick since leaving America, and there was no way to clean anything. "It's like living in a heated sewer," Amos had written in one of his stories. There were twelve toilets for twelve hundred men, no water for drinking and none for washing. Richard Harding Davis, the most famous correspondent of the day had reported, "The ship's water smells like a frog pond or a stable yard, and it tastes like it smells!"

Amos tried to comfort O'Dell. "We'll land day after tomorrow. It'll be better then."

But it was not, for on June 22, the landing at Daiouirí, eighteen miles east of Santiago, proved to be as unpleasant as the voyage.

Amos scrambled over the side of the transport into a waiting longboat. Like bucking broncos, the small boats bounded and rolled in the waves. Several men jumped too soon and crashed when the boat lurched upward, while others waited too long and dropped into the trough between the waves.

When they were fully loaded, several of the longboats were roped in line and towed by a Navy steam launch. The journey was wet and choppy, and the wind-tossed spray soaked Amos and O'Dell to the skin. O'Dell turned gray, and vomited all over himself, and he was not alone.

Upon reaching the shore, they had to wait for a wave to lift the boat level with the rotting wooden pier, then leap across. It was dangerous business, and Amos saw two black cavalrymen drown when they missed the wharf. Horses and mules were pushed overboard to find their own way ashore, and the first thing Amos did when he landed was to gather Roosevelt's mounts, Prince and Little Texas before they followed the lead of several others who swam out to sea and drowned.

For two days Roosevelt and the other officers of the Rough Riders worked to pull the men together. The overall commander of cavalry, General "Fighting Joe" Wheeler, had commanded Confederate cavalry in the Civil War. General Wheeler was no less hot-headed and ready for trouble when he led the men out on June 24, than when he'd led his grayclad troops against Grant. The strike force would be heading for a pass in the mountains called Las Guasimas, which lay between the army and Santiago, the ultimate objective.

When Captain Bucky O'Neill, former mayor of Prescott, Arizona, came by and spoke with Roosevelt just before the assault, Amos was standing close enough to hear their conversation. "Colonel, we'll get our chance today! Fighting Joe won't be able to resist a chance to hit the garlics."

"Capital!" Roosevelt grinned, and he turned to Amos. "I'll ride Prince today, but bring Little Texas along in case he goes down." He looked at the men and nodded approvingly, and when the column moved out, the men followed the narrow jungle trail joking, laughing, and arguing at the top of their lungs.

O'Dell was eager. He poked Amos in the ribs with a sharp elbow. "Bet I get more of 'em than you, buddy!"

But Amos had considerably more imagination than the little soldier. "What if they get you, Faye?"

O'Dell stared at Stuart, then laughed. "One of them get *me*? Not a chance!"

"It could happen."

"Nah! We're gonna whip 'em, Amos!"

Amos licked his lips, for he knew that any of them could go down. "Wish I'd paid more attention to my ma. She's a Christian. If I die, I'll be in hell right off, Faye."

O'Dell stared at Amos. "Hey, you're fighting for your country. Anybody who dies fighting for his country goes to heaven. Didn't you know that?"

Amos shook his head. "Those fellows waiting for us up there . . . they're fighting for their country, too. Everybody dies, Faye. But Ma says it's only saved people who go to heaven."

"Saved? What's that mean?"

Amos stared at Faye, surprised. He'd grown up listening to revivalists, and his mother had read to him from the Bible all his life. "Why . . . saved is believing in Jesus."

"Well, I'm saved then." O'Dell shrugged. "I've always believed in Jesus."

"No, it's more than that, I think," Amos said. He was searching the terrain in front, watching for the glint of sunlight on steel barrels. His nerves were tense, and he saw that General Wheeler was sending out more scouts. "What Ma says is that a fellow has to give up his bad ways and do what God says. But she says, too, that you got to be converted." Just talking about it took some of his fear away, and he told O'Dell what he could remember of the sermons he'd heard. The small man seemed intrigued by the one on being born again.

"Born again?" Faye mused. "I guess it'd take something like starting all over to get me ready to meet God. I've done some pretty bad things—"

Suddenly there was a shrill z-z-z-z-*eu* overhead, followed by a sharp *crack*.

"Mausers!" Roosevelt yelled.

The hidden Spaniards opened fire, and a man five feet in front of Amos grabbed his face, which exploded like a red flower, and he dropped to the ground. Others were falling. But Roosevelt was so excited that he jumped up and down. Amos saw a bullet hit a tree inches from his head, sending splinters everywhere.

"Look at that!" O'Dell said in wonder. "He *likes* it!"

The Rough Riders were pinned down, the Mauser bullets bowling them over. The Mauser packed a terrific punch. The force of a bullet striking an outstretched arm was enough to spin a man around in his tracks before he hit the ground. Amos heard the chugging sound made by the slugs as they plowed into the flesh of his companions.

It was Fighting Joe Wheeler who saved the day. The feisty little cavalryman could contain himself no longer. The Civil War never far from his mind, he loosed the rebel yell and shouted, "Come on, men! We'll put the Yankees on the run!"

With a wild cry, the Rough Riders charged. The Spaniards broke and fled down the trail to Santiago. One of them who was taken prisoner said, "These gringos . . . *muy loco*! When we shoot them, they scream and run *at* us! They even try to catch us with their hands!"

Amos and Faye had joined in the wild charge, and when it was over, they collapsed, winded and drained. Amos looked back over the ground they'd covered. It was strewn with bodies, both Spanish and American.

Faye caught his breath, then shook his head. "Lots of our guys didn't make it, Amos," he said soberly. The slaughter had done something to him, and he muttered, "Wonder if they were born again, like you said?" When Amos didn't answer, he studied the faces of the dead and wounded. "Makes a guy feel funny, don't it?"

All day the work of burying the dead and treating the

wounded went on, but the way lay open to Santiago. It was rough going, Amos and Faye discovered, for the trail could not handle the wagon and mule trains hauling their supplies. They were forced to eat "embalmed" beef and beans soaked in hog fat, and when opened, the cans smelled like garbage pails in the damp heat.

At night the land crabs sought them out—ugly creatures that moved about noisily in search of food. Amos came awake with a wild scream when one of them crawled over his face that night, and he was not the only one. The red ants, too, had a bite like an electric needle, so that Amos finally climbed a tree to escape the vermin.

As they marched on, Amos listened to the officers as they talked about what lay ahead. Captain O'Neill, a tall, good-looking man with black hair, took time to explain it to a small group of the soldiers as they cooked supper on the last night of June.

"There are two hills—San Juan and Kettle—surrounded by trenches and barbed wire. The Spaniards' main defense runs along the crest of San Juan Ridge. Then there's a village called El Caney, with wire and trenches and a fort with loopholes. Here's what we've got to do to get through to Santiago—" He pulled a rough map from his pocket, and the men crowded around to take a look.

O'Neill frowned. "It's uphill, and will be tough going."

That night Amos wrote his mother and Rose. He waited until the next morning, then gave the letters to Faye, saying with a casual shrug, "If I drop, Faye, see that these get back, will you?"

O'Dell stared at him. "Oh, blast it, Amos!" he snapped. "Nothing's going to happen to us!" He jammed the letters into his pocket, muttering, "You and your talk about hell! Gives me the willies!"

Amos wanted to ask if he could carry any message for O'Dell, but saw that his friend didn't want to talk about dying.

The two of them moved out with the regiment, and soon

discovered that before attacking the hills, they would have to march down a narrow jungle trail. "Every Spaniard in the country will zero in on us," Amos whispered. "They can pick us off like sitting ducks."

At that moment he and the rest of his fellow soldiers looked up to see a horseman in a black business suit, watching them as they set out. Amos stared, not quite able to believe his eyes. It was William Randolph Hearst! He was recognized by a soldier, who yelled, "Hi, there, Willie!" and the cry was taken up and shouted from one end of the column to the other.

"Guess he came out to see his war in person," Amos said grimly, knowing that in one sense, it really *was* Hearst's war. But he saw, too, that the publisher wasn't so arrogant for once. His long face was pale, and he looked sick. *Maybe he sees what his "nice little war" really means,* Amos thought. He made no attempt to speak to Hearst, for the line was moving rapidly now.

Ten thousand men crowded the jungle trail, with the Spaniards waiting for them. As Amos pressed forward, the air suddenly vibrated with the screech of Mauser bullets. Amos felt his mouth go dry and his stomach tie up in knots.

The Rough Riders were not riders at all now, for the territory was too rough for cavalry. They fought their way through, finally coming to the foot of Kettle Hill. As they lay down, taking cover, Captain O'Neill stood up straight, ignoring the rain of fire and smoking a cigarette.

"Sir, better get down!" Amos called out.

O'Neill laughed and blew a cloud of smoke. "Sergeant," he began with a smile, looking down at Amos, "the Spanish bullet isn't made that will kill me!" But he was wrong. At that instant a slug struck him in the mouth and came out the back of his head. He was dead before he hit the ground.

One of the men next to Amos began to retch, while the firing from the Spanish line grew more intense. Just then, Lieutenant Jules Ord, who was at the apex of the enemy fire, stood up and yelled, "Good-bye, if I don't come back!"

Holding a pistol in one hand and a bayonet in the other,

he led the attack. "Come on! We can't stay here!" and shouting like lunatics, fifty men leapt up and raced toward San Juan Hill. Ord reached it first and was shot dead at once.

Theodore Roosevelt was right behind. "Bugler, sound the charge!"

The bugle sounded, and all but one man moved forward. Roosevelt saw him, and ordered him to his feet. "What? Are you afraid to stand up when I am on horseback?" he raged. Just then a bullet ripped into the man, narrowly missing Colonel Roosevelt. "Come on, Rough Riders!" Roosevelt screamed, and drove his horse up the hill.

Amos rose with the rest, almost mindlessly, for the battle-madness had taken them all. He stayed as close to Roosevelt as he could, and when a Spanish officer appeared, he saw Roosevelt drop him with one shot.

A cry went up, and the regiment surged forward, Amos with them. He saw Faye O'Dell go down, clutching at his stomach. Amos dropped beside him, and saw at once that there was no hope. The bullet had torn the boy's stomach wide open, and blood flowed from the wound, gushing redly.

"Amos!" Faye gasped, lifting one bloody hand to clutch at Amos.

"You'll be all right," Amos lied. "I'll get some help—"

"No—too late—" Faye's eyes were wide, and a trickle of blood dribbled from his mouth. "Amos . . . not ready to die—!" The little soldier arched his back, but he could not speak. He kicked his feet wildly, then he went limp.

"Faye!" Amos cried, weeping for his friend. But Faye was dead, and the officers were yelling at the troops to move on.

Amos got to his feet and plunged blindly up the hill. He got no more than ten feet before the world turned a brilliant, blinding red—and then it turned to black. There was time for only one thought as he fell. *First Faye . . . and now me. Oh, God—*

San Juan Hill was taken. Santiago fell a few days later, and on July 3, the Spanish fleet tried to escape from Santiago Harbor and was annihilated by the American Navy.

The Spanish-American War was over.

But Amos Stuart knew nothing of all this. He was in a coma, lying on the ground for many hours before medical help arrived. Even then he did not regain consciousness. If Theodore Roosevelt himself had not ordered the doctors to do their best for the wounded man, Amos Stuart would have died in Cuba.

He woke up on a hospital ship, his head bandaged, and with a raging fever. When the orderly saw he was awake, he called the doctor, who came to look at him. After a brief examination, he nodded. "You'll live, Stuart. I didn't think you would."

After the doctor left, Amos lay there, his mind wandering most of the time. He thought often of Faye O'Dell . . . and how the small trooper had gone out to meet God without being ready.

I ought to be grateful it wasn't me, he thought. But he found that the war and O'Dell's death had left its mark, and as his body mended, his spirit grew hard.

Part 2
1899–1900

9

ROSE FINDS A CHARMING MAN

From the moment Rose waved Amos off to war, she had the feeling that somehow she had made a grave mistake. For the first few weeks after he left, she went about her work at Charlie's Place with a vague feeling of unrest. During this time she went often to see Anna. It was the closest thing to a real home in her life, for the older woman had become like a second mother to her.

"I wish you would-a quit that saloon," Anna said, shaking her head. "It's no good for young-a girl to be all alone in a place like-a that!" The two women were sitting on the back steps of Anna's house. Summer had fallen on New York like a heavy blanket, and the sun beat down on the bare yard, which had been pounded as flat as concrete by the feet of children at play.

"Oh, it's all right, Anna." Rose shrugged. "It's better than the factory."

"Maybe it's not so hard, but . . . you be careful, Rose."

The brief warning stirred something in the young woman, and she gave a fleeting grimace. Her long black hair lay down her back, for she had washed it in the rainwater Anna collected in a barrel as it fell off the roof. She was prettier than ever, Anna noted. Regular food had caused her to fill out, and she was wearing one of the new dresses she had bought for herself at Eddy Sparks's urging. It was light-blue cotton with white trim, and the color made her green eyes appear blue.

"You mean . . . men?" she asked after a delay. "I know,

Anna. Eddy does the best he can to keep them away. But they're always there." She smiled then, and reached over and patted the older woman's shoulder. "As long as I've got you and Eddy to preach at me, I'll be all right." She got up, stretched, and sighed. "It's almost three o'clock. I've got to go back to rehearsal."

"You come-a back tomorrow, you hear? We fix a big chocolate cake. Make you fat and pretty . . . like-a me!" Anna grinned.

"All right, I will." Rose hugged Mary Elizabeth and the other children, then left to go back downtown.

It was a long walk, so Rose treated herself to the luxury of a cab ride. The streets were crowded, and she watched with interest as one of the new horseless carriages came chugging down the street. It was an odd-looking contraption to her, though she had seen many of the vehicles since coming to New York. The cabdriver gave the noisy affair a sour look, turned to her and said grumpily, "Them things will never amount to anything. Be glad when folks lose interest, and we can have the streets back like we're supposed to!"

Rose got out of the cab in front of Charlie's Place, paid the driver, and went inside. It was a little cooler there, and she went at once to the dressing room. The rehearsal was only for her act—a new number Eddy wanted to try—so the other girls were not around. She put on the older dress she used for rehearsals, then went out to find Eddy.

"Hello, Eddy," she said, seeing him seated at the piano. He had been kind to her, and she had grown to trust him a great deal. But she saw at once that he was upset. "What's the matter, Eddy? Don't you feel good?"

Sparks ran his fingers over the keys in a series of dissonant arpeggios, unaware that he was doing so. "I'm not sick, Rose," he said, doing his best to smile at her. "Well, maybe I am a little . . . but it's not something a pill or a doctor would be able to fix."

Rose was confused, for the actor had always been a cheerful sort. She asked cautiously, "Is it something about your family?"

"No, they're all right." Sparks shook his head, then said glumly, "Well, you've got to hear about it anyway, so I might as well tell you now. Charlie told me this morning that he's got a new company coming in to take our place. Tomorrow will be our last night here."

Rose felt her stomach begin to knot up, and she bit her lip nervously. "Why did he do that, Eddy?"

"Oh, we've been here longer than most, Rose. People like a change."

"But . . . do you have another place for us to go?"

"Well . . . not yet, but I'll find something." He reached over and patted her shoulder awkwardly. "Sorry about this, Rose. Don't say anything to the other girls yet. I'll tell them myself."

"All right, Eddy."

Rose made it through the performances without betraying her roiling emotions. But when Eddy told the girls afterwards that they would be finished after the next evening's performance, she could see they were as unhappy as she. One of them, a small girl with blond hair named Eileen, said to Rose, "This is a bad time to be out of work. Nobody's looking for singers and dancers now . . . they've already got plenty."

"Eddy will find something for us," Rose said with more confidence than she felt.

But after the final performance, Eddy's face was sober as he met with them. "I haven't been able to get a booking yet. I've got a line on a spot in Cleveland, but it won't be open for three weeks." He looked haggard and tired, but he smiled and tried to be encouraging. "Give me your addresses, all of you, and I'll get word to you as soon as I find something."

Rose went to her room, fighting off the fear that rose in her at the thought of the future.

"I'm going back home, Rose," Lillie, her roommate, said before going to bed. "This is no life for me. Take my advice and do the same."

The next day Rose began looking for work, but discovered very quickly that there was none available . . . not for her, at least. She had no real friends in the entertainment world, and no marketable talent—at least for the legitimate stage.

One of the men she spoke to that first day, a heavyset man with a balding dome and a kind heart, said, "Little lady, you can't sing and you can't dance and you can't act—not enough for the stage, I mean." He hesitated, not wanting to hurt her, but finally said honestly, "All you have going for you is your good looks. But this town is full of good-looking young women, and I'd hate to see you go the way most of them go. Be better if you get a job as a typewriter or a teacher."

But those things were beyond Rose, and she knew nothing else to do. That night when she went home, she had to struggle to control the fear that choked her and brought a trembling to her hands. She walked the floor all night, unable to sleep, trying to think of something. Finally, she fell into bed. *I won't be able to afford this room now. I'll have to find a cheaper place.*

For a week, she searched for work as hard as any miner ever sought for gold, but found nothing. Nothing, at least, that she could bring herself to take. Several times she was approached by men who offered her a job in their saloons or dance halls. But the glitter in their eyes frightened her.

At the end of the week, when the rent was due, she was confused and paid up for another week without thinking. She had spent most of her income on clothing and had less than twenty dollars left. She ate little that week and exhausted her strength by going to downtown shops, looking for almost any sort of work.

She had seen Anna only once during this time, and when Nick came by early one afternoon, saying, "Mama says to bring you home," she was ready. Noting the slight hollow in her cheeks, he added carelessly, "She's promised to make some of that lasagna you like so much. Come on, let's go."

It was a good evening for Rose. Anna stuffed her until she

couldn't swallow another bite, and the children clamored over her. As she left with Nick, Anna hugged her. "You come-a home, Rose! We miss you!"

Nick put her in a cab, and all the way back to her room, he chattered idly. Rose could never make out exactly what it was Nick did for a living, but whatever it was, he was prospering. His cheeks were glowing with health and he was wearing a fine suit and seemed to have plenty of money. When he walked her upstairs to her room, he took some money out of his pocket and pressed it into her hand.

She tried to refuse and he grunted, "Aaaa, shut up and take it, Rosie! Plenty more where that came from." He closed her fingers over the bills, kissed her cheek, and grinned. "You miss ol' Amos, don't you?"

"Yes; I'm afraid for him."

"He'll be okay," Nick said quickly. "Don't let this get you down, Rose. Something will turn up."

Rose lived for a week on the money Nick gave her, but it was almost gone by Saturday. Now she had no money for rent, and the thought of having to leave the room brought panic to her. Finally she came to a decision. *I'll have to go back to work at the factory.*

She rose the next morning, as depressed as she'd ever been in her life. The joyless future at the factory offered nothing but misery. Knowing she'd have to walk, she decided to have a good breakfast first.

Going to the restaurant that offered the cheapest meal, she ordered, and when the meal came, she ate it slowly, knowing such treats would not come again soon. Afterward, she walked all the way to the factory, a distance of six miles, and got her old job back with no difficulty.

The manager remembered her and nodded. "Sure, you did good. Come in Monday morning at six."

"Thank you, Mr. Berlin." Rose left the factory, hating the thought of spending her days in the bleak building that reeked of hopelessness.

With half a day on her hands, she decided to go back to
Anna's. She was packing her suitcase when a knock came on
the door. Surprised, she opened it and found Tim Quincy, a
general handyman at Charlie's Place, standing there.

"Letter for you, Rosie," he said. "It's from Eddy Sparks."

"Thank you, Tim." Rose smiled, and as soon as he left,
she tore open the envelope, hoping it was a job offer. Instead,
it was only a brief note, scrawled in a careless hand. *Rose, I
haven't found anything, but I talked to a fellow here who'll maybe
give you a job. He's taking a show on the road and needs a good-
looking gal for a small part. Don't pay much, and you'd have to do
the costumes and props. His name is James Hackett. He said he'd
be at the Crescent Hotel Saturday and for you to come by. Hope it
works out. Be careful with Hackett. He's a ladies' man.*

The note was signed "Eddy." Rose stared at it for a long
moment, then whirled and began to undress.

It will be better than the factory, she thought. *As long as I can
eat and have a place to sleep, that's all I need.* She took extra pains
with her appearance, putting on her best dress and fixing her
hair in the most attractive style. Then she left the room and
headed for the Crescent Hotel.

James K. Hackett was a mediocre actor—a fact appreciated by most of his colleagues, but not clearly discerned by
Hackett himself. He was, however, a quick study, able to mas-
ter long speeches with ease, and he was one of the finest-look-
ing men on the stage. Unfortunately, he acted every role in
exactly the same fashion, overdone and highly dramatic. No
matter what emotion the scene called for—gentleness, anger,
fear—Hackett came on like a storm, sawing the air with his
arms and eating the scenery.

The height of his career had been his short stint on the
road with Maude Adams in the role of Mercutio. Unbe-
knownst to him, he had not been Miss Adams's first choice,
but when forced to choose a substitute, she had thought
Hackett would do if she could get him to modify his histri-

onics. She soon discovered that she was mistaken. It was not entirely the actor's fault, for he was like a horse with only one gait—full speed at all times.

Hackett had left the play in Boston, and when Miss Adams was asked who would replace him, had replied caustically, "Go out on the street and bring in the first man you see!"

Hackett had one friend who had two splendid advantages—a great deal of money and no judgment at all in theatrical matters. His name was Gerald Partain, and he admired Hackett excessively. He had never made a dime on his own, but his father had left him so much money that he was having difficulty throwing it away fast enough to impoverish himself, so when Hackett came to him with a request for funds to put together a company and take it on the road, Partain was delighted.

While Partain was not a critic of the theater, he was a student of beautiful women, and it may have been Hackett's lady who brought him in as a paying partner. Partain had seen Lylah Stuart in her minor role, had been introduced to her by Hackett, and was convinced that the show—featuring the two in starring roles—would be a smash.

After they had left Partain, Hackett had grinned. "He's like a gold mine that never gets played out, Lylah. A good chap with no sense whatsoever . . . but plenty of money." He had embraced her possessively, promising, "You're going to be a star, sweetheart. No way we can miss!"

Lylah was new to the theater, but already knowledgeable enough to understand that James Hackett would never be a star. He might do as a rung on her own ladder, however, and she had allowed him to kiss her before asking, "What play are you thinking of, Jim?"

"*Sherlock Holmes*, I think. It's a great role for me."

And you'd make a hash of it! Besides, there's no good role for a woman in that one. Lylah had put her arm around Hackett's neck, smiled secretly, and said, "Let's talk about it, Jim—"

After considerable persuasion, Hackett had agreed to do a

play called *The Runaway Girl*, in which there was a great role for a rising young actress.

Hackett was basically a lazy man, loving his time on the stage and the applause of the crowd, but hating the multitudinous details that go with taking a show on the road. It had been Lylah who had plunged in and pulled the show together, and it had been Lylah, not James Hackett, who got the good reviews.

Hackett had grown jealous, and after a three-month tour, had staged a rousing fight with Lylah, accusing her of *using* him. Lylah had laughed in his face. "That's just wonderful coming from you, Jim!" she said bitterly. "You've never done a thing in your life that cost you anything. But I won't be *using* you anymore. Good-bye and bad luck!"

Without Lylah, the show lost its luster, and Hackett had closed it almost at once. Going back to his gold mine, he'd said, "Gerald, the time is ripe for something really *new* on the stage—"

Hackett easily persuaded Partain to put up the money for a new play, and this time he chose *Dr. Jekyll and Mr. Hyde*, which had been done in a highly successful manner by the famous Richard Mansfield two years earlier. It was more or less a one-character play, which suited Hackett exactly. It would mean a very small cast, consisting of one more man and two women. And it was for one of the women's roles that he'd agreed to interview a young woman recommended by Eddy Sparks, an old friend of his.

"She's not a trained actress," Sparks had warned Hackett, "but she needs a job bad. She's a good looker, though . . . see?"

Hackett had taken the picture Sparks handed him and made up his mind on the spot, though he didn't say so. "Have her come by to see me at the Crescent next Saturday, Eddy, but warn her the pay's not much."

And when Hackett opened the door to his hotel room and

greeted the young woman who stood there, he knew he had
to have her.

"Miss Beaumont?" he smiled, stepping back. "Come right
in. Here, take this chair." He ushered her in, seated her, then
proceeded to turn on his charm, which was highly developed
and seldom failed.

"I've heard such fine things about you from Eddy." He
smiled warmly. "Too bad the troupe had to break up. Have
you found anything yet?"

"No, Mr. Hackett," Rose said nervously. She had made it
a rule never to be alone with a man in his room, but this time
there had been no choice. Still James Hackett seemed nice
enough, and as she sat there listening to him describe the
play, she began to relax. Finally she said, "Mr. Hackett, I'm
not an actress. I have no experience except with Eddy
Sparks's company . . . and all I did in that was dance a little."

Hackett waved his hand with an eloquent gesture. "Of
course, Rose . . . may I call you that? Good! Well, Eddy told
me, and really what I'm offering you is not a part in the play so
much as a job helping with the costumes and the tickets . . .
things like that." Hackett knew that if he didn't find someone
to do these menial chores, he'd have to do all the work Lylah
had taken on herself, and he had no intention of doing that.
"The role you'll play is very minor—not more than twenty
lines in all—and it doesn't call for any great ability. That's why,
as I think Eddy must have mentioned, the pay is not large."

"Oh, I don't mind. I'll do *anything*, Mr. Hackett!"

Rose had no idea how appealing she was as she leaned forward in that pleading stance. She was aware that men found
her attractive, but was one of those rare women of real beauty
who did not dwell on the matter. There was not a trace of
pride in her character, as she said simply, "Please give me a
chance."

Hackett hesitated. "You have a husband? No? A family?"
He listened carefully as Rose explained that she had nobody,
and this relieved him. He'd been forced to face more than

one jealous husband and one or two offended fathers and brothers in his time, but this one was free of all encumbrances.

"Well, I don't see why not," he said. Getting to his feet, he moved to the oak dresser, took out two glasses and a bottle of wine. As he poured the wine, he said easily, "I'll have to give you some training, of course, but I see no reason why we can't work this thing out."

"I–I don't drink, Mr. Hackett," she said when he offered her a glass.

"Well, that's *splendid*, Rose!" he said heartily. "A good idea, but this is only wine, not liquor. I insist . . . a toast to the success of our new venture!"

Rose took the glass reluctantly. She had been practically raised in a saloon, and had seen the worst that drunkenness can do to a human being. *It's only wine*, she argued, and managed a smile. "Well . . . just one, then."

"To the play—" Hackett said, and then favoring her with his most ingratiating smile, held his glass high, adding, "And to us, Rose—"

The wine was strong, and Rose got to her feet at once. "If you'll tell me what to do, I'm ready to start, Mr. Hackett."

Hackett noticed that she had her back braced and was eyeing him cautiously. *Like a deer watching a big wolf*, he thought, but said aloud, "We'll meet the rest of the cast later. First, we'll go have a late breakfast and I can tell you about your part."

Hackett got his coat and slipped into it, but before he opened the door, he let his hand fall on Rose's shoulder. She looked at him with alarm, and he removed it immediately. "I'm glad you came by this morning, Rose. I think we're going to have a splendid time."

Rose was glad when he motioned her forward with a little bow and did not see the glitter in his eyes as he followed her out of the room. She could not know that he was a man who found innocence a challenge and that he had already started planning his strategy to claim her as one of his many triumphs over virtue.

10

LYLAH GOES HOME

After eight weeks on the road with an abysmally bad play, Lylah was drained emotionally, physically, and financially. The play, *Old Heads and Young Hearts*, was a piece of sentimental claptrap, cheapened by the histrionics of the actress who played the leading role—Georgia Cayvan. Herbert Kelcey, her co-star, was not bad, but was unable to keep the performance from sinking into a sticky, saccharine morass each night as Georgia shed enough tears to float a battleship.

The troupe had performed in forty towns, most of them one-nighters, with a few two-night stands. The cities and towns had become nothing but a blur to Lylah. And life was a dreary ritual—perform, pack the scenery and costumes, fall into a strange bed for a few hours of sleep, get up with an awful groggy feeling, catch a train to the next town, set up the stage, perform—then do it all again.

The men she met were all after the same thing, of course. Actresses were considered only slightly better than prostitutes, she discovered, and when Lylah did agree to have dinner with one of them, she spent most of the evening keeping her guard up. Many of them commented on the glamorous life she led, to which she wearily replied, "If you like working long hours, living in cheap hotels, eating poorly cooked food, getting by on starvation wages, and living on the razor's edge, not knowing from one day to the next if you'll have a job—why, yes, it's *very* glamorous."

The end came in St. Louis, when the show failed to attract more than twenty in the audience. Todd Blankenship, the manager, had paid them off—not as much as they had been promised, but all that could be scraped together. Lylah was weary of travel, and when Blankenship pulled her aside, she was ready to hear what he had to say. "Lylah, I can't promise a thing, but I'm on my way to Chicago to put together a show for Al Kendal. Think I can find a place for you."

"I'd appreciate that, Todd. How long will you be gone?"

"Three weeks at least."

Lylah thought quickly, adding up her assets and finding them short. "I'm going home to see my folks, Todd. I'll give you my address. When you need me, write, and I'll come."

"Sure, Lylah. I'll try to get you something better than you had in this clinker!" Shaking his head with disgust, he added, "You've got more talent in your little finger than Georgia's got in her whole body!"

Lylah had taken the southbound train out of St. Louis, so weary she had slept sitting up in the day coach. She'd longed to take the sleeping car, but was short of money.

"Fort Smith! Next stop—Fort Smith!"

Startled by the conductor's shrill announcement, Lylah looked out the window. The low hills flew by, then the train slowed as it began passing through the outskirts of the town. As she watched the farmhouses and isolated shacks appear out the window, then the real beginnings of the town, she wondered what sort of welcome she'd receive. She hadn't written to her family for a long time, ashamed to do so. But when Amos had found her and practically forced her to write, she'd written a short note, which her mother had answered at once. She still had the letter, would always have it, for it had restored her hope. Her mother had written in a thin hand:

> You're our daughter, and when God gave you to me, he gave me a special blessing. Your pa and all of us love you. Nothing can ever change that, my dear daughter, nothing in the world!

And this house is your home, any time you want to come. We long to see you. Come when you can, for you are ours and always will be.

Lylah took the letter from her pocket and read it again. It was an anchor for her. How many times she had wanted to quit and run back to the house surrounded by the mountains, longing to forget all about show business!

But she had not, for there was something in her that would not let her rest, and she knew deep inside that she would never again have a simple, safe life such as she had known as a girl.

The train ground to a stop, expelling great clouds of steam, and Lylah got off the coach and took her suitcase. Seeing a man with a wagon, she walked over to him. "Can you take me to the Bible Institute? I'll be glad to pay."

"Why . . . shore I kin—" The man nodded. He looked at her carefully, taking in the cut of her dress, her quite obvious charms. "If you're aimin' to go to that preacher's school," he offered when he'd helped her in and taken his seat, "you'll have to git a different dress."

Lylah laughed. "Why, I've already been to Bethany!"

The driver looked her over with a skeptical eye. "Then you done gone and backslid, missy," he pronounced firmly. "Ain't none of the young women from there looks anything like you!"

He introduced himself as Hiram Moon when she gave her own name. He was a tall, lanky man of no more than thirty, and Lylah sensed that he was a kindly sort.

Moon took in the lustrous eyes, the full tempting lips, the curving figure. "My wife would kill me if she found out I was squirin' you around, but she can't kill me but once, now kin she?"

When they pulled up in front of the school, Moon leapt out and helped her step down. "No charge." He shook his head when she attempted to pay him. "Man needs to spend all the time he can with upstanding young folks from the Bible Institute." He grinned and shook his head. "My Molly will sure hear about this little trip. You know how people are—always gossipin' about folks. Well, good luck now."

Lylah thanked him, thinking of his words, then went at once to the dean's office, where his secretary looked up, instantly assuming an air of distaste. Miss Saddler was a plain woman with brown hair and No written on her face. Now she said, "So . . . *you're* back. I wouldn't think you'd have the gall!"

"And a good morning to *you*, Miss Saddler," Lylah said cheerfully. Looking around the office, she shook her head, thinking of the times she'd spent in this office. The Dean had seen the rebellious spirit in her and had tried to help her. He was a fine man, Lylah knew, and she had always regretted the difficulties she'd caused him. "I'd like to see Donald," she said.

"He's in Greek class," Miss Saddler snapped.

"Well, I'll just wait, if that's all right."

It was certainly *not* all right, Lylah saw, for a dark cloud gathered on Miss Saddler's face. But Lylah smiled sweetly, and sat there patiently for fifteen minutes. When a bell rang, she rose. "Don't bother getting up, Miss Saddler. I'll find Donald myself." She left the office, walked out, and saw the students filing out of the classroom.

"Hey . . . it's Lylah!" somebody cried, and instantly she was surrounded by her former classmates, caught up in a flurry of hugs and handshakes. But she noticed that Donald Satterfield was not among them.

As soon as she could, she went over to join him. "Don, will you talk with me for a few minutes?"

"All right, Lylah." He was not smiling, and there was pain in his eyes. "We can walk outside if you like."

They left the classroom building and strolled down the cobblestone walk under the large chestnut trees. "We can sit here, I guess," Satterfield said, motioning to a painted bench.

Lylah sat down, and as he joined her, said quickly, "Don,

I should have written you. I treated you terribly. But . . . I just couldn't. I was so ashamed."

Satterfield's expression thawed, and he said at once, "It's all right, Lylah. I just hated to see you take the way you did. There's no happiness in it for you."

There was, Lylah saw, no point in arguing with Don. She ignored his statement, put her hand on his, and said softly, "Can you forgive me, Don? I didn't want to hurt you, but I would have gone crazy if I'd stayed here."

"Why, you know I couldn't refuse you anything, Lylah."

Realizing that Don Satterfield meant exactly what he said, Lylah could not stop the tears that misted her eyes. She was not accustomed to finding such devotion in men. "You ought to use a horsewhip on me," she murmured, trying to smile. "Maybe if you had, I'd be a better woman."

Don shook his head, turning the subject aside. "Tell me, Lylah, what you've been doing."

She told him, not knowing that it gave him great pain to hear it. Satterfield had loved her for a very long time, and as he listened, the death knell sounded for his hopes. Lylah, he saw, would never be for him. He had given his life to God, and she would never accept that kind of existence.

He said nothing, however, until she had finished, then, "I'll borrow a buggy and take you home."

"Oh, Don, you don't have to do that," Lylah protested, but he insisted.

An hour later they left Fort Smith and spent the day on the dusty roads that led to the mountains. Stone County was well named, for the rugged mountains of the area broke through the shoulders with bare rock. As they rolled through the narrow passes, they seemed to be enclosed with stone walls, green and mossy from the waters that washed over them.

It was a hard trip, and when Satterfield finally pulled the weary team to a halt on the ridge overlooking the valley where the cabin rested, the sun was settling behind a western line of hazy mountains. Then he spoke to the team, and thirty minutes later they drew up into the yard.

The door opened, spilling out first the smaller children, then Owen and Lylah's parents. "Lylah! Lylah . . . you're home!" Lenora and Gavin struck her with flying hugs, and as soon as Lylah had kissed them both, Logan was there to claim her attention.

Then she turned to Owen, who looked much bigger and taller, grabbed him in a fierce hug, whispering, "Oh, Owen—"

Owen gave her a hard hug, then stepped back, and there was her mother, with two-year-old Christie in her arms, blue eyes trained on the newcomer. "Oh, Ma!" Lylah gasped and fell into her mother's arms. She clung to her, struggling to keep back the sobs that bubbled up inside her, before she turned to face her father.

She was most afraid of him, though he had never been hard on her as a child. But she had heard him speak harshly of young people who dishonored their parents, and now she faltered under his gaze. Unable to say a word, she dropped her head, wishing she'd never come. *He hates me,* she thought, and was about to turn away, when he stepped forward and took her in his arms. "Welcome home, Lylah—"

Lylah welcomed her father's strong arms. But even as she held on to him, she thought, *I'll never be as good as they are . . . not in a million years. They've got something that was left out of me.*

By the time she'd had a supper such as she hadn't eaten for months, and recounted some of the things that had happened to her, it was late. Don Satterfield had slipped away to see his own people—and to avoid being thanked, Lylah suspected. Finally the younger children were put to bed, and only Lylah was left at the table with her parents and Owen.

"How long can you stay, Lylah?" her brother asked.

"Well, maybe two weeks or so. I've got a job coming up in Chicago." Lylah watched disappointment sweep over Owen's features, and after he got up and left to go to bed, she asked, "What's wrong with Owen, Ma?"

Marian tucked a lock of hair away, her face growing sad. "He's like you and Amos, Lylah. The others all like the farm, but Owen's like a caged animal. He's only fifteen, but he's done a man's work ever since Amos left."

"He'll be the next to go, I guess," Will said heavily. He shrugged his shoulders, putting the thought away, and asked briskly, "Well, what do you think about that big brother of yours, daughter? Ain't he a caution!"

"Amos?" Lylah stared at her father. "I haven't heard from him in weeks. What's he done?"

"Done?" Will pounded the table with the flat of his hand. "Why, he's up and gone to Chinee . . . that's what he's done!"

"China!" Lylah exclaimed. "What in the world?"

"We got this letter from him last week," Marian said, rising to fetch an envelope from the washstand. She handed it to Lylah. "Read it."

Dear Ma and Pa and all of you (she read quickly). This will come as quite a shock to you, I'm afraid. By the time you read this, I'll be on the high seas headed for China! Yes, that's right—China!

I'm as surprised as any of you, I guess. I've been doing a lot of traveling for the *Journal*, covering different stories. Well, three days ago Mr. Hearst called me into his office and set off a bombshell.

"Stuart," he said, "Things are happening over in China. I want you to go look into it." Well, I was so shocked, he had to laugh at me; then he said, "You've done a good job, and besides, I can't spare any of my best men. Go do the best you can. Find out what the people over there are thinking. Don't spend all your time with government officials. Talk to the people in the rice paddies and in the streets."

So this is good-bye for a while. I've tried to reach Lylah, but couldn't locate her. When she writes, tell her where I am. Don't worry about me. You prayed me through the Spanish-American War, Ma, so you can surely get me through a little boat trip and a visit to China!

Owen, hold the fort! I think of you all the time. When I come
back, you and I will go on a trip. I'll let you name the spot, so
be thinking about it, pal! The rest of you mind Ma and Pa, and
I'll bring you all a present from the mysterious East!

Lylah put the letter down, and her face was grave. "He
didn't mention Rose."

"Rose? Oh, the girl he was stuck on before he went to war?"
Marian said. "He's never said a word about her since he came
home."

"No, and that's what worries me." Lylah nodded. "If he
was over her, he'd talk about her . . . say *something*. But he's
never mentioned her name."

"Where is she now?" Will Stuart asked. "She went on the
stage, didn't you say?"

Lylah hesitated. "Yes, with a man named James Hackett."
She started to say more, then suddenly changed her mind.
"Amos is getting on in his profession. I'm proud of him."

"So am I." Marian rose and stretched. "Time for bed."

At the door, she turned and smiled at her daughter. "I'm
proud of *all* my children, Lylah."

Sitting in the stern of the small boat, Amos Stuart wished
he'd never even *heard* of China! He had been ill all day, his
stomach rejecting even the thin rice gruel the boatman's wife
offered him. "No . . . just leave me alone," he muttered, which
was translated instantly by a young Chinese boy he'd hired
in Shanghai.

Amos lay back and tried to ignore the spasms in his stomach, thinking of what to do next. He'd gotten off the liner a
week earlier and started to implement the plan he'd concocted on the ship. It was a plan based on Hearst's idea to interview the common people. Instead of going to the Embassy,
he had looked up an interpreter and set out to travel the country in an attempt to discover what the small people of the
massive land were like.

His guide and interpreter had been a blessing, for the youth was the product of a Methodist mission school in Shantung. He was only nineteen, but quite a scholar, especially knowledgeable about the history of China. Every night when they paused, Lee Sang Pei found lodging for them and, after their meal, lectured his American employer on the history and nature of the country.

"It is very simple, Mr. Stuart," Lee said one night after Amos felt a little better and was able to sit up. "England wants tea . . . my people want opium."

Amos had stared at the young man. "Lee, East-West relations *can't* be that simple."

"I fear it is so," Lee said, a gloomy light in his dark eyes. "Your people crave tea, and my country supplied that need. But the English grew alarmed at all the silver coming into China, so despite the opposition of many of your good people, opium has made up fifty percent of all British exports to my country since 1875. You must have heard of the Opium War? It was started by the English when my government confiscated twenty thousand chests of opium illegally brought into China. Many of your most courageous leaders, including William Gladstone, stated that a more unjust war was never fought, which is saying a great deal, I think."

Amos listened as the young man explained how America had become involved. "All the European nations saw China as a rich prize to be seized. All of them got footholds in my country. And now that America has grown up and won its war with Spain, it too wishes a slice of the profits."

"What do the people think?" Amos asked. "I mean, the working people, not the government."

Lee hesitated, then asked, "Do you really want to know, Mr. Stuart?"

"Yes!"

Lee studied him, then called the boatman over. He spoke rapidly, and the man nodded almost violently, beginning to speak.

"My name is Liu Mok. All my ancestors have been weavers of cloth. We are proud of our work! We cheat no man, and sell at a fair price. But now that is all gone! The merchants in the cities buy cloth from the *yang kuei-tzu!*"

The man spoke at length, then Lee interpreted his words, adding, "*Yang kuei-tzu* means 'foreign devils,' Mr. Stuart."

"Ask him what he is going to do."

Lee spoke, and when the man answered, he turned to face Stuart with concern and anger on his face. "He says he will become a Boxer."

"A Boxer?"

"A secret society, sir," Lee explained. "Secret societies are common in China. For people like this man, they provide an organization that can bring pressure on the rich and powerful. They blend with my culture, with the Chinese taste for mystery which runs through our history."

"What do these Boxers do?"

"It is hard to explain, Mr. Stuart—" Lee hesitated. He nodded toward the boatman. "To uneducated peasants like this, the Boxers are heroes, giving battle to wicked men in high places. They are very flamboyant, thought to be spirit soldiers—immortal, heaven-sent, come to sweep the empire clean of all foreigners. The Boxers do all sorts of things to strengthen this view—cloaking themselves in vivid costumes, practicing ritualistic mumbo jumbo and making passes with their arms like professional prizefighters."

Amos was feeling sick again and lay back. Lee sat beside him, saying nothing. The boat glided along in the water, making a gurgling sound, and Amos dozed off.

The next morning Amos felt much better. "I think I would like to find out more about the Boxers, Lee," he said.

The young Chinese shrugged. "That will not be difficult. They are displaying their power at every opportunity." He spoke to the boatman, then told Amos, "Tomorrow there is a demonstration by the Boxers in a valley not far from here."

The two arrived at the village just in time to witness the

ceremony. More than once, Amos was accosted by armed men, all muttering *"Yang kuei-tzu"* and brandishing their long swords. But Lee pacified them by promising that Stuart would spread the word of the Boxers' superiority and invulnerability.

A holy shrine had been erected at one end of the valley, and now a line of Boxers, red ribbons on their chests fluttering in the gentle breeze, stood to one side as if bewitched, oblivious of their surroundings. The villagers crowded together some distance away as a stocky Boxer addressed them.

Lee interpreted quietly: "Spirit Soldiers are protected by heaven. No harm can come to them." He waved an arm. "Those you see have become *hsien*, they are immortal. They have practiced the way of *hsien*. Watch!"

Amos stared as a handful of men shouldered their rifles and cut loose with a volley. Three of the Boxers toppled over, dead or dying. The remainder were unhurt. Another volley was fired. Some of the Boxers waved their hands, as if to turn the bullets aside, and this time none fell. Now the riflemen laid aside their weapons and took swords in hand. With fierce shouts, they charged, brandishing the long knives. The peasants gasped at the ferocity of the thrusts, yet the line of Boxers never wavered or broke.

"See!" cried the stocky leader triumphantly. "Boxers are immune to steel and bullets!"

"What of those who fell?" one of the peasants inquired timidly.

"Fool! They were not real Boxers. They lacked the true faith. Perhaps they were the spies of the foreign devils," he added, casting Amos a suspicious glance.

Lee quickly guided Amos back to the boat.

Later, when they spoke of what had happened, Lee spoke with a voice of prophecy. "You will go on to see much of China . . . perhaps you will speak with the Empress herself. But you will learn no more than what you have seen these past few days."

"You think the Boxers will lead a rebellion, Lee?"

"Yes . . . and I will be one of the first they will kill."

Amos stared at the young man. "Why, you're no foreigner!"

"I am a Christian. The Boxers dislike Christians most of all foreigners, though the church has done more for the poor people than anyone. But when the time comes, the Boxers will slaughter every Christian in China. Do not doubt it, Mr. Stuart."

"Are you afraid, Lee?"

"No! If they kill my body, they will send my soul to be with my blessed Lord!"

Amos Stuart traveled thousands of miles in China, and did indeed have an interview with the Empress. But as he left the shores of China, he thought, *Lee was right! When the revolt comes, it will be the Boxers who lead it . . . and God help the poor Christians when it happens!*

11

DECLINE OF A WOMAN

July of the year 1899 set all records for high temperatures in New York City. The scorching sun heated the concrete so that eggs could be fried on the sidewalks, and asphalt melted into a semi-liquid black tar. Butter became a thin yellow liquid that had to be poured rather than spread with a knife. Crowds flocked to Coney Island, seeking relief, and more people slept on balconies and in back yards than in the steamy houses.

Perhaps it was the heat that caused James Hackett to explode with anger when his play ground to a halt—a total failure. That at least was one excuse, though the actor needed little to set him off. His tour with *Dr. Jekyll and Mr. Hyde* had been a flop, and when he had tried in desperation to attract audiences with another play, a comedy called *The Ugly Duckling*, the result had been even worse, if possible.

Hackett was unable to face up to the fact that he had no talent whatsoever for comedy; therefore, he placed the blame for the failure of the play on the other actors and actresses in his company. Most of them were mediocre talents at best, for Hackett was stingy and paid pitifully small wages. In desperation, he had brought the show to New York and had spent every cent he had to put the play on in a small theater. The first performance had been well attended, for Hackett had some reputation. But by the end of the week, the ticket sales had trickled down to a handful, and Hackett was forced to call the play off. He had slashed out at the cast savagely, then refused to pay their salaries.

Rose had stood by helplessly, the only one of the troupe to feel guilty. She had been given a difficult role, one calling for great ability, and was simply lost. No one but James Hackett would have allowed an inexperienced actress to even attempt such a thing. Now he made it plain that much of the debacle was her fault.

Cursing and raving in their hotel room, he threw clothing into a suitcase. "If you'd given me *anything*, the play would have made it!" he raged. "But, no, you didn't even't *try!*"

"I–I did try, Jim—" Rose whispered. She stood with her back pressed against the wall, her face pale and her lips trembling. "I'm just not an actress, but I told you that."

Hackett glared at her, his face red with anger. "Oh, so it's *my* fault, is it?" He slammed the suitcase shut viciously, then came to take her arm in his powerful hand. "I gave you every chance, but you couldn't stay away from the bottle, could you?"

"You . . . gave me my first drink, Jim—"

Her answer only infuriated him further, and he jerked her cruelly so that she cried out with pain. "That's my fault, too, is it? You *agreed* to take that first drink! But you couldn't handle it like a lady. Guzzling gin all day long, so drunk you couldn't remember your name, much less your lines!"

Rose closed her eyes, trying to ignore the pain in her arm. Hackett was not wrong, and the memory of how she had slipped into drinking brought her shame as it always did. He had pursued her with single-minded attention, and she had succumbed, an easy prey for the actor's wiles. She had been totally dependent on him, and when he had insisted on her learning to drink, had unwillingly allowed herself to be persuaded.

But Rose had no tolerance for liquor, and before two weeks had passed, Hackett had gotten her drunk. She had awakened in his bed with nothing but nightmarish memories of the seduction and had wept for hours. Hackett had been somewhat shamefaced about his actions, but not enough to give her up. She was beautiful and filled a role in his play, so he satisfied her with intimations that someday they would be married. No promises—he was too clever for that! But it was an old game to him, and he played it well.

As the weeks went by, Rose discovered that alcohol had the power to make her forget and began drinking secretly. Liquor was easily available, and she fell into the trap without thinking, increasing the amount of liquor, until even Hackett began to suggest that she taper off. "A little liquor will do you good, Rose," he'd say, "but you're on your way to becoming a drunk. You've got to learn to handle your drinking."

But she could not . . . and that reality brought fear into her heart. Every day she would promise herself, "Not one drink today!" But as curtain time drew near and the dread began to rise in her, she would give the drunkard's classic excuse, "Just *one* drink, and I'll be all right!" But one drink became two, and by the time the curtain went up, she was always half-drunk.

Now as she stood with her eyes closed, unable to break away from Hackett's grasp, she could not answer a word. Finally, he shoved her away, stepped back, and stared at her. The sight of her made him feel guilt . . . insofar as he could feel such a thing.

Reaching into his pocket, he pulled out a billfold, stared at the thin sheaf of bills, then frowned and pulled out a few of them.

"Here's forty bucks," he said gruffly. "Sorry it had to turn out like this. You're a sweet kid, Rosie, but I made a mistake trying to make an actress out of you." It was as close to an apology as he would ever make, and he turned quickly and picked up his suitcase. "So long, Rose," he said, and headed for the door.

"You can't leave me, Jim!" Rose cried. "What will I do?"

Hackett hesitated, then shook his head. "You'll find something, Rose. I'll keep my ears open. Besides, you can always get a job hustling drinks."

Rose blinked as the door shut, then went to the bed and sat down abruptly, her knees weak. She sat there trying to think, but the fear that came blotted out all thought.

Finally she got up, went to the dresser and picked up the bottle. She started to pour the amber liquor into a glass, but suddenly put the bottle to her lips and swallowed convulsively. She coughed and gagged, hating the taste of it. Still holding the bottle, she moved to the window and stared down at the street below.

She thought of the past months with bitterness. Ever since she had given in to Hackett's lust, she had felt dirty and unclean. Now that he was gone, she felt even more soiled. What should she do? If she refused to work in a bar, the bottle factory was her only option. She was getting drunk very quickly, but the liquor didn't obliterate the memory of the hard grinding labor and the miserable existence that accompanied that job. She thought of Anna but knew she could never face her—not now, not ever again.

Then she thought of Amos, and tears stung her eyes. She took a long drink from the bottle, but his face seemed to rise before her. How many nights she had tried to sleep, and he had come floating out of the past, so clear at times—like a daguerreotype. It had been natural for her to think of him, for he had been kinder to her than any man she'd ever known. And he had loved her.

Why did I ever let him go? The anguished question came to her lips, as it had a thousand times, but she could never find an answer. Now that it was too late, she saw clearly that she had loved Amos Stuart. She remembered the gentle touch of his lips on hers, the glow of his fine eyes as he spoke of his love for her. What more could she have wanted? Why had she been such a fool?

She sat there hating herself, bitterly reviewing the steps that had brought her to disgrace. Finally she lay down on the bed, her head swimming with the liquor, her heart dark with the knowledge of the disaster she had made of her life.

When she awakened, she saw that the sun was going down. She was sick then, as she always was, and when that was over, she stared at her face in the mirror, pale as death, her hair stringy and limp. Taking a deep breath, she got up, swayed wildly, then began to take off her gown. She washed in the cold water, did her hair as carefully as she could, then stood staring at the cosmetics she used for the play. She had never liked to paint her face, and thought that women who did so were vulgar and tawdry.

But now she reached out a trembling hand and applied the makeup liberally. When she was finished, she put on a dress Hackett had insisted on buying for her. She disliked it, for it was cut too tightly around the waist and bosom and was a shade of bright green that she knew was far too gaudy. She put on a hat, studied her reflection in the mirror, and felt her heart sink. She looked cheap, and knew that any man who saw her would think her easy. She gave a longing glance at the bottle of whiskey, but shook her head and left the room.

She walked through the lobby, stopping when the desk clerk called her name. "I was wondering...," the clerk began with some embarrassment. "That is, will you be keeping your room, Mrs. Hackett?"

"Yes, but my name isn't Mrs. Hackett," Rose said, looking him directly in the eye. "I'm Rose Beaumont." She whirled and left the hotel, and went at once to Charlie's Place.

The owner, Charlie O'Steen, stared at her when she approached him, asking for work.

"Why, Rose, I don't use actors anymore," he said, waving his hand around the room. "Costs too much. Most of my customers come to drink nowadays, not to see a show."

"I need a job, Mr. O'Steen," Rose said evenly, "but I'm no actress. I did work here with Eddy Sparks' company, though."

Charlie gave her an appraising look. "Well, you're a good-looking woman, Rose. I'd like to have you work for me. Sit down and we'll talk about it."

Rose sat down, only half listening to him. When he finished speaking, she said, "That's fine with me, Mr. O'Steen."

"Call me Charlie." The saloon keeper got to his feet and stuck out a beefy hand. "Come back at six, Rose."

As Rose left his place, she was aware of having crossed an invisible line. She felt afraid, for she knew that her life would never be the same. She was realistic enough to know what being a dance hall girl meant. It was like being plunged into an alien world, where all she had loved was gone, and as she stepped outside the saloon, she knew she was lost.

The summer in New York ended so abruptly that Amos had no feeling whatsoever of autumn. It seemed to him that one day the sweltering summer heat was sucking all the energy out of him, and the next, he was stepping outside his apartment building to be met by a cold gust whipping around the corner, numbing his face and hands. "More like December than October," he observed to the cabdriver waiting in front of the building.

Amos hurried down the street, enjoying the sharp wind, thinking of what it would be like to be out in the hills with Owen after a deer. He thought often of the Ozarks, and especially of Owen. His kid brother seldom wrote, but the letters from his mother were filled with news of all the children, and he sensed that she was concerned about Owen. *He's going to the dances and playing music with your father,* she had said, and that was enough for Amos to know she feared that this son had the same streak in him that ran in William Stuart.

Amos arrived at the *Journal* and walked quickly to his desk—a small cubicle just off the pressroom. Taking off his coat and hat, he sat down and began to write. The roar of the presses drowned out all the street noises, which was all right with Amos. When he wrote, he became oblivious to everything around him. It was not enough to speak to him, his editor had discovered. One had to grab Stuart and literally drag his mind away from the words that flowed out of him.

For two hours he wrote steadily, then with a grunt, put his pencil down and leaned back. His back ached, and he had to uncramp his fingers slowly as he read what he had written. The words pleased him, and a smile touched his lips as he thought of how Al Paxton, his editor, would scream!

Whatever excuse the United States may have had for the war with Spain, there is not a shred of justification for invading the Philippines. These small islands might be on the planet Mars as far as most Americans are concerned, yet all of us enjoy the natural resources that come from there, including rice, sugar cane, and spices. All we need to know, however, is that the Filipinos are fighting a revolution against Spain for their liberty. Sound familiar? Can you think of any other nation which rose up against an oppressive nation and won its freedom—say, in 1776? What could be more fitting than to see this great nation rush to the aid of Emilio Aguinaldo, the leader of the Filipino people?

But what would you say if you learned that our leaders, far from trying to aid that small nation gain its freedom, is making plans to invade the Philippines and steal it for personal gain?

Pretty strong stuff! Amos thought, and his smile faded. He knew that Theodore Roosevelt was leading the movement to annex the Philippines. Roosevelt, who had been elected governor of New York in November by a landslide after the Spanish-American War, had struck out against those who opposed expansion, the Anti-Imperialists, with all his might. This group included men such as ex-President Cleveland, William James, Andrew Carnegie and, surprisingly enough, Mark Twain. It was their contention that the move to annex the Philippines sprang out of a lust for power, money, and glory abroad. But Roosevelt countered by proclaiming, "We are a conquering race. We must obey our blood and occupy new markets, and if necessary, new lands. In the Almighty's infinite plan, debased civilizations and decaying races must give way to the higher civilizations of the nobler and more virile types of man."

Amos took the sheaf of papers, put on his coat and hat, then left after dropping them on his editor's desk. He left because he knew exactly what would happen. *Al will take the column up to William Randolph Hearst, who will scream and throw it into the wastebasket. He'll tell Al to fire me, and Al will beg him to give me one more chance.*

It had gone that way several times, and Amos knew that he was walking on a razor's edge. Hearst was a tyrant, and more than one brash young reporter had found himself ushered out on the streets after displeasing the publisher. The possibility should have troubled Amos, but it did not—not much, at least.

He was sick of working for Hearst, and knew that he was a fool for feeling that way. How many young men would give their left arm for a chance to work for the *Journal*, the most powerful newspaper in America? But every day since coming back from the War, Amos Stuart had been conscious of a nagging doubt about his place.

The sight of men dying suddenly—blotted out without a moment to make their peace with God—had scarred him. He thought every day about his friend Faye O'Dell and at nights had bad dreams about the young man. Often he woke up in a cold sweat, petrified with fear, thinking, *What if it had been me? I'd be in hell right now!*

He glanced across the street, and the sight of his favorite restaurant reminded him that he was hungry. He turned and started to cross the street, wondering how to get his stories by Hearst. He was so deeply immersed in thought he scarcely noticed the woman who came out of the saloon next to the café. He did observe that she was drunk, a fact that never failed to disgust him. He had to pass within five feet of her and noticed that she had stopped and was watching him. The streets were thick with prostitutes, and Amos did not bother to look at her. "No!" he snapped, confident he knew what she wanted, and brushed past her.

He did not turn, but if he had, he would have seen the stricken face of the woman he'd asked to marry him. Instead he disappeared into the café, and Rose moved on down the street, swaying and mumbling to herself. A man came up to walk beside her, a smile on his face, and without even looking at him, she took his arm and allowed him to lead her, still stumbling, until they disappeared into one of the sleazy hotels on a side street.

12

"FROM THE GUTTERMOST TO THE UTTERMOST!"

C aptain Hugh Pentecost wore the dark uniform of the Salvation Army with the same pride that he had worn the crimson-and-white uniform of His Royal Majesty's Coldstream Guards. Six feet three and slender as a rapier, he had left the British Army, sacrificing a brilliant career after having been converted in 1890, in a street meeting conducted by General William Booth, the founder of the Salvation Army.

After leaving the Coldstream Guards—to the everlasting chagrin of his socially prominent family—he joined the Salvation Army, throwing himself into the work of saving lost souls with all the ardor he'd exhibited in battle against the foes of the Empire.

"I'd rather win one soul to Jesus than win the Victoria Cross!" Pentecost would exclaim, his light blue eyes flashing. "God won't look us over for medals or diplomas, but for *scars!* God saves us from the guttermost to the uttermost!"

He had joined with Bramwell Booth, the son of the founder, in mounting an evangelistic assault on the Devil's strongholds in London and had so favorably impressed General Booth that in 1897, Pentecost was chosen to begin a work among the poor in New York City.

The captain hit the slums of the Fourth Ward—the most notorious section of all, filled with drunkards and prostitutes—and in a short time had become a familiar figure to the denizens of the skid rows and slums, his tall erect figure attracting attention wherever he went. Very few knew that if he had chosen to stay in England until the death of his father, he would have been "Sir Hugh" instead of "Captain Pentecost."

The Fourth Ward, where the captain had chosen to set up his banner, was an old section of the city. Wave after wave of immigrants was pouring into New York, and the early settlers who had become the new rich and middle class were abandoning their neighborhoods and moving uptown. Their decaying homes were fast becoming slums or were being replaced by tenements—rookeries with scores of families crowded into what were designed to be single-family dwellings.

Much of the Fourth Ward was one street after another lined with grog shops, houses of ill repute, dance halls, billiard parlors, and saloons. Every night one could count on a murder every half mile, a robbery every one hundred sixty-five yards, and six outcasts at every door.

There had been many attempts to reclaim these derelicts, including the famous Water Street Mission begun by Jerry McAuley—a former prisoner of the infamous Sing Sing Prison. McAuley had died in 1884, but one of his converts, Sam Hadley, had been successful in expanding the work. Captain Pentecost had become good friends with Hadley, and on December 22, the two men were sitting in Hadley's office, discussing the work.

Hadley, a stout man with a heroic mustache that compensated for a receding hairline, was standing in front of a glowing coal stove, warming his backside, while Captain Pentecost was sitting in a chair, tilted back against the wall of the sparsely furnished office.

"Good service, Hugh." Hadley nodded his approval. "But you always preach a good sermon."

Captain Pentecost smiled wryly. "I've wondered how large the crowd would be if we didn't give them a free meal first, Sam."

"Doesn't matter why they come. It's our duty to do what we can for them. Food and shelter for a night, and they hear the gospel." Hadley grinned at his guest, adding, "You gave it to them red-hot and sizzling tonight, Captain."

Pentecost frowned, and a dissatisfied look crossed his thin aristocratic face. "That was a mistake, I think. These people don't need to be convinced that they're sinners on the way to hell. They know *that* already, Sam. I wish I could preach a good old hellfire sermon to some of the rich people on Fifth Avenue."

"Not much chance of that." Hadley shrugged. "Not many wealthy people respond to the Gospel. They're like the rich man Jesus told about in the parable, building more barns to put their money in. No, we're seeing more souls saved in the Fourth Ward than the rest of the city ever thinks about seeing."

Pentecost nodded, then got to his feet and stretched. "Well, I've got to go home. I'll see you next Thursday night. And I'll preach about the love of Jesus when I come."

"Good night, Hugh. And I *still* say it was a fine sermon!"

Pentecost pulled on his heavy wool coat, wrapped a red muffler around his neck, then pulled his billed cap down over his face. When he stepped outside, the cold air struck him like a blow, but he liked cold weather. He suffered every summer, hating the sultry temperatures that turned New York into an oven. But now as the snow that had fallen during the service stuck to his boots, he looked up to see the flakes swirling madly as they fell. "Come on down, snow!" he grinned. "Cover this dirty old town!"

Strolling down the street, he knew that as much as he himself enjoyed the winter spectacle, it was a trial for the poor, many of them unable to afford the cost of coal.

The preacher's head was swarming with plans, as usual, as he made his way from Water Street, turning right on Dover and headed for the Army Headquarters. So completely was he engrossed in his thoughts that he was startled when a commotion across the street attracted his attention.

Two figures were barely visible by the yellow glare of the gaslight, so heavy was the snowfall now. A man was shouting something, and as Pentecost wheeled and crossed the deserted street, he heard the man curse, then saw him shove the other person, yelling, "I'll not be puttin' up with ye! Go sponge on somebody else, do ye hear me?"

Pentecost came up behind the speaker, the sound of his boots muffled by the soft four-inch blanket of snow, and touched him on the shoulder. "What's the trouble here?"

The burly fellow whirled around with his hands held up, fists clenched. "Do ye want a bit of it, then?" he grunted. "Come on, put up yer dukes! I'll teach ye to sneak up on a feller!"

Pentecost drew himself up, his frosty blue eyes piercing the other's gaze. "No need for that. I just want to help. What's the matter?"

The man peered at Pentecost and then suddenly lowered his hands. "Oh, it's the preacher." He shrugged his beefy shoulders, adding, "I been at this one a week to pay up on her room, but she drinks it all up fast as it comes in. I can't afford to keep her, so it's out she goes!"

At that moment, the woman suddenly slumped, her legs giving way under her. As she sprawled on the snow, Pentecost sprang toward her, supporting her head. Leaning forward, he smelled the rank odor of raw gin, but when he touched her face, it was burning hot. "Why, this woman is sick!"

"Not a bit of it! Just drunk, that's all," the man said in disgust. "She's always drunk." He drew himself up defensively. "Now don't give me any sermons, ye hear me? I've kept her for five weeks, with nary a penny paid. Christmas or no, she can't stay here no more!"

Pentecost knelt in the snow, trying to think, and finally he put his arms under the woman's knees and lifted her, coming to his feet. "Merry Christmas, brother." He nodded, then turned and walked into the dancing flakes.

The man stood there, flummoxed. He'd expected the preacher to try to shame him, and now he was angry and didn't know why. "Yes, and she'll do the same to you as she done to me!" he shouted at the disappearing form, even now almost swallowed by the whiteness. "She ain't nothin' but a drunk and a tramp . . . and she won't never be no better!" Then he wheeled about and stomped back inside, muttering about how things had gone to the dogs in the Fourth Ward.

Pentecost carried the unconscious woman as far as Pearl Street, where he found a cab at the curbside. "Salvation Army Headquarters," he directed, then lifted the woman into the cab. He got in beside her and as the cab moved silently down the velvet-covered street, held her in his arms.

Now, what in the world will I do with her?

He was still pondering the answer to that question when the cabbie leaned over and announced, "Headquarters, sir."

The tall man got out, paid the fare, then pulled the woman into his arms and walked with her toward the door of the brownstone building with the small sign—*Salvation Army*—painted on it. He was forced to juggle her around as he opened the door, but as soon as he was inside and had shut the door with his hip, he was relieved to see the familiar figure of one of his coworkers.

"Well, and what is it you've dragged up now, Captain?"

Maggie Flynn's voice was thick with the accent of old Ireland. She was a short woman, compactly made and suited for hard work. Her squarish face was not pretty, but comfortable, and her dark blue eyes and red hair made an attractive combination. She had been in the service of the Lord's Army in New York since its beginning, and Hugh Pentecost was the object of her special devotion. Not a romantic notion, no, for she had long ago decided that she was too plain to be a wife. She now admired one thing in a man—devotion to Jesus—and Hugh Pentecost had that quality in abundance.

"She got thrown out on the street, Maggie . . . and she's

sick." For once the ever competent Captain Hugh Pentecost
was at a loss. There was no place for homeless women—a
cause he and Maggie had been trying to launch for two years
with no success. "I couldn't think of anything to do but bring
her here."

Maggie Flynn snorted. "Well, and should you have left her
to die in the streets? Come on and put her in my bed." She
marched down the hall to her room, which contained a single cot on which Pentecost laid the unconscious woman.
"Now, you get to bed," Maggie commanded, beginning to
roll up her sleeves.

"Shall I try to find a doctor?"

"You'd not be gettin' one to come here. There's no money
in it." Maggie moved to kneel beside the woman, felt her
brow, then put her head on the woman's breast. She listened
intently for a long time, then got slowly to her feet, a bleak
expression on her face.

"What is it, Maggie?" Pentecost asked quickly.

The woman looked down at the still form, then shook her
head doubtfully. "Pneumonia, I think." She shook her head,
adding, "From the looks of her, she's lived like the Devil himself. Thin as a stick and eat up with whiskey."

"Well, the Lord our God is able," Pentecost said slowly.
"Nothing is too difficult for him."

Maggie stared at him, then nodded. "It'll be God who does
it if she lives, I'm thinkin'. Now, you go to bed."

"Can't I help?"

"You can pray . . . and that's all anybody can do, Hugh."

"Well . . . if it ain't Santa Claus!"

Nick Castellano flung open the door to find Amos Stuart
standing on the stoop, his arms full of packages. His head
was frosted with snow, and he was grinning sheepishly. "No
reindeer, Nick, but lots of presents for everyone. I—"

A series of shrill cries drowned out whatever he had
planned to say, and he was seized by a troop of young Castel-

lanos and dragged into the parlor, where Anna grabbed him
and kissed him noisily.

"Amos . . . you come-a back!" she cried, and tears began
running down her cheeks.

"Don't cry, Anna!" Amos pleaded.

"Aw, she cries over cookbooks." Nick grinned and pum-
meled him on the arm. "You sorry outfit! Why didn't you tell
me you were in town?"

Amos surrendered his packages to Anna, who began slapping hands at once. "Got in two days ago . . . just in time for
Christmas. I can't make it home to Arkansas, so I decided to
force myself on you."

"You come-a with me!" Anna spoke up. "I gonna feed your
face! Nick, you keep-a the kids away from the presents."

The next few hours were precious to Amos. He'd become
fond of the Castellanos and felt like a brother to Nick. After
a stupefying meal, they moved into the parlor. "I know it's
the night before Christmas, but I'm leaving for a short trip
home tomorrow, so you open my presents now, okay?"

"Yea!" The kids agreed enthusiastically, and soon the floor
was littered with fancy wrapping paper. Anna was stunned
by the beautiful pure silk dress he had chosen for her, and
ran off at once to try it on. When she came back, she yelled,
"It fits! How you find my size, Amos?"

"Had it special made, Mama Anna."

Nick was pleased beyond words with his gift—a set of ex-
quisitely carved chessmen. He loved the game, and he and
Amos had fought many a battle over the old board and crudely
carved wooden pieces.

"Hey, Amos, these things must have cost a mint! You
shouldn't have done it!"

"Give 'em back if you don't like 'em." Amos grinned,
pleased that he'd wrestled the gifts all over China and on the
long voyage home. He watched with pleasure as the youngsters shouted their delight.

"It's the *best* Christmas we ever had, Amos!" Eddie assured him.

But it was Mary Elizabeth who touched Amos most. She was only a few months older than when he had left, but in those brief weeks had ripened into a real beauty. Her gifts were a red blouse of pure silk and a delicate fan made of ivory. At his insistence she tried on the blouse, and when she came back, he whistled. "Why, Mary Elizabeth . . . you look *beautiful!*"

The girl flushed and dropped her eyes, and when the children were all shooed out at last, Nick said, "Watch out, Amos. I think Mary's got her eye on you."

"She's grown up, Nick," Amos acknowledged, but to him she was still a child.

Anna glanced sharply at Amos, but said only, "Now, you sit down and tell us all about China."

They drank coffee and talked until midnight, when Amos yawned and called it quits for the night. "I'm done in. Got to catch a train at eight in the morning. And as soon as I get back, Hearst is sending me to cover the war in the Philippines."

"I thought the war was over," Nick said in surprise.

"Not even started yet, Nick. We've sold the Filipinos down the river . . . pretended to save them from Spain, but now we're going to take their country." He saw his hosts were shocked, and shook his head sadly. "It's going to be a nasty business. We'll win because we're stronger and have the guns, but I'm ashamed to be a part of it."

They spoke of the war, and finally Amos asked about his old friends. He listened as they spoke of this one and that, but finally asked nervously, "What about Rose? You ever see her?" Amos didn't miss the look the two exchanged. "What's the matter?"

It was Nick who answered, though with considerable reluctance. "Well, pal, I wasn't going to tell you about her. She's . . . gone wrong."

"Wrong? How?"

"She took up with an actor—fellow named Hackett. He got her started drinking and then kicked her out. She got a job at a dance hall, but didn't keep it."

"She was such a good girl." Anna twisted her handkerchief nervously. "It's that man's fault!"

"I dunno, Mama," Nick said, doubt in his voice. "She didn't have to go the way she did. She could have come to us for help." He shrugged. "I didn't know about her until she was pretty far gone. Soon as I heard, I looked her up, but she wouldn't talk to me."

"She was ashamed, Nicky!" Anna insisted vehemently.

"I guess so . . . but she's on the streets now, Amos."

Amos kept his composure, but inside he was profoundly shaken. He remembered Rose's merry eyes, her quick laughter, her innocence. Most of all, her innocence. How could a young woman go bad so quickly?

He rose to his feet, saying evenly, "I'm sorry to hear it. She had good stuff in her."

After the good-byes were said and Amos was gone, Anna narrowed her eyes. "Nick . . . he's hurting, Amos is."

"I know, Mama." Nick's dark eyes glowed with anger, and he said, "I'd like to wring her neck! He ain't gonna get over this easy."

"No. I think he's still loves Rose."

"Well, he better forget her, Mama. She's a bad one now!"

All the sounds were soft, muted and indistinct, as though filtered through layers of cotton wool.

She learned to recognize one voice in particular, a strong woman's tone that came more often than the rest. The other voices came and went, but this one was always there, speaking in measured cadences. Though she couldn't understand the words, somehow she always grew peaceful when she heard that voice.

She was hot at times—so hot the very covers seemed to scorch her flesh, and she would thrash around wildly, trying to escape the heat. But strong hands held her down, and then the cool touch of water could be felt, bringing relief to her fevered flesh.

At other times, icy chills racked her body, and she shook so hard her teeth chattered. Then the voice would come—soothing and firm—like a warm blanket that drove away the cold.

Occasionally, she would sink down into a dark pit, blacker than ebony, and it was then she would cry out in fear. For in that darkness ugly, foul things picked at her with spectral fingers, trying to absorb her into their hideous shapes.

But the worst was the nightmare that came over and over. In the dream she seemed to be watching a woman who was walking along a narrow pathway over a cavernous cleft in the earth. Smoke and fire and the cries of the damned rose from the cleft, and she saw the woman about to fall over the edge. Always she would run to help her, but when she took hold of the woman and turned her around . . . she saw that the woman had her own face!

It was this dream that brought her out of her deep coma. She came awake, crying out with dry lips, and opened her eyes. Light was flooding in from a window, and she blinked, momentarily blinded.

"Now, then . . . you're out of it, dearie!"

Rose recognized the voice, for it was the same one that had meant safety and warmth. She blinked again. The woman belonging to the voice had a broad face and wore a kind smile. Rose tried to speak, but her lips were parched, and she could only croak, "Where am I?"

"Now, then, take a little water." The woman reached over and picked up a glass, and when she put it to Rose's dry lips, said, "Don't gulp so hard . . . there's plenty more."

Rose drank thirstily, then lay back on the pillow. Looking around the room, she saw nothing familiar and grew afraid. She could not remember coming here.

"My name is Maggie. Don't try to talk too much, dearie. You've been very sick, but you're going to be all right now."

"What's . . . wrong with me?"

Maggie shook her head soberly, then smiled, "Well, it was pneumonia, but the Lord Jesus put his hand on you and brought you out of the valley of death." Then she got up, saying, "Now, to get some solid food into you."

Rose lay there as the woman left, and by the time she came back with a steaming bowl of soup, Rose was ready with her questions. "How did I get here?'

"You eat and I'll talk," Maggie ordered, and while she spooned the soup into Rose, she gave her a quick history of what had transpired. "It was Captain Pentecost who brought you in . . . carried you like a baby, he did!"

"Who is he?"

Maggie laughed softly. "You'd best be thinking he's an angel, dearie, for if he hadn't brought you in, you'd not be alive, I'm thinking." She watched as the girl finished the soup, then saw that her eyes were drooping. When they closed, it was in a natural sleep, not the fevered coma.

Getting to her feet, Maggie stretched wearily and left the room. She found Pentecost speaking with two of the officers. "She's come to, Captain."

"She going to be all right?"

"Unless she has a setback."

Pentecost cast a sharp look at the lassie. "You've worn yourself out, Maggie. Go get some sleep. I'll sit with her until Glenda comes in from the street service." Maggie started to object. "That's an *order*, Maggie!" barked the captain, and she surrendered without another word, going to bed and falling asleep at once.

Pentecost went to sit beside the sleeping girl. She was, he saw, a beautiful woman . . . or had been before sin and disease etched their mark on her. But despite the evidence of hard living, he found it hard to believe what she had been.

He sat there, off and on, for most of the afternoon, and was about to doze off when she spoke.

"I–I'd like to get up."

Pentecost started, then bent over her. "Why, I think you'd best wait for a little while, young lady." When she didn't argue, he asked, "What's your name?"

"Rose. Rose Beaumont."

"Is there anyone you'd like me to notify, Rose? Somebody who needs to know where you are . . . someone who'd be worried about you?"

"No," she whispered. "Nobody is worried about me."

When the girl turned her head to one side, Pentecost could see a single tear rolling down her cheek. He reached out and took her hand, and when she gave him a startled glance, he spoke gently. "Yes, Somebody is very worried about you, Rose."

"No!"

"Oh, yes." The fatherly figure bent closer, and there was love and compassion in his blue eyes. "*Jesus* loves you. He's always loved you, Rose, and now he's brought you here so that you can learn to love him, too. Will you let me tell you about him?"

Rose's heart seemed to contract at the name *Jesus*. She had heard of Jesus, but he had always seemed as remote to her as George Washington. Now, with the life only feebly pulsing in her, she seemed to hear something familiar. There was something about that name—Jesus—that drew her, and she whispered fervently, "Yes, please, tell me!"

The tall man began talking, reading from time to time from a small Bible. For a moment only, Rose felt her old reserve go up. This man was a stranger, and she had been hurt by men. Yet, somehow she knew he was different, and she lay there, listening.

He told her how he had led a wild life as a soldier. "But one day I heard that Jesus loved me . . . and for the first time in my life, I knew what it was to be loved," he said. "I had a fine family, but they were not demonstrative people. I had everything a man could want, but I was miserable. Then I heard General Booth say that if I would let Jesus come into my heart and become Lord, he would bring peace, forgive all my sins, and make me fit for heaven." The captain told how he had put his trust in Jesus that day, and from that moment, he had known peace. Finally he asked gently, "Would you like to trust Jesus, Rose?"

"He . . . wouldn't want me, not after what I've done!"

"Oh, yes, he's the friend of sinners," Pentecost assured her. He spoke for a long time of God's limitless love. "Rose, I think you've been looking for love all your life, but you've been looking for it in the wrong places. Now you've found One you can trust. He'll never let you down, no matter what! He died for your sins, Rose. He wants you to be his own treasure. Will you let him come in and make you pure and ready for heaven?"

It didn't happen all at once. Rose couldn't believe what Pentecost was telling her. It was too good to be true! The time rolled on, and finally, a great longing was birthed in Rose. "If I could only start over . . ." she said brokenly.

"That's exactly what Jesus wants! 'Ye must be born again' is his commandment." Seeing that Rose was yielding, he pressed in. "Rose," he said, "I believe God is speaking to you right now. And it's very simple, so simple even a child can understand how to do it. The Bible says, 'Whosoever shall call upon the name of the Lord shall be saved.' Anybody can do that! The question is . . . *will* you do it? If I pray with you, will you call on God, asking him to save you, to forgive your sins?"

Rose felt desperation rise, along with doubts, but she managed to nod. Pentecost began a fervent prayer in her behalf. While Rose knew no prayers, she began to cry, "Oh, God, save me! I want to be different . . . help me in the name of Jesus!"

Maggie Flynn entered the room, groggy with sleep, but

seeing the joy in Rose Beaumont's eyes, began to shout, "Glory to God! A sinner's come home! Glory to God and the Lamb forever!"

Pentecost was fighting tears, but he knew what had happened. He gripped Rose's hand, whispering, "Now, you're a handmaiden of the Lord, dear Rose. A brand-new creature."

Rose lay there, unable to speak. She knew so little. Nothing at all about religion. But she knew one thing . . . something . . . someone had come to her, and it was like nothing she'd ever known before!

She looked up at the pair leaning over her, and tears bright as diamonds starred her eyes. "It's–it's so peaceful. For the first time in my life, I'm not afraid." A smile came trembling to her lips, and she whispered, "Is it always going to be like this?"

Pentecost smiled. "All Christians have problems and trials, Rose, but Jesus is there now, and he will make the difference!"

Rose Beaumont had no idea what she would do, where she would go, how she would live. But her voice held a new note of confidence. "As long as Jesus is with me, I won't ever be afraid again!"

13

OUT OF THE PAST

Amos's visit to Arkansas lasted for a month before he returned to New York, expecting to be sent to the Philippines to cover the war that was shaping up there. But for three months Hearst had kept him busy with routine details, which suited Amos, for he had no desire to see the vicious war he felt was inevitable. Therefore, he was caught off guard, when Hearst called him into his office one morning in May. He reported at once and found the publisher tense and nervous.

"Stuart, forget the Philippines," Hearst said curtly. "I'll send Yates to cover it." Amos stared at him, and Hearst explained, "You're going to China!"

"China!"

"Yes." The publisher began to pace the floor, his hands clasped behind him, his words tumbling out. "We're in real trouble over there—bad trouble! And nobody seems to see it, or give it a thought."

"What's happening, Mr. Hearst?"

"You saw some of it the last time you were there, Stuart. I've been reading your reports again. I didn't pay much attention to them at the time, but your warning about the Boxers . . . well, I think they're going to explode."

"What's set them off?"

Hearst frowned. "It's not any *one* thing." He stopped pacing, took a seat behind his desk, and lit a cigar while he collected his thoughts. Expelling a cloud of bluish smoke, he began to lecture Amos as if the reporter were a large crowd in a hall, an irritating habit of the man.

"The world has suddenly discovered that China is a big market, and all the nations are fighting over the pie. England won the Opium War and got a slice. The United States got a slice at Wanghia, and France got her share. The ports were thrown open to foreigners—something new in Chinese history."

"And that means the end of many small craftsmen," Amos broke in, remembering the boatman he had met. "They can't compete with the factories."

"Exactly right! So the Chinese fear what's happening. The ruler of all China is a vicious snake of a woman—the Empress Dowager, Tzu Hsi, and she hates foreigners with all her evil heart! She's made no secret out of that, publicly vowing to rid China of all of them."

"She'd go to war?"

"No, she's got no navy and the Chinese army is weak and corrupt. But there's one strong force in China—the Boxers! That very name means 'Fists of Righteousness'."

"A rough bunch, sir."

"So you say in your reports. Well, the Empress has placed the blame for China's woes not on the rotten ruling class, but on foreign invaders—and she's going to use the Boxers to get rid of them, or so I suspect."

Amos had learned that William Randolph Hearst had a peculiar genius for smelling out potential news stories. It was this quality that had made him the foremost publisher in America, and Amos asked, "What do you want me to do, Mr. Hearst?"

"Get to China as fast as you can!" Hearst snapped. "The situation there is explosive, and I want the *Journal* to have a man on the spot. I've booked passage for you on the *Cora Adams*. She sails day after tomorrow." Hearst hesitated, then got up from his desk and came to stand beside Amos. There was something uncharacteristically awkward in the way he put his hand on the younger man's shoulder. "Amos, be careful. I wouldn't want to lose you." Then, as if he had done something shameful, he whirled on his heel and returned to his desk. "Now, get out of here! I've got work to do!"

Amos disembarked from the *Cora Adams* early on the morning of May 28, 1900. Almost as soon as his feet touched Chinese soil, Amos Stuart was aware of a decided difference in the country. On his previous visit, he had been an object of curiosity, most of it friendly. But as soon as he stepped off the gangplank, he heard the hissing taunts of the Chinese who loitered on the dock: *"Yang kuei-tzu!"*

They're calling me a foreign devil, Amos thought. He stared at them, and whereas the lower classes would have dropped their gaze, they now glared at him, eyes blazing with hatred. *I'd hate to be caught out alone on a dark street with these fellows!*

He ducked his head, then made his way to the street, where he hired a rickshaw to take him to the railroad station. Though the rickshaw coolie said nothing, Amos sensed the same distaste manifested by the men on the dock. And on the way to the railroad station, his approach was heralded by jeers and catcalls coming from the people in the crowded streets. *Things are worse than Hearst or anyone else suspects,* he mused.

Amos took the train from Shanghai and for two days and nights was bounced over the irregular tracks en route to Taku, a city which guarded the upper mouth of the North River. Once again, he experienced the same animosity from the train crew and the passengers that he had encountered earlier. Being the only white man on the train, he felt isolated and at times even afraid. Only the conductor spoke some sort of pidgin English, but when Amos tried to learn why the anti-American feeling was so great, the man clammed up, refusing to speak.

Amos was exhausted when the train finally pulled into the station at Taku but hurried to make contact with the naval force lying off the Taku Bar. There he found seventeen men-of-war, situated twelve miles offshore. It was this force the Empress feared, for she had nothing to match it.

The shore was swarming with activity, and with difficulty Amos located Admiral Seymour, the officer in charge of the fleet. Seymour was a short, spare man with pale blue eyes and a crusty manner. He was not overly happy to see Amos at first, but when he discovered that Hearst himself had sent the reporter, he thawed slightly. "Perhaps Hearst can draw some attention to this mess!" he snapped. "Lord knows we're in trouble!"

"What's happening, Admiral?" Amos asked.

"It's a sorry business," Seymour said in a clipped manner. "The Boxers are out of control, killing and looting all over the country—mostly missionaries, but any white person will do. They butchered a young English clergyman named S.M. Brooks in Shantung Province last December. It gets worse every day." He gestured toward the soldiers and marines who were being bullied into order by non-coms and said, "We got a message from the Embassy at Peking last night that they're expecting an attack, so we're getting a rescue force together."

"But . . . if the Chinese attack the Embassy, it'll mean war!"

"It should, but the Empress is a crafty old woman," Seymour said. "She's watched this trouble build up for some time, and she wants to get the foreigners out. So she's come out in favor of the Boxers. That bunch has already brought North China to a state of anarchy. The armies of the Empress are badly equipped and poorly trained, so she's gotten the Boxers to do her dirty work. It's a devilish thing, Mr. Stuart! Straight out of hell! And Tzu Hsi has joined in with the dark powers of the spirit world!"

"But our country will never stand for an armed attack on our people!"

"It won't be the official army who attacks, it'll be the Boxers. You can't declare war on bandits . . . not if they're in another country." Admiral Seymour grew impatient. "The company is moving out. Do you want to come along? May be dangerous."

"Count me in," Amos agreed at once.

The force that left Taku was not large. Amos joined the officers and men who were packed into the small boats that would take them to Tientsin. He found himself seated with a group of United States marines, and got acquainted with Sergeant Joe MacClintock and a young private named Willie Summers.

MacClintock was a veteran marine, and Amos soon learned that he was worried about his men. "Most of them ain't never heard a shot fired," he said confidentially to Amos. "I wish we had a few more salty old veterans."

"You think it'll be a fight, Joe?"

"Bound to happen."

Willie Summers listened to this and puffed out his chest. He had only one ambition in life—to be a real marine—and had left Pittsfield as soon as he was old enough. The training at Parris Island had been tough, but he had come through it well, and was thrilled when he found himself slated for sea duty on a destroyer headed for the Orient.

"You watch me, Sarge," he piped up, a grin on his freckled face. "I'll get me a dozen of them Boxers! See if I don't!"

For some reason the young fellow reminded Amos of Faye O'Dell, and he couldn't help hoping that the lad fared better than the hapless O'Dell. While the three of them stood on the deck, the Chinese who watched from the shores of the narrow river, hurled insults.

"Beware the Fists of Harmonious Righteousness!"

"All foreigners are to be assassinated!"

"Go home, foreign devils!"

Amos ate in the officers' mess, where the younger officers pumped the Admiral for information, but Seymour only said, "We may get through to Peking without trouble. I hope so."

Two hours later, however, the stillness was broken by rifle fire. Amos was on deck, talking with MacClintock when a loud *ka-whong!* sounded, and something struck the cabin behind him. He stared at the shoreline, but MacClintock yanked him below the rail, shouting, "Attack! Get your rifles!"

The men came bursting out of the hatches, firing blindly toward the source of the gunfire. Some of them slid over the sides into the shallow river and waded ashore. Bullets kicked up geysers of water around the crouching marines, but they returned the fire.

Finally the Boxers gave way and Admiral Seymour, who had watched the action, said to his second-in-command, "I intend to be in Peking by nightfall!"

But he was wrong. When the troops disembarked from the boats and crowded into waiting trains to make the journey to Peking, Amos kept close to the marines.

"This should be a pleasant journey," he heard one officer say.

"Expect so," said another. "Hope we get to see some action."

He got his wish—and more!

The train had traveled no more than ten miles before it ran into an ambush. The marines were hustled off the train and drawn up into battle lines. MacClintock shouted, "Stuart, better get out of this!" But Amos paid no heed.

For the next few hours, the Boxers charged again and again with a ferocity such as none of the Americans had dreamed possible. There seemed to be no end to it, and in the end, the attacks went on for two days. The railroad had been ripped up in front of them, so there was no way for the force to go onward except on foot, and that was impossible.

Some dispatches from the fleet advised Seymour that the Imperial Army had joined with the Boxers. "This is no longer an isolated attack by some peasants, but a planned military campaign by national troops," he told his officers. We'll have to go back to Tientsin and relieve the garrison there."

"But what about the legations in Peking?" an officer demanded.

Seymour heaved a sigh. "I'm afraid they'll have to take their chances." He calculated a minute, then said, "I think we must try to get them word that we won't be coming . . . at least, not until I can raise a sizable force. Send a small group of marines. Have them use that guide, Ho Sin. He can take them through the back country."

"Dangerous work," the lieutenant said thoughtfully. "If the Boxers catch them, they'll be butchered."

Seymour shrugged. "We'll have to risk it."

When Amos discovered that Sergeant MacClintock was going to Peking with a message, he volunteered. "I'll go along, Joe."

"Your insurance paid up?"

"Sure!"

"Can you shoot?"

"I did some of that going up San Juan Hill."

His answers satisfied the sergeant. "All right, Amos, let's go pay our little visit to Peking!"

Amos Stuart never forgot the next five days. The guide Ho Sin tried to make the small force turn back many times, for he was shattered with fear. But Sergeant MacClintock kept him under guard night and day, knowing that he would abandon them at the slightest opportunity.

"We'll travel by night," MacClintock informed his men— only ten in all, including Willie Summers, who had practically begged to be allowed to go. "We stay with the roughest country and keep out of sight. Anyone sees us, we take them with us so they can't give no alarm."

Amos had little hope of a successful mission, for the land was flat and filled with small villages. But they ate cold rations, made no fires, and at dawn on the second day of June, Ho Sin pointed at the shadowy outline of a city.

"Peking!" he announced, and a cheer went up from the patrol.

They hurried across the farms surrounding the city, and when they reached the streets, MacClintock shouted, "Here, now, you're marines! Look the part!" Willie Summers puffed out his chest and stepped up his gait as the small group marched into the heart of the city.

MacClintock had seen a map of the city and knew exactly where they were going. He showed the map to Amos as they made their way down the streets. "Look, Stuart, here's a map of Peking. The Captain gave it to me. We're supposed to go to the legation quarter."

"There it is, not far from the palace." Amos pointed to a spot on the map. "I don't think they're going to be too happy to see us . . . not with the bad news we've got to give them."

"I can't help that," the sergeant grunted. Then he looked up. "Look . . . a welcoming committee."

Amos had seen the small group of men and women even before MacClintock spoke. An undersized man wearing steel-rimmed glasses led the group, and there was a smile on his rather bland face. "Welcome to Peking," he said, his voice high-pitched and clear. "I'm Lemuel Gordon. I presume the other forces are not far behind?"

Sergeant MacClintock saw that they were all expecting good news, especially the women. Reaching into his pocket, he took out the communiqué he was carrying and handed it to Gordon. "Message from Admiral Seymour, sir."

As Gordon opened the sealed envelope, a woman with a baby in her arms smiled in relief. "Your men look worn out, Sergeant. You need food and rest." She turned to the small man and her smile faded. "What's the matter, Lemuel?"

Gordon cleared his throat and turned to face the small group who had accompanied him. "There will be a slight delay, I'm afraid. The Admiral has met more opposition than he had expected. He's taken the main force back to Tientsin until the units arrive from home."

"But . . . that's impossible!" The speaker had arrived just in time to hear Gordon's statement. "I'm Sir Claude Mac-Donald, Sergeant, commander-in-chief here in Peking. What's the meaning of this message?" MacDonald was tall and slender, and his mustache bristled with aristocratic dignity. He cut an impressive figure, but he did not impress Sergeant Joe MacClintock.

"Sir, the Imperial Army has joined forces with the Boxers," MacClintock said. "It's going to take a fair-sized army to cut its way here to Peking."

"But . . . what are we to *do*?" Helen Gordon spoke with a touch of hysteria. "We're going to be attacked at any moment!" A cry of alarm went up from the group.

"Now, we must not give way to our fears," Lemuel Gordon said quickly. "God hasn't forgotten us."

"But apparently Admiral Seymour *has*," Sir Claude snapped. Then he regained his erect bearing. "Well, then, Sergeant, I'll have your men shown to their quarters. We can use you, that's certain."

"Sir, this is Mr. Amos Stuart," MacClintock put in quickly, "a correspondent for the *New York Journal*." He turned away, speaking to his men as they trooped off in the charge of one of the men.

Sir Claude stared at Amos in amazement, then laughed shortly. "Well, Mr. Stuart, you may write a story, but I'd like to know how you're going to get it out of Peking."

"I'd like to be of any help I can, sir," Amos said respectfully.

"Any military experience?"

"Well, I served in the war in Cuba with Roosevelt."

"Ah? Well, we certainly can use you," Sir Claude said with a little more warmth. "Come along, we'll find you a room."

An hour later Amos had bathed, changed clothing, and was sitting with Gordon and Sir Claude in a rather ornate room in the American Legation. Just as they settled down to a meal, they were joined by a tall, fine-looking man of about forty.

"A colleague of yours, Stuart." Sir Claude smiled and introduced him. "Mr. George Morrison, foreign correspondent for the *London Times*. He's also a medical doctor, strangely enough! Mr. Amos Stuart of the *New York Journal*, George."

Morrison shook hands warmly, his keen eyes bright. "Good

to see you, Stuart. Just heard about your beastly trip from Sergeant MacClintock. Rather a hair-trigger affair, wot?"

"Did you get the women, Morrison?" Sir Claude interrupted.

"Yes, Sir Claude, but it was a close thing!" Morrison shrugged as he caught Amos's look of inquiry. "I rode out a few days ago to look things over," he explained, as calm as if he'd decided to go for a ride in Central Park. "I took the route to Fengtai, and the reports are true. Fengtai is about wiped out, and the people are running like rabbits. Nothing to be done, so I started back, but I remembered that Squiers's wife and that young woman named Polly Smith were close by, in a villa in the Western Hills overlooking Fengtai. Thought they might be trapped, so I went by and picked them up."

"Good thing you did, George," Lemuel Gordon said warmly, admiration on his round face. "They'd have been killed out of hand if the Boxers had gotten wind of them."

The men ate hungrily, and then Sir Claude and Gordon excused themselves, leaving Amos and Morrison to get better acquainted.

"I know I'm your competitor, Mr. Morrison," Amos began, "but anything you can tell me about this business will be appreciated."

"Why, certainly! And let it be George and Amos, eh?" Morrison sat back, and the two drank tea as he filled Amos in on the situation. "You've got to understand that there are two distinct groups here in the city, and they don't get along too well. First, there are the missionaries—every brand you can imagine. The poor Chinese can't make head nor tail out of the differences between them." Morris allowed himself a small smile before going on. "But they've done a magnificent work in China—mission schools, orphanages, hospitals, that sort of thing. Of course, the Boxers charge them with terrible practices—all lies."

"What's the other group?"

"Oh, the diplomatic corps." Morrison stood up and, stepping over to a wall, pointed to a map hanging there. "The Legation Quarter is here."

Amos rose and joined him, peering at the map.

"But do you think the Boxers will attack the legations, George?"

"Afraid so."

Amos turned to face Morrison. "Can we hold out?"

"Hard to say. There are thousands of Boxers armed to the teeth, and only a few hundred of us. Very few fighting men." He raised one eyebrow and smiled crookedly. "Are you wishing you'd stayed in New York, Amos?"

"I find this all very stimulating," Amos said with more confidence than he felt.

"Ah, well, we'll do what we can." Amos heard the door open behind him, and Morrison smiled over his shoulder. "Come in and meet our newest recruit."

Amos turned and saw the face of the young woman who had entered, just as Morrison said, "Miss Rose Beaumont, may I present Mr. Amos Stuart of the *New York Journal*."

Amos had been hit once in the stomach with great force. It had taken his breath so completely that he could not speak, not if his life had depended on it.

This was another such moment. And as he faced Rose, he was unable even to respond to her low greeting. "Yes, Mr. Morrison. Mr. Stuart and I have met before."

Amos stood there, staring at Rose, unable to believe his eyes. His mind went totally blank, and he could not make sense out of whatever it was Morrison was saying. He knew that his face had gone pale, and there was an emptiness, a sort of nausea in his stomach as he stared at the woman he'd loved so much.

Rose! Rose! something cried inside him, but it was a faint thing. Finally Amos managed to nod in acknowledgment. "Yes . . . we've met before, Miss Beaumont and I."

14

THE FISTS OF RIGHTEOUSNESS

D espair lay over the Peking legations after the message from Admiral Seymour. Streets were deserted and native help grew scarce. Word of new outrages, of destruction of foreign property, or of wanton murders heightened the tension.

The Boxers invaded the Tartar City, that section of Peking north of the legations, and by night the sky was illuminated by flames from burning sections of the city. The night wind carried the agonized cries of the Christian converts unfortunate enough to fall into the hands of the *I Ho Ch'uan*—Fists of Righteousness.

Life within the legations was increasingly strained during this waiting time of neither war nor peace. The missionaries were inundated with two thousand Roman Catholic Chinese, plus a number of Methodist converts who needed shelter. This was not done without some heated discussion, and Amos was in the meeting held in one of the large rooms after the evening meal, when the problem was brought up.

Sir Claude was opposed to accepting the refugees. "They will create a problem," he insisted angrily. "The compound is already overcrowded, and many undesirables will no doubt be in their number. And how are we to feed and house them?"

Lemuel Gordon argued mildly that they had no choice in the matter, for to turn them away would be to condemn them to certain death. George Morrison, though not a missionary himself, supported Gordon's view. The argument swayed

171

back and forth, and strangely enough, it was Amos who provided an answer.

He was sitting with his back to the wall, acutely conscious of Rose, across the room. Once she turned and caught him watching her, and he flushed, jerking his head away. But when both sides had given their arguments, he spoke up. "I'm not a part of the work here, Sir Claude, but there's one factor you might want to consider."

"And what is that, may I ask?"

"I think we all believe that this legation is going to be hit by trained soldiers. Who's going to get this place ready to withstand that attack? We're so few. But with the help of these people, we could dig trenches, erect bomb shelters, make barricades, and do all the rest of the hard work that defending a fort involves. In my judgment, sir, we need *them* about as badly as they need *us*!"

It was exactly the right thing to say, and over Sir Claude's protests, the matter was settled. "Sir Claude, you're the commander-in-chief, and we'll gladly obey you in all things political," Lemuel Gordon spoke up. "But in this case, we must do what we think is best."

The meeting broke up, and Gordon came over at once to speak to Amos. "Come home with me, Amos. I think we need to make plans for the fortifications."

"What about Sir Claude?"

A glint of humor sparked Gordon's eyes behind the spectacles. "Well, we'll do the work and let him take the credit."

Amos laughed, liking the man tremendously, and accompanied him to the small house where he lived with his wife, Helen, their infant son, Charles, and Sally, their four-year-old daughter.

"I brought Mr. Stuart by so we could make some plans, dear," Gordon explained.

Helen Gordon, a delicate woman in her mid-twenties, had not attended the meeting, but had stayed home with Charles, who was sick. "I'm glad you've come, Mr. Stuart. Sit down and I'll make some tea." Now she turned to her husband, worry etched on her thin face. "The baby isn't doing well, Lemuel. He's still got a high fever and he won't eat."

"We'll get Dr. Morrison in to look at him." Gordon took the child from her, then nodded toward a chair. "Have a seat, Amos . . . may I call you that? And you must call us Lemuel and Helen." He sat down in a cane rocker and began rocking the baby, who cried restlessly.

Amos relaxed, speaking easily with Lemuel while his wife made the tea. Returning with a tray, she served them and sat down to listen, sewing curtains as the men talked about fortifying the legations.

"The Boxers wouldn't really dare attack the legations, would they?" Helen asked. "I mean, Admiral Seymour will be here with an army soon."

Amos and Gordon exchanged a brief glance, silently agreeing that it might be well to let her think the army would arrive soon, though each of them knew it would be a long, long wait.

"My dear—" Gordon began, but was interrupted by a knock at the door. He got to his feet, opened the door, and stepped back with a smile on his face. "Why, Rose, come in!" He turned to Amos. "I understand you and Miss Rose are old friends."

Amos stood to greet her, saying evenly, "We knew each other in New York City."

Upon seeing Amos, Rose halted abruptly, her cheeks flushed with color. "I–I didn't know you had company, Reverend Gordon—"

"Oh, come in, Rose!" Helen called out quickly. "I need a favor from you."

"I stopped by to see if you wanted me to sit with the baby for a while."

"No, I think the doctor needs to look at him. Would you mind finding Dr. Morrison and asking him to look in on Charlie?"

"Why, of course."

"I'd better go with you, Rose," Gordon said at once. "It's

not safe for you to be out alone. Boxers have been seen inside the legation."

"Oh, Lemuel, you're so tired!" Helen said, then a thought
came to her. "Why don't you join us, Rose, while we visit with
Amos, then he can walk you back to Dr. Morrison's quarters."

Amos had no desire at all to spend an hour with the Gor-
dons, especially with Rose present. Rising, he volunteered,
"I'll be glad to get the doctor," waving away Gordon's protest
that they weren't through making plans. "We can do that
later," he said. "I'll look for the doctor . . . but if he's not in
his room, I may have trouble finding him. May take awhile."

"I'll go back with you, if I may," Rose said suddenly, and
before Amos could think of a way to prevent it, she stepped
to the door and waited for him. "I'll come back and sit with
Charlie tomorrow so you can rest, Helen," she added, then
left the room.

Amos had no choice but to follow her outside.

She turned and walked toward the canal that ran from
Legation Street to the British legation. With the setting of
the sun there was a coolness in the air, and the only lights
were the yellow flames of lanterns hung along the banks of
the canal. This was usually a busy thoroughfare, but since the
crisis it was almost deserted after the sun went down.

Amos walked stiffly beside Rose, unable to speak. He had
not spoken to her since the first moment they met. Had, in
fact, gone out of his way to avoid her. The first night after
their initial meeting, he had lain awake on his bed, tossing
and turning for hours. He had thought that the bitterness and
anger that had churned in him since Rose dropped him had
gone, but he had been wrong—very wrong!

How can she face me? he had thought as he lay on his cot. *She
treated me like a dog! And how can she be here, pretending to be a
missionary? Nick sure wouldn't lie to me about what she became,
would he?*

A dog howled somewhere in the distance, and Rose said

quietly, "He won't be howling much longer. He'll be in some-body's stew."

Just then they came to one of the small bridges that arched the canal, and she said abruptly, "Amos, I have to talk to you." Without looking to see if he was following, she turned and walked up the wooden bridge, then leaned on the waist-high rail and stared down at the water.

Amos came to stand beside her, saying nothing, curious as to what she might have on her mind.

"It was a shock when I walked into the office and saw you, Amos," she said quietly. She waited for him to answer, but when he did not reply, she added simply, "I wanted to turn and run away."

"Why?" Amos asked harshly.

"Because of the shameful way I treated you, of course." Rose was wearing a simple dark green dress, cut in the Chinese fashion. She wore her raven hair up, and her green eyes were sober as she turned to face him. "I knew that sooner or later I'd have to face you. Amos, I'm so sorry about the way I behaved. Can you ever forgive me?"

Amos was torn. His first inclination was to say, "Yes, I for-give you, Rose!" She looked so small standing there beside him, so fragile and as beautiful as ever. He remembered the times he'd spent with her—the soft kisses, the warm light in her eyes as she murmured to him.

But he had had long months to hate her, too, and now the old bitterness welled up inside him. "Why did you do it?" he demanded. "Couldn't you have waited just a few months? Was what you felt for me so weak it wouldn't even last *that* long?" He saw her flinch as the words cut deep, and he took a perverse satisfaction out of it. *Let her hurt a little!*

Rose received his reprimand without reply, her lips quiv-ering, the pain in her eyes betraying her vulnerability. When he had finished, she said, "I'm guilty of all you say, Amos. I–I know you can't believe this . . . but even when I was moving away from you and from all that was right, there was something in me that told me not to do it."

As she spoke, Rose felt tears beginning to burn her eyes and willed them away, determined that Amos would not see her cry. Turning back toward the rail, she put her hands on it and stared down into the depths of the murky green water. "I suppose you know what happened to me . . . what I became?"

"Yes, I heard."

Rose thought she could hear a note of sadness, of regret in his voice, but could not be sure. "What you heard was true, Amos. All of it."

Fireflies had begun to gather on the bank of the canal. Stuart watched them as they blinked—miniature amber torches dotting the gathering darkness. The night birds were out now, sweeping and wheeling. Something in the sadness of their plaintive cry struck a responsive note in him, and he said, "It . . . doesn't matter now."

"No, Amos, it doesn't matter." Rose's voice was almost a whisper. "God has forgiven me . . . but I'll never marry."

Amos blinked in surprise. "Why not, Rose?"

She bowed her head for a moment, then turned to look into his eyes. "It would be asking too much of a man to forget what . . . I've been." As she spoke, it seemed to Amos that she was shutting some sort of a door, and it brought a curious lonely feeling to him.

"Some men could forget."

"No. No man's that good." Rose shook her head. Then she smiled. "But I'm happy, Amos. Can I tell you why?"

"Yes."

As Rose spoke, confirming his worst suspicions, then telling how she'd been saved by a miracle, Amos knew she was telling the truth. She *was* happy! "What brought you here?" he asked when she had finished.

"Oh, one of the missionaries came through New York,

preaching about the need for missionaries in China. God spoke to me . . . and here I am."

Amos stared at her, unable to comprehend her joy. He waved his hand toward the city walls. "The Boxers will be hitting that wall soon. I don't think there's much chance for any of us. You came to an odd place to find happiness."

"Happiness isn't a *place*," Rose replied. Her lips curved in a faint smile, and she had no idea how provocative that gesture was to the man who stood there watching her. "Happiness is when everything is going right for you in the world. But when things start going wrong—" She touched her breast. "Joy in the heart makes the difference. Joy is from God, Amos. It's one of the fruits of his Spirit. And the joy he gives isn't tied to circumstances. A man or woman can lose everything— health, family, possessions, even life itself—but a believer can't lose her joy."

"I guess I don't understand." Amos felt uncomfortable, more uncomfortable than he had ever felt in his life. Suddenly he found himself telling Rose about Faye O'Dell, and when the story was finished, he shook his head sadly. "He died without knowing God, Rose. I . . . wish he hadn't!"

Rose sensed Amos's heartache. She stood there, praying for wisdom before she answered him. "We can never know about things like that, Amos. All God requires is a hungry heart and a cry. That can happen in a moment. Your friend . . . isn't it possible he might have cried out to God at the end?"

"Y–yes, I suppose so," Amos faltered. It was a new thought for him, and he stood there in the darkness, his face twisted with the pain of the old memory. "I hope you're right, Rose," he muttered, then brightened. "I'm sorry about what I said. And I'm glad you're happy, Rose."

"Thank you, Amos." With an impulsive gesture, she touched his hand. "You're right about our situation. If God doesn't perform a miracle, we'll all die in this place." She was quiet and calm and lovely as she gazed steadily up at him. "I'm praying you'll find God here, Amos." Then she turned, saying briskly, "Let's go find Dr. Morrison."

Amos followed her off the arching bridge and alongside the canal, where the yellow lanterns made ripples of amber light in the dark water.

For the next three weeks, the missionaries and the diplomats hungered for knowledge of what was happening outside the city. They knew nothing of the struggles Seymour was having to pull an army together. They all nourished a certain optimism, none of them able to believe they would be left to fend for themselves.

Then on June 19, this optimism was shattered.

At 5:00 P.M. scarlet envelopes were delivered to each of the foreign ministers. The notes were identical: "Within twenty-four hours, Your Excellency, accompanied by the legation guards, who must be kept under proper control, will proceed to Tientsin in order to prevent any unforeseen calamity."

Morrison stared at the note, which had been handed to him by one of the diplomats, then showed it to Amos. "That's it, I'm afraid," he said tonelessly. "I hope we've made our fortifications strong."

There was no thought of leaving Peking. If to stay meant massacre, to leave the compound meant destruction. At once activity in the legations increased. A detachment of marines aided in the evacuation of the Methodist compound. Seventy-one missionaries and a large number of converts, including 124 Chinese schoolgirls, were brought into the quarter and lodged in the small chapel of the British legation.

The British compound, commanding a good field of fire and not dominated by the Tatar Wall, had been selected as the key defensive position. Crowded into it were some nine hundred persons, plus a large number of ponies, mules and sheep, and one cow—all this in three acres of land with a normal population of sixty people.

It was a frantic scene. Carts containing household furniture jammed into the area, and peasants swarmed about, unloading their belongings. One building was assigned to the French, another to the Russians, a third to the Imperial Customs. A group of men huddled over maps and planned strategy. Dr. Morrison made space on the tile floor for his mattress, heaping his supply of books nearby.

Then as darkness fell, heavy firing commenced in the east, near the Austrian legation. Amos was standing beside Sergeant MacClintock, and the two of them turned to face the sound of the guns.

"Well, looks like the siege of Peking has begun," the marine remarked. "God help us all!"

Amos was thinking about the sheet of paper that Sir Claude had shown him earlier. This sheet listed the total strength of the legation guards. With his reporter's sure memory, he could see the list clearly:

	Officers	Men
American	3	53
British	3	79
German	1	51
Austrian	7	30
Russian	2	79
French	2	45
Italian	1	28
Japanese	1	24

He thought of the masses of enemy troops, some of them well armed, that now ringed the city, and said with a wry smile, "God will have to do it, Joe. Otherwise, we don't have a prayer!"

The siege seemed to last forever, though by actual count, only five weeks had passed by the time the fighting finally ended. Each day life had grown more oppressive. Food was in short supply, sanitation impossible, privacy forgotten. To make matters worse, the defenders never got a clear look at their attackers, hidden in the streets and buildings of the city. Rooftops and trees limited the view from the legations to less than one hundred yards, and this blindness increased the sense of isolation.

Casualties had mounted steadily as machine gun and rifle fire ripped into the legations. It was on a hot afternoon in July that Amos—on guard with the marines—was suddenly aware of something happening down the street.

MacClintock had seen it too, and whispered, "Stay alert now. They'll be coming soon."

"Maybe they won't charge," Willie Summers offered hopefully. "Maybe they'll pull back." He was thinking of home and secretly wishing he were there.

Sir Claude MacDonald came hurrying forward. "Look . . . the Boxers are wheeling an artillery piece into place!"

MacClintock shook his head. "We're in trouble, Stuart. We've got nothing that can reach that gun. It's one of them new Krupp cannons!" The cannon barked and over to the right, a section of the wall blew up. "Keep your heads down!" MacClintock ordered.

The defenders could do no more than crouch in the rubble as the rapid-fire cannon spoke again and again.

MacClintock looked at his men, his face mask-like. "That gun's got to be knocked out. I'm goin' . . . but nobody has to go with me." He threw himself over the wall without hesitation, and Amos followed. Even as he went over the wall, he was thinking, *Why am I doing this?* He noted that Willie Summers, his face pale as paper, was one of the three marines who had come tumbling after him. *He's as scared as I am*, Amos thought.

The five men dodged into an alley. "We'll get on top of that building—see?" MacClintock said. "We can pick those gunners off from there."

"But they'll just start again when we pull back, Joe," Amos argued.

"Yeah, so I'm going to spike the cannon! Now, you birds get into position. When you knock the gunners out, I'll go fix that cannon so them Boxers can't ever use it."

Amos shook his head. "You can't make it! There's lots of riflemen supporting that gun. They'll cut you down!"

"You knock them off if they try it, Stuart." MacClintock grinned at Willie, who was staring at him. "Summers, I appoint you corporal," he said. "You're in command . . . now get going!"

Summers swallowed, but he drew himself up proudly. "Come on, let's get those jokers!"

Amos and the marines scrambled to the roof of the building the sergeant had mentioned and lay down flat. "Gosh!" Summers breathed. "Sarge was right . . . look at that!"

Looking down, Amos saw that they commanded a clear view of the cannon crew, who had no idea they were in danger.

"Now, get the crew, then keep your eyes open," Summers ordered. "Them Boxers will pop up to get a shot at Sarge! I'll take the officer. Bibb, you take the guy with the red scarf—" He went on identifying the enemy soldiers. "We'll all fire on my signal. Don't miss! When the five soldiers go down, I'm hoping them Boxers will think the gods have turned against them. All right, aim . . . fire!"

Amos drew a bead on the chest of one of the Chinese soldiers, and at the signal, pulled the trigger. It was almost mystical—or so it must have seemed to the onlooking Boxers—for every member of the crew fell to the ground, either dead or wounded.

"There goes Sergeant MacClintock!" Summers yelped. "Now . . . get them Boxers!"

Amos fired as rapidly as he could find a target, and the effectiveness of the marines' fire drove the Boxers from the scene, leaving twenty of their men on the ground. Meanwhile,

MacClintock made a wild dash for the cannon. They saw him attach something to it, then light a match and touch it to a fuse. He whirled and was halfway back to safety when a bullet from an unseen sharpshooter knocked him down. At the same instant, the explosive he'd fixed to the cannon went off with a tremendous roar.

"Willie . . . cover me!" Amos yelled.

He threw down his gun, darted down the stairs, then turned into the open field. As the rifles of the marines chattered, two more Boxers fell from the branches of a tree.

Reaching MacClintock, Amos was relieved to see that the sergeant was alive. He had a bloody thigh, but he was conscious. "Come on, Joe, climb aboard!"

Amos yanked the marine to his feet, bent and lifted him to his shoulders, then began to run. MacClintock was a heavy man, but Amos wasn't aware of the extra weight. His feet struck the dust, sending up tiny puffs. Near his head, like bees humming was the whine of bullets. The wall was only ten feet away. He kept on, spurred by the thought of safety. "He got him! He got him!" He could hear the marines clearly.

Then he was at the wall . . . but even as he reached it, a giant fist struck him a tremendous blow in the side. Amos pitched forward, pushing MacClintock to the ground, then crawled in front and grabbed the sergeant's wrists. "Come on, Joe!" he grunted, and with one final lunge, the two cleared the distance.

"You hit, Amos?"

Looking up, Stuart saw Willie Summers's pale face, his freckles standing out like a badge.

"He got it in the back," MacClintock said in a thin voice. "Better get both of us out of here."

At that moment, reinforcements arrived—twenty Italian guards. The officer took one look at the two wounded men and snapped, "Get them to the hospital. We'll take care of things here." His dark eyes gleamed, and he nodded, "We saw it all. There'll be a medal for both of you."

Amos felt himself losing consciousness, the pain razor-sharp. He forced his eyes open and studied the officer, then whispered something.

"What did he say?" the officer asked.

Willie Summers grinned. "He said he'd rather have a ticket to the good old U.S. of A!"

Amos drifted off into a warm oblivion, unaware of his jolting ride to the field hospital, where Dr. Morrison dug the slug out of his side. Nor did he know Rose when she bathed his face and sat beside him all through the night.

15

HOME AT LAST!

Amos awakened slowly, reluctantly coming out of a deep sleep. His mouth had a sour taste, and when he tried to lick his lips, they felt like dry paper. A sudden desire for water overtook him, and when he opened his eyes, his surroundings swam into focus.

He was lying on a single cot in a room with only one window through which he could see no more than an inky blackness. A single coal oil lamp, turned low, penetrated the darkness, and when he turned his head, he squinted, making out the forms of several men in cots like his own.

Next to his bed was a small table. Seeing a glass there, his thirst became acute. He rolled over on his side, but as he reached for the glass, pain exploded in his side like a bomb. Involuntarily, he expelled a grunt of pain and fell back, gritting his teeth until the wave of agony subsided.

"Amos . . . are you awake?"

The whisper was followed by a cool hand on his brow, and he opened his eyes again to see Rose bending over his cot. She was wearing a white dress and had appeared so suddenly and in such a spectral light that, for one confused moment, Amos thought he was dead. Then the touch of her hand reassured him, and he nodded. It took an effort to speak, but he mumbled, "Drink . . . !"

Picking up the glass, Rose poured some water into it, then carefully supporting his head, put the glass to his lips. "Be careful," she warned. He gulped thirstily, draining the glass, and when she refilled it, he drank that as well. "How do you feel?"

"Rotten." Amos found, however, that the water had lubricated his mouth sufficiently for speech. Although his head was pounding and his right side throbbed with every movement, he began to struggle to sit up. Rose helped him into a sitting position, and he stared at her from hollow eyes. "I remember getting hit," he said. "How long have I been out?"

"Just since yesterday," Rose replied. "Are you hungry?"

"Yes!"

She smiled at the urgency in his tone. "That's a good sign. I'll go get you something to eat." She left the room, and he lay there quietly until she returned with a tray. "This is still warm," she said, handing him a bowl. "Do you need me to feed you?"

"No, I can do it." He took the bowl and was astonished to find how hungry he was. As he ate, he asked, "No sign of the relief force, I take it?"

"Not yet."

She waited until he was finished, then said, "Breakfast will be in a couple of hours, then you can have something else. I did find a little coffee." She handed him the cup. "Everyone is talking about what a heroic thing you did, Amos, saving Sergeant MacClintock's life." He shrugged and sipped his coffee, and she realized her praise had made him uncomfortable. "The sergeant is in the cot on the end."

"How is he?"

"Oh, not bad. Both of you were lucky, the doctor said. No bones hit. You'll be up and around in a week."

Amos drank the coffee slowly, savoring the strong flavor. Except for the sound of heavy breathing, the room was silent. From the small window came a sound of a gun firing, distant and muffled. Rose sat beside him, watching him, and he wondered how long she'd been in the room. The light from the lamp gave her skin a mellow glow and sculpted the planes of her face, giving an oriental cast to her eyes, deep in the sockets. She had always been quiet, Amos thought, and now he saw how attractive and reassuring that quality was. He disliked talkative women, those who couldn't bear a single instant of silence, and there was something pleasant about the way she just sat there, letting time run on.

Finally he said, "Have you heard from Nick or Anna?"

"Anna writes me sometimes. She's worried about Nick. Did you know he had been arrested?"

"No . . . but I'm not too surprised. He's in with a hard bunch."

The food had made Amos drowsy, and he lay there, relaxed. He found that the bullet had done more than tear his flesh; it had weakened his spirit in a way he could not explain. For one thing, his anger with Rose was gone, and he wondered about that, for it had been with him for a long time. He was very weak, and as he slipped off, he reached out his hand and mumbled, "Rose?"

"Yes, Amos?" She leaned forward, took his hand and waited, but he was already asleep. When she tried to pull her hand away, he tightened his grip, and she let her hand rest in his. For a long time, she sat there looking down into his face. He was thinner, and the wound had dealt him a hard blow, but she still thought he was fine-looking. Not handsome, but his features were strong and gave the impression of sensitivity. With her free hand, she brushed a lock of his hair back from his forehead.

He's a good man, she thought, letting her eyes rest on his face. *I can never have him now . . . but I can always remember that he loved me once.* The thought saddened her, and she gave his hand a squeeze, released it, then rose and left the room.

The siege continued without respite. Sir Claude estimated that the Boxers had fired more than two hundred thousand rounds at the compound, and the result was a steadily mounting casualty list, with thirty-eight fighting men killed by the end of July, and fifty-five more badly wounded.

With no sign of relief and supplies dwindling, the embattled prisoners found it almost impossible to keep their spirits up. The huge walls surrounding them loomed larger, seeming to close in each day.

"It's like–like being in a big *rat trap!*" said Willie Summers, who had come in from his post to eat with Amos. "If we could just get a good shot at those . . . ," he broke off abruptly, glancing at Rose Beaumont, who appeared with a bowl of soup.

She put the bowl in front of him, smiled, and said with a glint of humor in her greenish eyes, "Finest Mongol pony soup in town, Willie."

Summers looked down at the mixture and shook his head in disgust. "If anyone had ever told me I'd be eatin' pony soup . . . "

Amos was amused at the young marine. "Better than bird's nest soup," he commented, lowering one eyelid in a sly wink at Rose.

Summers stared at Amos, jaw dropping. *"Bird's nest?"* he demanded. "Well, if that ain't just like these Chinamen!" Nevertheless, he ate his soup with gusto, then shoved back from the table and regarded Amos. "When you comin' back to work?" he asked. "Seems like you been soldierin' on us long enough."

"We heroes have to take care of ourselves, Willie." Amos grinned, for he had learned to make light of his accomplishment. He had healed rather slowly, for the bullet had not gone squarely in, but had turned, ripping a gaping tunnel in his side and back. For the first week, every movement had been pure agony, but when the flesh began to knit, he could move about with some degree of ease . . . as long as he didn't make any abrupt motions.

The days passed slowly, but even in the midst of constant crisis, Amos was undergoing some sort of metamorphosis that puzzled him. For long hours he lay on his cot with nothing to do but think. He could sleep only so many hours, and even at night he lay silently pondering what was happening to him. By nature an introspective man, he was aware that something unusual was going on inside. Even that mystified him, for he had been a man of the mind, assuming that only mystics or people with great religious inclinations, like his mother, were moved in the "spirit."

In his enforced idleness, Amos came to understand something that he would never have known if his busy life had not been brought to an abrupt halt. Sorting out the skeins of his history, he began to realize that his restlessness for the past few years was rooted in a kind of inner emptiness. This came as a shock, and at first he shook off the idea. But as he pondered the matter, he realized it was true.

"A man has to have something more than work," he mused. "He can fill his life up with things, but those things don't ever seem to be enough. Guess that's why I've been chasing all over the world . . . looking for something over the next hill."

Finally he realized that Rose was at the core of his problem, and it didn't take him long to conclude that the bitterness spawned by her betrayal had been a cancer eating away at his spirit. For long hours, he thought of the early days when he'd fallen in love with her and of the wonder of that love. Then came the war . . . and nothing in the war had been more devastating than his rejection by Rose.

But she wasn't all of it. He had never forgotten the times when God had seemed to reach out and touch him. He thought again of that time when he had asked God for a job and had been given one instantly! He thought of his mother, how she'd faced every difficulty with a serenity that was baffling to him.

And he thought of Faye O'Dell, whose bones now lay in a shallow grave in Cuba. Despite Rose's words, he still grieved over the lad.

And now, sitting at the table as Rose and Willie bantered with each other, he thought he saw in Willie some of the same vulnerability he'd seen in O'Dell. He had never inquired into the boy's belief about God, and when he brought his thoughts back to the present, his attention sharpened as he heard the two speaking of religion.

"Guess I'll go to heaven," Willie was saying. "I ain't done lots of bad stuff."

Rose shook her head slightly. "That's not the way to get to heaven, Willie. Jesus said, 'I am the way, the truth, and the life. No man cometh unto the Father, but by me.' That's why Jesus died—to save sinners. And we're all sinners, Willie."

"But . . . some are worse than others!"

"Yes, that's true, but it's not how *bad* our particular sins are. As a matter of fact, some of the things we think are the very *worst* sins may not be as bad in God's eyes as some of the *little* sins," Rose said pensively. "We think it's terrible to kill a person . . . and it is, of course. But I've known people who were so cruel to their family for years that God must have wept. Yet they were in good standing with man. No, we're all disobedient to God, and the only way to get back in good standing with *him* is to have our sins forgiven."

Willie shook his head. "Miss Rose, I'm just dumb, I guess. But I can't see how a man dying two thousand years ago can make *me* good."

Amos nodded. "I've wondered about that myself," he murmured and was aware that Rose turned her eyes on him at once.

"I know it's difficult to understand," she said earnestly. She hesitated, then asked, "Did you know that the Jews sacrificed a lamb to God? Well, the Book of Hebrews says it's impossible for the blood of animals to take away sin."

"Why'd they do it, then?" Willie demanded. He was leaning forward, his eyes riveted on Rose.

"Because God commanded them to. But for hundreds of years, with thousands of lambs slain, not one sin was ever washed away by the blood of those animals. But all the prophets God sent kept telling the Jews to hope, that one day a Messiah would come, One who would save his people. And in the Gospel of John, the first chapter, we learn that all those prophecies came true. 'The next day,'" she recited with glowing eyes, "'John seeth Jesus coming unto him, and saith, Behold the Lamb of God, which taketh away the sin of the world.' And that's what Jesus did—he took away the sin of the world."

"But why do the preachers talk about hell if Jesus took away sin?" A look of bewilderment crossed Willie's face. He had been afraid for days, not of death so much as the shadow that lay beyond death. He had admired the calm assurance of Rose Beaumont and the other missionaries and longed for that same peace.

"Jesus said one time, 'Ye will not come unto me that ye might have life.' Come to Jesus—that's what you have to do, Willie," Rose explained. "It was all I *could* do. I was so deep in sin I knew I could never make things right. I could only cry out to Jesus . . . and the instant I did, he came into my heart. Ever since that moment, I've had peace."

Willie looked down at the table, his face drawn. His lips were trembling, and he was embarrassed by his display of emotion.

But Rose had seen this happen many times. She drew her chair close to his and began to tell him how to find Christ. After a brief time, Amos heard her ask, "Would you like to be saved, Willie? To know that you're going to heaven when you die?"

Willie's shoulders were tense, but he nodded his head.

"Then pray in your heart. God wants to save you. Just ask him to as I pray."

Amos was astonished. He sat there staring at the two. And then he became aware that his own hands were trembling and his heart was beating faster. He felt short of breath, and then the impulse struck him to do exactly what Willie seemed to be doing—he wanted to call on God!

Instantly it was clear that this was the root of his troubled spirit. He knew that for years he'd been running from God.

And he had the awful feeling that if he didn't call out to God now, he would never be able to do so. It was, somehow, his last chance!

Amos resisted the overwhelming sense of urgency . . . or he tried to, but he could not control his trembling, and as Rose kept on mentioning Jesus, the very *sound* of that name brought tears to his eyes.

Suddenly he knew that this was not merely a matter of life or death—this was for all time, for eternity. A sense of fear that he might miss out on the greatest of all things swept over him, and he began to pray. It was not a neat, orderly prayer, but a desperate cry, as from a man going down for the last time.

Amos never knew how long he sat there, for he lost all sense of time and place. But as he prayed, a strange sensation of peace began to grow inside him. At first it was a very tiny thing—buried in his doubts and fears—but somehow it swelled until it filled his whole soul.

He looked up, his eyes filled with tears, to find Rose looking at him, and he whispered, "I–I just asked God to save me!"

Willie's cheeks were damp with tears. "Me, too, Amos!"

Rose put out her hands, and each of the men grasped them as she began to praise God. She began quietly enough, but soon the joy that rose up in her could not be contained. Other men, hearing her, came to gaze at the three. Before long, the small dining room was full, and Rose began to tell them all what had happened. "Amos, are you saved?" she asked unexpectedly. "Has Jesus come to your heart?"

Amos looked around at the curious faces and smiled. He nodded and his voice was full of the joy that kept welling up in him in great waves.

"Yes . . . I called on God right here at this table. I–I don't know how it happened, but I do know that everything in this world is different!" He turned to Rose and lowered his voice as he added for her ears alone, "*Everything* is different, all new and fresh!"

Rose stared at Amos, knowing that he was no longer the

man he had been. There was a gentleness in his eyes that had been missing, and she knew that he was saying more than his words implied. She hoped that soon he would be coming to her as a man comes to a woman.

Amos did come to Rose, but not until several days had gone by. Not that he kept his distance, for the two of them had long talks as she taught him—along with Willie Summers—how to study the Bible. As word spread, the little group grew to ten, then fifteen.

Still, Amos said nothing personal to her, and Rose reluctantly put away her expectations.

They were both shocked, along with the rest of the compound, when Sir Claude called the leaders together and issued a grave warning. "We must attack the Boxers," he said. His face was thin and etched with the pressure of the siege. "If we do not, they will be over the walls by tomorrow. We must prove that we are still a fighting force."

"It must be done," Dr. Morrison agreed, "and at once!"

That night seventy-five men gathered to make the attack, and Captain Meyers, an Englishman who had been given the command, faced them. "This is a desperate enterprise. We must drive the Boxers back if it costs us every man in the attempt. Now . . . follow me!"

Amos had joined the group, despite warnings from both Rose and Dr. Morrison. He himself knew his decision was because of Willie, for the two had grown very close. Now as the men moved forward, he whispered, "Stay close, Willie."

"Sure, Amos!"

They hit the Boxers with all they had, taking them off guard, and the world seemed to be filled with explosions and gunfire.

Amos fired and reloaded as rapidly as he could and was glad to hear the captain cry out, "That's it, men! Now, back over the wall!"

Amos and Willie were among the last to retreat, and they

had almost reached the wall when a blast of machine gun fire shattered the night.

"Duck, Willie!" Amos yelled, but even as he did so, he saw his friend's figure driven backward by the force of the bullets. "Willie!" he called again, and as the slugs flew around him, Amos dropped to the ground beside the boy. Amos didn't even hear Captain Meyers ordering the men to get the machine gunner, for he was gently holding Willie's head.

Blood was running from the young marine's mouth, and Amos could see that his friend's body had taken three or four slugs. There was no hope, he saw, and he thought Willie was already dead.

But the young man opened his eyes and whispered faintly, "Amos . . . good thing . . . I got saved—"

"Willie! Willie!" Amos moaned.

"It's okay, Amos." The eyes opened wide and a smile curved the boy's bloody lips. "I'll see Jesus first. Don't ever . . . forget how we got . . . saved—"

Then his body jerked slightly, his eyelids closed, and Willie Summers died in Amos's arms.

At the funeral the next morning, Amos could barely hold back the tears as Lemuel Gordon spoke briefly. He heard little of the sermon and afterward walked the streets, thinking of many things. When darkness came, he found himself seeking the comfort of familiar faces. Rose was startled when Amos appeared at her door. "Come and walk with me, Rose," he said, and something about him compelled her to agree.

He led her to the same bridge where they'd talked once before, and again they leaned on the rail, peering down at the rippling water. For several minutes he did not speak, and Rose wondered what he was thinking, why he'd brought her here.

Then he turned and cupped her shoulders in his hands. His eyes were filled with pain, yet there was a quiet joy in him, too. "Rose, I love you. I've never stopped loving you."

"Amos—!"

"No, don't talk, just listen," he said swiftly. "The past is over . . . for both of us. Everything starts all new and shiny when we come under the blood . . . that's what you taught me. So we're both new. Nothing in the past counts."

She tried to speak, but he cut off her protest in the simplest way possible—with a kiss. He drew her close and lowered his lips to hers, and it was as if nothing else existed for either of them. She stopped struggling and returned his kiss, and in his arms, all her doubts fell away.

When Amos lifted his head, his eyes were shining. "Rose, I can't lose you again. Will you marry me?"

"Yes! Oh, yes, Amos!"

A frog on the bank below suddenly announced his presence with a deep cry, then plunged into the canal, sending circles over the face of the dark water . . . but neither of the two on the bridge heard him.

Two days afterward General Alfred Gaselee, in charge of the relief expedition, led his troops into the city. He came clattering in on a black charger, swung to the ground, and was met by Lady Claude MacDonald, who had by some miracle donned a lace-trimmed gown and broad-brimmed hat for the occasion.

Looking as if she had just come from a garden party, Lady MacDonald offered her hand, saying graciously, "General Gaselee, how good of you to come—!"

The legation was relieved—and the Boxer Rebellion was over.

Part 3
1905-1908

16

DEATH IN THE HILLS

A mos and Rose disembarked from the train at Fort Smith just after dawn on a Wednesday in October of the year 1905. The steam engine had bulled its way through heavy snows for much of the journey from New York, but Amos was relieved to see that only white patches of old snow marked the hills that shouldered their way up around the town.

"I need to rent a rig for a few days," he told the stationmaster, then added, "unless there's a stage going to Mountain View."

"Nope, nothing that way." The grizzled fellow shook his head. "You can rent a rig right across the street—Parsons' Stables. Tell him Fred Hoskins sent you. He'll give you good rates." He peered over his steel-rimmed glasses, sizing Amos up. "You from the city?"

"Am now. But I grew up in Stone County."

"Ho! You tell Parsons that! He's an honest man, but he does favor his own folks."

An hour later Amos was driving a pair of spirited grays out of Fort Smith. "I'm glad you got a covered carriage, Amos," Rose said, glancing over her shoulder at the children who were playing in the back.

As usual, it was Maury who was making up games and demanding she be allowed to change the rules. At three, she was a year younger than Jerry and had come into the world with a crown of flaming red hair and a temper to match. Jerry was sitting patiently, allowing Maury to have her way. He was dark, with his mother's crow-black hair and green eyes. Seeing her look around, he asked, "How long will it take to get to Grandma's?"

"A long time," Amos spoke up. "If you get sleepy, wrap up in the blankets and take a nice nap."

Both children spoke at the same time—Maury's defiant "I'm not going to take an ol' nap!" and Jerry's cheerful "Sure, Daddy."

Rose and Amos exchanged rueful smiles. But in less than two hours, the carriage ride had lost its novelty, and the night's sleep they'd missed, along with the rhythm of the road combined to lull the children to sleep.

Amos was silent, and Rose didn't intrude on his thoughts. They knew each other so well, in any case, that she had no need to ask how he was feeling. The telegram that had come had been blunt, in the fashion of mountain people: *Come home. Mama is dying.*

As soon as they had heard, they had bundled the children up and had caught the first train out of New York. Now, as they made their way through the foothills of the Ozarks, her husband, Rose knew, was berating himself for not having visited his people in over a year. She watched him covertly, though he was so lost in his world of thought he would not have seen her gaze.

Finally she could not keep still any longer. "Amos, don't blame yourself. Mr. Hearst has kept you so busy. You couldn't have gotten home when you were off all over the world."

Amos turned to her, a deep furrow creasing his brow. He studied her, then found a small smile. "Know me pretty well, don't you?" He put his arm around her and drew her close. "How about a little kiss now that our chaperones are asleep." He kissed her. Even after more than five years of marriage, Rose still felt like a girl when Amos embraced her. She pulled away, happy to have brightened his mood. "I'm praying for your mother," she said. "We've seen God do great things, Amos."

"Yes, we have." He sighed and shook his head. "She's been sick so long, though. I wish I could have talked them into moving to a drier climate—Arizona, maybe."

"She'd never leave the hills, Amos. You know that."

They made good time, the children waking up at noon. Stopping at a country store, Amos bought crackers, cheese, and pickles, and when the owner said, "Got some of them new drinks—Coca Cola," Amos ordered four of them. "You all headed far?" the storekeeper asked.

"Just north of Mountain View . . . over in Stone County," Amos replied. At that, the four loafers who were sitting around the potbellied wood stove looked up curiously. "My people live on a farm . . . Will Stuart's my father."

"Do tell . . . Will Stuart!" one of the loafers piped up. "I've played with your pa at many a dance. Let's see, you'd be Will's oldest boy, but I disremember your name?"

"Amos Stuart."

"'Course! Well, now this is extra fine. Goin' home for a visit, are you?"

Amos glanced at Rose, then nodded. "Yes. I haven't been home in a year."

"You watch out for that brother of yourn." The man nodded knowingly. "That boy is a *hoss!* Plays the banjo better 'n any man in Stone County."

"Does pretty good with the girls, too," put in one of his cronies with a snort. "Him and Horace Wayfield had a rambunctious fight over to Baytown over that Perkins gal—the oldest one."

"Wasn't her a'tall! It was the middle one—Trudy!"

The two argued that out, then the first speaker said, "Anyhow, Owen whupped the tar outta Horace! Didn't think there was a man in the hills could do that."

Amos smiled briefly as the men jawed on about Owen's

exploits, and he realized they were carefully refraining from mentioning his father's own adventures.

After lunch, Amos loaded his family into the buggy and drove the grays hard to make up the time. The roads were frozen, and the ruts caused the buggy to bounce roughly.

Finally, they pulled up over the last ridge. "There it is," Amos said. Though the children were excited, he was dreading what was to come. His lips tightened. "I just hope we're in time."

Owen was waiting for them as they pulled up to the cabin. He had been all day, and now he stepped forward, towering over Amos. He put out his hand, crushing his brother's hand in his massive palm. "Glad you got here, Amos," Owen said. "And you, too, Rose."

"How is she?" Amos was almost afraid to ask, but Owen nodded soberly. "Still holding her own. Come on inside."

"Is Lylah here?" Rose asked as they moved toward the cabin.

"Not yet. She called Johnson's store. Said she'd be here in the morning. She was way out to California."

The main room of the cabin was full to overflowing. His father wasn't in the room, but all of Amos's brothers and sisters came to greet him. He was shocked at how much they'd all grown. Logan, at nineteen, was the smallest of the boys. He had rich chestnut hair and his mother's dark blue eyes. The boy greeted them shyly, as always, then stepped back. At thirteen, Lenora had been a child—now at age fourteen, she was fast becoming a woman in the way of mountain girls. Gavin, twelve, was the "black" Stuart, a throwback to his father's grandmother, and Christie, eight, was as blond as Gavin was dark.

After Amos and Rose had greeted them all, Owen said, "Come on in. Ma's been asking for you."

"The children—?" Rose asked tentatively.

"Bring 'em in." Owen nodded. "Ma wants to see them."

He turned and led the way to his parents' bedroom, followed by Amos, Rose, and the children. A single lamp burned on a walnut washstand, and Will Stuart got up at once and came to them.

"Amos—Rose—" He gave them an awkward embrace, then said huskily, "Glad you made it, boy!"

He was a fine-looking man, Amos thought, little changed despite his fifty-three years. His face showed signs of recent strain, but it had always been his wife who bore the brunt of the responsibility in the family.

"She's awake, Amos," Will said and stepped back to let his son advance to the bed where his mother lay.

Beneath the quilt that covered her, her body seemed scarcely to make an indentation in the feather tick. Was she breathing? Amos could barely make out the slight rise and fall of her frail chest.

"Ma? It's me—Amos." He saw her eyes open, and she smiled up at him. "I–I'm glad I got here, Ma."

Marian Stuart should have died three days earlier, but she had told the doctor sternly, "I won't go until I've given my blessing to Amos and Lylah—and that's that!"

She reached out with a thin hand, the blue veins startling against the ivory skin, and stroked his face. "I knew . . . you'd come, son," she whispered. Her hand was so light on his face, like a feather, and Amos bit his lip. "Tell me . . . are you still following Jesus?"

"Yes, Ma. He means everything to me and Rose."

Rose came forward, still holding the children's hands. "Amos is the best husband in the world, Marian," she said. "You taught him well. No man was ever more thoughtful of his wife and family than Amos Stuart."

For one instant the sick woman's eyes moved to her own husband, and Will Stuart dropped his head, his lips trembling. But Marian's words were for the children. "You big people go away," she said. "I have something to say to my grandchildren. Something private . . . just between us."

Amos smiled, and they all filed out of the room.

"What is she telling them, I wonder," Will asked, pacing outside her door.

Just as he spoke, Owen held up his hand to signal silence. "Listen!" They all broke off, listening hard. "It's a car coming, I think." Owen had always had the keenest hearing of any man Amos had ever known. "May be the doctor. He's got one of them automobiles."

Owen moved to the door, and the others followed him. An automobile was no novelty to Amos or Rose, but few of them had yet penetrated the hills of Arkansas. Automobiles were rich men's toys, for the most part. Still, it looked like a man named Henry Ford had come up with a way to make them less expensive. Just two years ago, in 1903, Ford had founded his little company, and Model A Fords were beginning to be seen all over the country.

"That's not the doctor," Owen said as the machine crested the ridge and came chugging down the rutted road. It was almost dark, and only when the automobile was twenty feet away did he grin and shout, "It's Lylah! Drivin' that contraption her ownself!"

It *was* Lylah, Amos saw, and when the racket of the engine stopped and she got out, he joined the rush to greet her.

"Now don't eat me alive!" Lylah laughed, hugging them all—or trying to. "My lands, Pa!" she gasped, giving them an appraising look. "What have you been feeding this bunch!"

"Cold water cornbread and possum, Sis!" Owen put his hands under Lylah's arms and lifted her high, then spun her around as she squealed.

When he set her down, she looked up into his face and shook her head. "Owen, you'd better stay in these hills, because those city girls will grab you for sure!"

She let them lead her into the cabin. "You boys . . . bring the packages in. I missed your last two Christmases, so I brought presents enough to make up for it!"

But as soon as she stepped inside, Lylah turned to her father. "Did I get here in time, Pa?"

"Yes." Will nodded. "She's . . . just been holding on to see you and Amos." He stared at this flamboyant daughter of his, never quite able to believe that she was part of him. She had left home with a raw kind of beauty, but not like this!

Lylah had fought her way to the high ranks of the world of the theater—not that Lillian Russell and Maude Adams were worried. Still, Lylah had starred in two very good plays with long runs, and producers always mentioned her name when it was time for casting a play.

She stood out in the cabin like a peacock among yard chickens, her wealth of auburn hair and strange violet eyes taking their breath away. Even in New York, Amos knew, she commanded attention in any crowd.

But now the violet eyes were hollow from lack of sleep, and lines of fatigue tugged at the corners of her full lips. "Can I see her, Pa?"

"Sure, Lylah." Will nodded. "She's with Amos's young 'uns right now. Sit down and rest for a minute."

Lylah stretched her back. "I've sat down halfway across this country. My bottom's dead!" She saw the shock on the faces around her and laughed. "I see I'll have to watch my language around here."

Will got her some coffee, and they all hovered around her. She told them about some of the exotic places she'd been, and Amos and Owen smiled at each other.

When she finally slowed down, Owen spoke up. "I remember when you left here to go to Bible school, Lylah. I caught you smoking a cigarette out behind the barn."

A giggle rippled around the room, and Will smiled faintly. "Seems like a million years ago since you left here, daughter."

Lylah gave her father an odd look. "Yes, it does, Pa."

They stayed up all night, or most of them did. The younger children went off to the sleeping loft, and Amos and Rose were assigned the only other full-sized bed.

But Amos and Owen and Lylah sat beside the fire most of the night. Amos told of the war and the Boxer Rebellion, making little of his own role. Rose and Lylah moved to Marian's bedroom in shifts, taking care of the sick woman's needs.

Morning came and with it the neighbors. Amos and Lylah had forgotten how it was with hill people.

Amos shook his head. "They feud like cats and dogs . . . but when one of their own is in trouble, there's nobody like them!"

One of the first to arrive was a woman of no more than thirty, a widow named Agnes Barr. She came into the cabin with a great deal of energy, insisting on cooking a meal. "These children have to be fed, Will," she said firmly. "Now you just sit down and let me take care of things."

"Who is she, Owen?" Lylah asked quietly.

"The widow Barr," Owen said, and both Lylah and Amos turned to stare at him, for there was a bitter edge to his voice. He said nothing more, but it was enough.

When Amos and Lylah were alone, she said fiercely, "She's one of Pa's women, Amos! I could *kill* her for coming here at a time like this!"

"You don't know that, Lylah," Amos protested weakly. But he knew Will too well, and he'd seen the guilty look on his father's face.

"She's after Pa!" Lylah snorted. "I knew it as soon as I saw her!"

And though Will Stuart made a few feeble attempts to get Agnes Barr to leave, they could all tell his heart wasn't in it. Agnes was a full-bodied woman, lush and ripe, and though she would be fat and blowsy in a few years, right now she had an animal magnetism men like Will could not resist.

Finally Lylah could stand it no longer. At one o'clock, she marched up to the woman. Amos was alarmed. What would his sister do?

But Lylah had certain skills against which Agnes Barr was helpless. "Thank you for your help, Mrs. Barr," she said sweetly, taking the woman's arm and propelling her toward the door. "The family needs to be alone now. Don't bother to come back. We'll make out somehow."

Lylah did not miss the poisonous glance she received from the woman, but it lasted only a moment. Then Mrs. Barr composed herself and replied, "Of course. I was about to leave. Will . . . send for me if you need me."

The air was thick for a moment after the woman left, but then Owen whispered loudly to Lylah, "I was hoping you'd knock the heifer down with a stick of stove wood!"

Just after midnight, Lylah came into the main room, her face twitching in a spasm of grief. "Come on . . . she's going—"

They jumped to their feet. Amos found that his legs were trembling and was grateful when Rose slipped her hand into his, whispering, "I'm here, Amos!"

They circled the bed, and at first they thought they were too late. Marian's face was smooth, not lined as it had been for years. The evidence of pain was gone from her features, and she looked almost like a young woman again.

Will was sitting beside her, his face working, tears running down his cheeks. Marian slowly opened her eyes, and when she saw him weeping, she said, "Will . . . I love you!"

"Oh, Marian . . . I've been—"

"Don't say it, Will. It's all right. We've had a fine family. Be a good father to them, Will."

Stuart dropped his head and clenched his teeth. He knew they all thought of him as a failure—which was true enough— for he was a weak man. He'd intended to change—to be a good husband and father—but now it was too late.

Marian looked slowly around the circle, taking in each face, studying it carefully. She began speaking of her love for them all, calling every name, giving each one a kind or encouraging word. She sounded almost prophetic, like Jacob blessing his children, Amos thought.

Finally she said her farewells to the younger children, then asked for her three oldest to stay.

When only Owen, Lylah, and Amos were left, Marian began, "Amos, my firstborn . . . you're so much like me. Take care of the little ones. The world is getting worse . . . it will take a strong man to keep them safe . . . promise me!"

"I promise, Ma!"

Marian kissed him, then turned to Lylah. Her eyes were luminous, and she spoke in a whisper. "You have chosen a hard way, daughter. But my God has told me that you will find your way back to him."

Lylah put her head down on the shrunken bosom and wept wildly. It was Owen who picked her up, and then Marian took his free hand. She held it for a long time, and the only sounds in the room were Lylah's muted sobs.

"Owen—," the dying woman whispered, "you've had to pay the price for holding the family together. You're the one who wanted most to see the world . . . but you stayed and helped your father and me. You've been bitter, son, but God is going to reward you greatly—" Her breast heaved as she struggled for breath, and she lifted herself up in the bed, gasping. "Owen, my son, never . . . be bitter."

Then Marian Stuart gazed on her children one last time. She smiled, her face more serene than they had ever seen it. She closed her eyes, calling, "Jesus . . . Jesus!" And then she slumped back against the pillows.

Will cried aloud and fell on her body, weeping. But Amos, Lylah, and Owen knew that their mother was at last free from pain and grief, as she had never been in life.

"Let us never forget," Amos whispered as he held his mother's worn hand, "how well she endured her going forth."

17

NIGHT AT THE CARNIVAL

L ylah . . . I've got to talk to you!"
Amos had come to the Minerva Theater where Lylah was rehearsing for her new play, *Girl of the Golden West*. He had waited impatiently in the wings until the scene was over, then took her arm as she came to him.

"What's wrong?" she asked at once, noting his look of agitation.

"I've just received a letter from Pa," he said. "He married that woman—that Agnes Barr."

"He *couldn't!*" Lylah exploded. "And Ma not in her grave two months!" Anger swept over her for a moment, then she sighed. "Yes, I guess he could, Amos. I knew it was going to happen. She was after him even while Ma was dying."

They stood there, angry and bitter, each knowing that nothing good would come of the marriage. "She'll make life a nightmare for the kids," Amos said gloomily, "and there's nothing we can do about it."

"I'll write to Pa," Lylah said as Amos turned to go, "but he's a fool where women are concerned." She hesitated, then looked at her brother, a dark wisdom in her violet eyes. "I'll tell you something else, Amos," she said in a hard voice, "Agnes Barr's the kind of woman who can't let men alone. You mark it down . . . inside of six months, she'll be cheating on Pa!"

Lylah was right–and wrong. Agnes Barr did not last even six months before she grew restless. She loved dances and insisted that her new husband take her to every party within fifty miles of the farm.

At first, Will was delighted with this arrangement, for he had always felt guilty over leaving his family to play his music. But Agnes just smiled and ran her hand through his hair. "We're lucky to have older children to stay home and take care of the young ones, honey. Besides, we're still on our honeymoon!"

After two months of chasing around frantically to every barn raising and dance in Stone County and some even farther away, Will Stuart began to feel his years. "We've got to settle down, Agnes," he said wearily after the pair returned from a three-day circuit, where he'd played every night. "I can't ask the boys to do all the work . . . and the house is a wreck."

"It won't kill your kids to clean the house," Agnes said, tossing her hair. "And those boys are big enough to work the place."

Will stared at her, but he had learned that Agnes wasn't as gentle and agreeable as he'd thought. Still he was a man who hated confrontation and merely said, "Well, I've got work to do. I'll take you to the dances close by . . . but we can't go way over to Fort Smith every time there's a frolic."

Agnes had made a quarrel of it, finally storming off for a visit with one of her old girlfriends, Ada Thomas. She'd stayed overnight, and at supper Will had been silent, saying only, "Your ma's gone for a visit. Be back tomorrow, I expect."

Owen stared at his father, but said nothing.

Later that day Lenora confided in her brother. "Owen, I don't like her. She's mean! I wish she'd stay gone forever!"

Owen put his arm around the fourteen-year-old, unable to offer much comfort. "We'll just have to get along with her, Lenora," he said slowly. "The more you cross her, the worse she'll get."

"I wish Ma—" Lenora broke off, tears springing into her eyes, then pulled out of his embrace and ran away, sobbing.

For all practical purposes, Owen had managed the farm for years. Not that Will Stuart was a poor farmer, but his heart simply wasn't in it. It had been Owen who had planned everything, and most of the time he had taken care of the finances—such as they were. His first clash with Agnes came when she demanded to handle the money.

"That won't do," Owen said evenly. "You don't know how to buy seed or how much to ask for cotton at the gin."

Agnes went off in a huff, and later that day, Will came to Owen with a hangdog expression on his face. "Son, I guess we'll have to let her handle things now."

As Owen predicted, Agnes soon spent all their cash on clothes for herself and ran up a big bill at the store for useless notions. So he threw himself into spring plowing, trying to ignore the misery he could see in the faces of his brothers and sisters. Owen didn't mind hard work, and as long as he was busy, he could think of other things. Mostly he thought of travel, of seeing things in the big world beyond the Ozarks. He'd read every travel book he could get his hands on and thought longingly of what it would be like to see the world, as Lylah and Amos had. The names of cities fascinated him, and he would put a map on the floor and stare at it for hours, reading the names of the rivers and mountains and small towns. Agnes laughed at him and called him a fool for dreaming of places he'd never see, and he put the maps away, looking at them only when she wasn't around.

And she was away much of the time. She began going to parties on her own, and once, when Will refused to go, she ventured to the county fair. Owen discovered from some of his friends that Agnes even went to some of the dances with her old friends. He suspected that his father knew this, too, but Will never mentioned it.

As the days of summer grew longer, Owen became more and more restless. He began to drop in on some of the dances, where he was always welcomed for his music. He took his younger brother Logan with him on some of these excursions, and the two of them grew close. It occurred to Owen that Logan had the same feelings for him that he himself had had for Amos when he was growing up.

Dale Truman, the science teacher at the school in Mountain View, was a particular friend of Logan's. He'd pointed out to Will Stuart that the boy had a fine head for math and science and urged him to send his son to the university at Fayetteville. Such a thing had been out of the question, of course, but Logan did frequently spend weekends with the teacher.

Late one Friday night, when Logan was away, Owen was sitting at the table poring over maps, when he heard a team approaching. His stepmother had gone to town, and everyone else was in bed. Rising at once, Owen picked up a lamp and went out on the front porch.

"Owen?"

"Yes. Who is it?" Owen stepped to the ground, held up the lamp, and recognized Dale Truman. "What's wrong, Mr. Truman?"

"It's Logan. He's been badly beaten." The teacher, a tall man of about forty, leapt to the ground and hitched the team to the porch railing. "I got Doc Willis to patch him up, and he gave me some morphine to kill the pain. I dosed him pretty good, so we may have to carry him in." The two men moved to the back of the wagon and together picked up the unconscious boy.

"Let's put him on the couch, Mr. Truman," Owen said when they got him inside.

They laid Logan down, and Owen stared at his face. The boy's eyes were swollen shut, and his lips were puffed out. "Who did this to him?" Owen asked from between clenched teeth.

Truman shook his head sadly. "It wasn't a local fight. A carnival came to town this morning . . . sort of a medicine show. I took my family and Logan. There was the usual sideshow, and one of the acts was a man called Iron Mike. He performs feats of strength—bending iron bars, picking up weights, that kind of thing. Then there's a boxing match. Mike takes on anybody in the crowd who's game. Anyone who can last three rounds with him gets fifty dollars."

"And Logan took him on?"

"Yes. I wasn't there when he did it, Owen. I was on the merry-go-round with my children. But someone told me what Logan was doing, and I ran over to the tent to talk him out of it." Truman shook his head. "I was too late. The fight had started. It was awful! He cut Logan all to pieces! He could have knocked him out any time, but he wanted to hurt him!"

Owen nodded, a thoughtful look in his eyes. "The carnival . . . will it still be in town tomorrow night?"

Truman stared at the young man, understanding at once what he intended to do. "Don't try it, Owen," he warned quickly. "That fighter outweighs you by thirty pounds and he's strong as a bull." Then he saw that his argument was falling on deaf ears and sighed. "Yes, it'll be there."

"Thanks for bringing Logan home, Mr. Truman. Will you stay the night?"

Truman declined, explaining, "I've got to get back to my family." Reaching into his pocket, he pulled out a brown bottle. "If the pain gets bad, give Logan a couple of drops of this. He didn't lose any teeth, but he's got a couple of bruised ribs, so make him lie in bed for a few days."

After the schoolteacher left, Owen got a blanket and made himself a pallet on the floor beside the couch. He slept on it very little, however, for a cold fury was building in him. The Stuarts suffered from their quick tempers, but Owen had never before been filled with anger. That night, however, he understood how a man could kill.

The next day, Logan was better. He was able to eat some hot mush and drink a little fresh milk.

Will Stuart was furious—not so much with the man who had wrecked Logan, but with the young man himself. "Don't

you have bat sense?" he demanded, shaking his finger at his
son. "The man's a professional brawler! Nobody's got a
chance against him in the ring!"

"Well, Pa," Owen said, angry enough to challenge his father, "you'd better not bet on that . . . because I'm going to
that carnival tonight and whip his tail!"

Will stared at Owen and knew at once that argument was
useless. His second son, he well knew, was easy to manage,
agreeable to a fault. But once his back was up, there was no
changing his mind. The family all grew quiet, and Will studied his son's set jaw. Finally he grinned, saying, "All right. I
haven't been to a carnival myself for many a year. We'll all
go!" He looked over at Logan. "If you can make it, son, you
can go too. I'd like you to see your brother in action."

The children were ecstatic, and there was no more work
done that day. They all piled into a wagon, and on the way to
town, Will wondered if he was doing the right thing. "If that
feller starts cutting you up for fun, Owen," he said as they
pulled the wagon up at the edge of the field where the carnival was located, "I'll put a spoke in his wheel!" He pulled
back his coat, and Owen was startled to see the butt of the
Colt .44 in his belt.

"You can't do that, Pa!"

Will shrugged. "Oh, I won't kill him . . . just mebbe shoot
a leg off his carcass."

At that moment Owen felt closer to his father than he'd
ever felt. "You're a caution, Pa!"

Then they all got down, and for an hour, the Stuart youngsters had the best time of their lives! Neither Gavin nor
Christie had ever seen a carnival, and Logan and Lenora,
though they had been once before, had never ridden a ride.

Again Owen felt a warm feeling for his father when Will
said, "I've got a little cash I've been saving, kids. We're going
to ride every ride and eat everything they got! Come on!"

Owen stayed with Logan in the wagon while the family

explored the carnival. "I'm right proud of Pa, Logan," Owen said once. "The young ones will never forget this."

Logan peered at his brother through puffy slits. "Neither will you if you get in the ring with Iron Mike, Owen. Don't do it." He winced as he moved on the wagon seat. "I know you've licked everybody in this part of the world, but he's different. He knows lots of tricks."

Owen grinned at Logan. "Maybe it'll be your turn to sit up with me, baby brother." He sat loose and easy in the wagon, not in the least nervous.

Logan, though tall and wiry, weighed no more than 140 pounds. Owen himself weighed 185 and was hard as nails. He had never lost a fight, for he was quick as a cat and tough as boot leather. He was aware that he would take some punishment, but that didn't matter. He had a strong sense of family and knew he'd get in the ring with Iron Mike if he died for it.

It was growing dark as the family came back, and his father gave him a worried look. "Owen, Mr. Truman told everybody what you're planning to do. I think the whole town's here to see the fight."

"Well, let's go give it to 'em," Owen leapt to the ground lightly, gave Logan a hand down, then led the way to the tent where the barker was already beginning his speech.

"Step right up!" he cried in a shrill voice. "Colonel Franklin Fletcher's world-famous show now offers for your entertainment . . . Iron Mike! The strongest man in the world!"

A heavyset man wearing a purple robe stood on the platform and looked over the crowd with a contemptuous sneer on his thick lips. About forty, he was past his prime, but when he dropped the robe and bent an iron bar, Owen saw that though he had some fat around his middle, he was still a powerful man.

When the crowd went inside to watch Iron Mike and the other performers, Logan explained, "When this is over, he'll offer to box anybody in the crowd."

Owen took the children inside. Before long he himself was fascinated by the thin Greek named Populis, who rammed a sword down his throat. "Ah, that thing folds up in the handle!" jibed a man in the front row. Populis smiled and removed the handle, then handed it to the man for his inspection. When he handed it back, satisfied, Populis swallowed it again, and the crowd laughed at the scoffer. The performer lit a torch and, for his grand finale, put the flaming brand in his mouth, bringing a scream from Lenora.

Owen was amused at the acts, some of which seemed very good. He especially enjoyed the three young women dancers. But it was Iron Mike whom he watched most closely. The strong man bent a spike in his hands, put ten men from the audience on one end of a rope, then laughed at their efforts to upset him. He lifted massive weights, and the muscles of his thick body writhed like serpents.

Finally the show was over, and Owen moved outside and found his father and the others. Truman tried once more to persuade him to reconsider. "Owen, you're crazy to try this. That pug will cut you to pieces!"

But Owen only shook his head, and at that moment the barker began his spiel. "Now Iron Mike has a challenge for you sporting men. Fifty dollars in hard cash for any one of you gentlemen who can stay just three short rounds with him! Which one of you needs fifty dollars? Step right up and be a hero to your lady friend!"

"Go on, Owen!" somebody shouted. "Beat the sucker's head off!"

Owen moved to stand before Iron Mike. The fighter's tawny eyes reminded him of a tiger. "Better go home, sonny." The man grinned, exposing yellow teeth, and he peered at Owen more closely. "You the brother of that kid I pounded last night?"

"Sure am."

"I heard you was comin'." Iron Mike laughed and said to the barker, "Hey, Sid, we got us a grudge match here. I whipped this hayseed's brother last night, so he's come to take his revenge on poor old Mike!"

The man named Sid brightened at once. "Come up here, young man," he cried, not failing to hear the cheers that went up. Apparently many of the boy's friends were here, and the barker smelled money to be made. He quickly learned Owen's name and made much of the fact that he was a home-town boy. There was little need for his pitch, though, for the crowd was ready.

"Fifty dollars for only three rounds," he repeated.

"I've got thirty dollars here says I stay," Owen said. He then looked at the fighter and asked, "You got any money, bum?"

"Why, you—"

Owen shrugged. "Put up or shut up."

"Cover him, Sid," the fighter growled from between clenched teeth.

"I'll just hold the stakes . . . and the fifty dollars." Sid turned to see a big man with a star on his lapel climbing up on the platform. "I'm Sheriff Peek. Let's have that cash . . . and I'll be watching to see that we have us a square fight."

Sid threw the fighter a despairing look, but he had no choice. He handed the money to the sheriff, and Owen did the same. But when Sid was close enough, he muttered under his breath, "Mike, let him stay and take the purse and the bet."

"What?" Mike grunted in shocked anger. "I'll kill that kid!"

"You can kill him in the *second* bout," Sid whispered rapidly. "Look, we can clean up, Mike! If he wins, he'll be cocky. You can challenge him, and we'll put up big dough. Then you can let the hammer down on him."

Iron Mike shook his head stubbornly. "Nothin' doin', Sid! He's a punk kid and I'm going to tear his head off . . . after I rough him up!"

A pretty girl in a brief spangled costume appeared. "I'll show you where to change, big boy." Owen recognized her as one of the dancers in the show. She led him to a back section of the tent and gestured toward a trunk. "Find yourself something in there." Then she touched his arm and gave him a coy look. "If you win, you and I might do some celebrating."

Owen grinned. "Suits me. What's your name?"

"Cecily."

She left, and from a pile of dirty clothes, Owen dug out a pair of short pants that fit him. He went at once to the tent where a boxing ring was set up—the first he'd ever seen. Except for the ring itself, every square inch of the space inside the tent was occupied. He shoved his way through the crowd, receiving a pat on the shoulder from some of the men, an encouraging word from others.

The amber glow of the lanterns overhead bathed the ring in pale light, and Owen saw that a big man dressed in a white suit was waiting with Iron Mike.

"I'm Colonel Franklin Fletcher, my boy," he said in a sonorous voice. "It will be my pleasure to referee this bout myself."

Fletcher, Owen saw, was a drinking man, albeit a handsome one. He was at least sixty, six feet tall, and portly. He looked much like Buffalo Bill, Owen thought, with his long white hair, mustache, and goatee.

The preliminaries were simple. After the gloves were on, Colonel Fletcher simply told them to fight fair. Then he stepped back, and a bell clanged, signaling the beginning of Round 1.

Iron Mike came roaring out of his corner, leading with a left, which was only a feint, for he threw a tremendous right that would have broken Owen's neck if it had landed. But it didn't land. Owen simply pulled to one side and let the burly fighter sail by. Iron Mike hit the ropes, and whirled at once as the crowd shouted at him.

He stared at Owen, then nodded. "You're fast, kid. I'll remember that."

Owen watched as the big man lifted his hands and came

at him flatfooted. He was an old hand—no doubt about that—completely confident in his skills. Sure he was overweight, but good enough for the yokels he faced each night. He was a knuckle-scarred man, flat of lip and flat of nose, with cruelty in his yellow eyes. Owen watched him plant his feet solidly, anchored by his vast bulk, and Owen began to circle the fighter at a distance. Suddenly he whipped back in the opposite direction and saw Mike stop and reverse himself. Mike's footwork was slow, and he knew it, for he let out a huge roar and came rushing forward, his head down and his big hands stabbing out in feinting punches. Owen slid by him again, hooked a hard jab into the man's belly, swung from the toes, and caught Mike on the side of the head with a solid right.

The blow would have put most men down, but Iron Mike never lost his balance. Instead, he whirled and struck Owen on the chest with a blow that had a crushing effect, turning him cold. It was a warning of the awesome power that lay in that massive frame, and Owen began to back away, knowing he could not match the man's strength. For the rest of the round, he moved away, dodging and weaving, as Iron Mike threw punch after punch. There was no way to dodge them all, and when the bell sounded, Owen sat down on the stool with sore ribs and a bleeding lip.

His father was there, offering him water from a bottle, and mopping his face. "He's a gorilla, Owen . . . stay away from him!"

"Sure, Pa." Owen studied the massive form of Iron Mike as he rested. *Got to hurt him . . . and got to do it quick. He'll run over me if I don't.*

Getting to his feet, Owen was on his toes like a runner, and when the bell sounded, he leapt across the ring, lifting his right hand and taking the fighter by surprise. Iron Mike, puffing from his efforts to catch up with Owen, came to his feet slowly . . . just in time to catch Owen's right glove in the mouth. All of Owen's weight was behind that punch, and

Mike's head was driven back as if he'd been struck by a railroad tie. He reeled backward, crashing into the ring post.

Sid shoved him forward, hissing, "Get him, Mike!" And though the older fighter was practically out on his feet, his instincts came to his aid.

Owen went in for the kill, but no matter how desperately he tried, he could not finish him off. The old veteran kept him at bay, using the skills learned in a lifetime of brawling. He sparred lightly until his mind cleared, then, holding Owen's gloves beneath his elbows, he suddenly butted Owen in the face with his bullet head.

Fiery lights exploded in Owen's brain, and he felt the bones of his nose crunch. He couldn't see for the tears and knew that he was helpless. But even as he waited for Iron Mike to finish him, a shot rang out!

Someone screamed, and Iron Mike stepped back in alarm. "No! Don't shoot—!" he begged the tall man who was aiming the biggest gun he'd ever seen in his life.

Owen wiped the blood from his face and wheeled around to see his father holding the .44 steadily on Iron Mike. The crowd grew silent, and Will Stuart said softly, "You foul my boy one more time . . . and I'll put you in hell!"

Colonel Fletcher stepped forward at once. "Sir, put the revolver away, if you please. I declare your boy the winner of this round!"

It meant nothing, for Owen still had to go the full three rounds. But he wanted to reassure his father. "It's all right, Pa!" he called out, then turned to face Iron Mike. "You're a dog, Mike!" he taunted.

The colonel stepped back and Mike came at him. A cold fury spurred Owen Stuart, and he moved like a cat, side-stepping the big man's rushes. Iron Mike was not accustomed to this much exertion, and his chest was heaving with the effort. He gasped as he struck out, and his blows, though powerful enough to knock a horse down, were slow and Owen danced aside easily.

The bell rang, and Owen didn't sit down to rest. He wasn't even breathing hard, and when the last round began, he moved toward the burly fighter, catching him with a straight left that stopped him in his tracks. He feinted to the left and, when the fighter moved in that direction, Owen came up with a tremendous uppercut, catching Mike on the chin. His teeth clicked, his head snapped back, and he reeled backward. Owen was on him like a June bug, slashing him with blows from every angle. For the rest of the round, he delivered punches that cut the flesh, then smashed the thick body with a thunderous right.

When the bell rang, the big man was out on his feet. Blood running down into his eyes from cuts to his eyebrows blinded him. A gap showed in his teeth between puffy lips. He kept pushing his gloves forward from sheer instinct, but when the bell sounded, Sid had to come and lead him to his corner.

The crowd went wild, but Owen was watching the old fighter and, in spite of himself, felt pity for the man. Iron Mike had only one thing to be proud of, and Owen had taken that away from him.

Owen made his way back to the dressing room, anxious to escape the crowd, and when he was pulling his shirt on, Cecily came through the tent and smiled at him. "You ready to celebrate with me, Owen?" she purred. Her eyes were slitted, and she reminded him of a feline about to enjoy a saucer of cream as she ran her hand over his chest.

Owen grinned recklessly. "Sure. Why not?"

Afterward he thought of that moment, wondering what his life would have been like if he'd refused the woman and gone home with his family. But there was never an answer for things like that.

He introduced Cecily to his father, winked, and said, "You go on home, Pa. Cecily and me . . . we've got some celebrating to do." Then he put his hand on his father's shoulder—the first gesture of affection he'd shown toward him in years. "Thanks, Pa . . . for what you did for me tonight."

Will felt a moment of pride, and he suddenly wanted to hug this strapping son of his. But he didn't really know how, and merely nodded, "Sure, son. We Stuarts got to stick together." Then he turned and moved away.

Cecily's hand was insistent on Owen's arm. "Come on . . . let's start the celebration!"

The celebration was fine. The two of them wandered around the carnival grounds for a time, Cecily presenting Owen to her friends as if he were a trophy. Then the two of them went to a dance being held in the town square. Owen had never danced with any woman like this! She clung to him, pressing herself against him. And later she produced a bottle of raw whiskey, which she made him sample.

It was potent stuff, and by midnight, Owen was drunk. "Let's get us a place to *really* celebrate, honey!" Cecily said and took the bills from his pocket.

She seemed to know what she was doing, so Owen could only follow her in a daze. He stumbled as she helped him up the step leading to a two-story frame hotel, the Excelsior, and tried to pull himself together as she paid for a room.

Owen's head cleared a little on his way up the narrow stairs, and as Cecily opened the door, he walked in blinking. Someone screamed, and Owen drew back in confusion.

Cecily grabbed his arm and said to the couple in the bed, "Hey, we got the wrong room . . . sorry!"

Owen felt Cecily's grasp as she tried to pull him away—but he could not move. He was drunk, but not so drunk that he could mistake the woman who raised up, covered herself with a sheet, and cursed him vilely.

It was his stepmother, and Owen stood there rooted, unable to turn. The man tried to hide his face, but Owen recognized one of the town's prominent figures—no less than his honor the mayor, Alfred Jaspers, a notorious womanizer.

Owen grew sick, turned and stumbled from the room, with Agnes's screams striking his ears. Ignoring Cecily, he staggered down the steps and left the town, seeking only darkness and a place to hide—someplace to forget what he'd seen.

But he knew nothing could remove the memory of that sordid scene. And as he stumbled along the road, he knew also that he could no longer live in the same house with his stepmother. By the time he reached the house, he knew what he had to do.

Agnes was sly, however. She was home by daybreak and at once retired with Will to the bedroom. The children heard the sounds of an argument, and when the door opened, Will called to Owen, "Son, I've got to talk to you. Come outside."

As they left the house, Owen got a glimpse of Agnes, who was smiling in triumph, and knew that she had concocted some story to clear herself. As soon as they were outside, Owen told Will what he had decided. "Pa, I'm leaving home." He said it to save his father embarrassment, for he knew what the woman had made his father agree to.

Will Stuart looked old and tired. He shook his head, and could say nothing but, "I'm sorry, son. It's got to be."

Owen put a good face on it. He stayed for three days, telling the children that he'd decided to see what the world looked like. When he left, the little ones cried, and the older ones bit their lips to hold back their tears.

He gave Logan thirty dollars he'd won on the fight, saying, "Buy the kids a treat from time to time. I'll send more when I get a job." He had no prospects as he walked away from the only home he'd ever known . . . but he was happy.

He caught a ride from Mountain View to Fort Smith without a single idea in his mind. As they came to the outskirts of the town, the old man who'd picked him up said, "Well, lookee there, bub. Carnival's come to town."

Owen smiled as he saw the banner which read: COLONEL FRANKLIN FLETCHER'S FAMOUS ELIXIR. "Guess I'll get out here," he said. "Thanks for the ride."

The first person he saw when he walked onto the grounds

was Cecily. Her eyes opened wide, and then she grinned. "Come for more celebrating, Owen?"

"No, I've come for fifty dollars."

She laughed. "Already spent it. Maybe we can work out something else. Come on and eat."

Owen followed her to the cook tent and was greeted by none other than the colonel himself. "Why, it's our young friend . . . sit down! Bring this man a steak."

"Watch out for him," Cecily warned Owen. "He wouldn't give you a steak if he didn't want something."

Colonel Fletcher protested, but after the meal, he called Owen over. "Come to my wagon, Mr. Stuart. I have a proposition for you."

"Never mind the wagon. "What's your offer?"

"Why, I've lost the services of Iron Mike, and it's your fault," Colonel Fletcher stated. "Mike decided to retire. So I'd like for you to join our little troupe. If you can lick Mike, you can lick anybody. How about it, my boy?"

Owen thought it over for almost ten seconds. "I'll take it, Colonel."

"Wait a minute, you fool!" Cecily yelped. "Make him pay you more than he paid Mike!"

"Now my dear—"

"Let's you and *me* go to your wagon, Colonel," Cecily said. "I am now this man's manager . . . and I'm saying he doesn't put on one boxing glove until we've talked terms!"

The pair left, arguing about money, but Owen was content. In his mind he could picture the map he'd pored over for years. Now he'd see those little towns and those big mountains for himself.

Owen Stuart was free at last to see the world!

18

ALLIE

The April sunshine warmed Owen as he sat with his back braced against the canvas of the smaller of the two tents. Sleepy and relaxed after having helped set up both tents, he let his fingers run over the frets of the five-string banjo he held, singing softly:

> Shine on, shine on, harvest moon up in the sky,
> I ain't had no lovin' since January, February, June or July.
> Snowtime ain't no time to stay outdoors and spoon,
> So shine on, shine on, harvest moon, for me and my gal.

The new tune by Nora Bayes and Hack Norworth had taken the country by storm, and Owen liked its sentimental flavor. He sang the last line again: "Shine on, harvest moon, for me and my gal," then strummed a progression of chords.

As he plucked out the tune once again, he smiled, thinking how Colonel Fletcher had seized on his musical ability when he had first joined the troupe nine months earlier. "Why, my boy, the Holy Book tells us that we are not to bury our talents, does it not?" And on this righteous foundation, Fletcher had cleverly utilized Owen's fine singing voice and ability to play the guitar and the banjo (with no extra pay, of course!). He had come up with the name 'Kid Nightingale' for Owen, and when Owen joined Sid on the platform, he did as much to draw in customers as Sid's fast patter. He'd sing one of the new fast show tunes, such as "You're a Grand Old

Flag," George M. Cohan's newest hit, or "In the Good Old Summertime," the new waltz everyone was dancing to. Then, after Owen had polished off his opponent, he would slip off his gloves and sing some ballad requested by one of the ladies in the audience—usually a maudlin one, such as "Sweet Adeline."

The colonel knew how to get the most out of his people, and Owen's rugged good looks and talent brought the young ladies— and some not so young ones!—into the tent like lemmings.

It had been, for Owen, a glorious nine months. The hard work of setting up and breaking down the tents and gear, the all-night journeys to the next town, the nightly bouts—often repeated as many as three times to catch all the customers— all of this was child's play to him. Once he even admitted to Cecily, "It's a good thing the colonel doesn't know it, but I'd do this for nothing!" She had stared at him in blank disbelief, saying emphatically, "Don't ever tell that old skinflint, Owen. He'd take you up on it!"

Now as he sat enjoying the fine New England sunshine, he thought of all the small towns the show had reached. Colonel Fletcher had bought four used railroad cars, and the troupe had modified them into sleeping quarters and storage for the equipment, so they had played only towns served by the railroad. Owen thought of them now as he sat strumming his banjo with a practiced hand—the Cajun towns in southern Louisiana, the austere New England towns with their inevitable steepled white churches, the homely towns of Kansas, the blistering villages of Texas and New Mexico, the towns crouched in Colorado under the mighty Rockies. He had soaked them all in, almost gluttonous in his aching desire to see the entire country.

He had saved no money, for what he didn't require for his own needs, he sent back to Logan, instructing him to use it for some fun for himself and the younger ones. When Logan had asked him how he could fight so many tough men, he'd written his brother:

I go two or three bouts every day, Logan. I was pretty tough to start with, and I've picked up tricks that you only get with experience. Most of the men I box with are strong and wild. I let them wear themselves out flailing away, and almost never get hit. Of course, from time to time, a pro sneaks in, and then it's tough, but there's not enough money in it to tempt professionals. The hard thing is having to hit them back. I hate that! What I do is let them fight themselves out, then at the end of the second round, I pound them in the stomach. It takes the wind out of them, but doesn't cut them up.

As he sat there he thought about how much he'd like to go home for a visit, but that couldn't be for at least six more months when the colonel was taking the show south again. Just then his thoughts were interrupted when Colonel Fletcher pulled up in his Model A and heaved himself out.

Fletcher took great pride in his automobile, though his driving skills were limited, and rarely did they leave a town without one of his misadventures putting a fresh scar on the shiny black finish! He'd even had the workers adapt one of the railroad cars so the machine could be carried from town to town.

"Ah, there you are, Owen!" he called out, walking over to hold out a newspaper. "You'll be interested in a piece in this paper, my boy. Front page—an editorial by your brother."

Owen took the paper eagerly. Amos never sent him copies of his work, but he was getting famous, so Owen got them when he could, collecting them in a scrapbook. The story read:

> We are now midway through the decade. Only five years ago people were in awe of the turn of the century, as if the hand of God was turning a page in human history. Cannons were fired at midnight in Berlin to mark the moment, and one listener heard the sound "with a kind of shiver: one knew all that the nineteenth century had carried away; one did not know what the twentieth would bring."

Well—what has it brought?

Violence, for one thing. This new century was born brawling in the Boxer Rebellion, in the Philippines, in South Africa. And every one of the great nations is on a trigger edge, ready and even *willing* to plunge into a war that could engulf the entire world. The fuse is burning, and when the charge goes off, not a single living person on planet Earth will be unaffected by the apocalypse.

We have money and bigness. Morgan, in 1900, bought out Carnegie to form with a hundred other firms the corporate colossus U.S. Steel—the world's first billion-dollar holding company.

But something has gone wrong with the system. The great mechanical and material achievements of the recent past have twisted society out of shape. In a country like America, with its dream of freedom and plenty, 1.7 million children put in 13 hours a day in dark factories for a pittance. Thousands of women live pinched lives, exhausting themselves with 12-hour workdays for which they are paid barely a dollar.

The God of the Old Testament is often inaccurately painted by liberals and unbelievers as a harsh, cruel deity, but he gave commandments that the ancient Jews must leave part of their harvest for the widows and the poor. It is our leaders—men like Morgan, Vanderbilt, and Ford—who must learn compassion for our people!

Owen whistled softly. "Strong medicine, Colonel!"

"Indeed, but all true, every word!" The showman was tremendously proud of having the brother of one of the premier journalists in America in his show and never failed to mention the connection when introducing Owen. He was also a fierce supporter of Teddy Roosevelt, and it was his dream to meet the president someday. "Is your brother still seeing President Roosevelt from time to time?"

Owen nodded. "Yes, he interviewed him last week. I guess Teddy has a soft spot for his old Rough Riders. He doesn't like William Randolph Hearst or his paper, but he likes

Amos." He laughed suddenly, remembering a letter he'd had from Amos in which he related an incident he'd witnessed involving the president.

"Amos said he was with the president earlier this year when he went to Cambridge for his twenty-fifth reunion. President Eliot never liked Teddy, Amos says, but felt obliged to invite him to stay at his house. So Amos went along. He said Roosevelt took Amos to his room, then when the president pulled off his coat, Amos saw a big pistol in his jacket. And he said when they went downstairs and President Eliot asked Roosevelt if they would be having breakfast together, Teddy said, 'Oh, no, I promised Bishop Lawrence I'd take breakfast with him . . . and . . . goodness gracious!' clapping his hand to his side, 'I've forgotten my gun!'"

The story delighted the colonel, who laughed heartily. "And there was the president of the United States rushing off to see the bishop, while the president of Harvard was horrified by the highest official in the land carrying a loaded gun!"

"Which is illegal in Massachusetts." Owen grinned. "Anyway, I wrote Amos that if we ever play anywhere near Washington, he'll have to get us an audience with the president. Amos mentioned it to Teddy, and know what the president said? He said, 'Bully! Capital! And I'll have a boxing match with the young fellow!'"

"He's a fighter, that Teddy Roosevelt!" Colonel Fletcher said, admiration shading his tone.

"Yes, and Amos is afraid that'll get us into a shooting war someday." Owen nodded. "Well, Colonel, guess I'll go into town and pick up a few things at the store."

"Take the Ford, my boy," Fletcher said generously. "It's too far to walk."

"Thanks, Colonel."

Owen had learned to drive the Model A, and it gave him great pleasure to use it from time to time. He had figured out how to crank the engine without breaking his arm and was so strong that it was not difficult for him. He set the spark, gave the crank a mighty pull, then leapt into the seat and manipulated the controls expertly, sending the Ford chuffing down the road that led to town.

As he sailed along, he spotted a hobo jungle set back from the road, close to a small stream, and marked the spot. When he arrived in the town, he parked the Ford and explored the main street. He mailed his letters to Amos, Lylah, and Logan, then ambled back down the street, stopping at the drugstore on impulse.

It was a long, narrow shop, with glass-lined cases around the walls and a long soda fountain flanked by steel stools along one wall. He studied the list of offerings carefully:

SODA FOUNTAIN

Ice Cream Soda	10 cents	Grape Lemonade	15 cents
Plain Soda	5 cents	Orangeade	5 cents
Root Beer Float	5 cents	Lemon Phosphate	5 cents
Sundae	10 cents	Buttermilk	5 cents
Cantaloupe Sundae	15 cents	Egg Milk Chocolate	10 cents
Egg Drinks	10 cents	Coffee	10 cents
Tonic Water	10 cents	Cakes	5 cents

DRUGS

Witch Hazel	25 cents	Corn Plasters	10 cents
Aruica Salve	10 cents	Wart Remover	10 cents
Bromo Seltzer	10 cents	Castoria	35 cents
Wine of Cardui	$1.00	St. Jacob's Oil	25 cents
Cough Syrup	25 cents	Hair Balsam	50 cents

"Guess I'll have a grape lemonade," Owen said. He sipped the sweet beverage, wishing he could buy one for his sisters and brothers and reminding himself to tell Logan to take them all in to the drugstore at Mountain View for a treat.

Owen strolled out of the drugstore and stepped into the general store, which smelled pleasantly of leather, cloth, and fresh vegetables, and spent half an hour picking out a few things. He thought of the hobo jungle and bought some cans of beans and bacon—something he often did, for he liked to talk to hobos.

When he came to the counter, his eyes lit on an advertisement for store-bought cigarettes. There, as big as life, was a picture of Lylah, smiling at him and holding up a package of Bravo cigarettes. According to the caption under her picture, she was saying, "I always smoke Bravo cigarettes! Why don't you try them?"

When the clerk came to tally his purchases, Owen asked, "How much for the picture?"

The clerk blinked in surprise, but grinned and said, "Take it, buddy. Just don't tell the boss." He stared at the picture and shook his head. "She's the cat's pajamas!"

Owen put his supplies on the floorboard, cranked up the Model A, and drove out of town. As he made his way along the road, he saw a broken tree limb stuck in the ground with a tin can on top—the sign of a hobo jungle, Owen had learned from his talks with the tramps. He found the camp beside a small stream, where about twelve men were sitting around while one man tended a large kettle, stirring its contents with a tree limb that had been stripped clean of bark.

"Well, sir, you're just in time for dinner," said the cook. He was a very fat man with a pair of bright black eyes, and he wore castoff clothing, none of which fit, and a black derby on his head.

"We can't feed everybody who comes down the pike!"

Owen looked over to see a hulking tramp glaring at him. The man was a troublemaker, Owen knew instantly, but he smiled and held up the box of groceries. "Something for the pot."

"Why, that's handsome of you, sir!" the cook said. "Very handsome!" He began to pull out the contents, examining them with a flourish. "I'm Wilber Watterson, sir. And you are—?"

Owen gave his name, then sat down and listened as Watterson kept up a running line of chatter. Owen liked to talk with the hobos and had decided that if he ever lost his job, he'd join their ranks. They led a hard life, exciting and dangerous, dodging the railroad crews. But they quickly became expert at begging, learning all the tricks of reaping a harvest from the people of the small towns along the railroad line.

By the time Watterson had finished his mulligan stew to his satisfaction, Owen had most of the tramps pegged. They were all, he saw, afraid of the beefy-shouldered tramp who had challenged him—Red Bennett by name. The man was not old, but his face was cruel, and he would have no mercy on a man, Owen understood instinctively.

"Come and get it, gentlemen!" Watterson called.

Owen stepped aside to let the others go first, then accepted a tin can offered by the cook and ladled out some of the stew for himself. It was surprisingly good, and he said so.

"Ah, Mr. Stuart, when I was a younger man, I was a chef at Antoine's in New Orleans!" Watterson began to eat hungrily, but the food flowing down his throat seemed to have no effect on the words that flowed steadily from his lips.

He was right in the middle of an outlandish story about how he had once entertained the czar of Russia, when he paused abruptly and looked across the camp. Owen turned to see two small figures, obviously tramps themselves, emerging from the woods. They were wearing baggy pants and coats, and both had soft hats with the bills pulled down low over their foreheads.

"Well, now—" Watterson grinned. "Our company is growing all the time!"

"We don't need no kids around here," growled Red Bennett. "You punks beat it!"

The young tramps halted, and Owen saw that the taller of the two could be no older than fifteen or sixteen, and the other nearer twelve. The older one had rosy cheeks and large dark eyes, and strands of blond hair escaped from beneath the soft cap. "We ain't beggars," this one said defiantly. "We got some beans for the pot."

"Get outta here." Bennett scowled. "Kids mean trouble." He swiped at his mouth with his hand and came to his feet when the pair didn't move. "You deaf? I said beat it!"

But the older tramp looked around and spotted Watterson. "Here, take these and put 'em in the pot."

Watterson caught the two cans of beans deftly. "It's okay, Red. No trouble."

But Bennett moved quickly for a man his size. Stepping up to the small pair, he took the older one by the arm and snarled, "You want a fat lip?" Then he struck the youngster with the flat of his hand, the blow making a *splat* as it landed. The blow drove the youngster back, and the soft hat went flying.

All the tramps were shocked to see a mane of yellow hair spilling around the fallen tramp's shoulders, and Bennett exclaimed, "It's a girl!" He moved quickly, grasping the young woman's arm and yanking her to her feet.

She was, Owen saw, a rather pretty girl—or would be if she were cleaned up and fed properly. He got to his feet, sensing trouble.

Bennett began to pull at the girl, grinning broadly. "Why, sure you can stay, sweetheart! We'll have us a party, just me and you—ow!" At that, the smaller tramp had run forward and kicked Bennett on the shin, and the big hobo put him down with one vicious swing.

The girl cried out, her eyes wide with fear. There was no mistaking Bennett's intention, and Owen stepped close and brought the edge of his palm down on Bennett's forearm, knocking the big man's arm downward, so that the girl staggered back.

"Hit the road, Red," Owen said, watching the big tramp carefully. Such men usually carried knives or guns, and he stood close enough to strike again if he saw evidence of either.

But Bennett was confident of his own huge fists and cursed Owen roundly, then struck out with a looping right. Owen barely moved his head enough to let the blow slip by, and while Bennett was off balance, he pivoted on his right foot and drove as hard a punch as he'd ever thrown in his life at the man. The force of it started in his right foot and traveled up his leg, where the V-shaped torso channeled the surge of power into the swelling deltoid muscles. His arm moved forward like a piston, exploding on Bennett's mouth with a fearful power. It was even more devastating, for it caught the big man coming in.

A solid meaty sound accompanied the blow, and Bennett's head was driven backward. He dropped to the ground with blood frothing from a split lip, and he lay on the ground, his legs twitching convulsively in the dust.

For one moment, there was total silence as the tramps stared at the bulky form of Red Bennett. Then Watterson whooped and did a little dance. "By gum! Never thought I'd see the day! John L. Sullivan ain't got nothin' on you, son!"

Owen stared down at Bennett's broken figure, then turned to the two young people. "He's going to be mean when he wakes up. You two better come with me."

There was no argument, and Owen said to Watterson as he turned to go, "If Red gets any ideas about getting even, tell him the next time, I'll break his neck."

"Don't think he'll be in shape to do much along those lines, Mr. Stuart." Watterson grinned. "He'll be thinking more about his teeth!"

Owen walked back along the path in silence. Only when he got to the car did he speak again. "What's your names?"

The girl had picked up her cap and was stuffing her hair under it. Her dark blue eyes were fixed on him. "My name's

Allie Dupree, and this is my brother Joey." She eyed the car, and when she turned back to face him, she squinted with suspicion. "Thanks for what you done . . . but it don't get you no place with me!"

Owen studied her thoughtfully. Even the baggy clothing did not conceal her rounded figure, and he sensed her bitter distrust of men—a distrust born of experience, no doubt. She had a square face and a determined chin, but there was nothing masculine about her, for her features were delicate and smooth.

"Okay." He shrugged indifferently and moved to crank the car. It started at once, and he got in. "Good luck."

But when the car jerked forward, the boy whispered something to the young woman, and she cried out, "Wait!" Owen stopped the car and turned to her, his brow lifted questioningly. "Well . . . maybe we could use a ride."

"Sure. Pile in." Owen waited until they had scrambled into the front seat, the boy in the middle. "You ever drive one of these things, Joey?" he asked, looking down at the boy, who was a smaller edition of his sister, with the same blond hair and dark blue eyes.

"No . . . but I'm going to someday. I'm going to learn to drive and work on automobiles."

Owen laughed at the determination in the youthful tone. "Maybe the colonel will let you practice on this one," he said, the youngster's eyes moving to meet his instantly. "Well, here we go—"

Owen had no plan for the pair past getting them out of the hobo camp and away from Bennett. But he saw that they were both hungry and, as soon as they got back to base, he took them into the cook shack. "Couple of visitors, Colonel."

That was all it took, for Fletcher could be a generous man. He waved them to a seat, and Owen sat beside Joey, who gulped his food down hungrily, then asked, "Can I go look at the car, mister?"

"Sure . . . but don't start the thing." Owen smiled. And

when the youngster vanished as if by magic, he turned to the boy's sister. "He sure does like machinery, doesn't he, Allie?"

The young woman had eaten with more mannerly reserve than Owen had expected. She was finishing her second piece of pie and now looked over at him, her eyes softer and more vulnerable than before. "I–I'm sorry about what I said . . . you know, when you offered us a lift." She bit her underlip in a feminine gesture, adding, "It's just that . . . I've had to fight off lots of men."

Owen nodded. "No offense, Allie. I'm glad I was there to help." He sipped his milk. "Where do you think you'll head now?"

Allie's shoulders drooped, and she shook her head. Fatigue was evident in every line of her body, and Owen thought he saw her shoulders shaking as if she were crying. *Poor kid's about past going! She can't be much older than my sister Lenora.* He sat there studying the girl, then came to a decision.

"Look, Allie," he said, "why don't I ask the colonel if you can hang around for a few days with the show?" Then he quickly added, "Always lots of work with a show like this. You could earn your bed and board until you get rested up."

He watched the girl grow very still and feared at first that he had offended her again. But then she turned to face him, and he saw tears spilling out of her eyes and running down her cheeks. Hastily, she yanked out a dirty handkerchief and wiped them away. Then she cleared her throat and said huskily, "Thank you, Mr. Stuart. I guess . . . Joey and me are about ready to drop—"

"Been there myself, Allie," Owen said. "You have another piece of pie, and I'll fix it up with Colonel Fletcher."

The matter was not hard to arrange, for there was plenty of work, and when Owen assured the owner that the pair would pull their own weight, Fletcher agreed at once. "But they'll be your responsibility, Owen," he warned.

"Go get Joey, Allie," Owen said when he returned. "I'll

find you a place to sleep." He saw the relief flare in her eyes, and soon he had located a spot and some bedding.

He introduced them to the others, who had a cheerful word for the pair. All but Cecily, who stared at Allie with a calculating expression. "Got yourself a lady friend, Owen?" she asked later when she found Owen alone.

"Oh, Cecily, she's just a kid!"

"Oh, yeah? You're either blind or stupid, Owen Stuart!" she snorted, and whirled around, leaving him puzzled.

Just before Joey went to sleep, he asked hopefully, "Can we live with these people for a while, Allie?"

"I hope so, Joey." She stretched out on the spot and whispered, "Mr. Stuart . . . he's a good man, isn't he, Joey?" But her brother was already asleep, so she closed her eyes and joined him.

19

"I'M NOT YOUR SISTER!"

Allie and Joey quickly made a smooth transition to carnival life. They were both keenly alert, strong, and unafraid of hard work, so that by the end of the second week, they had made a place for themselves with Colonel Fletcher's troupe.

Joey proved to be handy with anything mechanical, able to fix almost anything that was broken with little or nothing in the way of tools. He explored every nut and bolt in the few rides the show carried and became adept, not only at setting up and dismantling the rides, but also at patching them together with wire or whatever was handy. He was a bright, cheerful lad and became a favorite almost at once.

With Allie, it was a little different. She was touchy, especially where men were concerned—a trait that Cecily professed to find hypocritical. "She's just putting on airs," the dancer told Owen. "You have to watch that kind more than any other."

"Aw, the kid's had a rough time, Cecily," Owen said. "I'm glad to see she's not one of the easy kind."

As soon as he made the remark, he knew it was the wrong thing to say. Cecily flared up immediately. "Oh, and I *am* easy, is that it?" she raged at Owen. But both of them knew she had been exactly that—easy—and without any guilt over their affair.

Allie never knew that the reason she had little trouble from the hands was because Owen had spoken to each of them with a smile and an implied threat. "I'm responsible for Allie and Joey," he had explained firmly. "Just thought I'd pass it on, because I'd sure hate to have trouble with any of you guys." His casual comment was taken seriously, for nobody wanted trouble with Owen Stuart.

As soon as Allie found that she was safe from unwelcome attention, she relaxed. And when it was discovered that the young woman was an excellent cook, she moved into the role of assistant chef. "Not as good as me, no," Beaudreau admitted to Colonel Fletcher, "but she is one big help, you bet!"

Other talents began to emerge as the show rolled on, and soon Allie was busy mending costumes, selling tickets, operating one of the concessions, and doing the less strenuous chores involved in setting up and taking down the equipment.

Three weeks after the youngsters had joined the show, Owen sought her out one day as she sat outside the sleeping car, sewing a patch on one of his shirts. Looking up quickly, Allie smiled. "Hello, Owen. I've got your shirt ready."

"You don't have to work on my old clothes, Allie," Owen protested, taking the garment. He examined it, then nodded, pleased with the work. "Can't hardly see the tear! My ma could sew like that."

He squatted down beside her, and as they talked, covertly studied the girl. Allie had never worn a dress since joining the show, and he supposed she didn't own one. Besides, he reasoned, it would have been unwise for a girl to have worn a dress in the hobo jungles, and Owen figured she had deliberately chosen to dress in shapeless men's clothing to lessen the danger.

Today, however, a hot August sun was beating down on the parched ground, and Allie had shed the dark coat and rough trousers and was wearing a thin, worn tan cotton shirt and a pair of faded boy's pants. The youthful curves of her body were startlingly evident to Owen. "How old are you, Allie?"

Looking up, she saw him staring at her and flushed. "Almost

sixteen." She bit off the thread with sharp white teeth, put the needle and thread into the sewing kit, folded the shirt, then turned her dark blue eyes on him. "Why?"

"Just wondered." He looked over to see what Joey was arguing about. The boy was talking to Leo Miller about the merry-go-round, and his voice carried across the distance. "If we cut these rods shorter, Leo, the blamed thing won't keep breaking down like it always does. Now look—"

Owen grinned and nodded toward the pair. "Joey's quite a mechanic, isn't he?" Then without waiting for an answer, he came out with what he'd come to say. A pleased light was in his eyes, and he turned to watch the girl's face as he said, "Got a surprise for you, Allie."

Allie was immediately on guard. "What is it?" She had been out in the world long enough to consider every offer a man might make as suspect.

Owen understood this and kept his voice light. "I had a talk with Colonel Fletcher about you and Joey. He's generous in some ways and tight as a jug in others. I told him the two of you ought to be paid, and after he got through arguing—just out of instinct, I think—he agreed to pay you ten dollars a week, apiece." He saw Allie's eyes open wide and was pleased. "Not enough for what you two do—but we'll negotiate a raise from time to time."

Allie was suddenly ashamed of her suspicions. She knew Owen must have seen the stubborn, wary expression on her face and realized that he'd seen a lot of that side of her. *He's so big and strong I've been afraid of him*, she thought, trying to think of a way to say what she felt. *I've been expecting him to bother me all this time, like the others . . . but he's never even once tried to touch me.* Joey had told her she was an old grouch around Owen, adding that she needed a thrashing after all the big man had done for her. Now she suddenly realized her brother was right.

"I . . . Joey and I, that is—" She floundered helplessly, aware of Owen's warm blue eyes on her, and finally met his gaze and blurted out, "I'm sorry for the way I've acted for the last three weeks. I've been an ungrateful pest!"

Owen was surprised, but rallied quickly. "Oh, you haven't been that bad, Allie."

"Yes, I have, too! I've treated you like all the rest who try to—" Allie flushed, unable to finish, then she took a deep breath that swelled the front of her thin shirt. "I guess I've lived with my guard up for so long it's just hard for me to let myself be friends with any man."

"I know. And I admire you for it, Allie, the way you've kept yourself straight and taken care of Joey. Why, not many—"

"What's the conference about?" Cecily had emerged from the sleeping car and, seeing the pair, came to stand over them. She was wearing a bright red dress, a wide-brimmed white hat, and a pair of extremely high-heeled red shoes.

Allie got up at once, her eyes cautious, and Owen joined her. "I just talked the colonel into putting Allie and Joey on the payroll. Reminded him how Lincoln had freed the slaves."

"Yeah? That old skinflint actually came across?" Cecily snorted. She stared coolly at Allie. "Watch out for that old goat, kid. He don't throw money around for nothing."

Owen saw that Allie was not going to answer, so he spoke up. "You going to town, Cecily? Hey, Allie, let me give you an advance on the princely salary you're going to be drawing. Get Joey, and the four of us can go buy the stores out."

Cecily stared at Owen. "I did enough baby-sitting before I left home. See you later." She flounced away, headed for the center of town.

Owen sighed. "Well, how about it, Allie?" Then he said idly, as if he'd just thought of it, "Hey, maybe we can get you a pretty dress or something."

Allie understood at once that he was trying to offer her a way to buy some new clothes without hurting her feelings. "Oh, I don't need a dress, but I'd like to see the town."

"Come on then." Owen nodded. "Let's pull Joey out from under that merry-go-round and go see the sights!"

Joey was more than willing, and the three of them walked to Main Street, where farmers had come in from the country with their vegetables. The wide street was crowded with wagons and a smattering of noisy automobiles.

Owen advanced Joey enough money to buy himself a set of used wrenches—the beginning of a large set of tools. And although Allie protested at first, she was persuaded to buy a few personal things. Then Owen found a beautiful ivory comb and brush set and, over her protests, insisted on buying it for her.

When he had paid for it and handed it to her, saying, "Pretty hair like yours deserves to be treated with care," Allie's cheeks turned pink, and she could only murmur, "Thank you, Owen!"

They had ice cream at the drugstore, then as they were on their way out of town, Joey spotted a sign and cried out, "Look! A nickelodeon! Can we watch it, Owen?"

Owen agreed, but as they drew near, he saw that something was different. "Hey, this isn't a nickelodeon!" he exclaimed. "This is that new kind of picture show—moving pictures!"

Thomas Edison and George Eastman had invented a machine that produced motion pictures back in 1899, but they had to be viewed individually, the viewer turning a crank while looking though a porthole of sorts to see the short films. The nickelodeon craze had spread quickly, every city installing the machines in parlors, where patrons could watch the films—people sneezing, walking, swimming, or other physical activities—but there was no story involved. Edison himself foresaw no widespread use of the invention, but a man named Edwin Porter in 1903 had been struck by a brilliant idea: *Why not tell a story—and show the picture on a screen where a roomful of people can see it?*

"The Great Train Robbery!" Joey read the sign with excitement. "See a cast of forty, starring George Barnes as the Wicked Train Robber!"

Owen was amused at the boy's eagerness, but paid the admission, and the three of them walked into a small room with a white sheet stretched across the wall. They took their seats, and soon the lights dimmed and the flickering forms began to enact the drama.

It was a simple story, involving a train holdup, but nothing like it had ever been seen. When Barnes capped the action by aiming his gun directly into the camera and firing, several people scrambled to get out of the way. Joey yelled in alarm, "Look out!" And Allie grabbed Owen's arm with a gasp. Then it was over and Allie quickly released her hold, embarrassed.

"Looked real, didn't it?" Owen grinned as they walked outside. "My sister Lylah thinks it'll put real theaters out of business. She's an actress and claims she's going to get in on the ground floor of this new kind of thing." He shrugged. "I don't guess it'll ever get very big, though. Not like a real show."

They made their way back in time for Allie to help with the evening meal. Owen was preoccupied with the show, and that night he took on a huge man—one with no skill, but he was so tough that it took all Owen had to put him away. In the process he got a cut over his left eye. "Let me put some plaster on that," Allie offered when the match was over. She led him to the cook's tent where the first aid kit was kept and said bossily, "Now, you sit down and let me wash that out."

Owen, accustomed to ignoring small injuries, grumbled, "It's not worth fooling with." But he allowed her to bathe the cut with a strong antiseptic. "Ow!" he yelped as the alcohol touched the wound. "That's worse than the cut!"

"Be still . . . you're worse than Joey!"

As Allie worked on the cut, her face was no more than a foot from Owen's, and he saw that her skin was as smooth as anything he'd ever seen. She was intent on the job, and her lips were pursed delightfully. *Going to be a fine-looking woman someday*, Owen thought.

"You're as good at doctoring as my sister was," he said when she had finished, patting her shoulder awkwardly. "Pretty nice, having a sister again to take care of me."

Allie was putting the first aid kit away, but when she turned to look at him, she had an odd expression on her face. Her full lips grew taut and she said distinctively, emphasizing every word, "I'M NOT YOUR SISTER!"

She left the tent, her head high in the air, leaving Owen to stare after her. "What's got *her* back up, I wonder?" he muttered.

In the small cubicle she shared with Julie, one of the dancers, Allie got ready for bed, then sat down in front of the mirror fastened to the wall. Picking up the velvet-covered box Owen had bought, she took out the brush and comb, admiring the delicacy of the workmanship. Pulling out the pins, she let her hair fall free and began to comb it.

I'll use some of the rainwater we saved and wash it tomorrow, she thought. There was a sensuous pleasure in pulling the brush though her thick hair, and she studied her reflection as she worked. She considered the image with something like embarrassment, for she had not been interested in her appearance for a long time.

What she saw was a young woman with honey-colored hair cascading down her back, the bluest possible eyes, and a firmly rounded bosom. A thought came to her—secretly and without warning—and it moved her so greatly she impulsively lifted one hand to touch her burning cheek. She shook her head, half angry with herself for the thought, and put the comb and brush set away.

She turned out the lamp and lay there in the stifling cubicle, thinking of the afternoon and how much Joey had enjoyed it. That pleased her, and she smiled. *Owen will help him*, she thought, and found a great deal of security in the knowledge that all the burden for her brother was no longer rest-ing on her shoulders. Her last thoughts were of Owen and the musky scent of him as she'd worked on the cut above his eye. But the memory of how it had affected her was unsettling, and she put it out of her mind and drifted off to sleep.

The summer seemed to fly by for Allie. She had never been so content—at least not since her childhood days. The show moved across the northern states, and as October brought the hint of winter in its brisk winds, Colonel Fletcher turned his eyes toward the warmer climates. By November, they were tracing their way along the Gulf Coast of Texas, moving eastward until they arrived at Pensacola, Florida, a week before Christmas.

Neither Allie nor Joey had ever seen the ocean, and it was Owen who took them to the beach. A few brave swimmers were daring the white-capped waves, and Owen asked, "Want to try it?"

"No!" Allie replied firmly. Eyeing the bathers, she said in a prim tone, "I wouldn't be seen in public dressed like that . . . or *un*dressed, you might as well say!"

Owen stared at the figures on the beach, noting that the costumes covered the women almost as thoroughly as a dress. "Looks to me like those girls are wearing *too many* clothes, Allie." He grinned as she sniffed, adding, "They've got on more than Cecily and the other girls wear when they're dancing." This didn't make Allie any more sympathetic, and he decided that her tastes were just too refined for a brute like himself.

A week before Christmas, Colonel Fletcher called the troupe together. "I've decided to cancel our bookings for the next two weeks. We've been at it too long without a break. I'm giving you all a little Christmas bonus, so Merry Christmas . . . and be back on January 6!"

Owen had caught a glimpse of Allie's face as the Colonel was making his announcement and had seen the dismay that washed over it. Quickly he went to her as she and Joey were turning to leave. "Hey, this is great! Now we can all have Christmas together at my home place, just like I told you."

Allie and Joey stared at him blankly, and Owen snapped his fingers in a gesture of annoyance, "Well, I'll be! I forgot to tell you, didn't I?"

"Tell us what, Owen?" Joey asked.

"Why, I've been making plans for you two to go home with me . . . to Arkansas," Owen lied with a straight face. "Didn't want to say too much, 'cause I wasn't sure the colonel was going to let us off. But I *did* mention it, didn't I?" he asked anxiously.

"No, you didn't," Allie said evenly. "It's nice of you, but we wouldn't want to impose on your family."

"Why, they're *expecting* you both!" Owen had been a man to deal strictly in truth, but was fast discovering that he had a rare and rudimentary talent for lying and pure deception. He spoke quickly, spinning his web of deceit even tighter. "Well, if you don't want to go, I guess I can't make you. But my folks will sure be disappointed! Come on, now, we can have a great time! Joey, you ever shot a deer?"

"No—"

"I guarantee you a six-point buck!"

Owen couldn't have been more accurate with his aim, for all he had to do was sit back, and by the end of the day, the pair had come to look him up. "Joey is driving me crazy," Allie said. "I can't let him go alone. So . . . if you really want us to come . . . I guess we can."

"Great!" Owen said. "We'll get a train out of here tomorrow." He rushed off, sent a wire to Logan, which cost a great deal of money because he had to explain his lies, and wound up with another one. "Tell them you've been expecting them. Tell the older kids and Pa to give them a big welcome."

They caught a passenger train out of Pensacola the next morning, and as it pulled out of the station, Owen grinned and draped his arm around Joey's shoulder. "Better riding inside than on the rails, isn't it, Joey?"

"Yeah, it sure is!"

It was a difficult trip, but they were travel-hardened by now. They crossed the Mississippi delta, the endless cotton fields bearing nothing but dried sticks, then turned west across Arkansas. Stopping in Little Rock, they changed trains and, late on a Friday night, pulled into Fort Smith.

"Too late to go to the place tonight," Owen said. 'We'll get a room and try to catch a ride to Mountain View tomorrow morning."

The hotel clerk at the Arkansas Hotel had plenty of rooms, but he hesitated, not knowing what arrangements the trio might want. His was a delicate and sensitive task, and finally he gave up and blurted out his question. "One room, or two . . . or three?"

"One will do us, I guess," Owen said. He signed the register, and the three of them walked upstairs to room 214. He opened the door and stepped back. It was a nice enough room, much better than their quarters in the train—a double bed, a washstand, a walnut chest.

Owen threw his suitcase on the floor, then sat down and tested the bed. "I've slept on worse."

Allie was nervous, not liking the arrangements. She was ashamed to complain, though, and was tremendously relieved when Owen glanced at her and said, "Tell you what, Allie, you and Joey take the bed. I'll go liberate a cot and some blankets. You two can wash up and hit the sack. I guess you're pretty tired of sitting on those hard benches."

When Owen left, Joey undressed and fell into the bed, going to sleep at once. Allie quickly undressed and put on a flannel nightgown, one she'd borrowed from the cook's wife. It was too large for her, but warm, and she sat down to brush her hair. She had almost finished when she heard the key in the door. She made a dive for the overcoat Joey had gotten from one of the hands and managed to get into it just as Owen came through the door with a roll of blankets.

"Not in bed yet?" he asked in surprise. "You're not as tired as I am, then."

"I—I wanted to brush my hair," Allie stammered. "It hasn't been brushed in two days."

"Get busy then, Allie." Owen nodded. He began to make a pallet on the floor, and when it suited him, he sat down and pulled off his shoes. He was tired, but paused to watch Allie comb out her long hair. The strands had a golden sheen in the yellow glow of the lamp, and he admired how it lifted like fine silk as the comb went through it. There was something graceful about Allie's actions, as she drew the comb again and again through her hair.

He grew sleepy and lay down, saying huskily, "Knew you'd find a use for that comb and brush. Good night, Allie."

She hurriedly put up her hair, then rose to turn down the light. Seeing that Owen was sound asleep, his deep chest rising and falling, she allowed herself a moment to study his face. At rest, his features were relaxed, and he looked very young, she thought. The blanket had fallen off, and she carefully lifted it and placed it across his chest. At her touch, his eyes opened slightly, and he muttered, "Thanks, sister."

Allie looked down at him and her lips compressed into a thin line. "I'm not your sister!" she muttered, then turned the lamp out and fell into bed, asleep almost before her head hit the pillow.

The visit was a resounding success, better than Owen had hoped.

Joey got his deer, a fine buck, and Owen knew he would never forget the sight of the boy kneeling beside the animal.

He was about to speak of it to Allie late one afternoon. The snow had fallen, and she was delighted with it, insisting on accompanying him as he walked to check a small trap line Logan ran. They found nothing in the traps, which pleased Allie.

"I hate to think of those poor animals caught in those

awful things!" she said as they walked back through the woods.

Suddenly Owen reached out and grabbed her arm. She looked up in surprise, then glanced in the direction he was staring. Her heart almost stopped, for not thirty feet away, a mountain lion had dropped from the limb of a tree. He was an elegant animal—clipped ears, green eyes, a beautifully shaped head. Struck dumb at the sight, Allie could not move, except to lean against Owen weakly.

The great cat stared back at them with all the arrogance of a Nero, then turned and padded away silently.

"Beautiful!" Owen breathed, then glanced down at her. "Didn't scare you, did it?"

"Y–yes!" Allie gasped. "I've never seen a lion . . . not even in a zoo."

Seeing that she was trembling, Owen was instantly attentive. "Let's sit down on that log." He didn't mention the lion, but told her about Joey getting the deer until she grew calmer. "You know, I don't have one of those cameras that make pictures. But I've got something better, Allie. When I see something I like, I study it and try to remember it. Then I sort of put it in a secret room in my head, and when bad things happen, I go to that little room, and I look at my pictures—all the nice things that have happened. And now I know if I live to be an old man, living in a shack without a soul to care for me, I'll go to my room of pictures and see Joey beside that deer, his eyes like stars."

Allie gazed at him and whispered, "That's really nice, Owen." She got to her feet, and he rose with her. Then, jamming her hands in the pockets of the coat she'd borrowed from Logan, she cocked her head. "But you are a terrible liar, Owen Stuart." She smiled at the shock registering in his features. "You never wrote your people to ask if Joey and I could come, did you?"

"Why . . . sure I did—" Owen said weakly. Then he saw

her shaking her head and knew it was no use. "Well, I *meant* to!" he muttered. "Who told you?"

"Your stepmother."

Owen's face clouded and bitter words sprang to his lips, but he bit them back, saying only, "I'm sorry, Allie. She's not a . . . hospitable woman. My real ma would have loved you." He kicked at the snow, then looked at her. "Are you mad? About my lying?"

"No. Everyone has been so nice . . . well, *almost* everyone . . . your father, your brothers and sisters. I'm glad we came."

Relieved, Owen reached out to draw her close in a hard embrace. He smiled down at her. "I just decided to put another picture in my room, Allie—one of you when you were watching that lion. Your lips were open and your eyes were bigger than I've ever seen them." He tightened his grip, adding, "That'll make a great picture for my little art gallery, Sis."

Allie stiffened. "Owen Stuart . . . you are so—!"

"I'm so . . . *what*, Allie?" Owen asked, when she broke off.

Allie bit her lip, then took his arm. "You're the nicest man I've ever met . . . and the peskiest! Come on, I'll race you to the house!"

When they got ready to leave the next day, Logan drove them to Fort Smith in the wagon. At the station he shook Joey's hand, then said to Allie, "Don't be a stranger, now. Make him bring you back in the spring." He caught her off guard by leaning forward and kissing her on the cheek.

As they were pulling out of the station, Owen grinned at Allie. "Watch out for that one. He'll probably come courting you."

"Why don't *you* court Allie, Owen?" Joey piped up.

"Why I'm old enough to be . . . to be—"

Allie gave him a disgusted look. I know . . . you're old enough to be my *brother!*" she snapped. "Too bad I have to travel around with old man Stuart . . . tripping over his beard!"

The train clattered along, breaking the solitude of the mountains from time to time with shrill shrieks of the whistle. When they got back to Pensacola, Owen said cautiously, "Are you mad at me, Allie? Did I do something wrong?"

"No. Everything is fine," Allie said, summoning a smile. "It was the best Christmas we've ever had, Joey and me. We'll never forget it." She saw the relief soften his features and added, "You're a kind man, Owen Stuart. Not too bright in some ways . . . but you're young enough to be taught."

"Sure, Allie," Owen nodded, not understanding her, but happy that she was not angry any longer. "It's great to have you and Joey with me. Just like brother and sister, aren't we?"

She stared at him and nodded with resignation. "Yes, Owen, just like brother and sister."

20

Wings of Silk

Amos Stuart had taken off his coat, but the blistering sun beating down on the giant ditch that stretched out before him was closer to earth than he was accustomed to. Mopping his brow with a soggy handkerchief, he trudged along with his fellow reporters, silently resenting the natives of Panama who, by contrast, seemed cool and comfortable. *Like to see how they'd make out in a New York snowstorm* was the thought that occurred to him.

By now, he'd nearly covered the world, having become known as William Randolph Hearst's star reporter for the *New York Journal*, and when he'd been ordered to write a story on The Big Ditch, as the Panama Canal was called, he'd told Rose and the children good-bye, which was getting harder since they were older—Jerry now seven and Maury six. And slogging along in the sticky mud produced by a thundershower that morning, Amos found himself rehashing a familiar theme—*Got to leave this globe-trotting to the young fellows. Man with a family can't do what he's supposed to do, traipsing all over the world!*

The group halted, and as one of the officials situated them in a reserved section just under a huge mechanical digger, Amos mentally reviewed the history of the Canal. People had dreamed of connecting the Atlantic and Pacific oceans for hundreds of years, and in the nineteenth century there were a number of unsuccessful attempts to construct a canal across Central America. The Spanish-American War had demonstrated such a need. Amos remembered that during the war the American battleship *Oregon* had been forced to steam all the way around the tip of South America to join the Atlantic fleet.

When Roosevelt decided to forge ahead with the project, two sites were proposed—one across Nicaragua and Costa Rica, the other through Panama. The three countries had competed for the location of the Canal, and Panama had won. Amos had tried to convince the public that they were using scare tactics, primarily by distributing Nicaraguan stamps that illustrated volcanic activity in that country.

As Amos was lost in his thoughts, the man who was responsible for The Big Ditch appeared—President Theodore Roosevelt himself. He was wearing a white suit and a sun helmet, and as he passed by the press corps, he greeted them as always, baring his teeth in a smile and waving his hand. Then he saw Amos and came close enough to say, "Stuart, need to see you for a minute after we get this business out of the way."

The other correspondents cast resentful looks Amos's way, and Richard Harding Davis, Amos's chief rival, demanded, "How is it you always have these nice private little chats with Teddy, Stuart? What have you got on him?"

"Simple, Davis." Amos smiled blandly. "It's because my heart is pure."

A shout of derision went up from the other reporters, but they all settled down when Roosevelt climbed up into the cab of the giant steam shovel and, for the next hour, played with the monstrous machine with obvious delight.

Amos moved closer to Davis. "Look at him, Richard . . . like a boy with a new toy! And that's exactly what he is— partly, anyhow. He's been a great president, and a lot of his success has been his enthusiasm. Whether it's boxing or hunting big game or breaking up trusts like Standard Oil, Teddy gives it everything he's got."

"I think you're right, Amos." Davis nodded in agreement. "It's going to be pretty dull for fellows like us after Novem-

ber." A look of disgust crossed his face. "Who could make a
story out of Taft? The man weighs three hundred pounds and
never did an exciting thing in his life. Our headlines will read:
PRESIDENT TAFT EATS ENTIRE WATERMELON!"

"You think Taft will win?"

"Win? Why, Teddy handpicked him!" Davis snorted.
"Amos, you know as well as I that anybody Roosevelt en-
dorses will win." He sighed and gazed fondly at his leader.
"He's been the only lovable president this country has ever
had . . . and he'll likely be the last."

"Don't worry, Richard," Amos said. "He'll be back. The
only reason he's not running this term is that he promised not
to. But you wait until 1912—Teddy will be in that race if he
has to crawl up out of a sick bed to do it!"

After the ceremonies, Amos waited around until the president was free and motioned to him. "Stuart, I've got some
big things to do . . . and I need some help," Roosevelt said in
his typically blunt fashion.

"You need help getting ready for the election of 1912, Mr.
President?"

Roosevelt bared his teeth and laughed heartily. "That's
what I've always liked about you, Amos," he said, "always
ahead of the pack. What I want is someone to follow me
around and help me write my biography. Want to tackle it?"

Caught off guard, Amos's mind was blank for a moment.
It was a great opportunity, but he knew at once he couldn't
do it. "Mr. President, that's the best offer I've ever had," he
replied, "but I'm tired of roaming. I'm going to get a steady
job and stay home with my wife and children."

Roosevelt was genuinely disappointed, but shrugged in acceptance. "We both have that problem, Amos. I miss my family every day I'm gone." The two men shook hands, then the
president asked, "What's your next story?"

"The Army is interested in the Wright airplane. There's
going to be some kind of trial of the thing in Fort Meyers,
Virginia, right away. Mr. Hearst wants me to cover it."

"Bully!" Roosevelt burst out. "That invention will change the world, you mark my words!" He turned and left with the other officials, and Amos went to his room to pack.

As his ship pulled out of Panama that afternoon, Amos thought of the president and felt a great sadness. *We'll never have another president like Teddy Roosevelt.*

"Aw, Owen, it's only a few miles from here," Joey begged. "If you'd borrow the colonel's automobile, we could see the flying and be back in plenty of time for the show tonight."

Owen stared at the boy, who stood before him with a determined expression on his face. Joey had gotten up that morning, all excited about the story he'd read in the newspaper—Orville Wright's new airplane was scheduled to be flown on September 17, 1908 at Fort Meyers, which was only ten miles from Cooperville where the show was set up.

Owen was tired and preoccupied and said rather shortly, "The colonel won't let us have his car. He's going to use it himself for some advance stuff he needs to do."

"No, he ain't," Joey said stubbornly. "He's going to go tomorrow. He told me his own self he wasn't going to go." He turned to see Allie approaching. "Allie, you got to make Owen take us to see that airplane over at Fort Meyers!"

She was amused. "I'm not his boss, Joey."

"He'll do it if you ask him . . . he always does everything you ask him to do!"

Owen blinked at the outrageous statement and said resentfully, "Oh? Is that what you think, Joey? Well, we'll just see if she can make me." He turned to face Allie and folded his arms, glaring at her. "Go ahead . . . let's see if you can get me to Fort Meyers."

Allie had no desire to go see the airplane, but she loved to manipulate Owen. It was so easy! He was so partial to her and Joey that he would do practically anything they asked, and now she was determined to get him to change his mind.

She allowed a look of disappointment to crease her smooth

forehead. She moved closer, looked up at him, and blinked her enormous eyes, having learned long ago that he was fascinated by her eyes and thick lashes. She knew also that he hated to disappoint her. "Oh, Owen, don't pay attention to Joey," she said. "He's never satisfied, no matter how much you do for us." Then she sighed and turned away. "It's just that—" she began with a little catch in her throat. "Well . . . never mind."

"What is it, Allie?" Owen asked anxiously. "Something wrong?"

"Oh, no, Owen," Allie said quickly. "It's just that I've never seen an airplane. But . . . we'll see one someday, I suppose." She reached up and pushed a lock of his hair back from his forehead. "You look so tired. Why don't you go take a nap." She sighed heavily. "Come on, Joey, leave Owen alone, you hear me?"

"Now wait a minute—" Owen said, and then blustered, "It just happens that *I've* been wanting to see one of those blamed things myself!" He reached out and thumped Joey on the head. "I was thinking about going over there all the time. Now let this be a lesson to you, Joey," he said sternly. "You can't always have your own way about everything. Now I'm going to see if the colonel will let us have the automobile, and if he won't, the whole thing's off!"

When Owen stormed off, Joey winked at his sister. "Boy, he sure taught *me* a lesson, didn't he, Allie?" He gave her an admiring look. "Don't ever tell Owen to stick his head in a fire. He'd just up and do it if you said so!"

"Oh, hush, Joey!" Allie scolded, then giggled in a girlish fashion. "Poor Owen. We manipulate him something awful, don't we?"

"Sure!" Joey grinned. "And we make him do what we want, too!"

Joey got his first glimpse of the famous Orville Wright almost as soon as they got out of the car. "There he is!" he whispered loudly, staring wide-eyed at the man in the natty suit and black derby hat who was standing beside what seemed to be a huge box kite. "Can I go take a closer look, Allie?"

"Well, I guess so . . . but don't get in the way."

As Joey raced down the slight slope toward the airplane, Owen shook his head. "I wouldn't go up in that thing if they gave me a million dollars! Looks like a man could put his fist through it without half trying."

Owen was exactly right about that, for the plane was made of lightweight wood, covered with fabric. Basically it was the same type of craft the Wrights had used to make the first powered air flight in 1903, having two wings and a "tail" that protruded in front rather than extended toward the rear. A small gas engine drove two propellers by means of a bicycle chain, and the craft carried two men sitting upright, rather than one man lying flat on his stomach.

Joey moved in closer, and when one of the Army officers who spotted him said roughly, "Kid, get out of here—," he nodded and simply changed positions. But the officer slipped around on the other side, and Joey was suddenly pinioned by a large hand closing on his neck.

"Just a minute, Captain—" Orville Wright had seen the boy's capture and walked over to investigate. He was, Joey saw, a dark-skinned man with a jet black mustache. Despite his rather grim expression, Wright's lips turned up in a slight smile. "Well, young fellow, I guess you've been caught in the act."

"Yes, sir," Joey whispered meekly. Then he spoke up. "You can do it, Mr. Wright! I know you can! You just show these army men how it's done!"

Wright laughed aloud and addressed the officers who had gathered around. "I hope you gentlemen heard that!"

One of them, a lieutenant named Thomas Selfridge, agreed with Joey. "You're right, young man." He put out his hand, and the soldier who had been holding Joey released his hold. Selfridge gripped the boy's hand, a smile on his face.

"Guess you'd like to be making this flight in my place, wouldn't you, son?"

Joey swallowed hard, and a defiant gleam lit the sky blue eyes. He nodded. "Yes, sir, I sure would ... and someday I'm gonna be a flier, too!"

The men laughed, and Orville Wright was pleased. He had been worried about the flight, and he missed his brother Wilbur, who was in Le Mans, France, demonstrating a flying machine to the French authorities. The boy's sudden appearance had driven away some of the gloom that had oppressed him all morning.

Now he stood chatting with Joey for a few minutes. "I hope you do become a flier, Joey. When you get a little older, come and see me and my brother. We should be able to find a place for a bright young fellow like you."

Joey stared at the famous inventor, his face pale and very serious. "I'll be there, Mr. Wright. Save a place for me."

His earnestness made Wright smile. "Lieutenant Selfridge, why don't you show this budding young eagle our airplane while I talk to these gentlemen?"

From the slope above, Owen and Allie had watched the scene with some apprehension, but when it became apparent that Joey had made a place for himself, Allie smiled. "He's in heaven, Owen."

"Hey . . . Owen."

Hearing his name called, Owen turned to see his brother Amos running toward him, waving his hands. "Amos!" Owen cried out, and Allie watched as the two men came together, shaking hands awkwardly. Then she saw Owen reach out and pull the smaller man forward in a bear hug. "Doggone it, Amos! Never expected to see you here!"

Amos gazed up into Owen's bronzed face, almost overwhelmed by his younger brother's size and strength. "You young Hercules!" he exclaimed, admiration in his tone. "What in the world are *you* doing here?"

"The show I'm with is in a town about ten miles from here."

Owen was experiencing a peculiar feeling as he looked down at Amos. In his mind's eye, his older brother had remained much larger physically, and it seemed strange to see that Amos was so—so *small!* But Owen let none of his conflicting emotions show in his face and, remembering that Allie was looking on, he turned to her. "Allie, this is my older brother, Amos Stuart. And this is Allie Dupree, Amos. She and her brother are with the show. The three of us came over to see the flying."

"Nice to meet you, Miss Dupree." Amos smiled. He was curious about the girl, who seemed to be very young, but asked no questions. "What do you do with the show?"

"Oh, I just help out here and there, Mr. Stuart," Allie said quickly. Then she changed the subject. "I've read so many of your articles. Owen keeps them all in a scrapbook and makes us all listen while he reads them out loud . . . oh, I didn't mean—!" she broke off in embarrassment.

Amos gave a delighted laugh. "That's all right, Miss Dupree. Better a captive audience than none at all."

"What are you doing here, Amos?" Owen asked. "Writing a story on the airplane business?"

"That's it. Airplanes are going to be really big, I think, so I wanted to get in on the beginning."

As the two brothers stood talking, Allie felt more and more out of place. "I'm going to walk around for a while," she announced. "I'll keep an eye on Joey, so you two can talk."

"After the flight we'll go get something to eat." Amos smiled. "I want to warn you about this baby brother of mine." When she walked away, Amos asked at once, "Who is she, Owen?" He listened as his brother told him how he'd found the pair and how the colonel had given them a job.

"How old is she?"

Owen stared at him, then said curtly, "Too young for what you're thinking, Amos. She's just a kid."

At once Amos saw that he'd overstepped his bounds and began to talk about Lylah and the folks. Gradually, Owen relaxed, and soon the two men were deep in conversation, keeping one eye on the flying machine.

Allie moved around among the small crowd that had gathered, never taking her eyes off Joey for long. There were far fewer people than she had expected, and she soon went over to stand beside a wagon that was drawn up near one of the outbuildings. As she leaned back against the wheel, a voice called out, "Hidee, Missy!"

Allie looked up quickly and saw a small man in a faded jacket, peering at her from the seat. He got out of the wagon slowly, every movement evidently painful, and when he was on the ground, he lifted a cane from the wagon and limped over to stand beside her. He could have been anywhere from forty to sixty, Allie thought. His hair was thick and his eyes were bright, but his skin was wrinkled with age or weather.

"The name's Ivory Bill Parker," he introduced himself. "Come to see the show, did you?"

"Yes. Will it be soon, do you think?"

"Ought to be, but Mr. Wright's got to please them officers." He leaned back against the wagon, grimaced with pain, then shook his head. "Sure is tough, a man like me having to cripple around."

"Did a horse throw you?"

"No, *that* threw me!" He jerked his thumb toward the back of the wagon, and Allie looked inside, seeing only a very large basket and piles of some kind of colored material. "Don't you know what that is, missy?"

"No. What is it?"

"Why, it's a balloon!" Parker shook his head sadly as he considered the basket. "Wish I'd never seen the blamed thing!"

Allie had seen several balloon ascensions and had been tremendously thrilled by them. Once in Topeka, Kansas, a man named Harkness had been hired by Colonel Fletcher to perform. The crowds had increased dramatically, for Harkness had not only ascended in his balloon, but had jumped out of it with a parachute.

An idea began to form in Allie's mind. "You fell out of your balloon, Mr. Parker?"

"No, I jumped too soon and broke both legs, missy. Been laid up for near four months. 'Bout drove me crazy! Just let me get back to Texas, and you won't see me in any more of these fool things!" He was a talkative man, and Allie was a rapt listener. Parker told her how a friend of his had convinced him that the two of them could get rich by buying a balloon and making parachute jumps. The only trouble was, according to Parker, his partner did none of the jumping and drank up all the profits.

Allie listened, careful not to betray her mounting excitement. "You'll be taking your balloon to Texas, I guess."

"No! I come here to sell the fool thing!" Parker looked around at the sparse crowd, then shook his head mournfully, "It's a washout, missy. These army folks don't want no balloon, and neither do these farmers."

For a while, Allie stood talking with the small man. But the idea that had come to her wouldn't go away. She felt silly, even thinking about it, but she knew that Fletcher Shows was having a difficult time. The year 1907 had been a bad one for the country. In October, the worst stock market crash since the Panic of 1901 had jarred the country. Millionaires such as E. H. Harriman had been hard hit, but the average American had been hit even worse. The crowds at the show had fallen off drastically, and within six months, the Colonel had let everyone go except the mainstays of the company. Allie and Joey worried a great deal, knowing that they were staying on only at Owen's insistence. Both of them had worked as hard as they could, but they had no money-making skills, nothing to help draw people to the show.

Standing beside Ivory Bill Parker, Allie made up her mind. Forcing all the arguments aside, she turned to the little man and said, "I've got a proposition for you—"

An hour later, Amos and Owen were joined by Joey, who

came rushing up, his eyes bright as stars. "I met Mr. Wright, Owen, and he says I can work for him when I get older!"

"No foolin'?" Owen grinned. He introduced Joey to Amos, then asked, "When's the thing going to fly?"

"Any minute now. You see that man with Mr. Wright? That's Lieutenant Selfridge. He told me all about the airplane, and he's going to fly with Mr. Wright."

A roar from the small engine broke the silence, and Amos said, "Looks like they're about ready."

"Sure wish I was in there with them." Joey sighed wistfully. "Lieutenant Selfridge said if I'd stay around, maybe he could get Mr. Wright to give me a ride!"

They watched as the kite-like affair began to move. Wright and Selfridge sat side by side, and the machine picked up speed as it moved across the field. It lifted off the ground gracefully, and a shout went up from the spectators. "By golly, that thing really works!" Owen said in awe.

The plane rose, then began to circle. "That's been the trouble with these things," Amos observed. "They go pretty well straight away, but nobody's been able to make them turn with any kind of success. Looks like the Wrights have got that whipped!"

The plane made three circles of the field, then something seemed to go wrong. Hearing a loud tapping, Wright appeared to try to shut off the power, but three seconds later the entire machine began to shake, almost throwing the two men from their seats! With the power off, the machine was out of control and apparently nothing he did with the levers had any effect. Then the plane nosed down and headed for the ground in a perpendicular dive.

"They're going to crash!" Joey cried.

For one electrifying moment, it seemed as if the plane might pull out of the dive. But there was no time, and the sound of the crash ripped through the air as the machine plowed into the ground.

At once the ground crew and the officers ran to the wreck

and began frantically working with the two men. "One of them was thrown clear," Amos said hopefully. "He ought to be all right. It's the one who's in the wreckage I'm worried about."

Amos moved in closer as they began to bring in the injured men. Recognizing one of the officers, he called out, "Are they all right, Major Little?"

The officer gave him a stricken look. "Mr. Wright is badly injured. A broken leg and some ribs, probably."

"What about Lieutenant Selfridge?" Joey asked.

Major Little stared at the boy, then shook his head. "Tom Selfridge is dead, my boy. His skull was crushed in the fall. He died instantly."

Amos saw the boy's eyes fill with tears and knew he had the lead for his story. He spent the next hour talking to the officer and crew. Owen stayed with him, shocked by the tragedy, but fascinated by the way his brother was able to piece it all together.

Amos looked harried. "I'd like to spend time with you, Owen, but I've got to get this story written."

"Sure, I know. But say, we'll be close to New York City in about two weeks. Why don't we get together then?"

"Great! I'll get Lylah to come with me, and we'll catch your act!"

Owen left and, when he got back to the car, he found Allie there, her arm around Joey. The boy's face was pale, and tear tracks still stained his cheeks.

"I guess we'd better get back," Owen said awkwardly, not certain of what to say to the boy. "We'll have to hurry to make the first show."

"Owen, you go ahead," Allie insisted. "Joey and I will be a little late."

"What's that, Allie?" Owen asked in bewilderment. Then he saw the horse-drawn wagon and the small man sitting on the seat.

"This is Ivory Bill Parker, Owen," Allie said quickly. "We'll ride back with him." She saw Owen's face take on a stubborn set and, before he could refuse, she rushed on. "He's our new partner. We're going into show business together."

"Show business? What's this fellow up to?"

"He owns a balloon," Allie explained, aware that Owen was glaring at the man on the wagon. "Colonel Fletcher will be glad to have Ivory Bill. You remember how well the show did in Topeka when the balloonist was there. Ivory Bill's had an accident, but Joey can handle the balloon."

Owen didn't like it. "And what exactly do *you* do, Allie?"

Allie looked him directly in the eye and said defiantly, "Me, Owen? Oh, I do the parachute jump."

21

EVERYTHING CHANGES

Everyone except Owen was highly in favor of the new act—especially Colonel Fletcher.

When Owen cornered the owner and expressed his feelings in a rather vehement fashion, Fletcher was astonished. "Why, Owen, I'm surprised at you." The colonel had been drinking rather more than usual, and he spoke carefully to avoid slurring his words. "This is a *splendid* opportunity for the young people."

"A splendid opportunity for Allie to break her neck you mean!" Owen had spent almost the entire two days since Ivory Bill Parker had burst on the scene, trying to talk Allie out of the enterprise—with no success whatsoever. Now he was arguing with the colonel, his eyes bright with anger. "What if she gets hurt . . . or *killed* . . . in that fool contraption? Could you live with that?"

But it was useless, for the colonel was a desperate man. Receipts were down and he was deeply in debt. Privately he agreed with Owen, but he was seventy-one years old and not a well man. Finally he put an end to Owen's arguments. "It's not my responsibility, Owen. If the girl wants to take the risk, it's her decision. Now let's hear no more about it!"

Owen left Fletcher's office and made his way toward the wagon where he found Allie and Joey engaged in inflating the balloon. It was a rather simple task, consisting of stretching out the fabric of the bag so that hot air from a portable gas furnace could flow into it. Joey and Allie were holding the

colorful balloon in place as Parker managed the furnace. Just
as Owen arrived, the hot air swelled the limp fabric so that
the balloon, tethered by guy ropes, lifted off the ground and
hovered over the little man.

"I want to talk to you, Parker!" Owen burst out.

But Allie took one look at his face and said, "Just a minute,
Owen—", and he was forced to stand there until the balloon
was fully inflated. Parker shut off the roaring gas. "Now, let
it go!"

"Let me go up in it, Bill!" Joey cried out, and at the man's
nod, he scrambled into the worn wicker canopy. "Let 'er go,
Allie!" he shouted as the balloon rose a full eight feet, then
was brought up short by a single rope tied to a stake.

Parker and Allie grabbed a pair of ropes dangling from the
basket and, as the little man loosed the anchor, the balloon
began to rise.

"It's too hot!" Parker shouted in alarm as he was jerked off
his feet and lifted into the air, a short distance off the ground.
Owen leapt to grab the rope and his weight brought the balloon slowly back to earth. When his feet touched, he held on
to the rope.

"That's the way!" Parker yelped. "Now, let it out!"

Owen gave him a sour look, but began to play out the rope,
hand over hand, commanding, "Go help Allie!"

It was not as difficult as he thought, and as he looked up,
he saw that Joey was peering over the edge, cheering him on.
"Let 'er go, Owen!"

Slowly the balloon rose, but was soon caught by a breeze
and began to drift toward the south. Owen, worried about
Joey, watched as it floated gently on the light breeze. He kept
his grip on the rope. "That's enough . . . let's bring her down!"
Parker yelled.

Out of curiosity, Owen eased his grip, and as he suspected,
both Allie and Parker were tugged upward, suspended by their
ropes. "Wonderful!" he said sarcastically. "Is this part of the
act, Bill? The two of you dangling from that thing?" He began

to haul the balloon down with powerful jerks, and finally it settled. Almost as soon as the basket touched the earth, the balloon began to collapse as the air inside cooled off.

Joey was out of the basket in an instant, his face flushed with excitement. "It was great! I could see for about a hundred miles!"

Owen stepped back from the folds of cloth, a disgusted look on his face.

"Thanks a lot, big fella!" Parker said quickly. He hastened on. "I have a winch I use to keep the balloon from getting away like that, but the youngsters were so anxious to try it out that I didn't take the time."

"Look, if you can't handle the balloon, how in the world do you think you can control a parachute jump?" Owen demanded. "If you want to break your own legs, Parker, that's your business . . . but I'm responsible for these young people, and I'm not going to put up with it!"

Allie and Joey had already discussed the fact that Owen would be dead set against the act. But both of them were determined, and now Allie came to stand in front of Owen. "I know how you feel, but it'll be all right." Her dark blue eyes were soft, for she knew that his anger was fueled by concern. "This is just something I have to do, don't you see? Joey and I can't go on forever, letting you support us."

Owen moved his shoulders in a gesture of impatience. "That's got nothing to do with it! Anyway, what if you get killed? Who'll look out after Joey then?"

But Allie and Joey had gone over all that, and now Allie put her hand on Owen's strong arm, trying to make him listen to reason. Though she argued long and hard, she had discovered a stubborn streak in the big man.

Finally Owen pulled away, saying angrily, "All right . . . go on and kill yourself then!"

"Aw, he'll come around, Allie," Ivory Bill said, noting the stricken look on the girl's face. Joey came up to add, "Sure he will. He's just afraid for you, that's all. But when he sees how easy it is, why, he'll be proud of you!"

Allie frowned, not sure about that. "I guess you'd better give me a lesson or two on parachuting, Bill."

Ivory Bill shrugged. "Only three things to know, and I can't help you with two of them. Lesson number one: Don't jump until I give you the signal."

"What about lesson number two?"

"Well, I can give the signal, Allie," Parker said slowly, watching her face, "but I can't *make* you jump. When you're up there all alone, I expect you'll find out it's pretty hard to turn loose. And there's nothing I can do to help you with that . . . nothing anyone can do, I guess."

"Aw, Allie can do it!" Joey said. "Now, what's the third lesson, Bill?"

"Just pull that ol' rip cord, kid! Most people don't have any trouble with that one . . . it's number two that causes problems!"

"Where's Allie?" Ivory Bill asked as Owen shoved his way through the crowd that surrounded the colorful balloon. "Go get her, Owen," he yelped nervously. "Joey and me will hold on here, but I think she may have got cold feet."

"All right, Bill."

As Owen plowed his way through the throng, he noted that at least it was a fine day for a jump—sunshine, only a slight breeze, and warm enough to be just comfortable. And the advance billing the colonel had put out seemed to have worked, for the fairgrounds had filled up as they hadn't in months.

"Allie?" he called as he reached the dressing room, but got no answer. "Allie, are you here?" He pushed his way through the flap and saw her, standing very still in the middle of the small space. Her face, he saw at once, was pale, and her lips were almost white as she pressed them together.

Why, she's paralyzed, Owen thought, and his first impulse was to rush forward and say, *Now, you see? That's enough of this foolishness. Get that silly rig off and let's forget this nonsense.*

But he had a forewarning that it would not be that simple. Stepping into the room, a thought flashed into his mind. *If she doesn't jump, she won't be able to try anything—ever.* He had seen enough of life to know that this was a universal truth. He'd seen men, thrown by a horse, who had lost their nerve, and he'd made it a point when anything frightened him, to put his head down, ignore the fear, and plunge right in again. *Better to be dead than scared all the time!*

An idea came to him, then, and knowing he had to get her mind off the actual jump, he put a frown on his face and said angrily, "Now you listen to me, Allie Dupree . . . you are *not* going to wear that outfit!"

Allie had been projecting herself to the moment when she'd be high in the air and had convinced herself that she would not be able to turn loose and drop into nothingness. She had made two practice jumps, and each time it had taken all she had to simply loosen her grasp. Ivory Bill had warned her: *It's different with a crowd yelling, Allie. I've seen one or two who could do it with nobody around, but they just froze when the spotlight was on them.*

She blinked at Owen's obvious displeasure and looked down at the costume she and Bill had rigged up. "What's wrong with it?"

"Why, it's disgraceful!" Owen glared at her, raking her with his eyes.

Allie was wearing a pair of new riding breeches that clung tightly to her slim figure, a pair of glossy black boots that came over her thighs, and a crimson silk blouse, that did nothing to disguise her womanly curves. Her honey-colored hair, tied by a single golden band, fell over her back, and a neckerchief of black silk was knotted at her throat.

Secretly Owen thought she looked beautiful, but he kept the frown intact as he continued his tirade. "That—that outfit is too tight," he insisted. "Now you go put on some decent clothes, or I forbid you to step out there in public!"

As he had planned, Allie was so angry over his criticism

that she forgot all about her fear. Color crept back into her cheeks and her eyes fairly sparked as she shot back, "There's nothing wrong with this costume, Owen Stuart! Your girl-friend Cecily wears about enough to keep inside the law, and you never say a word to *her!* You're just an old—" Allie faltered, unable to come up with a name vile enough to express her opinion. Then she threw her head back, stared up at Owen defiantly, and said, "You *dentist!*"

"Dentist?" Owen's jaw dropped and he could barely suppress a smile. "What kind of name is that? Never mind . . . you get out of that thing, or you can't do the act!"

"I'll do it . . . and I'll do it in *this* outfit!"

Allie shoved past Owen, ignoring him as he followed close behind, telling her she *just couldn't* wear such a thing, but she missed the gleam of satisfaction on his face.

"There you are!" Ivory Bill burst out as she appeared amidst the applause of the crowd. "Git in that parachute . . . and Allie, don't even *think* about it. Just put your mind in cold storage, and when you hear the gunshot, just let go and pull that ol' ripcord!"

Parker's advice was all that saved Allie, for as she got into the basket, she was suddenly aware of the crowd—every eye trained on her. She gasped as if a bucket of cold water had been dashed in her face. She had never been on a stage of any kind, had certainly never been the center of attention of hundreds of people. Now she saw them as individuals, not as a faceless mob, which made it worse. The men were staring at her boldly, some of them turning to make comments to their friends, and from their coarse laughter, she could imagine what they were saying! There was a glitter of expectancy in the eyes of other spectators. *They want to see me fall,* Allie thought. It was the same sort of thing that drew people to Owen's fights—the perverse thrill of seeing a man cut to bits or knocked unconscious.

She heard Colonel Fletcher begin his spiel about how dangerous this stunt was, how the young lady had performed be-

fore the crowned heads of Europe and such. Then she heard
Joey whisper loudly, "Smile, Allie! Wave at the crowd like we
practiced!"

Somehow Allie came up with a smile and waved at the spectators, but her mind was stretching ahead to that moment
when she would have to let go and dive at the ground. She
heard Ivory Bill call out, "Here we go, Allie!" and felt the balloon surge upward. The ground fell away, and everything
seemed to shrink. She was still smiling and waving, but as she
spotted Owen looking up with an agonized expression on his
face and growing smaller by the second, she tasted the metal-
lic tang of fear.

As the paralyzing emotion gripped her, Allie tried to take
Ivory Bill's advice. *Put your mind in cold storage!* She took her
eyes off the ground, knowing that she could never jump unless she did. The horizon was beautiful. The sun striking the
tin roofs of barns gave them a silver sheen, while far in the distance the hills lifted, clearing the earth with burly shoulders.
The muted sounds of the calliope and the yelling of the crowd
might have drifted to her in a dream as the breeze swayed the
canopy gently.

Allie grasped the shrouds and, keeping her eyes on the
horizon, put one leg over the rim of the basket, then the other.
Clinging tightly to the line that connected the frail basket to
the balloon overhead, she grasped the rip cord with her other
hand. She could still hear the crowd, their cheers thin and far
away, but put everything out of her mind. Her jaws were
clamped together so tightly that they hurt, but she was only
conscious of one thing—the sound of a gunshot.

It came sooner than she had expected it—a clear, short explosion—and, without thought, she turned loose the line she
was holding and launched herself away from the basket. The
wind whipped at her hair and terror gripped her throat, but
she yanked the rip cord with all her might.

There was one terrible moment, as she plunged toward
the hard earth below, when nothing seemed to happen. *It*

didn't open! The thought screamed through her mind. But
then she heard a popping sound, and the harness bit into her
flesh. The crowd roared as her plunge slowed abruptly, and
then she was swaying back and forth gently.

Thank you, God! Allie had never learned to pray, but this
cry came from the depths of her spirit. She looked down and
saw Joey dancing up and down, holding on to Ivory Bill. The
faces of the crowd looked very white, and Allie could now
smile and wave back at them.

She landed as Ivory Bill had instructed, her knees bending to take the shock of the landing.

It was Owen who got to her first, holding her in his arms so
that her feet cleared the ground. "You did it, Allie! You did it!"

Allie was very conscious of being pressed against Owen's
chest and for one moment could not speak. Then she smiled.
"I'll change the costume if you say so, Owen."

Owen set her down and gazed at her adoringly. "You look
beautiful, Allie! Just beautiful!"

Allie knew that this was one of the moments she'd always remember—a picture for her own room of memories. *A blue sky
with white clouds. The sound of a calliope. People applauding. Joey's
eyes proud and excited . . . and Owen Stuart saying, "You look beautiful, Allie! Just beautiful!"*

"Look at her, Owen!" Joey breathed, staring upward as
Allie swung back and forth on the trapeze suspended beneath
the basket of the balloon. A series of lanterns with reflectors
fastened to the sides of the basket cast yellow beams down
on Allie as she spun, making a giant swing on the bar. Then
at the peak of the swing, she let go, and a cry went up from
the spectators as she executed a graceful backward flip. As
always, whenever Owen watched Allie's jumps, he seemed
to die for a moment. And then her plunging form was arrested
so that he swallowed and remembered to breathe.

"That trapeze sure put the icing on the cake, hey, Owen?"
Joey talked rapidly as he and Owen reeled in the balloon.

When it was settled into place and the silk fell in shapeless folds on the ground, the boy went on, "Ivory Bill says I can do a jump pretty soon. Won't that be great?"

"Just dandy," Owen said shortly. "Then I can worry about *both* of you!" He left the midway without speaking to Allie, for she was busy signing autographed pictures of herself for a quarter apiece, smiling and joking with the group that had gathered about her.

As Owen moved through the crowd, he failed to see four people who were attempting to locate him. He had received a telegram from Amos, saying he would be down with Lylah for a visit, but Owen expected them later in the week.

"Hey, there he is!" yelled Nick Castellano, catching sight of Owen. But Amos caught his arm. "Wait, Nick, let's talk about this thing." There was a worried look on Amos's face, and he turned to Lylah for support. I feel pretty bad about this scheme of Nick's, Lylah," he said soberly. "I think we ought to at least tell Owen what's going on."

Lylah nodded. "I think so, too. I never liked surprises, and this one could backfire in a big way."

Nick began speaking very rapidly. He was a little heavier than he had been when Amos had first met him, and he was puffing from exertion. But he was rather proud of his idea, though he'd had to talk fast to sell both Amos and Lylah on the scheme.

When Amos had mentioned that he and Lylah were going to see Owen, Nick had conceived the notion of getting Owen out of the carnival business. "Look," he had told the pair, "I'm in with the big boys in the boxing game. All I have to do is ask, and they'll give Owen a bout."

"Professional boxing's different from what Owen's doing, Nick," Amos had protested. "I've seen some of the pugs walking around talking to themselves."

But Nick had been persuasive. He'd argued that they owed it to "the Kid," as he called Owen, to at least give him an opportunity. "Let me go along and take a look," he begged. "I know fighters pretty good. If I see the Kid ain't got it for the ring, why, I get a little vacation. But if he's got what it takes, Amos, he can make more from one bout in the Garden than he can in a year with that dumb carny. What kind of life is that—fightin' every yokel who comes along . . . and then only for peanuts? Now *that's* what's going to get the Kid hurt!"

In the end Nick had convinced them, but when they'd left New York in his Ford—one of the first of the Model T's to roll off Henry Ford's new line—there had been a new wrinkle. "This is Jack McVicker," Nick had said, indicating a large man with a flat nose and a heavy-duty chin. "He's a fighter, Amos. Went up against the big ones a few years ago—even Jim Jeffries. I decided it might be better if a real fighter looked Owen over, so Jack agreed to come, right, Jack?"

"Too right, mate." McVicker nodded. "Glad to help the young chap out. Might save him a lot of grief, y' know."

The fighter had a thick Australian accent, and both Amos and Lylah had to listen carefully. They were agreeable . . . until Nick mentioned that the plan was for McVicker to accept the challenge Owen gave every night.

"Got to test the lad out, y' understand," McVicker said when he saw the worried looks on their faces. "I'll not hurt him, if that's what you're thinkin'. Just see if he can hit . . . and if he can take a punch."

Amos and Lylah had agreed—at least halfheartedly—but now that the time had come, it didn't seem fair. "Let's let Owen in on it, Nick," Amos urged. "He's not expecting a professional boxer."

But Nick was persuasive, and McVicker assured them repeatedly that he was now a sparring partner for heavyweight contenders. "That means I do what I'm told, miss." He nodded toward Lylah. "This gentleman is paying me a hundred dollars to find out if his friend has any business in the ring, and that's all I aim to do." McVicker's light blue eyes were almost hidden in the squint caused by scar tissue, but he managed to convince both Lylah and Amos that Owen would not get hurt.

"Come on, now," Nick urged. "The ballyhoo for the show is starting!"

"Let's stay back out of sight, Amos," Lylah said. "It would make Owen self-conscious if he knew we were here."

The two of them watched as the barker whipped up the crowd and made the usual challenge. When McVicker called out, "I'll have a go!" Amos shook his head. "I don't feel right about this, Lylah . . . but it's too late to stop it."

He bought two tickets. They were finding their seats on the very back row, when Owen came out and stripped off his robe.

"Amos, look at him!" Lylah gasped, staring at the narrow waist that led up to the heavily-muscled upper torso. "Not like my little brother!"

"He's a tremendous athlete," Amos agreed, then added, "But look at McVicker."

The boxer had shed his robe, and a cheer went up from the crowd, for he was at least twenty-five pounds heavier than Owen. He had a slight paunch, but as the two men met when the referee bell rang, even Nick was nervous. "Jack's a good fellow . . . but I hope he remembers this is just a test. He put down the heavyweight champion of the world with one punch when he got mad once."

Lylah stared at him. "You picked a fine time to tell us!" she said indignantly. "If it gets bad for Owen, I'll go down and stop it myself."

The two fighters came out, and Owen saw at once that the man was a professional. There was no mistaking that shuffle and the manner in which McVicker kept his guard up. It was not the first time he'd faced a professional, but a warning went off in his head as McVicker threw a left that moved faster than it should from such a heavy man. It was a crisp, snapping blow that he caught on his forearm, but the power of it turned him cold.

McVicker's eyes glinted with approval, for not one boxer in a hundred could have blocked the blow so easily. He saw

at once that the young fellow was in magnificent condition—
the stomach flat as a board and not an ounce of excess weight
on his six-foot frame. McVicker moved forward and tried another left, then a hard right, but both missed as Owen dodged
and slipped to one side. *A fine defensive fighter,* the more experienced pugilist noted. *But can he do anything but duck?*

He found out soon enough, for Owen knew he couldn't
back away from this man for three rounds. He waited until
McVicker shot out that fine left jab, dodged it, then sent a
counter blow which caught McVicker flush in the jaw. Most
men would have gone down, but only a flicker of surprise reg-
istered in the big man's eyes, and he came roaring in, throwing blows from every angle.

Can't take this one out with one punch, Owen thought as he
backed away, parrying some of the blows and taking some on
his shoulders and elbows. They stung, though, and he ducked
into a right that caught him on the neck and sent him sprawl-
ing to the floor. He was not hurt, but the crowd yelled, expecting to see a knockout. Owen got to his feet slowly, and
by the time the referee wiped his gloves clean and stepped
back, Owen had a plan. He knew he could not beat the big
man . . . not unless he outsmarted him.

What will he expect me to do? Owen asked himself, and the
answer came. *He'll come roaring in to finish me off . . . and he'll
expect me to back away and try to last out the round. So I guess my
best chance is to do exactly the opposite. I may get killed, but he'll
whip me anyway—*

He had read McVicker's mind, and as soon as the referee
stepped back, the fighter went in with all guns blazing. He had
learned that after knocking a man down, it was wise to move
in for the finish, since a hurt man would usually back up.

But instead of backing up, Owen planted his feet and
launched a hard right that caught McVicker coming in. It was
a solid blow, with every ounce of Owen's weight behind it,
and it took the boxer by surprise. McVicker was halted, and

temporarily helpless. Owen saw it and leapt to finish him off
. . . but just at that moment the bell rang, ending the round.

McVicker stumbled back to his corner and plopped down
on the stool. He was an old hand and had been hurt before,
so that by the time the bell rang, he was able to come out with
his eyes clear. He moved carefully, however, expecting the
young fighter to rush in for the kill. That was all he needed,
for he had the old skills to do it. But he got no chance, for
Owen began to circle him, throwing crisp left hands that
McVicker could only partially block. The time ran on, and
the crowd went wild, but Owen refused to be stampeded.
When McVicker saw that his young opponent had no intention of coming to him, he grinned. *A smart boy, this one!* For
the rest of the round, he chased Owen but could not corner
him, and when the bell rang, he shook his head in bewilderment and went back to his corner.

"You got him, Owen!" Lyle Easterling exclaimed as the bell
rang for the last round. "All you got to do is finish him off!"

But Owen had seen the big man's power, and knew it
would not be that easy. He went out on his toes, intending to
outmaneuver the big fighter, but he had no chance, for
McVicker had a plan of his own. He wanted to see if the young
man could take a real punch.

It took the older fighter most of the round to land the
punch, and he received a pounding in the process. But finally
he tied Owen up and sent a whistling right that caught the
younger man on the jaw. He stepped back as Owen fell, then
turned and went to his corner. He was worried, because in
the heat of battle, he had hit the young man with all he had.

He glanced over at Nick who was yelling at him, his face
mottled with anger, and then glanced toward Owen. *Shouldn't
have done that*, he censured himself and was surprised to see
Owen stumble to his feet on the count of eight. McVicker
blinked in surprise, for he saw that the young man had been
hurt, but his eyes were clear and he was coming out with his
hand up in a good defensive position.

McVicker, relieved, used none of his formidable skill in the remaining few seconds. When the bell rang, he dropped his gloves, and said, "Bucko, you're a fine young boxer. Don't know as I ever seen one better."

The two boxers headed for their dressing rooms, but Owen didn't get the chance to dress. Amos, Lylah, and Nick came through the flap just as he threw off his robe. They surrounded him, Nick and Amos pounding him on the back, their eyes bright with excitement. Lylah finally shoved them out of the way and went over to Owen. "Bend down and kiss me, you gorgeous man!"

Owen was happy to see them and giddy with victory. "Look, get out of here and let me get dressed."

"Sure, then we can go get something to eat." Nick nodded. "Is there a good place in this tank town?"

"Yes . . . if the booth's not taken, Nick." They left, and Owen dressed quickly.

When he went outside to join them, he was surprised to see McVicker standing beside them. Owen cast a suspicious glance at Amos, who shook his head, protesting, "I had nothing to do with this, Owen . . . it's that guy there!"

Nick smiled and introduced McVicker, who put out his hand at once. "Glad to meet you, mate." He nodded, a smile on his battered lips. "I didn't keep the fifty bucks for staying the three rounds."

"What is this, Nick?" Owen asked.

"Why, I'm going to make you rich, Kid." Nick grinned, slapping Owen on the back. "Let's go get some steaks and we'll talk about it."

An hour later, the five of them were sitting around a table in the town's best and only restaurant. Nick had talked steadily, outlining his plan to make a professional out of Owen.

"I'm no professional, Nick," Owen smiled. He nodded at the fighter, adding, "Ask *him*, he can tell you. He'd have beaten my brains out if the bout had gone on much longer."

McVicker had said little throughout the meal, applying himself to his food while Nick talked. Now he looked across the table at Owen and shook his head. "That ain't exactly right, mate," he remarked in his gravelly voice. "I expect I might have beat you in a longer fight . . . but I can beat most fighters. Not braggin', but even if I'm past my peak, there ain't ten men fightin' today I couldn't take." He paused to pour his tea into his saucer, sipped it noisily, then said, "I don't usually tell young fellows to take up boxing. It's a hard life, and not many make any money at it. But I got to say, that with the right training, you'd be a contender, young fellow. You got the speed, you can take a punch, you can hit like a mule . . . and you're smart."

"You hear that, Owen?" Nick insisted. "Come on to New York. I'll be your manager and Jack here can train you."

Owen shook his head, and Nick set about to persuade him. The talk went on for a long time, and finally Amos said, "Nick, that's enough. You had your chance. Now it's up to Owen."

Nick saw that he was finished and said no more. They left at midnight, and Nick's last words were, "Now, Kid, the offer's still good. If you change your mind, come right to New York. It'll be the smartest thing you ever did!"

Owen thought no more of it and laughed as he told Allie and Joey about the offer.

But the laughing stopped three weeks later.

When Colonel Fletcher didn't show up for breakfast or lunch one day, one of the hands knocked on the door of his room. When he got no answer, he looked inside and found the colonel lying beside his bed—cold and dead.

The entire company grieved, for Colonel Fletcher had been fair and just to all of them. But it was soon discovered that he had been fighting a lost cause, for the show was in such debt there was no way to continue.

A week after the colonel's death, the show was dismantled for the last time, the equipment sold to pay off debts, and the crew scattered.

That afternoon, Owen came looking for Allie and Joey and found them watching the last of the rides being taken down. Owen had been quiet, saying nothing to anyone, except the people he'd worked with. His farewell to Cecily had been easier than he'd expected. She had cocked her head, regarded him through narrowed eyes, then said lightly, "It's been fun, Owen . . . but I guess we both knew it wasn't forever, didn't we? Look me up if you ever get to Chicago."

Owen could tell that Allie and Joey were both frightened. "Guess it's back to being tramps for Allie and me," Joey said.

"Yes, Owen," Allie added soberly. "It's scary—not having any place to go."

"Everything changes, I guess, but you've got a place . . . if you want it," Owen assured her. "I'm going to take Nick Castellano up on his offer to be a fighter. And I want you two to come with me to New York."

Hope leapt into Allie's eyes, and Joey's expression showed instant relief. Owen knew he'd made the right decision, but warned them, "It's going to be beans and bread, maybe for a long time. I probably can't do it at all. But we'll make out, the three of us." He looked down at the two. "Will you go with me?"

"Yes, Owen!" they both said at once.

Owen grabbed them around the shoulders and laughed out loud. "That's what I wanted to hear! Now, look out, New York . . . here we come!"

Allie found her eyes filling with tears and she dashed them away, glad of the feel of Owen's strong right arm around her shoulders. "Owen, can I keep my costume?"

"Why not? If I get knocked silly, you can put it on and parachute off the tallest building in New York . . . and I'll catch you when you land!" Owen laughed and gave them both a final squeeze. Then, arm-in-arm, the three of them walked away from the remains of Fletcher's show.

Part 4
1909

22

A Deal with Rocco

Madison Square Garden was packed, but the big tanned man in the expensive tweed jacket shouldered his way through the crowd, leading an attractive young woman and a wide-eyed boy to their seats on the front row. One tough-looking individual, who had been pushed to the side, turned and gave the newcomer a hard look. "Who's he think he is? I gotta good mind to teach him some manners!"

His companion grinned. "Go right ahead, Kelly. That's Owen Stuart, the heavyweight boxer. Go on . . . you've had a full life . . . give him a lesson in manners!"

Owen didn't hear the comment and would not have heeded if he had. After a year in the ring and more success than he'd ever dreamed, he had learned to ignore such comments. Jack McVicker had taught him that much, soon after he had come to New York. *Never pay any mind to the crowd, Owen . . . no matter if they're cheerin' or booin'. The man they cheer tonight is the chap they'll be heavin' rotten eggs at tomorrow!*

"Looks like we're just in time, Joey," Owen said as the three settled down. "I only hope Buffalo Bill doesn't miss his target and shoot one of us instead."

Joey shot a disdainful glance at Owen. "He don't *never* miss, Owen . . . not Bill!"

At that moment the music swelled, and a blinding flash from the overhead lights mounted over the grandstand spilled

over the sign—BUFFALO BILL'S WILD WEST SHOW.
From out of the shadows came a beautiful water-smooth silver stallion, bearing a man with a snow-white mustache and
goatee. He circled the arena, then swept off his hat in a salute
to the spectators as the stallion reared and pawed at the air.
The crowd went wild, and as one of the hands began throwing blue glass balls into the air and the old man began to shat-
ter them with his Winchester, Joey was on his feet, scream-
ing until his face was red.

"I wish I could get that excited about something, don't
you, Allie?" Owen asked, touching his shoulder to hers. When
she looked up at him and smiled, he shrugged. "Guess I'm
getting old. Sure is fine to see Joey having so much fun,
though."

"He'll never forget this day, Owen. It'll be a memory picture for him to keep."

The balls popped, and soon the earth was covered with
fine twinkling powder, and a pewter-colored fog filled the
arena. Then a panorama of the Old West unfolded, as the old
man, followed by Indians, bronc riders, clowns, and all the
symbols of a bygone era, paraded by. Finally, Bill Cody took
his place alone under the white lights in the center of the
great coliseum, and the band ceased playing, the noisy crowd
settling into respectful silence.

"This visit will be my last hail and farewell to you all," the
old Indian fighter said. His voice, for all the years he'd used
it to fill many tents and auditoriums, was still a milk-smooth
baritone. "Thirty years ago you gave me my first welcome. I
am grateful for your long devotion to me. During that time
many of my friends have long been gathered to the great, un-
known arena of another life. There are only a few of us left.
Last year, at the end of the performance, I merely said good
night. This time it will be good-bye. To my little friends in
the gallery and to the grown-ups who used to sit there, I thank
you once again. God bless you all."

For a moment the silence was so profound that Owen could

hear the jingle of the bit as the great stallion reared, and then as Cody disappeared into the shadows, a great burst of applause shook the Garden.

After the show, the three of them filed out of the Garden, Joey still in a state of euphoria as Owen hailed a cab and gave the cabbie instructions. As they clattered along the streets, Allie was quiet, and when Joey finally ran down, Owen asked Allie what was bothering her.

"Oh, nothing," Allie replied quickly. "Just tired, I guess."

"You're making too many jumps. Why don't you take a vacation?"

Allie shook her head, not wanting to tell Owen that she and Joey were barely scraping by, even though she was working every day. When they'd first arrived in New York, Owen had gotten a small apartment for her and Joey and had supported them. Objecting to this arrangement, Allie had gone to the manager of Coney Island with a proposition—doing her balloon act at the amusement park. She had gotten the job, but the pay wasn't much. She had had to buy the old rig from Ivory Bill, and while he'd given her a good price, she had to send a payment every month. Then, too, she'd insisted on Joey's going to school, and that had proven to be more expensive than she'd expected.

As they moved through the traffic toward the heart of the city, Allie became aware that Owen was studying her. *He knows me pretty well . . . about some things,* she thought, and asked quickly, "When do you have another fight, Owen?"

"Saturday night, over in Newark."

"Will you win?"

"Sure he will! Whatta you think, Allie, that he's gonna *lose?*" Joey asked indignantly. "Can I go with you, Owen . . . please?"

"Afraid not, Joey. It's no place for you."

"If it's good enough for you, I guess it's good enough for me!"

Owen shook his head firmly. "You stay with your books and learn all you can about airplanes. If you're going to ask Mr.

Wright for that job, you'll have to be pretty sharp." He reached
out and rubbed Joey's head playfully. "Don't want you to wind
up an old pug like me."

Allie listened to the two—Joey begging to go to the fight,
Owen steadfastly refusing. The argument continued until the
cab stopped in front of their apartment, and Joey got out.

"You work on that arithmetic, Joey," Allie said. "I'll be
home right after the jump."

Joey waved in agreement, and Owen said to the cabbie,
"Drive us to Stockman's Gym." The cab lurched forward and,
when they were almost there, Allie asked Owen if she could
come to the fight.

"Oh, you wouldn't like it, Allie." Owen shrugged. "It's not
like the bouts in the carnival. Lots of cigar smoke and too
much drinking."

Allie thought about that. "I wish you could do something
else to make a living."

Owen turned to her quickly, on the defensive. "Why, I'm
making a good living, Allie! I've won all nine of my fights . . .
and I've been able to send money home for the last three
months. As tight as money is, I figure I'm lucky." He grew
restive under her steady gaze, for he had been aware that she
didn't like the idea of his boxing. "Look, it's like Nick and
Jack McVicker both say—boxing is pretty bad for most of the
guys in it. But I'm good enough to keep from getting chopped
up, and that makes a difference. I'll stay with it awhile, and
maybe even get a shot at the title someday. Even if I don't,
I'll make a lot of money. Then I'll quit before I slow down or
get hurt."

"Amos doesn't like for you to fight," Allie said. "And he's
the smartest man I know. Neither does Lylah. You know they
don't."

Owen shook his head stubbornly. "They're just afraid I'll
get hurt . . . but I won't. Nick will take care of me, see that
I'm not overmatched. And Jack's teaching me all his tricks."
He reached over and squeezed Allie's hand. "Look, I don't

want you worrying about me. I'm going to make enough money to send Joey to college . . . maybe even Harvard. Isn't that worth a few punches in my ugly face?"

Allie frowned. "It's not an ugly face. And I know you're doing it for us and for your family. But what about *you*, Owen? What do *you* want . . . for yourself, I mean?"

The question caught him off guard, and he shrugged it aside. "I'm okay."

Allie looked down at his big hand on hers, then lifted her eyes to his. "Owen, I don't get scared anymore when I make a jump, but I never leave the balloon without thinking that something might go wrong. And what then? Is it all over?" She shook her head, a thoughtful expression in her dark eyes. "I don't think so. I think there's more than this little time we have down here."

"Rose been preaching at you?" Owen asked. "Yeah, sure, she has. Amos tries to tell me all the time about how I ought to get religion."

The cab stopped and Owen was glad, for it always made him nervous for some reason to talk about such things. "I'll come out and pick you up after the jump. We'll stop and have something to eat."

"All right, Owen."

"Take this lady to Coney Island," Owen ordered, handing the driver some bills. "This ought to take care of it." Stepping back, he waved at Allie, then as the cab rumbled off, he turned and entered the gym.

Instantly he was surrounded by the smell of resin and sweat, and his ears were assaulted by the rattle of speed bags and the thudding of gloves striking the big bags. Four regulation-sized rings were set up, and all of them were occupied with fighters going at each other hard. Almost everyone spoke to Owen, and he remembered how nervous he'd been the first day Nick and McVicker had brought him to Stockman's. He'd been convinced that the first man he took on in the ring would knock him cold, but he had quickly discovered he could hold his own with most of them.

The dressing room was almost empty, except for Dutch Longstreet, an older fighter who was getting into his ring garb. "Hello, Owen," Dutch grunted. The man had a nose like a saddle and a voice box full of rocks. "Nick tell you he wants me to spar wi' youse?"

"No, I haven't seen him yet, Dutch." Owen was troubled, for Dutch was getting on in years and had no business in the ring, even as a sparring partner. Owen had to control his feelings about the old fighter, for he believed Longstreet was just one step away from joining the ranks of zombie-eyed boxers who'd taken too many punches.

As he put on his trunks and robe, then headed back to do his bag work, Owen struggled with the fear that Nick was making a mistake. *I can't beat up on Dutch . . . Nick will just have to find somebody else.*

Owen looked around, but there was no sign of Nick, so he spent the next hour punching bags. He was skipping rope when he saw Nick come in, accompanied by a short, muscular man with a swarthy complexion. The fellow looked vaguely familiar to Owen. They were trailed by two other men, both wearing black derbies and loose-fitting coats.

"Hey, Kid." Nick grinned, coming up to slap Owen on the back. "How's it goin'?"

"All right, Nick."

"Hey, want you to meet somebody." Nick turned and nodded at the heavyset man, saying with a touch of pride, "This is Tony Rocco. Tony, this is my boy, Owen Stuart."

Tony Rocco—he's the one the cops have been trying to nail, Owen thought, and then remembered having seen his picture in the paper. "Hello, Mr. Rocco."

Rocco was a Sicilian and had a strange pair of eyes—dark and half-hooded by heavy lids. "Nick tells me you're gonna be the champ, Stuart," he said, speaking in a heavy accent.

Owen shrugged. "You know Nick, I guess. He thinks big."

Rocco grinned and nodded at the two men who'd stood back a few feet. "You hear that? Nick's been givin' us the business!"

"Aw, Mr. Rocco, the kid's *modest!*" Nick protested. "He's got dynamite in his hands—dynamite!"

"Well, let's see a little of it," Rocco ordered. He sat down in one of the wooden chairs under a ring, lit a cigar, and nodded. "Let's see some action."

"Sure, Mr. Rocco! Come on, Owen, I'll put your gloves on. Dutch, you ready?"

As Nick laced up the gloves, Owen said quietly, "Nick, you set this up with poor old Dutch, didn't you? But I'm telling you now . . . I'm not going to play along."

Nick jerked back, and his face was tense. "You *gotta* do it, Owen!" he said under his breath. "Rocco can help us! He's got connections . . . can get us a shot at the title!"

"I won't do it, Nick," Owen said evenly.

Nick glared at him, then when he'd finished tying the gloves, called out, "Gotta be just a boxing match today, Mr. Rocco. Couldn't get a first-rate sparring partner on such short notice."

"I didn't come to see no waltz, Castellano," Rocco grunted. "Let's see what the kid's got."

"I'll pay Dutch an extra hundred, Owen," Nick hissed. "What's one more knockout to a bum like him?" He skipped out of the ring, rang the bell, and sat there, his face drawn with anxiety.

Dutch Longstreet always gave all he had. He had no defense at all, never had had any, as his battered face bore witness. His success in the ring had come from taking all his opponents could throw and counting on a lucky punch to put them away.

He came roaring at Owen, who simply parried the windmill blows and made no attempt to do more than send a few punches that did no damage. He heard Nick calling out, "See that footwork? Light as a feather, ain't he?"

But when the bell sounded, Rocco was decidedly impatient. "Okay, so he can dance, Nick. Now let's see him *hit!*"

But Owen steadfastly refused to slaughter the old fighter and, at the end of the second round, Rocco got up and marched down to say to Nick, "What is this? You got me down here to see this kid do the two-step?"

Nick thought fast. Looking across the room, he spotted Sailor Lyons battering away at a hapless sparring partner and got an inspiration. Lyons was not a contender, for he was too slow for top-flight competition, but he was as tough as any fighter in the country. "Mr. Rocco, my boy don't do good with sorry competition. But what if he puts Sailor Lyons down for the count?"

Rocco's eyes glinted with interest. "Ain't been done but once," he said around his cigar. "I might be interested if your boy can do that."

Nick had to work fast, so he rushed over and interrupted Lyons. "Tony Rocco wants to see you in action, Sailor. I'll pay you a hundred to go three rounds with my fighter."

Lyons was interested. "No kiddin'? Who you handlin'?"

"That young guy there, Sailor. He's pretty good, I have to tell you."

"Who's he fought?" Lyons listened as Nick reeled off the names, but Sailor Lyons was unimpressed. "It's a go . . . but gimme the hundred first."

Nick slipped the fighter some bills, then raced back to say breathlessly, "Owen, you got to put the Sailor down! He's no pushover. In fact, he's tougher than anybody you've fought so far. Will you do it?"

Owen nodded. "Do my best, Nick."

Nick slapped him on the back, then stepped out of the ring. When the two men squared off, every man in the gym came to watch. "That kid ain't got no chanst with Sailor," one of Rocco's hirelings grunted.

So it seemed for the first round. Lyons had almost everything—including a good left and a thunderous right hook. His footwork was not fancy, but good enough, and he had a jaw made of concrete that he kept tucked behind a massive shoulder. He manhandled Owen badly during the first round, driving him around the ring. And when the bell sounded, Nick leapt into the ring as Owen came to the corner. "You gotta do better, Owen."

"He's strong as a bull, Nick," Owen said, not even breathing hard. "His right is slow, though. I can try to beat him to the punch . . . but if I don't, I'll be the one on the floor, not him."

"Do it!" Nick dodged out of the ring and watched as Lyons continued to throw rights at Owen. Midway through the round, it happened, and Nick saw it.

Lyons set his feet, started the right-hand attack, but Owen did not back away from it this time. Stepping forward, he beat Lyons to the punch. Owen's right jab struck Lyons, who promptly fell backward. He was not out, but the crowd yelled, for Lyons had not been decked over half a dozen times in a long career. Befuddled, he got up quickly, making the mistake of moving forward to exchange punches before his head was clear—exactly what Owen was hoping he'd do.

Nick stood gasping as Owen plowed into the big fighter, hammering him with hard lefts, and then catching him again with a right that downed Lyons again. Four times Lyons went down, and the last time he crawled to his feet, he was obviously helpless.

Owen stared at the man, his gloves up, then shook his head and walked away. "That's enough." He stepped out of the ring, his face reddened with the blows he'd taken.

Rocco stared at Owen, an odd expression in his dark eyes, and said to Nick, "He don't take orders too good, does he?"

Nick shrugged. "He's got a mind of his own. But he put Lyons out."

"Yeah, he did." Rocco stood there, turning the thing over in his mind, then said abruptly, "I'm goin' to get a steak. Come on, and we'll talk about it."

"Sure, Mr. Rocco! Lemme say a word to my boy!"

Nick rushed over to hug Owen. "What a terrific fighter you are, Kid! I mean, you're really somethin'—"

"Nick, he's trouble!" Owen interrupted. "Don't have anything to do with him."

"Rocco?" Nick was dumbfounded. He himself had lived on the fringe of the law most of his life, and Tony Rocco was one of his heroes. "Why, he's the man we need, Owen!"

"Nick, I'll fight for you . . . but not for anybody else," Owen insisted. "And when you tell Rocco that, he won't want any part of us. He has to control everything he touches, and he's rotten. I won't fight for him!"

"All right, Kid, all right, don't get excited," Nick said soothingly. He could always handle Owen, but now was not the time. "He's a sportsman, Rocco is, and he just likes to see a good boy. He'll get us some good fights, and that's all we need."

But when Nick broke the news to Rocco that he intended to keep all of Owen's contract, the gangster flared up, and it took all of Nick's powers to persuade Rocco that there was money to be made . . . and that later on Owen would catch on to how great it would be to have Tony Rocco in his corner.

Rocco finally agreed, but grudgingly. The last thing he said was, "That kid . . . he don't take orders too good. But he'll take 'em from me, Nick. Don' make no mistakes about that!"

23

"You're Not a Little Girl Anymore!"

Rose and Amos Stuart entertained rarely, but the evening with Allie and Owen was a definite success. The food was delicious and Amos was elated with the rave reviews of his new book. Owen and Allie came alone, for Joey had been invited by one of his teachers to visit the science fair.

The four of them were sitting in the parlor when Amos said suddenly, "Owen, I've heard something rather alarming about your fight with Spears next week."

"What's that, Amos?" Owen had been offered a shot at Jimmy Spears, one of the top contenders for the heavyweight championship. And though Nick hadn't mentioned it, Owen was fairly certain that Tony Rocco had been influential in getting the fight for him. It was the biggest break Owen had had, and he smiled at Amos, warning lightly, "Don't bet against me, Amos. I'm going to win."

Amos was very serious. He'd been in the newspaper business long enough to have many reliable sources. "The odds have gone up against Spears . . . which doesn't make any sense. Nobody understands it, but an informant told me day before yesterday that the big gambling figures are pumping the odds up for you to win. Then they'll bet against you . . . and you'll lose."

Owen frowned. "You always hear talk like that before a big

fight. Nothing to it. Insiders know I can beat Jimmy Spears. He's a good fighter, but Jack's got him down pat. He's showed me everything Spears can pull, and he's taught me what to do about it."

Rose leaned forward. "It's more than just this one fight, Owen—" She hesitated, then went on urgently, "You've been drawn into the wrong kind of life. Believe me, there's no happiness in it for you. The only real joy in this world comes from Jesus."

Owen looked at Rose, a woman he admired greatly. "Time for the sermon, isn't it, Rose?"

"Don't make fun, Owen," Allie broke in, putting her hand on his arm. "I think both of us need help."

Owen stared at Allie, admiring her new blue dress and the sweep of her hairdo. But he was annoyed with her for taking Rose's side. "I'm doing all right. All I have to do is keep on winning fights, and one day I'll be champion of the world. How could anybody do better than that?"

"Owen, it's not that way." Amos shook his head, wondering how to reach this brother he loved so much. He and Rose and Allie had seen Owen change in the last few months. His younger brother had been an easygoing fellow before that, seeming to want little. But Nick had managed to change Owen—for the worse. Amos said as much, but at that, Owen flared up.

"Nick's all right, Amos!"

"He's thick with Rocco, and *that's* not all right," Amos said, then knew at once that such tactics would get him nowhere. He softened his tone. "Rose and I are worried about you, Owen. The best man in the world is in danger when he's offered a pile of money. He goes deaf and blind to the real things, the important things."

"Amos, I'm not going to go crazy," Owen argued. He got to his feet, feeling the need to get away. "Look, it's been a great evening—just great. And I'm not saying you're all wrong. But it's my big chance, and I've just got to take it, that's all."

After Owen and Allie left, Rose said unhappily, "I made a mess out of that, Amos."

"No, sweetheart!" Amos folded her in his arms and kissed her cheek. "I don't think the finest preacher in the world could have done any better. Owen's just not ready. He's running from God . . . and I don't think he'll stop until he runs into something that's too big for him to handle."

"What might that be?"

Amos shook his head. "I don't know . . . but it'll have to be a pretty thick wall. Owen's a tough one, and it'll take something worse than he's ever faced to make him realize that some things are just too big for him. And when that happens . . . he'll look to God."

"That's right, isn't it?" Rose whispered, thinking of the past. "People only seek God out of desperation. When you're flat on your back, there's no way to look but up, is there, Amos?"

Nick stared across the table, incredulity spreading across his face. He'd come into the private dining room at a summons from Tony Rocco, excited and confident. *I've made it!* was his first thought when Sonny Costello, Rocco's right-hand man had stopped by his hotel room with the word that Mr. Rocco wanted to see him—"on the double."

Nick had dressed hurriedly, putting on his classiest suit, and had rushed over to the Astor, going at once to the private dining room. He'd found Rocco eating a plate full of raw oysters.

"Hello, Nick. Want some oysters?" Rocco had asked, then continued eating steadily.

Nick sat down and waited, trying not to watch Rocco, for there was something almost obscene about the way the swarthy gangster devoured the slimy mollusks. Nick hated oysters himself, and something about the way Rocco dropped the limp morsels into his mouth—tilting his head back and rolling them around on his tongue—was slightly sickening, though Nick had better judgment than to show his disgust.

Finally Rocco finished, drank thirstily from a glass of red wine, then turned his eyes on his guest. "Nick, you're gonna make a bundle."

"Sure, Mr. Rocco," Nick nodded. "It's a sure thing. Why, Owen will take Spears easy! Then in a year or so, it's a title shot!"

Rocco smiled, at least with his thick lips. He had a way of simultaneously lowering his heavy eyelids and his voice when he said something important, and he did so now. "We're gonna be smart, Nick," he said softly as he winked at his listener. "That boy you got . . . he could maybe be champion in a couple of years. The public don't like that black guy." By "that black guy," Nick knew Rocco was referring to Jack Johnson, who'd beaten Tommy Burns the previous year to win the heavyweight title. "They're already talking about a 'white hope' to dump him. And your boy might do it when he's got some more experience . . . but he ain't gonna be ready for that for a while."

"But after he takes Jimmy Spears—"

"He ain't *gonna* take Spears," Rocco whispered. "That's what I got you here for, Nick. Little change of plans."

Suddenly Nick saw it all. "You ran the odds up on Owen, didn't you?"

"Sure I did." Rocco grinned. "They'll be even higher by fight time tomorrow night. Everybody's sayin' there's gonna be an upset, that Stuart can take Spears. We can get good odds . . . and when Spears wins, we'll be in the long green."

Nick Castellano's quick wit was silenced. He stared at Rocco for a moment, knowing that the ground had just been cut from under him, but he tried. "Mr. Rocco, it won't do. My boy Owen . . . he ain't smart. He's some kind of a Boy Scout. He's got some kind of notions I can't get around. You saw how he was that first day in the gym," he went on desperately. "He wouldn't beat up on Sailor . . . not even when I told him how important it was."

"Yeah, sure, Nick, but this time he ain't got no choice. We're gonna go for the price on Spears. Besides, the kid don't have to hurt nobody, just take it easy, that's all." Rocco shrugged his beefy shoulders. "I don't think he can beat Spears at all . . . but you gotta' make it plain, Nick. He takes a dive—or things could be kind of unpleasant, for both of you."

Nick was a tough fellow, but he knew enough about the activities of Tony Rocco to feel a chill at the implied threat. Rocco had had men killed for less, and Nick knew it. He got to his feet, feeling sick. "All right, I'll talk to him."

"Sure, you talk to him . . . but don't make no mistakes on this one, Nick. Hate to have to send Sonny here to pay you and the kid a visit."

Nick looked into the reptilian eyes of Sonny Costello, a razor-thin Sicilian, and suppressed a shudder. "He'll be all right when I explain it to him, Mr. Rocco. After all, we can get a bet down and make a bundle, like you say." But as he left the room, Nick was already dreading his interview with Owen.

Rocco watched him go and sat there staring at the table for a time. Then he said, "Sonny, we need some insurance on this."

Costello leaned forward, listening intently as his boss spoke rapidly. "I'll take care of it, Mr. Rocco. No problem."

Owen stared at Nick for a long moment, then shook his head. "No, I won't do it, Nick."

At that moment, Nick knew he was in for a bad time. He was aware that Owen knew something about Tony Rocco, as everyone did—the result of stories in the papers about the gangster. But Owen had no idea how vicious and deadly Rocco really was, for the worst of the stories never made the newspapers. *He don't have no idea what we're up against,* Nick thought as he fought down the panic that had been rising in him all day. *Owen's still got some idea about playin' fair and stuff like that!*

It was a side of Owen Stuart and Amos, as well, that Nick had never been able to grasp. His own life had been shaped in the gutters of New York, and he'd survived only because he practiced the same sort of fierce and deadly methods used by others. He had, in fact, gotten better at it than most, but now he knew that Tony Rocco's power was too strong for their combined efforts.

"Look, Owen," he argued nervously, "I wish I hadn't gotten mixed up with Rocco, but that ain't the question. You don't know what he's like, but I do. He got where he is by puttin' anybody down who got in his way. Guys who crossed him . . . they just disappeared. Sometimes a fisherman will find a skeleton in the Hudson River, feet in cement. That's what'll happen to us if you don't lay down for Spears tomorrow."

Owen listened, but was not impressed. "We'll go to the police, Nick."

Nick was so shocked his jaw dropped. "Go to the cops!" he exclaimed. Such a thing violated the "code" he'd lived by for years. The police were the enemy, and any of his crowd that gave them anything was out of business. But he said nothing about this to Owen. "And what good would that do us? You think they're going to give us a bodyguard for the rest of our lives? I'm telling you, Owen, Rocco don't never give up . . . never! He might wait five years, but he'd rub us out if we crossed him."

The argument went on for a long time, and Owen finally said, "Look, Nick, it may not even be a problem. We've been talking big about how I'm going to take Spears, but we both know it's not that close. He's beaten some of the best fighters around, and no matter what the odds are, we both know I'd have to be lucky to get by him."

"That ain't good enough, Owen," Nick answered wearily. "It's got to be a sure thing. Rocco and his crowd will have a hundred thousand or more riding on this fight, and they don't want any doubts. I've got to go back and tell Rocco you've agreed to pull your punches."

Owen shook his head. "I won't do it, Nick. You should have told him from the beginning."

Nick got to his feet slowly, knowing further argument was useless. "I'll go try to have Rocco hedge his bets," he said. "It's not too late . . . maybe he'll do it."

Owen watched him go, then, feeling completely depressed, left his apartment and went to Coney Island. He got there at dusk, just when Allie was packing her parachute for her jump later. "Need any help?"

Allie looked up with a quick smile. "Hello, Owen. Let me finish this and we'll go for a walk." He watched as she finished packing the chute and tossed it into the wicker basket. "Now, how about a hot dog?"

"Not hungry. Let's walk for a while."

Allie led the way past the rides, and they began to stroll along the beach. It was cold, and the stretch of sand was occupied by only a few hardy souls, bundled in heavy coats. Allie saw at once that Owen was disturbed. "Worried about the fight?"

"No." A flock of birds high in the sky caught his eye, and Owen watched them as they soared and wheeled. Feeling the sharp bite of the wind, he thought suddenly of home. "If I were back home in the hills, I'd be hunting ducks," he said. "Nothing like wild duck and rice this time of the year." He rambled on, speaking of his boyhood days, and Allie listened quietly.

She was a good listener, having learned a great deal about Owen from soliloquies he sometimes delivered. She knew how close he was to Amos and Lylah, and how grieved he was over his father's weaknesses. Now as they moved along the gray sand, he began to reminisce about his mother. He often did, Allie knew, for Marian Stuart had been a powerful force in molding his character.

"Amos is a lot like Ma," he said slowly. "She loved two

things more than everything else—her family and God. That's the way Amos is." He took half a dozen paces, then said, "Wonder why Lylah and me aren't like that."

"You may be more like your mother than you think," Allie answered. "You admire her more than anyone . . . and that means you've got some of her in you, just like Amos has."

Her comment drew his attention, and he stopped short, turning to face her. "You're pretty sharp, Allie. Do you really believe that?"

His face, for all its toughness, had a wistful air. Allie knew him so well, and now she wanted to comfort him. "I never met her, but you've talked about her so much I feel like I knew her. You say Amos is like her . . . well, you don't know it, but you're like *him.*"

The darkness was closing in and the air was growing colder, but neither of them was aware of it. Allie spoke quietly but passionately, yearning to give some assurance to this big man she loved so much. Perhaps it was out of compassion that she reached up and cupped his face in her soft hands. "Oh, Owen! I wish I could make you see what goodness is in you!"

At her touch, Owen felt a strange sensation. He bent forward so he could see her face in the gathering darkness "You're . . . a sweet girl, Allie," he whispered, and then it seemed natural to lower his head and kiss her on the lips.

What had been intended as a gesture of thanks became something quite different. Allie's lips were softer than Owen had dreamed, and when she put her hands behind his neck, pulling him closer, a shock rippled through him. The firm curves of her body being pressed against him stirred old hungers. He drew her closer, his lips falling on hers hungrily as she surrendered to his embrace. The clean fragrance of her hair and the smoothness of her hands caused him to linger, and he was aware that she was returning his kiss with an intensity of her own.

It was a kiss of loneliness, for both of them had been cut off from much that others had known, and as they clung to each other, both Allie and Owen were reaching out to satisfy a vague but intensely strong need to share themselves with someone.

Finally Allie pulled back, trembling. "Owen—" There was such a brokenness in her tone that he knew she was weeping. He himself was shocked by the emotion her kiss had evoked, and he stood there in the darkness, knowing they had crossed some kind of boundary. Never again could he think of her as he had since the first day he'd seen her in the hobo jungle.

"You're not a little girl anymore," he murmured.

Allie took his hand in hers and held it to her cheek. She had been shaken fully as much as Owen, but now a great happiness filled her, welling up like a fountain. She had loved Owen for so long and now at last she knew that he saw her as a woman.

"It's cold out here, Allie," he said, interrupting her thoughts. "Let's go where it's warm. We need to talk."

Allie looked around at the hazy shoreline, then said in wonder, "I think I'll put this in with my collection of good memories—the first time you kissed me—" She giggled, adding, "But not the last!" Then she began to run, holding to his hand tightly.

24

THE END... AND THE BEGINNING

The call, which came only five hours before the fight, caught Nick completely off guard.

Earlier in the day, he had gone back to see Rocco and assure him that everything was set. "The Kid is goin' along, Rocco. We're covered."

Rocco had been doubtful, but Nick had talked convincingly, and finally the man had shrugged. "Okay, Nick. I'll take your word for it."

Nick stared at the squat figure. "You give me your word, Mr. Rocco? No rough stuff?"

"My word, Nick."

Nick was so relieved he had not noticed the glint in Rocco's hooded eyes and had left with the pressure easing. *I'll dope Owen up just before he goes into the ring* he decided. *Just enough to make him sluggish. He can't win against Spears unless he's in top form.*

On his way back to Owen's apartment, Nick had stopped by a drugstore and picked up a small bottle from the thin, balding druggist, who had warned, "About four drops of this will do the job, Nick. That's enough to slow a guy down. If you really want to put him out, give him six drops . . . but no more than that."

Letting himself in, he had found Owen lying on the bed, reading a newspaper. Looking up, Owen greeted Nick. "Hey, listen to this. Says here there's going to be the first aeronautic show ever put on here at the Garden on the 25th." He smiled and shook his head, adding, "Won't Joey be in hog heaven over that?"

"Yeah, he sure will." Nick hesitated, then asked, "You feelin' all right?"

"Sure, Nick." Owen put the paper down. "What about Rocco?"

"I talked to him," Nick said quickly. "He said he'd hedge the bets. Just go in and do your best, Kid."

Owen got up and came to put his hand lightly on Nick's shoulder. "That took a lot of nerve, Nick, facing up to Rocco like that."

Nick couldn't meet Owen's clear gaze, so he moved away to take off his coat. "Just get it off your mind. And when this bout is over, me and you are gonna take a little trip." He found a smile. "You've told me a thousand times about that farm of yours in Arkansas. What about if you take me there? Maybe I can milk a cow or somethin'!"

Owen was delighted. "Sure, Nick, we'll do that. You'll love it!" Nick was relieved when Owen seemed to forget about Rocco. He sat back and listened as Owen rambled on, marveling at how the big fellow seemed to lack any nerves whatsoever. *If I was gonna climb in a ring with a guy who could scramble my brains,* he thought, *I'd be looney!*

It was the phone that interrupted Owen's tale about how he'd bagged his first deer. Nick started at the suddenness of it, but Owen merely lifted the receiver and said, "Hello?"

An instant change came over Owen, and Nick knew something awful was happening. Owen's lips thinned. "I don't believe you—" He paused and stared at Nick while he waited, covering the receiver to whisper, "It's one of Rocco's men. Says he's got Allie, that he'll kill her if I don't—" he broke off, listened, and his face grew pale. "Allie . . . don't worry! It'll be all right—" He halted, listened hard, then said, "Look, I'll do anything, but don't hurt that girl!"

Nick stood there, his mind reeling with shock. As Owen pleaded with the caller, all Nick could think was, *But Rocco gave me his word!* He knew the man was a thug at heart, of course, but there was a lot of talk in their world about honor—to the family first, and then to friends. You might cut an enemy down, but you never betrayed a friend. It was deeply ingrained in Nick, a code that went all the way back to the old country.

And now Rocco had violated that trust. Rage flared up in Nick, his mind beginning to function again. "What did he say, Kid?" he asked quietly.

Owen swallowed hard, then shook his head. "If anything goes wrong, he said, he'll hurt Allie bad . . . then kill her." Owen shut his eyes. "It was somebody named Sonny. He . . . liked telling me what he'd do to her. And she was sitting right there the whole time he was talking—" Owen suddenly opened his eyes and grabbed Nick by the arm, his fingers a vise, doubling his other fist. "You told me it was all right, Nick!"

Nick made no move to defend himself, which would have been fruitless in any case. Looking up into Owen's blazing eyes, he said evenly, "He crossed me up, Kid."

Owen loosed his grasp and made a dive for the telephone. "I'm going to call the cops!"

"Wait a minute!" Nick grabbed at Owen. "That's no good! In the first place, you don't know where they're holding her. And even if you did find out, the cops would be too late. Sonny is a killer . . . but he's smart, too!"

"We've got to do *something*, Nick!"

"Yeah, we're going to do something, all right." The rage that had ignited in Nick had become a cold, icy determination. "Rocco gave me his word . . . his word! But he's going to be sorry. I'm going to make him crawl, Owen!"

Owen was alarmed at the raw hatred glowing in Nick's dark eyes. "What can we do? Nick . . . if anything happens to Allie, I'll—"

Nick put on his coat, then came to stand in front of Owen. "Kid, we've got to work together. You've got to go into that ring. Throw the fight! The girl's more important than any fight . . . right?"

"Sure, Nick! I'll do it!"

"Make a good job of it, Kid," Nick warned. "Don't just fall down. Take a beating if you have to."

"Yeah, sure, Nick . . . but what about Allie?"

"That's *my* job." Nick's thin lips turned up in a humorless smile. "If things go right, I'll have her at the Garden before the fight. But if you don't see us, don't worry. I'll get her out, Kid, I swear it!" Nick stared at Owen. "Can you believe me . . . after I lied to you?"

Owen nodded slowly. There was a deadly quality in his friend that he'd never seen before, though he realized suddenly it had been there all the time. "I know you'll do your best, Nick."

Nick whirled and left, saying, "Tell Jack what's happened, Kid. He'll know how to do the job!"

Nick went at once to his hotel room, where he opened the top drawer of his dresser and took out the heavy revolver he kept under his shirts. Whipping off his coat, he put on the shoulder holster, inserted the revolver and smiled grimly. *Sonny will be looking for a gun, so I'll give him one.* He reached back into the drawer and came out with a thin stiletto with a six-inch blade. Carefully he tested it with his thumb, nodded thoughtfully, then strapped a paper-thin sheath to his left forearm. He slipped the knife into the sheath, handle facing toward his palm. Then he put on his coat and stood before the mirror.

The revolver made a slight bulge, but the stiletto was invisible. He shot out his left arm suddenly, at the same time reaching over with his right, and the knife appeared in his hand, as if by magic. He did this three times, then slipped the weapon into place, saying aloud, "All right, Sonny, let's see how good you really are!"

The minutes dragged by on leaden feet for Owen as he waited in his room. He paced the floor, forcing himself to remain there, but he'd never known anything like the panic and fear that clawed at him. Once he cried out in helpless rage and struck the wall with his fist, not feeling the pain. *If it was just me I could stand it . . . but not Allie!*

The hands of the clock seemed to be frozen, fixed in place. Up and down he paced, and when he'd thought at least thirty minutes had passed, he was shocked to see that only five minutes had dragged by.

After two hours, he finally slumped down on the chair and placed his face in his hands, pushing against his eyeballs. His hands were shaking and nausea rose in him so that he had to swallow the bile that came burning to his throat. Without meaning to, he began to moan and, before he knew it, tears scalded his eyes. He had not wept for years, but now he was not even aware of the tears. A sense of loneliness overwhelmed him as he tried to fight off the thoughts of a world without Allie . . . and he knew he could never survive it. *If they kill her . . . I'll kill them all . . . and then myself!* Wild thoughts clawed at his mind as he sat there in dumb agony.

And then he knew what Amos and Rose had been trying to tell him. Amos had said, *No man is tough enough to make it on his own, Owen. Sooner or later he winds up with something he can't handle . . . and the man who doesn't have Jesus Christ to call on won't make it!*

As he sat there, pondering, he seemed to hear his mother's voice, and a wave of shock ran down his spine. He knew it was not an audible sound, but the memory of it was so vivid he froze. He remembered how she'd held his hand as she lay dying, and he seemed to hear her whisper as she had that night, *Owen . . . don't try to live in your own strength . . . it'll fail you. Let Jesus be your strength . . . trust Him when everything around you is falling down.*

Owen Stuart had always been alone, so he knew well what that was like. Many times he had longed for someone to be close to him. He had found this with Allie, but he realized now that no human being can fully fill the heart of man.

Suddenly he was aware that he was not alone in the room! He knew if he opened his eyes and looked around, he wouldn't see anyone . . . but the blind fear that had come to destroy him was fading. And he knew it was his time to find God.

Slowly he slipped to his knees and fell on his face. His tears dripped off his chin onto the carpet, and he cried out, "Oh, God . . . I can't make it by myself! Help me! I need you!"

Owen never knew how long he lay there, crying out for God. But when he finally got to his feet, every trace of the fear was gone, along with all the guilt that had been lurking in his heart for years. He stood there marveling at the peace that had come and said, with wonder in his voice, "You were right, Ma! Jesus *does* make the difference!"

He looked at the clock, then dressed carefully and left the apartment. All the way to the arena, he felt the fear trying to come back. But it was as if he had been placed in a large globe of light, and the darkness and fear and guilt were on the outside. Inside, Owen knew, was that Presence that had come as he lay on the floor, crying for mercy. And as he entered the door of the arena, he whispered, "Lord Jesus . . . it's all in your hands—", and he moved confidently toward the dressing room.

Allie did not flinch when the tall, thin mobster came toward her. He had amused himself by tormenting her, kissing her, and yanking her face back cruelly when she tried to avoid him. She had soon discovered that he actually *wanted* her to resist, that it gave him pleasure to hear her cry out with pain. So now she waited passively and, when he put his arms around her, she fought back the revulsion she felt and offered no resistance. He had a feral look, and the strong sickening-sweet lotion he used only made the stench of his unwashed body even more offensive.

Costello, angered at her passivity, shoved her back, cursing. When she struck the wall, the jolt caused her to blink, but she made no sound.

"I hope that pug don't throw the fight," the gangster grated. "You know what's gonna happen to you if he wins?" He began to tell her horrible things that reflected his sick mind. He paused in the telling only when a knock came on the door.

Costello leapt to his feet, a gun appearing in his hand. "Who is it?"

"It's me, Sonny . . . Larry. Open the door!" When the door opened, the thick-bodied man pushed through. "It's Castellano, Sonny. Says he's got to see you."

"What for?"

Larry shrugged. "He won't tell me. Says it's private . . . somethin' about the fight. You want me to run him off?"

"No, send him up . . . but shake him down first."

"Already did that, Sonny." Larry grinned, holding up a revolver. "He was wearing this under his arm."

Costello took the weapon. "Send him up . . . but keep your eyes open, Larry. He may have brought some friends along."

"Sure, Sonny." The thick-set gangster moved down the stairs and, when he faced Nick, motioned with a jerk of his chin. "Go on up . . . but no funny business, Castellano."

"Hey, no problem, Larry!" Nick slapped the man on the shoulder, got a cold look for his trouble, then with a laugh moved up the stairs. He touched the knife with his right hand, then took a deep breath and knocked on the door.

At Costello's invitation, Nick opened the door and stepped inside. The first person he saw was Allie, standing with her back against the wall. "Hey, doll, take it easy," he soothed. "Everything's goin' great! Couple of hours and you're outta here."

"What do you want, Nick?"

Nick turned to face Costello with a smile on his face. The tall man was holding the gun Larry had confiscated earlier, and his steely eyes were guarded. There was no hope as long as Sonny held that gun, so Nick went to a chair and slumped down. "Gotta drink, Sonny?"

"This ain't no saloon." Suspicion was part of Costello's makeup—a well-honed trait to which he owed his longevity in the violent world he moved in. He kept the gun in his hand, not pointing it at Nick, but ever a threat. Costello, Nick well knew, had the speed of a striking serpent and was fully as ruthless. "Get out, Nick," he said suddenly, sensing that something was not quite right.

Nick stared at him, allowing his face to register surprise. "Didn't Mr. Rocco tell you?"

"Tell me what?"

"Why, he wants me to stay here until the fight's over. Then . . . if it goes right . . . I'm supposed to take the girl home."

Costello's eyes narrowed. "He never said nothin' to me about that."

Nick snapped his fingers as if he'd just remembered. "Hey, I know what happened, Sonny. As soon as he decided to send me over, he started for the phone . . . to spill it to you. But you know how it is . . . the phone rang and, when I left, he was talking to the big boy in Chicago. You know how Mr. Rocco's been workin' on *that* little deal!"

Costello hesitated, and Nick yawned. "He'll call pretty soon. Now how about that drink?"

For one moment Costello paused, then nodded. "We'll wait for the call." He turned and moved to a table, putting down Nick's gun so he could pick up the bottle of whiskey and a glass. As he turned and moved toward Nick, he asked, "What if the Kid don't come through?" he asked. "The girl gets it?"

"That's what he said, Sonny." Nick sat, willing himself to remain calm, and began sipping the drink. He was very much aware that even if he got Costello, Larry was still waiting . . . a dangerous man. *Got to get closer,* he thought, and for ten minutes he slouched in his seat, speaking languidly and listening to Costello's measured replies. Finally he got up, crossed to the window, and looked out. "Gonna snow pretty soon. I hate cold weather!"

Costello was leaning against the wall, and Nick walked past him to get a refill from the whiskey bottle. Then he sauntered back, taking a careless position not five feet from Costello. Time was running out. Nick was afraid that Rocco might call—and then he'd have no chance at all. He was aware that Costello himself had a gun and that he'd been watching carefully to see if Nick would try to retrieve the weapon he'd left on the table.

He left my gun there just to see if I'd go for it, Nick suddenly realized, and a shock rippled through him as he realized that, if he'd made a grab for the gun, he'd have been shot down at once!

But now he saw that Costello had relaxed. He took out a cigarette, placed it between his lips—and just as he struck a match, Nick saw his chance and snatched the knife out of the sheath. Even as he drew it back over his head to throw it, Nick saw Costello's unbelievable reflex action. A gun leapt into his hand. *He was too quick for me!*

Almost in one motion, Nick threw the knife and rolled to one side, but the gun exploded, and it felt as if a fist had struck him in the face. There was no pain, but the left side of his face went numb. Nick hit the floor and rolled over, frantically kicking a chair out of the way. *He'll get me with the next shot!*

Nick came to his feet, his left eye blinded with blood, but he saw that Costello was not going to shoot anyone . . . not ever again.

The stiletto had penetrated his throat and, from the gush of blood, Nick knew that the razor-sharp edge had sliced through the big artery. A scarlet flower blossomed on the man's white shirt front.

Costello dropped the gun, reached up and grasped the handle of the knife, and pulled it free. There was a look of horror on his face, and he tried to cry out, but only a gurgling sound came from his throat. Frantically he clawed at his throat, trying to staunch the gushing stream of crimson, but he could not, for his heart was pumping the life's blood through the fingers of a dying man.

At that moment, Nick heard the sound of footsteps and whirled, making a dive for his gun. He picked it up just as the door burst open, and through the bloody veil that clouded his eyes, he saw Larry yank his gun from the holster. Without thought, Nick lifted his own weapon and pulled the trigger. A small black hole appeared in Larry's forehead, and he fell backwards, dead before he struck the floor.

Nick turned to Allie, gasping, "Let's get out of here!"

"You've been shot!" Allie cried out.

But Nick shook his head. "Never mind that—" The left side of his face was beginning to come alive with pain, and he could not see out of his left eye. Snatching a handkerchief from his pocket, he pressed it to his face. For one brief moment he stared at Costello, who was on the floor, his legs twitching as his life drained out. Nick took out a handkerchief, wiped off his gun, then stooping down, placed it in Costello's left hand. There was no strength in the limp fingers, and the gun dropped to the carpet.

Nick stood up and moved across to the body of the dead man. He picked up Larry's gun and stuck it in his pocket. By now Nick was sick at his stomach, and he held the handkerchief over his wounded face.

"Come on, doll, let's get out of here," he said, and the two of them stumbled down the stairs. They walked down the street, ignoring the curious glance of a couple on the other side.

"Nick, you've got to get to a hospital."

"Not right now, sweetheart," Nick said. He managed a grin. "First, we get you to the arena . . . and then I got one more call to make—"

★   ★   ★

When Tony Rocco woke up, he discovered that the night-mare he was having was real!

Rocco was not afraid of guns, but he had a deathly fear of knives. In his dream, he had felt the cold edge of steel on his throat. Now he came out of sleep instantly, and a voice that was as cold as the blade on his throat spoke. "Hello, Tony."

Rocco tried to move, but at once the blade bit into his flesh. He felt the blood running down his neck, over his chest . . . and a scream bubbled up in his throat. "Noooo! Don't cut!"

"Let's have some light." The gaslight blossomed, and the blade left his throat.

Rocco shaded his eyes, peering at the four men who sur-rounded his bed. Terror shot through him, and he began to beg, "Now, let's talk, boys! You know me! We can make a deal!"

"We're going to make a deal, Tony." Rocco sat up in bed and saw Nick Castellano standing beside him.

The left side of Nick's face was bandaged, and he held a slender knife in his hand.

"Marko . . . Pete!" Rocco called out in fear.

"Why, they're right here, Tony," Nick said, motioning to the two men on his left. And here's Alphonse.

Tony stared at his hirelings, and the glitter in their eyes told him he was no longer their boss. "You sold me out!" he whispered. It was a moment he'd feared, as did all his kind. Obviously Nick Castellano had gotten to his men. "Look, you guys," he babbled, "Whatever Nick promised you, I'll give you more—"

"You're a little late, Tony. The boys and I have decided to . . . restructure the organization. You'll still be up front, but I'll be with you all the time." He leaned forward and touched the tip of the blade to Rocco's cheek. "All the time, Tony, baby . . . and if something happens to me, one of my partners here will see that you get sliced up." Nick paused and then asked in a soft voice, "You wanna live, Tony?"

"Yes—yes, Nick! I'll do just what you say."

Nick Castellano's one eye glittered. He knew that he would probably never see out of his left eye, but one was good enough. "Sorry to be the bearer of bad tidings, but Sonny and Larry got into a fight and knocked each other off. We'll have to send lots of flowers to their funeral, won't we, Tony?"

"Yeah, Nick!" Rocco nodded quickly. He knew he was a dead man if he crossed Nick Castellano . . . and he wanted to live. "Yeah, sure, lots of flowers!"

The two figures walking along Thirty-eighth Street moved slowly. Snowflakes had begun to drift down, and the smaller figure moved in closer.

"Owen, are you very sorry about the fight?"

He looked up at the flakes, tracing their lazy path, not answering her for a moment. The flakes bit his lips, miniature fire, then melted. "Always liked snow," he said through puffy lips. Then he put his arms around her. "No, Allie. I lost, and that's that."

"If it hadn't been for Nick—" Allie began, then broke off, pushing the bad memories from her mind.

"He's quite a fellow," Owen murmured. "When the two of you came busting into my dressing room ten minutes before the fight, I thought I was seeing things!" Then he laughed softly. "And Rocco went to all that trouble for nothing. I had no chance to beat Jimmy Spears. He's way out of my class."

Allie said timidly, "Maybe next time—"

Owen held her tightly. "There's not going to be a next time, Allie. I've fought my last bout." He watched the joy erasing the worry lines in her face and smiled. "It's all different, Allie. Everything seems so clean and new! If I live to be a hundred, I'll never forget how Jesus came to me in that room and saved me."

Allie dropped her head, leaning against his chest. She said nothing, but he knew what she was thinking. Putting his hand under her chin, he tilted it toward him. "Feel left out, don't you, sweetheart?"

"Y–yes."

"Sure you do. So did I when I was around Amos and Rose and Ma. But it won't take you long to come in out of the cold. You're ready to find the Lord. And I'll be with you, Allie, all the way!"

"Will you, Owen?" Allie shook her head. "I've been so afraid."

Owen held her tightly and kissed her. Her lips were warm, even in the cold, and he said, "I think God's got something for me to do, Allie . . . and I think it's the kind of job that requires a wife. So, first, you say yes to Jesus . . . and then say yes to me!"

Allie felt her heart lift, knowing he was promising her what she most longed for. She touched his face lightly. "I'm ready, Owen!"

He laughed, and the two of them held each other as the snowflakes swirled around them. Then they turned and moved down the street, seeming to meld into one figure as they walked toward the light.

A TIME TO DIE

The story of the Stuart family continues in the next book of the American Odyssey Series. As America teeters uncertainly between war and peace, the family reunites one more time in the calm-before-the-storm shelter of the Arkansas hills.

Then, in London, Lylah finds bittersweet love. She is swept into the vortex of wartime Europe while her brother Gavin joins the French Foreign Legion.